William Harrison Ainsworth

Chetwynd Calverley

A Tale

William Harrison Ainsworth

Chetwynd Calverley
A Tale

ISBN/EAN: 9783337122096

Printed in Europe, USA, Canada, Australia, Japan

Cover: Foto ©Andreas Hilbeck / pixelio.de

More available books at **www.hansebooks.com**

Popular Authors in the

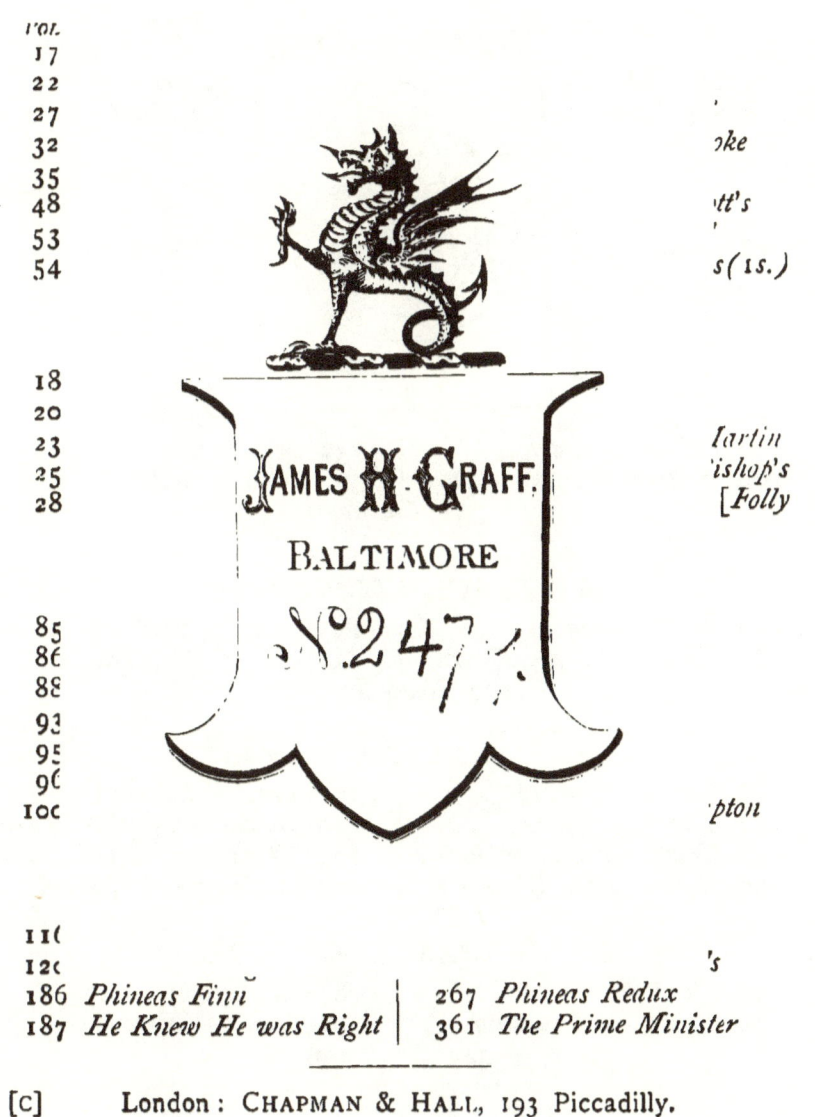

JAMES H. GRAFF.
BALTIMORE
No. 247

[C]   London: CHAPMAN & HALL, 193 Piccadilly.

Select Library of Fiction.

[D]   London : CHAPMAN & HALL, 193 Piccadilly.

CHETWYND CALVERLEY.

A Tale.

BY

WILLIAM HARRISON AINSWORTH,

AUTHOR OF

"CONSTABLE OF THE TOWER,"
"LORD MAYOR OF LONDON,"
"THE TOWER OF LONDON,"
"CARDINAL POLE,"
ETC.

NEW EDITION.

LONDON:
CHAPMAN AND HALL, 193 PICCADILLY.
1877.

In Memoriam.

---◆---

THOMAS GILBERT AINSWORTH.

CONTENTS.

———◆———

BOOK II.—THE HEIRESS OF BRACKLEY HALL.

BOOK III.—WALTER LIDDEL.

BOOK IV.—PROBATION.

BOOK V.—LADY THICKNESSE.

viii   *Contents.*

BOOK VI.—THE CLAUSE IN MR. CALVERLEY'S WILL.

CHETWYND CALVERLEY.

THE YOUNG STEPMOTHER.

I.

OUSELCROFT.

ONE summer evening, Mildred Calverley, accounted the prettiest girl in Cheshire, who had been seated in the drawing-room of her father's house, Ouselcroft, near Daresbury, vainly trying to read, passed out from the open French window, and made her way towards two magnificent cedars of Lebanon, at the farther end of the lawn.

She was still pacing the lawn with distracted steps, when a well-known voice called out to her, and a tall figure emerged from the shade of the cedars, and Mildred uttered a cry of mingled surprise and delight.

"Is that you, Chetwynd?"

"Ay; don't you know your own brother, Mildred?"

And as they met, they embraced each other affectionately.

"Have you been here long, Chetwynd?" she asked. "Why didn't you come into the house?"

"I didn't know whether I should be welcome, Mildred. Tell me how all is going on?"

"Then you have not received my letters, addressed to Bellagio and Milan? I wrote to tell you that papa is very seriously ill, and begged you to return immediately. Did you get the letters?"

"No; in fact, I have heard nothing at all from any one of you, directly nor indirectly, for more than two months."

"How extraordinary! But how can the letters have miscarried?"

"I might give a guess, but you would think me unjustly suspicious. Is my father really ill, Mildred?"

"Really very seriously ill. About a month ago he caught a bad cold, and has never since been able to shake it off. Doctor Spencer, who has been attending him the whole time, didn't apprehend any danger at first; but now he almost despairs of papa's recovery."

"Gracious heaven!" exclaimed the young man; "I didn't expect to be greeted by this sad intelligence!"

"You have only just come in time to see papa alive! Within the last few days a great change for the worse has taken place in him. Mamma has been most attentive, and has scarcely ever left him."

"She is acting her part well, it seems," cried Chetwynd, bitterly. "But don't call her mamma when you speak of her to me, Mildred. Let it be Mrs. Calverley, if you please."

"I don't wish to pain you, Chetwynd, but I must tell you the truth. Mrs. Calverley, as you desire me to call her, has shown the greatest devotion to her husband, and Doctor Spencer cannot speak too highly of her. She has had a great deal to go through, I assure you. Since his illness, poor papa has been very irritable and fretful, and would have tried anybody's patience—but she has an angelic temper."

"You give her an excellent character, Mildred," he remarked, in a sceptical tone.

"I give her the character she deserves, Chetwynd. Everybody will tell you the same thing. All the servants idolise her. You know what my opinion of her is, and how dearly I love her. She is quite a model of a wife."

"Don't speak of her in those rapturous terms to me, Mildred, unless you desire to drive me away. I can't bear it. I wish to think kindly of my father now. He has caused me much unhappiness, but I forgive him. I never can forgive *her*."

"I own you have a good deal to complain of, Chetwynd, and I have always pitied you."

"You are the only person who does pity me, I fancy, Mildred. It is not often that a man is robbed of his intended bride by his own father. It is quite true that Teresa and I had quarrelled, and that my father declared if I didn't marry her, he would marry her himself. But I didn't expect he would put his threats into execution—still less that she would accept him. I didn't know the fickleness of your sex."

"It is entirely your own fault, Chetwynd, that this has happened," said his sister. "But I know how much you have suffered in consequence of your folly and hasty temper, and I won't, therefore, reproach you. Whatever your feelings may be, it is your duty to control them now. Papa passed a very bad night, and sent this morning for Mr. Carteret, the attorney, and gave him instructions to prepare his will."

" I always understood he had made his will, Mildred. He made a handsome settlement upon—his wife ? "

" It is as I tell you, Chetwynd. Mr. Carteret was alone with him in his room for nearly two hours this morning ; and I believe he was directed to prepare the will without delay, and to return with it this evening."

" Indeed ! " exclaimed Chetwynd, gloomily. " That bodes ill to me—to both of us, in fact. He will leave all his property to Teresa—to his wife, I am certain of it."

" Nothing of the sort, Chetwynd ! " cried his sister. " Come into the house, and see him."

" If he has made up his mind to commit this act of folly and injustice, all I can say won't prevent it. Ah, here is Carteret ! " he exclaimed, as a mail phaeton entered the lodge gate, and drove up to the hall door.

The attorney and his clerk descended ; and, leaving his carriage to the care of a groom, Mr. Carteret rang the bell.

" Come in at once, Chetwynd, and you will be able to see papa before Mr. Carteret is admitted. Come with me—quick ! "

Chetwynd suffered himself to be persuaded, and passed through the drawing-room window with his sister.

But he was too late. The attorney and his clerk had already gone upstairs.

II.

TERESA.

CHETWYND, only son of Mr. Hugh Calverley, a retired Liverpool merchant, residing at Ouselcroft, in Cheshire, was somewhat singularly circumstanced, as will have been surmised from the conversation just recounted—but he had only himself to blame.

Rather more than a year ago—when he was just of age—he had fallen in love with his father's ward, Teresa Mildmay, a young lady of great personal attractions, but very small fortune—had proposed to her, and been accepted.

Teresa had lost both her parents. Her mother, Lady Eleanor Mildmay, daughter of Lord Rockingham, died when she was quite a child. Her father, General Mildmay, an Indian officer of distinction, was one of Mr. Calverley's most intimate friends, and hence it chanced that the latter was appointed Teresa's guardian.

General Mildmay's demise occurred at Cheltenham about two years prior to the commencement of our story. By her guardian's desire, Teresa then came to reside with his daughter at Ouselcroft. Though Mildred was two or three years younger than her friend, and they were very dissimilar in character, a sisterly affection subsisted between them. Originating when they were at school together at Brighton, their friendship had never since been disturbed. To Mildred, therefore, it was a source of the greatest satisfaction when Teresa took up her abode with them.

The two girls differed as much in personal appearance as in character. Both were remarkably goodlooking. Teresa Mildmay had a very striking countenance. Her features were classical in mould, her complexion dark, her eyes magnificent, and arched over by thick black brows. Her tresses were black as jet, luxuriant, and of a silky texture, and were always dressed in a manner that best suited her. Her figure was lofty and beautifully proportioned. The expression of her face was decidedly proud—too proud to be altogether agreeable. Nevertheless, she was extremely admired.

Teresa possessed great good sense and good judgment, and was looked upon by her guardian as a model of prudence and propriety. As he frequently consulted her upon household matters, and, indeed, asked her advice upon many other points, she naturally acquired considerable influence over him.

A very charming girl was Mildred, though her style was quite different from that of Teresa. She was a blonde. A ravishingly fair complexion, a dimpled cheek, a lip fashioned like a Cupid's bow, teeth like pearls—these constituted her attractions. Her figure was slight, but perfectly symmetrical, and nothing could be sweeter than her smile.

Such were the two fair inmates of Ouselcroft, before a change took place in the establishment.

Having proposed to his father's beautiful ward, as we have stated, and been accepted, Chetwynd, who could not brook delay, was anxious that the marriage should take place at once.

To this, however, the prudent Teresa objected. She was of a cold temperament, and reflection convinced her that she had not done wisely in accepting Chetwynd; but for several reasons she hesitated to break off the engagement. She did not like to lose a comfortable home, and hoped that the young man, who had hitherto been very careless and extravagant, might turn over a new leaf.

In this expectation, she was disappointed. Chetwynd was very handsome and agreeable, and had many good qualities, but his temper was excessively irritable, and he was reckless in regard to expense. His Oxford debts, which were heavy, had been paid by his father, and he then promised amendment, but did not keep his word. On the contrary, he continued his extravagant courses. Though intended for the law, he would not study, but led a mere life of pleasure—riding daily in the parks, and visiting all public places of amusement; and his father, who was a great deal too indulgent, did not check him.

On his return to Ouselcroft, after an absence of a couple of months, during which he had not deemed it necessary to write to Teresa, she received him very coldly; and provoked by her manner, he told her next day, when they were alone, that he did not think he should be happy with her.

"If you really believe so, Chetwynd," she said, " the marriage ought not to take place. I release you from your engagement."

The remarkable calmness—almost indifference—with which she spoke, piqued him, and he exclaimed :

" Very well ; I accept it ! There is an end of all between us ! "

Scarcely were the words uttered, than he repented, and would have recalled them. He looked appealingly at her, but she seemed so cold, that he became fortified in his resolution.

Mr. Calverley soon learnt what had happened from Mildred; but, feeling sure he could set matters right, he sent for his son, and insisted on his marrying Miss Mildmay, on pain of his severest displeasure.

Chetwynd refused point blank.

" You won't? " cried the old gentleman, ready to explode.

" I have already given you an answer, sir," rejoined his son. " I adhere to my determination ! Pray don't put yourself in a passion. It won't have any effect upon me ! "

" Very well," said Mr. Calverley, with difficulty controlling his rage. " Since you decline to fulfil your engagement, I'll marry her myself ! "

" Ridiculous ! " cried his son.

" Ridiculous or not, you'll find I shall be as good as my word."

" Pshaw ! The young lady won't accept you."

He was mistaken, however.

The young lady *did* accept the old gentleman, and so readily that it almost seemed she preferred him to his son. Within a month, they were married.

Before the marriage Chetwynd went abroad, and did not keep up any communication with his family. They ascertained, however, that he was at Bellagio, on the Lake of Como.

Apparently, Mr. Calverley had no reason to regret the extraordinary step he had taken. Teresa made him an excellent wife, and seemed quite devoted to him. She studied him in everything—read the news-paper to him of a morning, chatted agreeably to him when they drove out together in the barouche, played and sang to him in the evening, and, in short, kept him constantly amused. She managed his large establishment perfectly—better than it had ever been managed before. She quarrelled with none of his old friends—even though she might deem some of them bores—but always appeared delighted to see them. Above all, she continued on the most affectionate terms with Mildred, who had never disapproved of the match. Nothing could be more judicious than her conduct.

At first, everybody cried out Mr. Calverley was an "old fool;" but they soon said he was a very sensible man, and exceedingly fortunate.

He was not, however, destined to enjoy a long term of happiness. Hitherto, he had scarcely known a day's illness; but a few months after his marriage his health began rapidly to decline.

Teresa tended him with the greatest solicitude.

III.

MR. CALVERLEY.

REPAIRING to the invalid's chamber, we shall find Mr. Calverley seated in an easy-chair, his head supported by a pillow. For nearly a fortnight he had not left his bed, but he insisted on getting up that day.

He had been a fine-looking old gentleman; but he was now wonderfully reduced, and his attire hung loosely on him. Still his countenance was very handsome.

His young wife was seated on a tabouret by his side, watching him anxiously with her large black eyes. She was wrapped in an Indian shawl dressing-gown, which could not conceal her perfectly-proportioned figure.

" Give me a glass of wine, Teresa," he said, in a scarcely audible voice. " I feel that dreadful faintness coming on again."

She eagerly obeyed him.

With difficulty he conveyed the wine to his lips; but having swallowed it, he seemed better.

Taking his wife's hand, he looked at her earnestly, as he thus addressed her :

" I must soon leave you, Teresa. Nay, do not interrupt me. I know what you would say. It must be, my love. I cannot be deceived as to my state. You have been an excellent wife, Teresa—a great comfort to me—a very great comfort. You are aware I have given my solicitor, Mr. Carteret, instructions respecting my will. I will now tell you what I have done. I have the most perfect confidence in you, Teresa, and I know you will carry out my instructions."

" Be sure of it, my dear," she murmured.

" Teresa," he continued, speaking very deliberately, " I have left my entire property to you."

" To me ! " she ejaculated, a slight flush tinging her pale cheek. " Oh, love, it is not right you should do this ! I am amply provided for already by the handsome settlement you made upon me, and I tell you at once, if you leave me your property, I shall not keep it. I shall divide it between Chetwynd and Mildred."

A faint smile lighted up the features of the dying man.

"I had formed a correct opinion of you, Teresa," he said, looking at her affectionately. "I know the goodness of your heart and the rectitude of your principles."

Then, slightly changing his manner, he added, "I must now make an effort to explain myself, and I pray you to give strict attention to what I am about to say. I have left you the whole of my property, because I feel certain it will be placed in safe hands, and I mean you to represent myself."

"I listen!" she murmured.

"First, with regard to Chetwynd. I do not exactly know how he is circumstanced, but I fear he is in debt. He has always been extravagant. I think it will be best to continue the allowance I have hitherto made him, of six hundred a year, for the present; and if he marries, or reforms, let him have thirty thousand pounds."

"It shall be done exactly as you enjoin," said his wife, earnestly.

"Beyond the sum I have settled on you, Teresa," continued the old man, "I estimate my property at sixty thousand pounds. Of this one half is to go to Chetwynd, provided he reforms; the other half to Mildred, on her marriage, provided she marries with your consent. This house, with the plate, pictures, books, furniture, carriages, and horses, and all the lands attached to it, are yours—for life."

"Oh! you are too good to me!" she exclaimed, her eyes filling with tears.

"I have now told you all!" he said. "I leave you mistress of everything; and, since you know my wishes, I am sure you will act up to them."

"I will! I will!" she ejaculated, in broken accents.

"Enough! I shall now die content!"

He then closed his eyes, and his lips slightly moved, as if in prayer.

Teresa constrained her emotion by a strong effort; and, for a few minutes, perfect silence prevailed.

The door was then softly opened by an elderly man-servant, out of livery, who came to inform his master that Mr. Carteret had returned.

"Show him up at once, Norris," said Mr. Calverley, opening his eyes.

"His clerk is with him," said the butler.

"Show the clerk up as well," rejoined the old gentleman.

"Shall I withdraw?" asked Mrs. Calverley, as the butler retired.

"Perhaps you had better, my dear, till the will is signed," replied her husband.

Mrs. Calverley remained till the attorney appeared, and having exchanged a word in a low tone with him, left the room.

IV.

FATHER AND SON.

TALL and thin, and very business-like in manner, was Mr. Carteret. Sitting down quietly beside the old gentleman, and taking the will from his clerk, he proceed to read it.

Though conducted with due deliberation, the ceremony did not occupy many minutes, and when the attorney had finished reading the document, Mr. Calverley declared himself perfectly satisfied.

" All you have to do is to sign it, sir," said the attorney.

Accordingly, a small table was placed beside the invalid's chair, and the will was duly executed and attested.

" Pray call in my wife," said Mr. Calverley, as soon as this was done.

When Mrs. Calverley re-appeared, she was informed by her husband that the will was executed.

" Yes; the business is done, madam," observed Mr. Carteret, with a very singular expression of countenance.

" Shall I leave the document with you, sir ? "

" No; take charge of it," replied Mr. Calverley.

" Well, perhaps, it will be best with me," observed the attorney, glancing at the lady as he spoke.

He was in the act of tying up the instrument preparatory to consigning it to his clerk, when the door opened, and Chetwynd and his sister came in.

The old gentleman looked greatly startled by the unexpected appearance of his son, and did not, for a few moments, recover his composure.

Scarcely knowing what might ensue, Mrs. Calverley stepped between them.

" I was not aware of your return, Chetwynd," said Mr. Calverley, as soon as he was able to speak.

" I have only just come back sir," replied his son,

regarding him steadfastly. "I hope I have arrived in time to prevent you from doing an act of injustice to me and my sister?"

"You will have much to answer for, Chetwynd, if you agitate your father at this moment," interposed Mrs. Calverley. "You see what a critical state he is in!"

"I cannot help it, madam," rejoined the young man. "I must and will speak to him while he is able to listen to me. Pray, don't go, I beg of you, Mr. Carteret," he continued, to the attorney, who was preparing to follow his clerk out of the room. "It is proper you should hear what I have to say. I have reason to believe, sir," he added, to his father, "that you have left your entire property to your wife, and have made my sister and myself entirely dependent on her. If this is really the case, I entreat you to alter your determination——"

"I don't understand why you permit yourself to talk to me thus, Chetwynd," interrupted the old gentleman, his anger supplying him with strength. "At all events, I shall not tolerate it. Even supposing it were as you state, I have a perfect right to bequeath my property as I see fit, and you have not proved yourself such a dutiful son as to merit consideration on my part. Wait till the fitting season, and you will learn what I have done."

"No, sir; I won't wait till your ears are deaf to my prayers! I *will* speak while you are able to listen to me. I may have given you some offence, but do not carry your resentment to the grave. Bethink you that whatever you do now will be irreparable."

"I cannot bear this!" cried the old man. "Take him away! He distracts me!"

"Mr. Chetwynd," said Carteret, "I am extremely reluctant to interfere; but your presence certainly disturbs your father very much. Let me beg you to retire!"

The young man showed no disposition to comply.

"Perhaps, Chetwynd, when I have spoken," said Mr. Calverley, trying to calm himself, "you will either go or keep silence. I have done what, on mature consideration, and with the prospect of death before me, I deem best for you and your sister; and I am certain my wishes will be most faithfully carried out."

"What you say, sir, seems to intimate that you have placed us entirely in the hands of your wife," cried his son. "Why should you compel us to bow to her will and pleasure?"

"Because she will take care of you," rejoined the old man; "and, though you are two-and-twenty, you have not come to years of discretion."

"That is your opinion, sir. But, granting it to be correct, does it apply to my sister?"

"Your sister makes no complaint," said his father, looking affectionately at her. "She knows I have done all that is right. She is in good hands."

"Yes, I am quite sure of that, papa!" cried Mildred. "Pray don't think about me!"

"Chetwynd," she added to him, in a low tone, "I wouldn't have brought you here had I imagined you would make this terrible scene!"

"I really must interfere to prevent the continuance of a discussion which I am aware can lead to no beneficial result," interposed Mr. Carteret. "I would again beseech you, Mr. Chetwynd, not to trouble your father! I know he has good reasons for what he has

done.   Have you anything further to say to me, sir?"
he added to Mr. Calverley.

"Stop a minute, Mr. Carteret, I beg of you!" cried
Chetwynd.   "I am yet in hopes that I may move him.
Let me make one more appeal to your sense of justice,
sir!" he added to his father.   "I promise you it shall
be the last!"

"I cannot listen to you!" replied Mr. Calverley.

"You refuse, then, to alter your will?"

"Positively refuse!" rejoined the old gentleman.
"For heaven's sake let me die in peace!   Can you
not prevail on him to go," he added to his wife and
daughter.   "He will kill me outright!"

"You hear what your father says!" cried Mrs.
Calverley, in an authoritative tone.   "Go, I command
you!"

"Yes, I *will* go," rejoined Chetwynd; "but not at
your bidding!   You are the sole cause of this misunderstanding between my father and myself.   By
your arts you have cheated me out of my inheritance!"

"Ah!" ejaculated Mrs. Calverley.

"This is madness!" exclaimed Mr. Carteret, trying
to drag him from the room.

"Hear my last words, sir!" cried Chetwynd to his
father.   "I never will touch a shilling of your money
if it is to be doled out to me by this woman!"

And he rushed out of the room.

V.

THE OLD BUTLER.

PUSHING aside the attorney's clerk, whom he found on the landing, he hurried downstairs, and had just snatched up his hat in the hall, when he perceived the old butler eyeing him wistfully.

He had a great regard for this faithful old servant, whom he had known since he was a boy, so he went up to him, and patting him kindly on the shoulder, said—

"Good-bye, dear old Norris. I don't mean to remain a minute longer in my father's house, and I may never return to it. Farewell, old friend!"

"You shan't go out thus, sir, unless you knock me down," rejoined Norris, detaining him. "You'll do yourself a mischief. No one is in the dining-room. Please to go in there. I want to have a few words with you—to reason with you."

And he tried to draw him towards the room in question; but Chetwynd resisted.

"Reason with me!" he exclaimed. "I know what you'll say, Norris. You'll advise me to make it up with my father, and bow the knee to my stepmother; but I'll die rather!"

"Mr. Chetwynd, it's a chance if your father is alive to-morrow morning. Think of that, and what your feelings will be when he's gone. You'll reproach yourself then, sir, for I know you've a good heart. I've got you out of many a scrape when you were a boy, and I'm persuaded something may be done now, if you'll only condescend to listen to me."

" Well, I'll stay a few minutes on purpose to talk to you. But I hear Carteret coming downstairs. I don't want to meet him. I don't want to meet anybody—not even my sister."

" Then I'll tell you what to do, sir. Go up the back staircase to your own room. It's just as you left it. No one will know you're here. I'll come to you as soon as I can."

And he almost forced him through a folding-door into a passage communicating with the back staircase.

Chetwynd had disappeared before the attorney and his clerk reached the hall; but Mr. Carteret stopped for a moment to speak to the old butler.

" Ah, we've had a frightful scene, Norris ! " he said. " It will surprise me if the old gentleman survives it. I suppose Mr. Chetwynd is gone ? "

" I really can't say, sir. He was here a few minutes ago."

" Looking rather wild, eh ? "

" I'm sure he looked wild enough when he passed me just now," observed the clerk. " I thought he'd have thrown me over the banisters."

" Serve you right, too ! " muttered Norris.

" Nothing could be more injudicious, and, I may add, more unfeeling, than his conduct to his father," remarked Carteret.

" I'm sorry to hear it," said the butler ; " but you must make some allowance for him."

" I can make every allowance," rejoined the attorney. " But no good purpose can be answered by such violence as he gave way to. On the contrary, irreparable harm is done."

"Not irreparable harm, I hope, sir?"

"I very much fear so. He used language towards Mrs. Calverley that I don't think she will ever forgive It's of the last importance that he should be set right with her. Should you see him before he goes, tell him so."

"I will, sir—if I *do* see him. There's master's bell. Excuse me ; I must go upstairs."

"Don't mind me, Norris. I can let myself out. As I drive back, at Mrs. Calverley's request, I shall call on Doctor Spencer, and send him to see Mr. Calverley at once. That will save time."

"Very good, sir," replied the butler.

And he flew upstairs ; while Mr. Carteret and his clerk went out at the front door.

"Has anybody just left the house, Edward?" inquired Mr. Carteret of his groom, who was waiting with the phaeton near the door.

"No, sir," replied the man.

"I fancied he was not gone," thought the attorney. "I am glad I spoke to Norris."

VI.

SELF-EXAMINATION.

CHETWYND had become more tranquillised since he entered the room that had once belonged to him—and that might be said to belong to him still—since it had always been kept for him.

A comfortable bed-chamber, with windows looking upon the garden. Night was now coming on, but it was still light enough to see every object in the room, and Chetwynd examined them with interest—almost with emotion.

The furniture was precisely the same he had left; the narrow iron bed, without curtains, and covered with an eider-down quilt—the easy-chair on which he used to sit and smoke—the books on the shelf and the prints on the walls, were still there, as of yore. Nothing seemed to have been disturbed.

When he last occupied that room Teresa was his father's ward, and believing himself in love with her, he indulged in dreams of future happiness—for there seemed no obstacle to their union.

Now, all was gone. Teresa had become hateful to him. Yet, somehow or other, her image was associated with the room.

Throwing open the windows, he looked out into the garden, and, after listening to the singing of the birds, sat down in the easy-chair, and tried to lay out a plan for the future.

Impossible! His mind was much too confused for the task. He could decide on nothing. Never having done anything during his life but amuse himself, he had no idea what he should have to do when thrown upon his own resources.

Compelled to examine himself, he found his knowledge of business exceedingly limited. However, he had plenty of friends, and did not doubt they would help him to a situation of some kind.

The thought that most annoyed him was that he had well-nigh spent all his money. He had not enough to pay a passage to Australia.

At length, Norris made his appearance, and explained that he could not come sooner, having had a good deal to do in Mr. Calverley's room. Doctor Spencer had paid a visit to his patient, and had only just left.

"However, all is quiet for the present," said the butler, "and I will therefore beg you to come with me to my room, where I have got a little supper for you."

"I shall really be glad of it, Norris. I suppose we sha'n't meet any of the other servants?"

"No; I have taken care of that, sir," replied Norris.

In the butler's pantry, to which they repaired, they found a cold pigeon-pie and a bottle of claret on the table, and being very hungry, Chetwynd made a hearty meal.

"I'm sorry I cannot give you a very good report of what has been going on upstairs, sir," said the butler; "though your father is not so bad as I feared. He has been put to bed, and Doctor Spencer has seen him, as I told you. The doctor gave him some stimulant that helped to revive him, and has left a small phial with Mrs. Calverley, from which she is to administer a few drops to him, as she may deem fit. I hope he may last out the night, and I think he will, for he seemed better when I left him just now. Heaven grant you may see him again, sir!"

"I despair of doing anything with him, Norris."

"Never despair, sir,—never despair!"

"Well, that's a good maxim. Extraordinary things have sometimes been done when all has been deemed hopeless. Fresh wills have been made almost *in extremis*. It may be so in my father's case, but I don't think it likely."

"You must remain in the house to-night, sir. It's your last chance."

"*Is* there a chance, Norris ? "

"You shall judge for yourself, sir. When I was in your father's room just now, standing by his bedside, he spoke to me about you in a way that showed his good feelings towards you had returned. Evidently, he didn't want Mrs. Calverley to hear what he said; but she was in the dressing-room, though the door was partly open. He asked me, in a low voice, if you were really gone; and seemed much relieved when I told him you were still in the house, but begged me not to mention it to his wife. ' It may alarm, her, Norris,' he said. I couldn't say anything more to him at the time, for she came out of the dressing-room; but I shall have another opportunity to-night. Of one thing I'm certain, sir; but I shall have another opportunity to-night. Of one thing I'm certain, sir—you haven't lost your hold of your father's affections."

At this moment a slight sound outside caught Chetwynd's ear.

Wishing to ascertain if there was a listener, he immediately got up, and, opening the door, looked along the passage right and left; but it was quite dark, and he could distinguish no one.

"It was a false alarm," he said, as he came back. "For the moment I fancied it might be Mrs. Calverley."

" No fear of that, sir; she never comes down here."

" Let us go back to my room. I shall feel easier there. After what you've told me, Norris, I shan't think of leaving to-night."

" That's the right thing to do, sir," cried the butler, joyfully.

" Bring the bottle of claret and the glasses with you, and come along," said Chetwynd.

VII.

TERRIBLE SUSPICIONS.

In half a minute more they were in the old room up-stairs.

The blinds were drawn down, the candles on the chimney-piece lighted, the claret and glasses set on the table, Chetwynd was seated in an easy-chair, and old Norris had taken a place opposite him.

" Now, Norris," said Chetwynd, " I should like to ask you a few questions. In the first place, what is the matter with my father? Till I came here this evening I have never heard he was unwell. What is his complaint? What does Doctor Spencer say about him?"

" Doctor Spencer says it's a complete ' break up,' " replied the butler; " but I don't think he understands the case at all. Your father used to be a remarkably stout man for his years, as I needn't tell you, sir. I never recollect him having a day's illness till his marriage; and, indeed, he was as well as ever for three months, when he caught a cold, and then a very sudden change occurred, and I thought all would soon be over with him—but he rallied."

" Did he quite recover from his cold ? "

" No, sir, he was much weakened, and didn't regain his strength. He looked to me as if gradually wasting away."

" Why, so he was, I suppose, Norris. There is nothing but what is perfectly natural in all this ; yet you seem suspicious."

" I hope he has been fairly treated, sir."

" Why should you think otherwise ? "

" Because he has symptoms that 1 don't exactly like, sir."

Then lowering his voice, as if afraid to speak the words aloud, he added, " It looks to me almost like a case of slow poisoning ! "

Chetwynd seemed horror-stricken at the idea.

" You must be mistaken, Norris," he said. " It cannot be. Whatever opinion I may entertain of the person it is evident you suspect, I am certain she is incapable of such a monstrous crime. Have you mentioned your suspicions to Doctor Spencer, or any one else ? "

" I told Doctor Spencer I thought it a very strange illness, but he said there was nothing unusual in it— it was simply the result of a bad cold. ' It was quite impossible,' he said, ' that Mr. Calverley could be more carefully attended to than by his wife. She had really kept him alive.' I don't know what he would have said if I had ventured to breathe a word against her."

" Did you warn my father ?   It was your duty to do so, if you really believed he was being poisoned."

" My immediate discharge would have been the consequence," said Norris.   " And how could I prove what I asserted ?   Doctor Spencer thought me a stupid old fool; my master would have thought me crazy; Mrs. Calverley would have thought a lunatic asylum fitter for me than Ouselcroft ; and Miss Mildred would have been of the same opinion.   So I held my tongue, and let things go on.   Had you been at home, sir, I should have consulted you, and you could have taken such steps as you deemed proper.   But it is now too late to save him."

" If this were true it would be dreadful," exclaimed Chetwynd.   " But I cannot believe it.   It must have been found out.   Doctor Spencer, who is a very clever, shrewd man, has been in constant attendance on my father, and must have been struck by any unusual symptoms in his illness, but he appears to have been quite satisfied that everything was going on properly. To make an accusation of this sort, with nothing to support it, would have been culpable in the highest degree, and I am glad you kept quiet."

" Still, I can hardly reconcile my conduct to myself, sir," said Norris ; " but I fear I should have done no good."

" No ; you would have done great mischief.   I am quite certain you are utterly mistaken."

Norris did not seem to think so, but he made no further remark.

After a brief silence he got up, and said :

"I must now go up to my master's room, and see whether he wants anything.   Perhaps I may find an opportunity of speaking to him."

VIII.

DEATH OF MR. CALVERLEY.

LEFT alone, Chetwynd revolved what the butler had told him; and on considering the matter, he came to the conclusion he had previously arrived at—that there was nothing whatever to justify the old man's suspicions.

"I cannot imagine how he has got such a notion into his head," he thought; "but, according to his own account, he has not a shadow of proof to support the charge. Besides, setting all else aside, there is no motive for such a crime. She could not wish to get rid of my father. Perhaps she might desire to come into the property, but, even if she were bad enough to do it, she would never run such a frightful risk. No, no, the supposition is absurd and monstrous!"

At this moment the very person of whom he was thinking came in, and closed the door.

In her hand she had a small lamp, but she set it down.

She looked very pale, but her manner was perfectly composed, though there was a slight quivering of the lip.

Chetwynd arose, and regarded her in astonishment.

"You need not be alarmed at my appearance," she said. "I have no unfriendly intentions towards you. I heard you were still here, and came to speak to you. I am anxious to prevent further unpleasantness. You are acting very foolishly. Why should you quarrel with me? Whatever you may think, I mean you well."

By this time Chetwynd had recovered from his surprise, and, regarding her sternly, said :

"I have no desire to hold any conversation with you, madam; but my conduct requires explanation. I was about to depart, but have been induced to remain for various reasons. I have learnt matters that have determined me to see my father again."

The latter words were pronounced with great significance, but did not seem to produce any impression upon Mrs. Calverley.

"I do not wish to prevent you from seeing him, Chetwynd, if you will promise to behave quietly," she replied.

"I cannot let him go out of the world in the belief that you have acted properly to him," said Chetwynd, fiercely.

"Then you shall not see him! Nothing you could allege against me would produce the slightest effect upon him, but you shall not disturb his latest moments."

"You dare not leave me alone with him—"

"No," she replied, in a severe tone, "because you cannot control yourself. In my opinion, you ought to ask your father's pardon for your manifold acts of disobedience, and if you do so in a proper spirit I am certain you will obtain it."

"You venture to give the advice," he said. "But have you yourself obtained pardon from my father ?"

"Pardon for what?" she cried.

"For any crime you may have committed," he replied. "It is not for me to search your heart!"

"I disdain to answer such an infamous charge!" she rejoined, contemptuously.

" Have you not shortened his days ? "

" What mean you by that dark insinuation ? " she cried.

" My meaning is intelligible enough," he rejoined. " But I will make it plainer, if you will."

A singular change come over her countenance.

But she instantly recovered, and threw a scornful glance at Chetwynd.

" What have you done to him ? " he demanded.

" Striven to make his latter days happy," she replied, " and I believe I have succeeded. At any rate, he seemed happy."

" That was before his illness," observed Chetwynd.

" Since his illness I have nursed him with so much care that those best able to judge think I preserved his life. I saved him from all pain and annoyance, and his confidence in me was such that he has left all to my management."

" I know it, madam ; and you have been in haste to assume the power, but it may be wrested from your hands ! "

" Make the attempt," she rejoined, defiantly. " You will only injure yourself ! "

Just then voices were heard outside that startled them both, and checked their converse.

" Great heaven, it is your father ! " exclaimed Mrs. Calverley. " He has risen from the bed of death to come here ! "

Next moment the door was thrown open, and the old gentleman came in, sustained by Norris.

A dressing-gown scarcely concealed his emaciated frame. His features had the most ghastly expression, and bore the impress of death. But for the aid of the old butler he must have fallen to the ground

Behind him came Mildred, carrying a light.

"Why did you allow him to quit his couch?" cried his wife, in a voice of anguish.

"I remonstrated with him," replied Norris. "But I could not prevent him. He would come down to see his son."

"I likewise tried to dissuade him, but in vain," said Mildred,

"Chetwynd is here, is he not?" cried the old man. "I can't see him."

"Yes, I am here, father," he replied, springing towards him, and throwing himself at his feet. "Have you come to grant me forgiveness?"

"Yes, my son," replied the old man. "But first let me hear that you are reconciled to my dear wife —your stepmother. Answer me truly. Is it so?"

"Father!" hesitated Chetwynd.

"Stand up, my son," said the old man.

Chetwynd obeyed.

"Now, speak to me. Is there peace between you?"

"If you can forgive her, father, I will forgive her."

"I have nothing to forgive. She has been the best of wives to me, and is without a fault. These are my last words."

"Your blessing, father—your blessing!" almost shrieked Chetwynd.

The old man made an effort to raise his hands; but strength and utterance failed him, and he fell dead into his son's arms.

𝔈𝔫𝔡 𝔬𝔣 𝔱𝔥𝔢 𝔍𝔫𝔱𝔯𝔬𝔡𝔲𝔠𝔱𝔦𝔬𝔫.

Book the First.

MILDRED.

I.

SUITORS.

Mrs. Calverley had been nearly a year a widow.

She was still at Ouselcroft, and apparently meant to remain there. No change whatever had been made in the establishment, and old Norris was still in his place.

The will had not been disputed, and the widow was in possession of her late husband's entire property.

She intended to allow Chetwynd six hundred a year, in accordance with his father's request, and instructed Mr Carteret to pay him the amount quarterly; but he peremptorily refused to accept any allowance from her, and ordered the money to be returned.

He had remained at Ouselcroft until after the funeral, and then went abroad. As may be supposed, no reconciliation took place between him and his stepmother.

Hitherto the fair widow had lived in perfect retirement with Mildred, and was only to be seen arrayed in deep mourning in Daresbury Church, in the vaults of which her husband was interred; but she now began to pay visits, and receive her friends.

When Mildred re-appeared in society, after her temporary seclusion, she created quite a sensation.

We are afraid to say how many persons fell in love with her. She was still in mourning, of course, but her dark attire set off her fair tresses and exquisitely delicate complexion, and suited her slight graceful figure. Then her amiable and captivating manner heightened the effect of her charms, and rendered her almost irresistible.

During her father's lifetime she had been greatly admired, and was accounted, as we have said, the prettiest girl in Cheshire; but her beauty was more talked about now, and many a gallant youth thought himself excessively fortunate if he could obtain her hand for a waltz.

But Mildred was by no means a flirt, and had no desire to make conquests. On the contrary, she was a very quiet girl, and gave the herd of young men who beset her at balls and parties very little en-couragement. She did not care to dance much, and would only dance with those who pleased her, or amused her.

There was no sort of rivalry between the lovely girl and her beautiful stepmother. That there were already numerous aspirants to the hand of the wealthy young widow was certain; but it was equally certain she was in no haste to take another husband. She, therefore, felt no jealousy of Mildred, but was delighted to see her admired and sought after, and would willingly have promoted any advantageous match.

Mildred, however, made some objection or other to all who were recommended to her. Thus, when Mrs. Calverley praised young Mr. Capesthorne, and said he would have a fine old Elizabethan mansion, with a park attached to it, and asked if he wouldn't do, the young lady replied that she admired Mr. Capesthorne's old house, but didn't care for him.

Again, when Colonel Blakemere, who was about to return to Madras, and wanted to take a wife with him, paid her marked attention, and got Mrs. Calverley to back his suit, Mildred settled the matter by declaring she would never go to India.

However, these were nothing as compared with what followed.

It never rains but it pours, and offers now came by the dozen.

Mrs. Calverley received a number of little notes, the writers whereof begged permission to wait upon her, intimating that they had an important matter to lay before her, and at the same time making some slight reference to Mildred, that left her no doubt as to their object.

Before replying to any of them, she consulted Mildred; and, having ascertained her sentiments, agreed to see a couple of them on a particular day, and within half an hour of each other.

On the appointed day she was alone in the drawing-room, seated in an easy-chair, and wondering who would appear first, when Mr. Vernon Brook was announced by Norris.

Mr. Vernon Brook belonged to a good old family, but was a younger son.

Dark, sallow-complexioned, and long-visaged, he

piqued himself upon having a Vandyke face. To assist the expression, he scrupulously shaved his cheeks, and cultivated a pointed beard.

He had ridden over from his father's place, which was about ten miles off, and arrived in very good spirits, deeming himself sure of success.

Mrs. Calverley received him very graciously, and begged him to be seated. After a few words had passed between them, he came to the point.

" I've a question to ask you, my dear Mrs. Calverley, which I hope you will be able to answer in the affirmative. Your daughter—step-daughter, I ought to say— is a very charming girl, and I want to know if I have your permission to pay my addresses to her? "

He said this in a very easy manner, and as if quite certain the response would be favourable.

Mrs. Calverley's looks rather discouraged him.

" I must be allowed to consider the matter, Mr. Brook," she replied. " My late husband entrusted his daughter entirely to my care, and I cannot allow an engagement to take place unless I feel sure it would conduce to her happiness."

" But this would not amount to an engagement, my dear madam, though it might lead to one—at least, I hope so."

" It will be best to come to a clear understanding at first, Mr. Brook. I think it right to say that I see no objection to you. You have many agreeable personal qualities, and are unexceptionable in regard to family, but I am not exactly aware of your expectations."

Vernon Brook's dark cheek coloured, and he rather hesitated. He was not prepared for such a point-blank question.

D

"I am a younger son, as you are aware, Mrs. Calverley," he said; "and, like most younger sons, my expectations are not very great."

"I may as well speak frankly, Mr. Brook," she rejoined. "He who aspires to Miss Calverley's hand must bring a corresponding fortune. He must have a thousand a year, or a prospect of it."

"I am sorry to say I have neither the one nor the other, but I hope my want of fortune may not be a bar. I think we could be very happy together."

"Possibly; but the days of romantic marriages are over, and only exist in novels. I have dealt with you very fairly, Mr. Brook. Miss Calverley, as I have said, was left to my care by her father, and I shall act for her as he would have acted."

"But I have reason to believe Mr. Calverley would not have made it a *sine qua non* that a suitor to his daughter should be a man of property."

"You have been misinformed, Mr. Brook. No one can be so well acquainted as myself with my late husband's intentions."

"Then I am not to hope?"

"It would be useless, sir."

Mr. Vernon Brook arose, and was reluctantly preparing to depart, when Norris announced Sir Bridgnorth Charlton.

Thereupon he hurriedly bade Mrs. Calverley adieu, bowed stiffly to the new-comer, and made his exit.

II.

SIR BRIDGNORTH CHARLTON.

SIR BRIDGNORTH CHARLTON, Baronet, of Charlton Hall, in Staffordshire, a very fine place, was a person of considerable importance. He had been a member for the county, and was still a zealous politician. That he had not married earlier in life was owing to a disappointment he experienced, which had deeply affected him and caused him to remain a bachelor.

In age Sir Bridgnorth was not far from sixty, still handsome, though rather portly, and exceedingly gentlemanlike in manner. He had seen Mildred at a county ball, and, being much struck by her resemblance to his former love, the old flame was revived, and he determined to offer his hand.

Accordingly, he wrote to Mrs. Calverley, as we have explained.

Sir Bridgnorth had never been in Ouselcroft before, and after a few observations on the beauty of the grounds, he said:

"You will, no doubt, have conjectured why I have done myself the honour of waiting upon you, ma'am?"

Mrs. Calverley slightly moved.

"You have a very lovely step-daughter. It is not necessary for me to launch into her praises; but I may say I have only seen one person in the course of my life who has charmed me so much. That person would have been my wife had she not jilted me and wedded another. Miss Calverley shall be Lady Charlton if she will accept me.

"You do us great honour, Sir Bridgnorth!" observed Mrs. Calverley. D 2

"I don't know whether I am right, ma'am," he pursued; "but I prefer making this offer through you, instead of direct to the young lady, as you can put an end to the affair at once, if you think proper. I needn't enter into any particulars. You know my position; you know what sort of place I have got you know I can make a good settlement on my wife, as well as give her a title. The main question is—will Miss Calverley have me? Is she wholly free? for I would not, for the world, interfere with any other engagement. I have suffered too much myself not to be careful. I am not foolish enough to persuade myself she can love me; but I believe I could make her a very good husband, and hope she would be happy. I am quite sure she would be indulged."

He said this with an honest, manly sincerity, that produced a strong effect upon Mrs. Calverley.

In a voice of some emotion, she remarked, "My own husband, as I needn't tell you, Sir Bridgnorth, was considerably older than myself, and no one could be happier than I was with him."

"You encourage me to hope, madam, that the disparity of years may not prove an objection. Supposing the young lady to be entirely disengaged, may I be permitted to see her?"

"Most certainly, Sir Bridgnorth! I would much rather she answered for herself than I should answer for her. Ah! I see her in the garden! If you will step out with me to the lawn I will present you to her!"

Sir Bridgnorth willingly complied, though he felt some little internal trepidation. A variety of emotions agitated him.

Mildred was at the further end of the lawn, but she came to meet them, and he thought her even more charming in her simple morning costume than in evening dress.

"I had the pleasure of seeing you at the ball at Stafford the other night, Miss Calverley," he said, after the presentation had taken place. "You interested me exceedingly from the striking resemblance you bear to a young lady to whom I was tenderly attached in former days. I will tell you that little story some time or other should you desire to hear it. Meantime, it may suffice to say that I was actually engaged to her, but she threw me over for a better-looking man, and married him. It was a severe blow, and I did not recover it for a long time. I made up my mind never to marry, and for five-and-twenty years adhered to my determination. But see what our resolutions are worth! The sight of you dispelled mine in a moment! As I gazed at you, my youth seemed to return. I felt as much enamoured as I had done before, and it was with difficulty I could prevent myself from going up to you and saying, 'Behold your lover!'"

"I am very glad you didn't, Sir Bridgnorth," said Mildred.

"I knew you would think me a madman!" he continued; "and fearing I might be guilty of some indiscretion, I would not even be introduced to you. But I watched you throughout the evening, and your image has haunted me ever since. Feeling that my happiness is at stake, I have come here to plead my cause in person, and have just spoken to Mrs. Calverley. Now you know all."

"Not quite all, my love," said Mrs. Calverley. "I am bound to add, that, in making his proposal to you through me, Sir Bridgnorth has behaved in the handsomest manner."

"I am convinced of it," said Mildred; "but——"

"Do not crush my hopes at once," cried Sir Bridgnorth, in alarm. "Give me the chance of winning your affections. I don't desire an immediate answer."

"But I am very fickle myself, Sir Bridgnorth, and extremely liable to change my mind. You shall have no reason to complain of me as you do of your former love."

"I don't complain of her," he said, in a quiet tone.

"Then you are extremely forgiving; for, in my opinion, she used you shamefully."

"You must not say a word against her," exclaimed Sir Bridgnorth.

"Why not?" inquired Mildred, in surprise.

"For an excellent reason," he replied. "She was your own mother."

Mildred could scarcely repress a cry.

"I thought as much," said Mrs. Calverley. "Your fair inconstant was the beautiful Annabella Chetwynd, my husband's first wife."

"Exactly so," said Sir Bridgnorth. "I never beheld her since her marriage," he added, to Mildred. "No wonder, therefore, your appearance produced such an effect upon me. For a moment I thought she had come to life again. I shall always take an interest in you, and shall always be delighted to serve you. Since I cannot be your husband, you must allow me to be a friend."

" That offer I gladly accept, Sir Bridgnorth," she replied, extending her hand towards him.

He took it, and pressed it to his lips.

" You may rely upon me, as you could have done upon your own father," he said, with an earnestness that bespoke his sincerity. " Call on me when you will, I will answer the appeal. And now farewell ! "

" I hope you are not going, Sir Bridgnorth," said Mrs. Calverley. " Pray stay and spend the remainder of the day with us ! I am charmed to make your acquaintance."

" I shall be quite grieved if you go, dear Sir Bridgnorth," added Mildred.

" Since you ask me, I cannot refuse," he replied. " But my carriage is waiting at the door."

" I will give orders that it shall be put up immediately," said Mrs. Calverley. " It is so kind of you to stay."

And she went into the house to give the necessary directions.

III.

INQUIRIES.

MILDRED now felt quite at ease with Sir Bridgnorth. His manner towards her was so kind, that she almost began to regard him in the light of a father.

" Excuse me if I ask you a few questions relative to your brother Chetwynd," he said. " I am influenced by no impertinent curiosity, but simply by the desire to ascertain if I can be of any service to him. I am aware that a serious misunderstanding occurred between him and Mrs. Calverley at the time of your father's death ; and I have also heard that he absolutely refuses to accept any allowance from her."

" What you have heard is quite correct, Sir Bridgnorth," replied Mildred. " Mrs. Calverley desires to allow my brother six hundred a year, and has instructed Mr. Carteret, her solicitor, to pay him the amount quarterly ; but he declines to receive the money, being excessively indignant that my father should have left her the entire control of his property."

" But what has become of your brother ? What is he doing ? "

" I really cannot tell you, Sir Bridgnorth," she replied. " He came here just before poor papa's death, and remained till after the funeral ; but he shut himself up in his own room, and saw no one except old Norris, the butler, who is still with us. I had no idea he was going away so suddenly, for he did not acquaint me with his intention, or even take leave of me, or I would have tried to dissuade him from the step, though I fear I should have been unsuccessful. His mind seemed a good deal disturbed by painful circumstances that had occurred—chiefly, if not entirely, of his own causing—and I dreaded to excite him still farther. I have since reproached myself for my lukewarmness, but I acted under the advice of Doctor Spencer. After his abrupt departure, he wrote to me from an hotel in London, saying he was going abroad, and in all probability should not return for two or three years ; but Mr. Carteret found out that he was still in town, and sent him a cheque for three hundred pounds. The cheque was returned at once, accompanied by a letter, stating that he would accept nothing from Mrs. Calverley."

" His conduct is inexplicable ! " said Sir Bridgnorth. " But I suppose some effort has been made to communicate with him ? "

" Every effort has been made, but without any satisfactory result. He left the hotel I have mentioned with the expressed intention of going abroad. Whether he really did so, we have been unable to discover. We fear he has no resources. We know from Norris, whom he took into his confidence while he was here, that he had very little money."

" That is dreadful ! " exclaimed Sir Bridgnorth. " He was pointed out to me a year or two ago, at Ascot, and I thought him a remarkably fine young man ; but I was told he was very wild and extravagant—played and betted heavily."

" He has been very extravagant, Sir Bridgnorth. Poor papa paid his debts more than once, but could never keep him in bounds. That was the reason why he left him dependent upon mamma."

" So I understood," said Sir Bridgnorth ; " and I think he did quite right."

" I am sure he acted for the best," replied Mildred ; " and I am quite certain Mrs. Calverley would have carried out papa's intentions had she been able, but Chetwynd thwarted their designs by his fiery and ungovernable temper. Heaven knows what will become of him ! " she exclaimed, the tears starting to her eyes. " It makes me very unhappy to think of him."

" l fear I have distressed you," observed Sir Bridgnorth, much touched. " Perhaps I ought not to have spoken ? "

" I thank you sincerely for talking to me about my poor brother," she replied. " I may appear indifferent to him, but I am not so. I love him dearly, and would do anything for him. But I know not how to proceed. Such is the peculiarity of his temper—such his pride, that if I could find him, he would accept nothing from me if he thought it came from Mrs. Calverley. Even if he were starving, he would refuse aid from her."

" Well, I must try what I can do," said Sir Bridgnorth. " He can have no antipathy to me. The first thing is to discover where he is. I will see Carteret, and hear what he has to say."

" I thank you from the bottom of my heart, Sir Bridgnorth!" cried Mildred, with effusion. " You are, indeed, a father, both to poor Chetwynd and myself!"

Just then Mrs. Calverley reappeared.

" No more on this subject before mamma, I pray, Sir Bridgnorth!" said Mildred. " It would be painful to her."

" I will be careful," he replied.

Mrs. Calverley came to say that luncheon was ready. And they went into the house with her.

IV.

PORTRAITS.

The more Sir Bridgnorth saw of Mildred, the better pleased he was with her.

Mrs. Calverley did not produce quite so favourable an

impression upon him, though he thought her very beautiful, and very clever. She seemed to him wanting in heart—perhaps designing.

Taking this view of her character, he came to the conclusion that she had married Mr. Calverley for his money, and possibly might have alienated him from his son.

Three or four of Mildred's admirers called during the afternoon, and they all seemed surprised at finding Sir Bridgnorth so much at home at Ouselcroft. They could not believe that Mildred had accepted him—yet it looked rather like it.

The young lady, however, did not trouble herself much about them; but, leaving them to stroll about the garden with Mrs. Calverley, she took Sir Bridgnorth to the library, telling him she wanted to show him a picture.

It was the portrait of a very handsome young man, painted by a well-known artist of the day. The features were regular and finely formed, and very haughty in expression. The likeness was excellent, and Sir Bridgnorth recognised it at once.

"'Tis your brother Chetwynd," he said, "and wonderfully like him. I should have known it anywhere."

" He was extremely handsome then," observed Mildred; " but I fear he must be much changed now. At that time, he thought he should have all his father's property, and expected to marry the beautiful Teresa Mildmay."

"Yes; I know the story," said Sir Bridgnorth, "and do not wonder at his vexation at the double disappointment. He has suffered much for his hasty temper. Things look very dark just now; but let us hope all may come right in the end."

She then drew his attention to another picture.

"Your father. Yes; I see. Time was, when I should have turned away from his portrait; but I have quite forgiven him now."

"Since poor papa's death, Mrs. Calverley cannot bear to look at that portrait," remarked Mildred. "But for my entreaties she would have it put away, and she now rarely enters the room."

"That is not surprising," said Sir Bridgnorth. "The portrait awakens painful memories."

"But I am always pleased to look at it, and I loved papa dearly !" said Mildred. "I often come here by myself, and think I am with him."

At this juncture, their discourse was interrupted by the sudden entrance of the very last person they expected to see.

V.

THE POCKET-BOOK.

IT was Chetwynd.

He looked pale and haggard, and his features had a sombre and stern expression, very different from that depicted in the canvas before them.

He closed the door after him as he came in, and started on perceiving Sir Bridgnorth, whom he evidently had not expected to find there.

Uttering an exclamation of mingled surprise and

delight, Mildred sprang towards her brother, and flung her arms round his neck. While returning her embrace, he said in a low voice, "Who have you got with you?"

"Sir Bridgnorth Charlton," she replied. "He takes great interest in you, and has just been making inquiries about you."

"Not many minutes ago, I told your sister it would give me sincere pleasure if I could render you any service," said Sir Bridgnorth. "I did not expect so soon to have an opportunity of saying the same thing to you. I beg you will look upon me as a friend."

"I am greatly beholden to you, Sir Bridgnorth," replied the young man. "I have very few friends left."

"Mine are not mere idle professions, as you will find, if you choose to put them to the proof," said Sir Bridgnorth.

"You speak so earnestly and so kindly that I cannot but credit what you say," rejoined Chetwynd; "and I am the more inclined to believe you, since I have never done you a favour. Indeed, if my recollection serves me right, you have more reason to dislike than to befriend me."

"Your sister will tell you that the past is forgotten."

"Sir Bridgnorth has a noble heart," said Mildred. "You may speak freely before him. He knows all that has occurred, and is aware that you have refused to accept any allowance from Mrs. Calverley."

"And I may add that I sympathise with you," said Sir Bridgnorth.

"What has brought you back so suddenly?" said Mildred. "Are you in any difficulty?"

"In a most desperate difficulty," he replied. "I want two hundred pounds, and must have the money by to-morrow morning. I could procure it at once from Carteret; but I would rather shoot myself than accept a farthing from Mrs. Calverley. Can you help me?"

"*I* can," interposed Sir Bridgnorth, quickly. "Luckily, I have the amount about me. In this pocket-book," he added, producing one as he spoke, "you will find the sum you require. Repay me at your convenience."

"A thousand thanks, Sir Bridgnorth?" cried Chetwynd. "You have, indeed, conferred a very great obligation upon me, and I shall not speedily forget it. Ere long, I hope to be able to return you the money."

"Don't trouble yourself on that score; but let me see you soon. Come to me at Charlton."

"I cannot promise to visit you immediately, Sir Bridgnorth," replied the young man.

"Why not?" inquired Mildred.

"Do not ask me to explain," he rejoined. "I am scarcely my own master, and where I to make a promise, I might not be able to fulfil it. I must now begone."

"Stay!" cried Sir Bridgnorth; "can I not bring about a reconciliation between you and Mrs. Calverley? I think I could accomplish it, if you will consent to some arrangement."

"Never," replied Chetwynd. "And I beg that my visit and its object may not be mentioned to her."

"How did you discover I was in this room?" asked Mildred.

" Old Norris, whom I saw on my arrival, told me I should find you in the library, and I concluded you were alone ; but I have found a friend as well. And now I can answer no more questions."

" Ever mysterious and incomprehensible ! " cried Mildred. I do not like to part with you thus."

" You must ! " he rejoined. " It is necessary that I should be in London to-night."

He then bade them both farewell, tenderly embracing his sister, and renewing his thanks to Sir Bridgnorth.

Just as he was about to depart, the door was opened by old Norris, who called out, " Mrs. Calverley is coming to the library ! "

" I won't see her ! " cried Chetwynd, fiercely.

But there was no retreat, and he was compelled to remain.

In another moment, Mrs. Calverley appeared. Her astonishment at beholding Chetwynd may be imagined ; nor, though she strove to veil it, could she altogether conceal her annoyance.

" I did not expect to find you here, Chetwynd," she said.

" I came to see my sister, madam," he replied, haughtily ; " and, having had a brief interview with her, I am now about to depart."

And, with a stiff bow, he quitted the room.

As soon as she could recover her speech, Mrs. Calverley observed to Sir Bridgnorth, " You see with what impracticable material I have to deal. Any friendly overture on my part is always scornfully rejected. Well, Chetwynd must take his own course ; and if he suffers for his wilfulness, he has only himself to blame. Do you feel at liberty to tell me what he came about, Mildred?"

"I do not," she replied.

"You were present at the interview, I suppose, Sir Bridgnorth?"

"Quite unintentionally, madam," he answered. "And my lips are sealed."

This incident rather threw a damp upon the pleasure of the day.

Mrs. Calverley looked displeased, and Mildred appeared anxious and thoughtful, so Sir Bridgnorth ordered his carriage.

But before taking his departure, he had a little private conversation with Mildred, and promised to come over again to Ouselcroft on an early day.

VI.

BRACKLEY HEATH.

MRS. CALVERLEY had a very pretty pony phaeton, which she was accustomed to drive herself. Easy as a lounging-chair, and with the two long-tailed bay ponies attached to it, the luxurious little vehicle formed a very nice turn-out.

One fine morning, about a week after Sir Bridgnorth's visit, Mrs. Calverley and Mildred set out in the pony phaeton with the intention of calling on Lady Barfleur and her daughter, at Brackley Hall, which was about six or seven miles from Ouselcroft.

Usually, they were attended by a groom, but on this particular occasion he was left at home.

The ponies were full of spirit, and eager to get on, but the ladies would not indulge them, and proceeded quietly along the pleasant lanes, through a rich and fertile district, abounding in farms, where some of the best cheeses in the county are made.

To reach Brackley Hall, however, they had to cross an extensive heath, a great part of which was very wild and marshy.

But this brown and uncultivated tract, where turf alone was cut, and where there were two or three dangerous swamps, offered the charm of contrast to the rich meadows they had just quitted. Here there were no farm-houses, no cow-sheds, no large barns, no orchards; but the air was fresh and pleasant, and lighted up by the brilliant sunshine, even Brackley Heath looked well. At least, our fair friends thought so, and the ponies were compelled to walk in consequence. Yet there was nothing remarkable in the prospect, as the reader shall judge. The whole scene owed its charm to the fine weather.

On the left the heath was bordered by the woods belonging to Brackley Hall, and, through a break in them, the upper part of the fine old timber and plaster mansion could be descried.

On the right the country was flat and uninteresting, planted in places by rows of tall poplars, and a canal ran through it, communicating with the River Mersey.

In front, but at some distance, rose a hill crowned by the ruins of an old castle, and having a small village and grey old church in the immediate neighbourhood.

In bad weather the heath had a dreary and desolate

E

aspect. Here and there a hut could be perceived, but these miserable habitations were far removed from the road, and might have been deserted, since no smoke issued from them, and nothing could be seen of their occupants. A few sheep were scattered about in spots where the turf was covered with herbage; but they seemed wholly untended. Rooks there were in flocks from Brackley Park, plovers, and starlings. Even sea-gulls found their way to the morass.

While the ladies were contemplating this scene, which they thought highly picturesque, and comment-ing upon its beauties, they were startled, and indeed terrified, by the sudden appearance of two formidable-looking fellows, who had been watching their approach from behind an aged and almost branchless oak that grew near the road.

Evidently, from their peculiar garb, tawny skin, black eyes, and raven locks, these individuals were gipsies. They did not leave their purpose in doubt for a moment, but rushing towards the ladies with threatening gestures, shouted to them to stop.

Mrs. Calverley tried to whip on the ponies, but before they could start off they were checked by one of the gipsies, who seized the reins, while his comrade, addressing Mrs. Calverley, demanded her whip, and, as she hesitated to give it up, he snatched it from her, and threw it on the ground.

"Excuse my freedom, my lady," he said, in accents meant to be polite, but that sounded gruff and me-nacing. " We can't allow you to go till we've had some talk with you; but we won't detain you longer nor we can help. We wants any money you may have about you, together with ornaments, rings, watches, ear-rings, and sich like. Deliver 'em up quietly, and you won't be molested—will they, Ekiel?"

"No," replied the other ruffian, who stood at the heads of the ponies. "It would hurt our feelin's to use wiolence to two sich lovely creaters."

Meanwhile, Mildred, who wished to preserve her watch, which had been given her by her father, was trying to detach it from the guard, but could not accomplish her object without attracting the attention of the gipsy near Mrs. Calverley.

Dashing round to the other side of the carriage, he caught hold of the chain, and broke it, but failed to secure the watch.

Mildred screamed loudly, though she had little expectation of help.

"Look quick, Clynch!" shouted Ekiel, in a warning voice.

"Give me the watch without more ado!" cried the gipsy to Mildred.

But she spread her hands over it, and redoubled her outcries.

"Here, take my purse and begone!" said Mrs. Calverley.

"Thank ye, my lady," rejoined Clynch, quickly appropriating the purse. "But that's not enough. We must have everything you've got about you!"

"You shall have nothing more, fellow!" cried Mrs. Calverley, with great spirit. "And see! assistance is at hand! If you stay a minute longer you will be caught!"

And, as she spoke, a gentleman was seen galloping towards them, followed by a groom.

Baulked of their prey, the gipsies ran off, and made

for the morass, with the intricacies of which they seemed well acquainted.

A minute or so afterwards their deliverer came up.

A fine-looking young man, between twenty and thirty, and having decidedly a military air, but a stranger to them both.

VII.

CAPTAIN DANVERS.

"I HOPE you have lost nothing, ladies?" cried the stranger.

"The robbers have taken my purse," replied Mrs. Calverley; "and but for your timely aid, they would have carried off all our ornaments."

"My chain is gone," said Mildred. "But I don't mind it. They did not get my watch, which I value extremely. I owe its preservation entirely to you, sir," she added, with a grateful look at the stranger.

"I am happy to find I have been of any service to you," he replied, bowing. "Follow the rascals, Tom," he added to his groom, "and try to capture one or both of them."

"Impossible, I fear, captain," replied the groom. "They can go where no horse can go in that marsh, if they know the ground, as they seem to do. But I'll do my best."

And he speeded after the fugitives, who were still in sight.

"Hold the reins for a minute, Mildred, while I pick up my whip," said Mrs. Calverley.

" Allow me ! " cried the stranger.

And, jumping down from the saddle, he presented the whip to Mrs. Calverley, who gracefully acknowledged the attention.

" We are really very much indebted to you, sir," she said.

" You greatly overrate the service," he rejoined. " I have literally done nothing. Hearing cries, and perceiving you were stopped by robbers, I galloped on to your aid—that is all."

" May we learn the name of our deliverer? " she asked.

" I am Captain Charles Danvers," he replied ; " nephew to Sir Leycester Barfleur, of Brackley Hall, which you can see through the trees yonder. But I dare say you know the place ? "

" We were on our way thither, to call on Lady Barfleur, when we met with this alarming adventure," observed Mrs. Calverley.

An idea seemed suddenly to occur to Captain Danvers.

" Are you not Mrs. Calverley, of Ouselcroft? " he inquired.

She replied in the affirmative ; adding, " And this is my step-daughter, Miss Calverley."

" I felt convinced of it ! " he cried, again bowing. " I am indeed fortunate in obtaining an introduction to a young lady of whom I have heard so much."

" You can pay compliments as well as rescue ladies from robbers, it seems, Captain Danvers," observed Mildred, slightly blushing. " We should have met you, I have no doubt, at Brackley Hall."

" Very likely," he rejoined. " But I prefer an accidental meeting of this kind ; it is more romantic. I hope you are not going to turn back. If you are, you must allow me to escort you. But they will be delighted to see you, I am sure, at Brackley, and you can recount your adventure to them."

" And extol your gallantry at the same time, Captain Danvers," laughed Mildred. " I have quite recovered from my fright, mamma, so I think we may as well go on."

" Do, by all me. s ! " cried Captain Danvers, vaulting on his horse.

Mrs. Calverley assented ; and they were just setting off, when the groom was seen returning, so they waited until he came up.

" I see you have failed, Tom," said his master.

" Yes, captain," replied the man, touching his hat. " I'm very sorry, but it was no use attempting to follow them. I should have got over head and ears in a quagmire."

" Immediate information of the robbery must be given to the police at Frodsham," said Captain Danvers.

" It is scarcely worth while to take any more trouble about the matter," said Mrs. Calverley. " My purse had very little in it."

" And I don't care much for my chain, since my watch is safe," added Mildred.

The party then set off, but not at a very quick pace, for Captain Danvers rode by the side of the pony-carriage, and chatted with its fair occupants.

VIII.

BRACKLEY HALL.

CAPTAIN DANVERS has already been described as a handsome young man of about five-and-twenty, and it may now be added that he was tall, well-made, and had marked features—the manly character of his physiognomy being heightened by his brown moustaches.

A dark velveteen shooting-coat, boots of supple leather, that ascended to the knee, where they were met by a pair of knickerbockers—loose, Dutch-looking trousers—formed his costume, while his brown curling locks were covered by a black felt hat. Such as it was, the dress suited him, and both ladies thought it very becoming.

Captain Danvers was in a cavalry regiment, which was quartered at Madras, and he had recently come home on leave. His father, Sir Gerard Danvers, resided at Offham Court, in Kent, and was thought very wealthy. Unluckily Charles Danvers was not an eldest son.

The party had now entered the park, and were proceeding along a fine avenue leading to the house, which stood right in front of them.

Brackley Hall, which was in admirable preservation considering its great antiquity, dated back to the period of Edward the Fourth, or even earlier.

Constructed almost entirely of timber and plaster, it was remarkable for the singularity of its form. It was only three storeys high, the upper storey projecting far beyond the lower, but the summit of the building was occupied by a lofty gallery, more than a hundred feet in length, that looked externally like a lantern, since it had continuous ranges of windows on every side.

Most curious was the timber-work, the gables and lintels being richly carved, as was the porch. The immense bay windows, which constituted the chief beauty of the house, were framed with heavy transom bars, and exquisitely latticed.

In the court-yard was a chapel, surmounted in olden times by a tall, square tower, but this had been taken down.

The hall was surrounded by a moat, and approached by a wide stone bridge. Another bridge communicated with the gardens, which were extensive, and laid out in a quaint, formal style, with terraces, stone steps, fountains, quincunxes, clipped yew-trees, alleys, and a bowling-green. We must not omit to mention that the old mansion had the reputation of being haunted.

Adjoining the house was a grove of noble elms, wherein a colony of rooks had been settled for centuries.

About half a mile off, at the rear of the mansion, was a small lake, or mere, remarkable for the blackness of its water. But black as was the mere, it abounded with fish, and at certain times of the year was a great resort of wild fowl.

Captain Danvers had sent on his groom to the hall to inform Sir Leycester and Lady Barfleur that Mrs. Calverley was coming on to call on them, and also to explain what had occurred.

Consequently, when the ladies had crossed the bridge and entered the court, they found Sir Leycester and

Lady Barfleur, with the fair Emmeline, waiting to receive them, and they had no sooner alighted than they were overwhelmed with expressions of sympathy. Some of the servants who were assembled in the court seemed likewise greatly excited.

Sir Leycester, an old fox-hunter and rather choleric, was excessively wroth, and vowed he would never rest till he had caught the rascals. He had no idea whatever, he said, that the country was infested with such vermin, but catch them he would. Mrs. Calverley endeavoured to dissuade him from his purpose, but in vain.

" I only waited to see you, or I should have been off before," he said. " You'll excuse me quitting you so abruptly, since I am going on your business."

" But I'd much rather you didn't go, Sir Leycester," said Mrs. Calverley. " I'm afraid the gipsies may offer a desperate resistance."

" I'm sure they will," added Mildred.

" No matter ; I'll have them ! " rejoined Sir Leycester.

" If you really are going on this gipsy-hunt, my dear uncle, I'll go with you," said Captain Danvers.

" No, no ; I don't want you, Charles," rejoined Sir Leycester. " Remain with the ladies. You must stay till I return, my dear Mrs. Calverley."

She promised that she would ; and, after a word or two with Lady Barfleur, he proceeded to the stables, and ordered a hunter to be saddled immediately. He also told Booth, the coachman, on whom he could place reliance, that he should require him and a couple of grooms to attend him.

While the horses were being saddled, a footman

brought a brace of pistols, which Sir Leycester had sent for.

Armed with these, and accompanied by Booth, and one of his own grooms, together with his nephew's groom, Tom, he set out on the expedition, shaping his course towards the further side of the morass, where he expected to find some traces of the robbers.

IX.

LADY BARFLEUR.

LADY BARFLEUR had been a very fine woman in her day, and though her beauty was now somewhat passed, she was still a stately dame, and accorded extremely well with the old mansion of which she was mistress.

The drawing-room, to which she conducted her visitors, was a very splendid apartment, and merits a .brief description.

The ceiling was adorned with pendants, and the upper part of the walls was covered with a profusion of plaster ornaments, among which were the arms of Elizabeth and James the First. The dark oak wainscoting was richly carved in arches and pilasters, producing a very fine effect.

The principal feature of the room, however, was the magnificent fireplace. Rising to a great height, it was adorned with pillars and sculptured figures that supported the architrave, above which were emblazoned the arms of the Barfleurs.

The furniture was consistent with the antique cha-

racter of the room—none of it being of a later date
than the early part of the seventeenth century.

As Lady Barfleur moved slowly and somewhat stiffly
about this noble apartment, or seated herself in a high-
backed chair, carved in oak, black as ebony, she looked
as if she belonged to the same date as the furniture ;
and her hair, having become prematurely grey, aided
the illusion.

Not so Emmeline. She was a very charming representative of the young lady of our own period.

An exceedingly pretty brunette, she had splendid
black eyes, shaded by long silken lashes, and arched
over by finely-pencilled brows, lovely features, ripe
red lips, and teeth like pearls—and, as she was very
lively, the latter were often displayed.

She was not tall, but her figure was symmetry itself,
and Cinderella might have envied her tiny feet. She
was about the same age as Mildred, and they were
great friends.

At first, the discourse turned chiefly upon the robbery, which Lady Barfleur begged might be fully described to her ; but it was soon changed to other topics.

For awhile, Captain Danvers seemed undecided
whether to devote himself to the beautiful and wealthy
widow or her lovely step-daughter ; but at length he
began to pay exclusive attention to the former, probably
because she gave him most encouragement. Indeed,
Mrs. Calverley seemed more favourably inclined towards
him than to any other suitor since her husband's death.

Captain Danvers, it appeared, had only arrived at
Brackley a few days previously, and this accounted for
his not having met the ladies of Ouselcroft before.

Whether Mildred was altogether pleased by having

him carried off in this manner, we will not say. Not the slightest sign of annoyance was manifest. She laughed and chatted gaily with Emmeline; and when that young lady proposed that they should go and look at the gallery, she readily assented, and left Mrs. Calverley in quiet possession of the handsome captain.

X.

THE GALLERY.

ASCENDING a beautiful spiral oak staircase, the two young ladies soon reached the gallery, which, it has already been mentioned, was situated at the top of the house.

Like all the other rooms in the old mansion, the gallery was maintained in its original state. At all events, it had undergone no alteration since 1570, as appeared from an inscription above the door.

Exceedingly light and cheerful, as might be expected from the multitude of windows, it seemed of immense size. It had a wooden roof—the rafters being painted; and the panels were covered with tapestry, or hung with family portraits. In the room were several curious old cabinets.

"I am always charmed with this gallery," exclaimed Mildred, as she gazed around it in admiration. "If I lived here, I should spend all my time in it."

"You would get tired of it," rejoined Emmeline. "For my part, I prefer my own little chamber, with its carved oak bedstead, and beautiful bay-window."

"Yes, your room is very pretty, but not to be compared with this grand gallery."

"The gallery is too large to be pleasant," said Emmeline. "Indeed, I rarely come here, unless we have company. But do sit down. I want to have a little private and confidential talk with you."

"I hope you have some affair of the heart to communicate," said Mildred, as she sat down on an old-fashioned sofa, covered with Utrecht velvet, and just large enough for two, while Emmeline placed herself beside her, and took her hand.

"You must know, then," began Miss Barfleur, "that two or three years ago I had a *tête-à-tête* with a very handsome young man. We were seated on this very sofa. Mamma and several other persons were present, but they were too far off to overhear what passed."

"That is one advantage of a very large room," remarked Mildred. "But I am sorry this *tête-à-tête* occurred so long ago. I hope it has been renewed.

"No; and I fear it never will be renewed," sighed Emmeline. "But I have not forgotten it."

"Did it come to a positive proposal?" inquired Mildred.

"Not exactly; but if the gentleman *had* proposed I am sure I should have accepted him; and I feel I never can love any one else."

"You think so now. I suppose he is still unmarried?"

"Shortly after the interview I have mentioned, he was engaged to another person; but the engagement was broken off, and he is now free."

"Have you seen him again lately?"

"Not for a long, long time, Mildred; but I love him still, despite his inconstancy, and I should like to know something about him."

"Emmeline," said Mildred, regarding her fixedly, "you are not referring to my brother Chetwynd?"

"To whom else could I refer?" was the reply.

Mildred uttered an exclamation of surprise.

"I perfectly remember Chetwynd speaking of you in rapturous terms," she said, "and telling me he had had a strong flirtation with you in the gallery at Brackley Hall, but I had no idea you were at all serious on the occasion. Oh, what a chance of happiness he has missed! Had be been fortunate enough to possess you, how different would have been his life!"

"I loved him!" said Emmeline, with emotion; "and I don't believe Teresa Mildmay ever did."

"I entirely agree with you," remarked Mildred. "I have listened to your recital with the deepest interest, dearest Emmeline, and I wish I could give you a good account of Chetwynd, but I really cannot. I saw him the other day, but only for a few minutes."

"At Ouselcroft?" inquired Emmeline, eagerly.

"Yes. He came there quite unexpectedly, and left immediately."

"I am afraid his hasty departure doesn't look as if he had made up his quarrel with Mrs. Calverley."

"Alas! no; and I greatly fear he never will become reconciled to her. Perhaps you are aware he won't accept anything from her?"

"Yes; and I admire his spirit."

"Still he is very foolish. He is punishing himself, not her."

"But he adhered to his word. I shouldn't like him half so much if he yielded."

"Then your regard won't be lessened, for I feel certain he won't yield."

"I judged him rightly, you see," said Emmeline; "and I persuade myself he will triumph in the end. And now, dearest Mildred, before we finish our discourse, will you faithfully promise to let me know when you next see him or hear from him?"

"I won't delude you, Emmeline. I don't expect either to see him or hear from him. Sir Bridgnorth Charlton has very kindly undertaken to look after him, but he may not have an opportunity of doing so. Unlike anybody else, Chetwynd seems to shun those who love him or would serve him."

"I hope he won't shun me," said Emmeline.

"Not if he could be made aware that you take an interest in him; but how convey the information? He does not correspond with me, and I don't even know his address, or what way a letter could reach him."

"Then I must remain in the same state of uncertainty as ever," said Emmeline, in a despairing tone. "You give me small comfort, Mildred."

"I pity you from my heart, dearest Emmeline; but comfort you I cannot."

For a moment, Emmeline seemed overpowered by emotion. She then found relief in tears, and her head dropped on Mildred's shoulder.

"Think of him no more—think of him no more!" cried Mildred. "He does not deserve your love. I, his sister, say so."

Emmeline made no response, but continued to sob.

Neither of them were aware that Lady Barfleur had entered the gallery.

Greatly surprised at what she beheld, her ladyship stood still. Fortunately she did not hear the words uttered by Mildred, so she could only guess at the cause of this sudden outburst of grief.

At length she announced her presence by a slight cough, and Mildred perceived her.

"Calm yourself, dearest girl," she whispered to Emmeline. "Your mother is here."

"Here!" exclaimed Emmeline, looking up. "Yes, I see. Can she have heard anything?"

"I think not. But be calm, or you will betray yourself!"

Thereupon they both arose, and Emmeline did her best to repress her emotion, and succeeded in forcing a smile.

"You will scold me, mamma, when you learn that I have been so foolish as to weep at a very pathetic story told me by Mildred," she said.

"I am glad to find it is nothing serious," replied Lady Barfleur.

"Have you come to tell us that papa has captured the gipsies?"

"No; he has not yet returned," replied Lady Barfleur. "I came to let you know that Mrs. Calverly and Captain Danvers have gone to the garden. Perhaps you may like to join them there."

"Shall we, Mildred?"

"By all means," was the reply. "I shouldn't think I had been at Brackley unless I had had a stroll in the delightful old garden."

"Don't wait for me; I'll follow," said Lady Barfleur.

Glad to escape further questioning, the two delinquents flew down the spiral staircase, and hastened to the garden.

XI.

WHAT PASSED IN THE GARDEN.

" Do you know, Mrs. Calverley, I have never been at your place, Ouselcroft, and I hear it's uncommonly pretty."

This remark was made by Captain Danvers, as he was seated by the side of the charming widow on a bench near one of the fountains.

" Come and see it, and judge," she replied. " We shall be at home to-morrow."

" Give me the greatest pleasure to ride over," he said. " A country place is charming ; but I almost wonder you haven't got a house in town."

" I think of taking one," she replied. " Mildred has never been in town—never resided there, I ought to say. Her papa objected to noise and racket—didn't care for the parks or the Opera, and disliked large parties. I don't think he could have stood a season in town. I prefer quietude and the country myself. However, Mildred ought to be considered, and as she wishes to mix a little more with society than she is able to do here, we shall go to London for a time."

" 'Pon my soul ! you're exceedingly kind," cried the captain. " Miss Calverley is blessed with a most indulgent mamma—'sister,' I was going to say, but I recollected myself in time."

F

" I shall make her as happy as I can, so long as she remains with me," replied Mrs. Calverley. " When my late husband entrusted his daughter to my care, he knew I should do my duty to her."

" And your first duty," he remarked, with a smile, " is to get her well married. That will be easily accomplished, for I hear there are many *pretendants*. No wonder!—she is a most lovely creature."

" And will have a very good fortune," said Mrs. Calverley. " I make no secret that I mean to give her thirty thousand pounds as a marriage portion."

Captain Danvers was astounded. If she was to have such a fortune as this, he began to think he had better turn his attention to the step-daughter. He endeavoured to look indifferent, but Mrs. Calverley perceived that the remark had told, as she intended it to do.

" You are the most generous of your sex, Mrs. Calverley," he observed. " Few women, circumstanced as you are, would make so great a sacrifice."

" I don't consider it a sacrifice, Captain Danvers. I regard it as a duty. I simply represent her father. What he would have done, I shall do."

" I cannot withhold my admiration of conduct as rare as it is praiseworthy," said the captain. " I repeat, you deserve infinite credit for your generosity. But Mr. Calverley, I believe, left a son as well as a daughter? What will he say to this magnificent portion?"

" He has no voice in the matter," replied the lady. " My husband left the entire control of his property to me."

" A wise man!—a very wise man!" cried the captain.

" Chetwynd Calverley has been very wild and extravagant," said the widow. " It was necessary, therefore, to tie up the property."

" Quite necessary !—quite proper ! " remarked the captain. "Though I shouldn't like it myself," he thought. " Is Chetwynd satisfied with the arrangement, may I ask ? "

" Very much the reverse," she replied. " But that is immaterial."

" He doesn't know what is good for him," said the captain. " None of us do," he mentally ejaculated.

" Then you approve of the course I am about to pursue, Captain Danvers ? "

" Entirely, my dear madam—entirely," he replied. " I think it most judicious."

" And now you have asked me a good many questions, let me ask you one in return ? " said Mrs. Calverley.

" Delighted to answer any questions you may put to me," he replied, wondering what she was going to say.

" But don't answer this, unless you like," she observed.

" Let me hear it," he rejoined, fearing something unpleasant was coming.

" How is it that your lovely cousin, Emmeline, has not married ? I know she has had several very good offers."

" 'Pon my honour, I can't tell. I fancy—but mind its only fancy—she has had some disappointment."

" I should think that scarcely possible," observed Mrs. Calverley. " Why, she is an only child, and will be a great heiress ! "

"Well, that's the only solution I can give of the
mystery. I know Lord Bollington proposed to her,
and I know my uncle would have liked the match to
take place, but the young lord was refused."

"Possibly she has an attachment," observed Mrs.
Calverley, thoughtfully. "If so, it's a great pity."

"Here she comes, with Miss Calverley," said
Captain Danvers, as the two young ladies were seen
advancing along the terrace.

XII.

BRACKLEY MERE.

By this time, all traces of tears had disappeared, and
Emmeline's dark eyes looked lustrous as ever.

Judging from her lively manner, no one would have
dreamed that she nourished a secret attachment. But
she kept it carefully locked up in the recesses of her
heart, and had no confidante except Mildred.

Captain Danvers rose to meet them, but Mrs. Calverley retained her seat.

"We shall see now how he acts," she thought.

He did not leave her long in doubt. He immediately began an animated conversation with Mildred,
and kept by her side as they walked round the garden,
leaving Emmeline to amuse Mrs. Calverley.

No doubt the handsome captain could make himself
extremely agreeable if he chose, and he now exerted
himself to the utmost, and succeeded.

Having expatiated upon the beauty of the formal old
garden they were surveying, and saying how much he

preferred it to the landscape style, he turned the discourse to the amusements and gaieties of London, and soon found that Mildred was really anxious to spend a season in town ; whereupon he expressed the greatest satisfaction, as he should frequently have an opportunity of meeting her.

By this time Lady Barfleur had made her appearance, and as she could report nothing of Sir Leycester, she suggested a visit to the mere.

"It is a nice shady walk there through the wood," she said ; "and if you have not seen the mere, I think you will be struck by it."

"Not by its beauty, mamma," remarked Emmeline, " but rather by its blackness."

"Well, such blackness as that water boasts *is* a beauty," said Captain Danvers. "In my opinion, the mere is well worth seeing."

"There are all sorts of legends attached to it," said Emmeline. "Amongst others, there is a superstition, that when anything is about to happen to our house, a great piece of black oak, that has been sunk for ages at the bottom of the lake, floats to the surface."

"An idle story," remarked Lady Barfleur.

"You excite my curiosity," said Mrs. Calverley. "I should like to see this mysterious lake."

"You must excuse my accompanying you," said Lady Barfleur. "Captain Danvers will conduct you there."

"With the greatest pleasure," said the captain. "I hope you will go too, Miss Calverley ?"

"Oh, of course !" she replied.

So they all set off, with the exception of Lady Barfleur, who rarely got beyond the garden.

In a very few minutes, they had plunged into a wood, through which a narrow road led to the mere.

In some places, the path was overarched by trees, and the branches formed a delightful screen on that hot day.

Captain Danvers led the way with Mildred, and the path being only wide enough for two, the others were obliged to follow. As the wood seemed to inspire such a tone, his accents became low and tender.

Suddenly they burst upon the lake in all its sombre grandeur. The water looked intensely black, but when examined, it was found to be perfectly clear. The broad expanse was surrounded by trees, which, in some instances, advanced beyond the bank.

The surface of the mere was unruffled, for not a breath of wind was stirring, and reflected the trees as in a mirror. Occasionally, however, a fish would leap up, and the smooth water was, for a moment, rippled.

But the effect of the scene was not cheerful. An air of gloom brooded over the place, that impressed the beholder with melancholy. Both Mrs. Calverley and Mildred acknowledged the feeling.

At the point where the visitors had approached it, the lake was shallow, and occupied by a large bed of reeds and bulrushes; but, at the opposite extremity, the water was profoundly deep, and supposed, by the common folk, to be unfathomable.

On the left, and not far from where they stood, was a boat-house, and Captain Danvers offered to row them to the further end of the lake, so that they might have an opportunity of completely surveying it.

The proposal was gladly accepted.

Repairing to the shed, they embarked in a large

flat-bottomed boat, better adapted for fishing than moving rapidly through the water.

However, it answered the purpose. Captain Danvers took the sculls, and contrived to get Mildred next him. The clumsy craft moved slowly on, and was now and then stopped that the ladies might look around.

As they drew near the lower end, the lake seemed to become darker, and the trees that shut it in assumed a yet more sombre appearance.

Here it was deepest.

Captain Danvers was tugging at the sculls, but still making very slow progress, when the boat struck against something in the water that gave it a great shock.

The captain ceased rowing, and looking round to see what he had come in contact with, to his surprise and consternation, he beheld the blackened trunk of a huge oak.

Hitherto, the dusky mass had scarcely appeared above the surface, but on being thus forcibly struck, it rolled round in such manner as to display its enormous bulk, and then gradually sank.

All three ladies saw the ill-omened piece of timber at the same time as Captain Danvers.

Uttering a cry of fright, Emmeline stood up, and, pointing to it, exclaimed :

" 'Tis the black oak I told you of. One of my father's house is doomed ! "

The others looked aghast, but spoke not. Even Captain Danvers seemed struck dumb.

Without a word, he turned the boat's head, and began to row back.

While he was moving round, Emmeline sat down,

and covered her eyes, to shut the hideous object from
her view.

"It is gone," said Mildred, in a low tone. "Try
not to think about it."

"I ought to think about it," rejoined Emmeline,
scarcely above her breath. "It is a death-warning!"

"But not to you, dearest girl," said Mildred.

"I would rather it applied to me than to those I
love," she returned.

Silence prevailed among the party till they landed.
No more jesting on the part of the captain. He
looked very gloomy.

When they got out of tho boat, he tried to cheer up
his fair cousin, but did not succeed.

They walked back quietly to the Hall, where a
painful surprise awaited them.

XIII.

PURSUIT OF THE GIPSIES.

SIR LEYCESTER BARFLEUR, as we have shown, had
ridden with his attendants to the further side of the
morass, where he hoped to intercept the gipsies in
their flight, but he could discover nothing of them.

Posting himself with Booth, the coachman, on a
little mound near the marsh, he sent off the two
grooms to the huts previously mentioned, to ascertain
whether the fugitives had taken refuge there; but
his emissaries brought him no satisfactory intelligence,
and it was the opinion of the turf-cutters who in-
habited the huts that the gipsies had gone off altogether.

Sir Leycester, however, felt convinced that the rascals were somewhere about, and ordered his men to make a careful search, directing the turf-cutters to assist them.

Again they were all at fault.

Sir Leycester next tried the wood that skirted the heath, and sent the men on by different routes, fixing a place of meeting in the heart of the thicket.

He himself pursued the main road, attended by Booth.

" It's a pity we didn't bring those two Scotch deer-hounds with us, Sir Leycester," observed the coach-man. " If the gipsies have taken shelter in this wood, we shall never be able to find 'em without a dog of some sort."

" I believe you're right, Booth," replied Sir Ley-cester. " I don't like hunting men in that way. But what's to be done, if we can't catch them otherwise ? "

" It's the only sure plan," rejoined Booth. " We're wasting time now."

" Well, go and fetch the hounds," said Sir Leycester. " Ride to the keeper's lodge as fast as you can. If Rushton shouldn't be at home, go on to the Hall ; but use despatch."

" Shall I bring Rushton with me, as well as the hounds, Sir Leycester ? " inquired Booth.

" Ay, do," replied the baronet.

" And a bloodhound ? " asked the coachman, with a grin.

Sir Leycester signified his assent, and Booth gal-loped off.

He had scarcely started, when the baronet regretted the last order given, and called out to him not to bring the bloodhound.

Booth, however, was out of hearing.

Sir Leycester then proceeded to the centre of the wood, keeping a sharp look-out on either side as he rode along.

The others had already arrived at the appointed spot, but had nothing to tell.

The baronet felt very much inclined to swear; but, just at the moment, a burly farmer, named Marple, who used to hunt with him, came up, mounted on a well-bred horse.

On hearing what was going on, Marple told the baronet he had just seen a couple of gipsies, who appeared to be hiding on the banks of the Weever, and offered to take him to the exact spot.

"No doubt they are the rogues you are looking for, Sir Leycester," he added.

"No doubt of it!" cried the baronet, joyfully. "Come along!"

He then rode off with Marple, taking the two grooms with him, and leaving the turf-cutters behind, to wait for Booth and the hounds.

The river Weever described a wide half-circle round the east side of the wood, the spot referred to by Marple being about half a mile off.

As they rode at a rattling pace, they were there in a few minutes; but when they approached the river, they proceeded cautiously.

If the gipsies had not decamped, they felt sure of catching them, the Weever being here very deep, while there was no bridge within a mile.

But, cautiously as they came on, they had been descried, and perfectly understanding their design, the gipsies were endeavouring to escape by creeping along the bank of the river, which was here bordered by willows.

Having got nearly to the end of this screen, the fugitives stopped, determined, if hard pressed, to make for the adjoining wood, and being both extremely fleet, they had no doubt of accomplishing their purpose.

XIV.

THE BLOODHOUND.

It soon became manifest to the gipsies that their pursuers were following them, and searching carefully about among the willows; and they were still more alarmed by the report of a pistol, discharged by Sir Leycester, with the view of rousing them from the covert.

Accordingly, they dashed off; and so busily were their pursuers occupied, that a minute or two elapsed before their flight was discovered.

A piece of ground, level as a village green, and a couple of meadows, lay between them and the desired place of shelter, and they had gained the first hedge, and were scrambling through it, when they were perceived by Sir Leycester, who instantly shouted a view-halloo, and the whole party started in pursuit.

But not without reason had the gipsies reckoned upon their own speed.

Before Sir Leycester and his attendants cleared the first obstacle, they had leaped a five-barred gate, and were flying across the second field.

In half a minute more they had plunged into the thicket, and fancied themselves secure.

Sir Leycester, on the other hand, who was close at their heels, knew very well they had run into the trap and chuckled at the thought of their speedy capture.

Causing his companions to disperse, he went towards the centre of the wood, expecting to find Booth with the keeper and the hounds.

Meanwhile, the gipsies, being well acquainted with the thicket, made their way to its inmost recesses, where the brambles and underwood would render it difficult, if not impossible, for the horsemen to follow them.

They heard Marple and the others on their left and right, pushing their way through the trees, and vainly endeavouring to get near them. They, therefore, felt quite safe; the only unpleasantness being that they might be detained there till night.

But this feeling of security was quickly dispelled by some sounds they did not at all like. They first heard voices at a distance, accompanied by the crackling of small branches, announcing that some persons on foot were searching for them, and Ekiel remarked, in a low tone, to his comrade :

" Why, that's Ned Rushton, the keeper's voice. We're not safe here, if he's after us."

" Keep quiet," muttered Clynch. " He mayn't come this way."

Shortly afterwards, a low, ominous growl, not to be mistaken by the experienced, reached their ears, and filled them with alarm.

" Ned has got a bloodhound with him, Ekiel," said Clynch. " We must kill the brute ! Have you got your Spanish knife with you ? "

"Ay! but I daren't attack that hound."

"Give me the knife, then! I'll do it!" cried Clynch. "We must get out of this place as quickly as we can, and run for life."

"Run where?" demanded Ekiel.

"To the marsh," replied Clynch. "That's our only chance."

"That devil of a dog has taken all my strength out of me."

"Don't be afeared of him!" cried Clynch, unclasping the cuchillo, the point of which was as sharp as a needle.

Just then, a long bay proclaimed that the hound had got the scent, while the voice, stated by Ekiel to be that of Ned Rushton, was heard encouraging him.

The gipsies set off; but had not gone far when the formidable hound burst upon them through the underwood.

Quick as lightening, Clynch turned, and dropping on one knee, faced the enemy with the cuchillo in his hand.

For a moment, the hound fixed upon him a red, deep-seated eye, and then sprang at his throat.

But Clynch, whose gaze had never quitted the terrible animal, received him on the point of the knife, and drove the deadly weapon to his heart. With a fierce yell, the hound fell back.

Having thus liberated himself from his formidable foe, Clynch was making off, when Ned Rushton appeared.

Exasperated by the slaughter of his favourite, he discharged both barrels of his gun at the flying gipsy, but without effect. The shot rattled over the head of the fugitive, but did him no harm. Clynch quickly overtook his comrade; and, as soon as the ground became clear of underwood, they speeded off towards the morass.

XV.

THE DEERHOUNDS.

MEANWHILE, Sir Leycester had not been idle.

He had sent off Ned Rushton with the bloodhound to unkennel the gipsies; but would not allow the other hounds to be unleashed.

However, when he heard the shouts, and caught sight of the fugitives, one of them with a blood-stained knife in his hand, running towards the morass, he shouted to Booth to loose the dogs, and, cheering them on, started in pursuit.

The deerhounds quite understood their business, and rushed after the gipsies at a tremendous pace, followed by Sir Leycester, who vainly endeavoured to keep up with them.

Marple, Booth, and the two grooms likewise joined in the exciting chase.

After a good run, Ekiel dropped; and as the hounds had to be pulled away from him, the incident caused a short delay, that enabled Clynch to reach the morass.

There was for no time hesitation, so he took the first path that offered—a narrow footway that seemed to lead towards the middle of the bog.

He soon found he had made a bad choice, for the path grew narrower, and the ground became soft.

But the deerhounds were after him, and behind them came Sir Leycester, who had ventured to ride along the pathway, in spite of the warning shouts of Marple and the others.

Clynch ran on a little further, and then stood at bay, preparing to defend himself against the deerhounds with the cuchillo, which he had never relinquished.

At this juncture, Sir Leycester's horse missed his footing, and slipped into the bog, and in the effort to recover himself, threw his rider over his head, completely engulfing him.

Cries of consternation arose from all who witnessed the accident; but they could render no assistance.

Marple, who had all along been apprehensive of disaster, flung himself from his horse, and hurried to the spot; but only to find that the unfortunate baronet had disappeared.

" Call off these dogs, and I'll help you to get him out!" shouted Clynch.

In the hope of saving the baronet's life, Marple complied; and as soon as he was safe from attack, the gipsy flung away the knife, and, setting to work, did his best.

But his help was of no avail. The horse was got out; but Sir Leycester had sunk, and could not be found.

Plenty of other assistance soon arrived. Booth, the coachman; Ned Rushton, the keeper; the turf-cutters —all were there.

But though every effort was made, and every available appliance used, more than an hour elapsed before the body could be recovered.

It was then conveyed to the Hall—Marple having gone on before, to break the sad intelligence to Lady Barfleur.

End of the First Book.

Book the Second.

THE HEIRESS OF BRACKLEY HALL.

I.

THE LAST OF THE OLD CHESHIRE SQUIRES.

A TERRIBLE sensation was caused at Brackley Hall when tidings were brought there of the fatal accident that had befallen its owner. Sir Leycester had been an excellent master, and was beloved by all his household, and their regrets for his loss were heartfelt.

Lady Barfleur was completely stunned by the shock. Marple endeavoured to break the sad intelligence to her gradually; but his countenance and accents betrayed him.

Rising from the sofa on which she was seated, she seized him by the arm, and commanded him to tell her the truth.

Thus interrogated, he felt compelled to give a direct reply. But he regretted doing so, when he saw the effect his words produced upon her. She looked aghast, placed her hand on her heart, and, then, with a half-stifled cry, sank upon the sofa.

Marple had taken the precaution to station a female servant at the door; and he now summoned her to her mistress. Lady Barfleur had fainted.

Emmeline did not hear of the direful event till she returned from the lake; and she then instantly bethought her of the death-warning she had received. She managed to restrain her emotions till she reached her own room, whither she was accompanied by Mildred, who was almost equally shocked, and then gave way to a paroxysm of grief.

Mrs. Calverley was likewise much distressed. She could not help reproaching herself as being, in some degree, the cause of the accident; though she had endeavoured to dissuade the unfortunate baronet from pursuing the gipsies.

Feeling certain, under the present afflicting circumstances, that Emmeline would not be willing to part with Mildred, she settled in her own mind that the latter should remain with her friend for a few days. Moreover, she herself would spend the night at Brackley, if she could be of any use to Lady Barfleur. Such were her mental resolves.

Hitherto, she had remained in the garden. She now went into the house. It was all in confusion, the servants appearing quite scared. There was no one to whom she could speak, for Captain Danvers had gone off to the marsh.

The drawing-room was deserted. Nothing was changed there. But how different the noble room looked in her eyes from what it had done in the morn-

G

ing! Its splendour seemed dimmed. The great emblazoned shield over the mantelpiece looked like a hatchment.

After gazing round for a few minutes, she sat down. Melancholy thoughts intruded upon her. Perhaps, even feelings of remorse assailed her. But we shall not search her bosom. She began to feel some disquietude at being left so long alone, and wondered why Mildred did not come down to her. Possibly, she could not leave Emmeline.

Suddenly, her attention was roused by a disturbance in the entrance-hall, that seemed to betoken an arrival.

What it was she could not fail to conjecture.

Trampling of feet, as if caused by men bearing a heavy burden, and muttered voices, were heard. Then followed other sounds, almost equally significant, the opening and shutting of doors, and the congregating of servants in the hall.

She waited for some minutes, in the expectation of being summoned, but as no one came near her, she went forth.

The hall was empty, but the dining-room door stood open, and at it was stationed the butler.

The man had a very sorrowful countenance indeed. He bowed gravely as she approached, and motioned her to enter the room.

A very touching spectacle was presented to her gaze.

On a large carved oak table, covered with a crimson cloth, and placed in the centre of the apartment, was laid the body of the unfortunate baronet.

It was partially covered by a cloak; and the stains from the swamp in which he had been engulfed had been carefully removed from his face and grey locks. Strange to say, his features were not changed, but seemed to wear their customary kindly expression.

Around were grouped the different members of the household, all of whom looked deeply afflicted, and some of the female servants were weeping bitterly.

On one side stood Ned Rushton, with two of his helpers, behind him. Rarely did Ned's manly visage exhibit such grief as it wore on this sad occasion. After gazing steadfastly at his late kind-hearted master for some minutes, he cast down his eyes, and did not raise them again till the moment of departure.

On the other side stood Marple, who, though burly of frame, was as soft-hearted as a woman. He deeply lamented Sir Leycester, and well he might, for the baronet had ever been a good friend to him.

At the end of the apartment stood Captain Danvers, a quiet but not unmoved spectator of the scene. If his grief made little outward show, it was not the less deep and sincere. He was strongly attached to his uncle, from whom, indeed, he had some expectations, that might never now be realised.

But the principal figures in this touching picture have yet to be described.

Emmeline and Mildred were kneeling down in prayer, at the back, when Lady Barfleur entered the room. She had nerved herself, as she thought, for the ordeal; but on catching sight of the body, she uttered a cry that thrilled all who heard it, rushed up to her dead husband, clasped her arms round his neck, and fell with her head upon his breast.

No one ventured to remove her; and she was still in this attitude when Mrs. Calverley entered the room.

The dark oak ceiling, the dark oak panels, the dim windows, harmonised with the sombre character of the picture, which made an ineffaceable impression upon Mrs. Calverley.

The scene suggested many reflections.

In the room, where for many years he had exercised unbounded hospitality, and where his ancestors had feasted before him, lay the last male representative of the ancient house of Barfleur.

Sir Leycester had had a son, who died when quite young, and the title was now extinct. All the late baronet's estates and possessions would go to his daughter and sole heiress. But Emmeline thought not of the wealth she had thus suddenly acquired. She thought only of the irreparable loss she had sustained in the death of the father who had treated her with constant tenderness and affection, and whom she dearly loved.

But if no selfish thoughts occupied her, reflections somewhat akin to them occurred to one near to her, who well knew how she was circumstanced. Mrs. Calverley knew that Emmeline was her father's sole heiress, and looked upon her as a very important personage, over whom it would be desirable to obtain an influence. Such influence could be easily acquired by Mildred, to whom, it was evident, Emmeline was strongly attached.

Mrs. Calverley knew much, but there was one important matter of which she was totally ignorant. How could she have been aware that Emmeline cherished a secret attachment to Chetwynd?

The picture we have attempted to describe remained undisturbed for a few minutes, when the new-made widow recovered from the swoon into which she had fallen.

As soon as she could, Mrs. Calverley, who had come up, gently raised her, and helped her to quit the room. Emmeline and Mildred arose and followed.

Captain Danvers remained till the household had withdrawn, and then held a consultation with the butler, to whom the entire management of the house had been entrusted for the present by Lady Barfleur.

As Mrs. Calverley had foreseen, Emmeline would not part with Mildred; and she herself remained till the following day, having despatched a messenger to Ousel-croft with a note to her housekeeper, explaining matters, and desiring her to send back some things that she and Mildred required.

Passing over the dreary interval that comprised the inquest, and the examination and committal of the gipsies, we shall come on to the funeral, to which a great number of important personages—relatives, connexions, and friends of the deceased baronet—had been invited.

Sir Gerard Danvers, of Offham Grange and his eldest son Scrope, Charles's brother, arrived at Brackley Hall on the eve of the sad ceremonial.

Up to this time, Lady Barfleur had not quitted her room; but she could not refuse to see her brother and nephew, and she, therefore, dined with them. It was a *triste* party, as may be imagined, for her ladyship's presence cast a gloom over it. Emmeline looked ill; Mildred was out of spirits; and Mrs. Calverley, who had come over that afternoon, had to supply the conversation. Both Sir Gerard and Scrope thought her very charming.

Scrope was about thirty, tall, thin, dark-complexioned, and by no means so handsome as his brother; but he was exceedingly gentlemanlike, and would be very rich, and that was much in Mrs. Calverley's opinion; so she took some trouble to please him.

It was with difficulty that Captain Danvers could maintain a grave exterior. Mr. Carteret, the solicitor, who had acted professionally for Sir Leycester as he had done for Mr. Calverley, had been over that day; and when the will of the deceased baronet was examined, it was found he had left his nephew Charles five thousand pounds. Impossible, after such a windfall as this, that the captain, who was not over-burdened with cash, could look very dull.

Members of some of the oldest and best Cheshire families—Egerton, Cholmondeley, Leigh, Venables, Vernon, Brereton, Mainwaring, Davenport, and others —attended the funeral.

Sir Bridgnorth Charlton, who had been an old friend of the deceased baronet, was likewise invited, and came.

Before the funeral *cortége* set out, Sir Bridgnorth took an opportunity of speaking to Mildred, and said he would call upon her in a few days, as he had something to tell her respecting Chetwynd.

Sir Leycester was not interred in the little chapel in the court of the old Hall, where some of his earlier ancestors reposed, but in his family vault in the neighbouring church of Brackley, and was borne thither, according to custom, on the shoulders of the tenantry. Sir Gerald Danvers and his two sons followed on foot, with a long train of mourners composed entirely of the deceased baronet's retainers. The carriages of the important personages we have mentioned closed the procession.

A word respecting Sir Leycester ere we lose sight of him for ever.

Not inappropriately, he might be termed the last of the Cheshire squires, since he left none behind who so completely answered to the description of that traditional character.

He seemed to belong to another age—a ruder but manlier age than our own. Yet Sir Leycester, though sometimes coarse and careless of speech, could be most courteous.

His ancestors had always been loyal—always true to the Stuarts. Brackley Hall had held out against the Parliamentarians in the time of Charles the First, and Sir Chandos Barfleur was killed at the siege. His son Delves was just as faithful to the king's fortunes, and lost part of his property; but it was restored by Charles the Second, and again jeopardised in 1715. Circumstances prevented Sir Wilbraham Barfleur from joining the Rebellion of '45. From this date the Barfleurs became loyal to the reigning family.

Born in the latter part of the last century, Sir Leycester belonged to that epoch rather than to the present. He retained the manners of his sire and grandsire, and thus became a type of the old school—a type that has now completely disappeared.

In look, bearing, physiognomy, costume, manner, he differed from the present generation. But there was no better gentleman, no cheerier companion, no stauncher friend, no better rider to hounds, than Sir Leycester Barfleur, the last of the old Cheshire squires.

II.

ABOUT a week after the funeral, Sir Bridgnorth Charlton
rode over to Brackley Hall, in fulfilment of his promise
to call on Mildred.

Lady Barfleur was not well enough to appear; but
Emmeline and Mildred, who had been impatiently
expecting his visit, received him in the drawing-room.

They were attired in deep mourning; and, though
there was no personal resemblance between them, they
looked like sisters.

After some inquiries respecting Lady Barfleur, and
messages of condolence to her, Sir Bridgnorth looked
at Mildred, who interpreted his glance correctly, and
said:

"You may speak freely of Chetwynd before Miss
Barfleur, Sir Bridgnorth. She takes great interest in
him."

"A very great interest," added Emmeline. "I hope
you bring us some news of him?"

"Very little," replied Sir Bridgnorth. "And what
I do bring is not satisfactory. You desire me to speak
plainly about your brother, Miss Calverley?"

"Most certainly!" she replied.

"Well, then, you may remember, when I accident-
ally met him at Ouselcroft, I gave him a pocket-book,
containing a certain sum of money?"

"I am not likely to forget your kindness," replied
Mildred.

"It appears there was rather more in the pocket-
book than I thought," pursued Sir Bridgnorth—"bank

notes to the amount of three hundred pounds. I mention this, because your brother has most scrupulously repaid me the exact sum, of which he kept a memorandum."

"He behaved like a man of honour!" cried Emmeline.

"Undoubtedly. But I did not want the money back. I want to assist him. I want him to come to me—to talk to me."

"Will he not do so?" said Mildred.

"I fear not. I suspect he is still in difficulties."

"If so, he must be got out of them, and you must manage it, Sir Bridgnorth," said Mildred.

"But I can't manage it, my dear young lady. I don't know where to find him."

"But he *must* be found!" cried Emmeline.

"Easily said; but not so easily accomplished," rejoined Sir Bridgnorth, smiling at her vivacity. "I have used every endeavour, but can obtain no clue to him."

"Is he in London?" asked Mildred.

"I believe so," he replied.

"Surely then he can be discovered?" she remarked.

"I have not succeeded in discovering him, that is all I can say," rejoined Sir Bridgnorth. "And I have really taken a great deal of trouble in the business. He has been remarkably successful in hiding himself."

"Do not keep anything back from me, I pray you, dear Sir Bridgnorth!" said Mildred. "Is he without resources?"

"I cannot imagine so," he replied. "He must have had some funds to enable him to repay me, unless—" and he paused.

" Unless what ? " said Mildred.

" You enjoin me to speak the truth," replied Sir
Bridgnorth ; " and I will do so at the hazard of giving
you and Miss Barfleur pain. My idea is that he has
lost money at play. Mind, I have no proof of what I
assert. It is simply conjecture."

" I fear you are right, Sir Bridgnorth," said Mildred, heaving a deep sigh.

" In your opinion, Sir Bridgnorth," said Emmeline,
who had listened anxiously to the discourse—" in
your opinion, I say, has Chetwynd lost a considerable
sum of money at play ? "

" I fear so."

" Has he paid it ? "

" I fear not."

There was a pause, during which the two young
ladies regarded each other wistfully.

At length, Mildred spoke.

" Sir Bridgnorth," she said, " Chetwynd's debts of
honour"—and she emphasised the word—" must be
paid, and shall be paid, at any sacrifice, by me ! You
will do me the greatest kindness by finding out exactly
how he is circumstanced, what he owes, and, especially,
what are his debts of honour."

Emmeline looked earnestly at Sir Bridgnorth, as if
she felt equally interested in the inquiry.

Sir Bridgnorth was evidently troubled, and for
some moments made no answer.

" Excuse me, my dear Miss Calverley," he said ;
" if your brother is in a scrape, I think he should be
allowed to get out of it—as he best can."

" No ! " exclaimed Mildred, decidedly. " It is not
like ʼou, Sir Bridgnorth, to give such advice."

"No!" added Emmeline, equally decidedly. "He must be freed!"

"Upon my word," said Sir Bridgnorth, surprised, "whatever may have happened to him, this young man cannot be called unfortunate."

"Then act as a true friend to him, dear Sir Bridgnorth!" said Mildred. "Make immediate arrangements to get him out of all difficulties. You will incur no personal responsibility."

"None whatever," said Emmeline.

Sir Bridgnorth was much touched.

"I think you had better leave him to himself," he said. "But, since you won't, I must needs help you I'll do all I can. But I cannot proceed as expeditiously as I could desire. I have reason to believe Chetwynd is living in London under a feigned name. Since all private inquiries have proved unsuccessful, I will cause some carefully-worded advertisements to be inserted in the newspapers, that may catch his eye and bring him forward. Could he be made aware that a beautiful young lady takes an interest in him, I am sure he would speedily reappear. But fear no indiscretion on my part. Nothing shall be disclosed till the proper moment arrives." Then, addressing Mildred, he added : "As soon as I can ascertain the amount of his debts, I will let you know."

"Pay them, dear Sir Bridgnorth—pay them!" she rejoined.

"But they may be very large ?"

"Never mind; pay them!" cried Emmeline. "Mr. Carteret shall repay you."

"No man ever had such a chance," exclaimed Sir Bridgnorth. "If he does not reform now, he is incorrigible."

" I have no misgivings as to the future," said Mildred.

" Well, I sincerely trust all will come right," observed Sir Bridgnorth. " There seems every probability of it, I must own."

Just then Mrs. Calverley was announced.

" I must take my leave," said Sir Bridgnorth, rising hastily. " You shall hear from me soon, or see me."

" Let us see you, please ! " said both young ladies.

Before he could depart, Mrs. Calverley entered, and stopped him.

" Ah, Sir Bridgnorth ! " she exclaimed ; " I'm delighted to meet you ! I want to have a word with you."

Sir Bridgnorth evidently wished to get away. But she begged him to remain for a few minutes ; and he could not very well refuse.

Mrs. Calverley then went on to the young ladies. After the usual greetings had passed, she said to Mildred, " I have a letter for you ; or, rather, a packet. It arrived this morning."

Having given her the letter, she moved to a little distance.

Glancing at the superscription, Mildred turned pale.

" What is it that disturbs you ? " inquired Emmeline.

" A letter from Chetwynd," replied Mildred, in a low voice. " Come to my room, that we may read it together."

Emmeline signified her assent by a look.

Mrs. Calverley took no notice of what was passing, nough she must have perceived it.

Before leaving the room, Mildred went up to Sir Bridgnorth, and, addressing him in a low voice, said :

" You must not go, Sir Bridgnorth. I may have something important to tell you about Chetwynd."

" In that case, I will stay as long as you please," he rejoined.

Meanwhile Emmeline prepared to follow her friend.

" Will you mind my leaving you for a few minutes, dear Mrs. Calverley ? " she said.

" Don't stand on the slightest ceremony with me, my love," replied the other. " Besides, I want to have a little talk with Sir Bridgnorth."

The two young ladies then went out.

" I am now quite at your service, madam," said Sir Bridgnorth, as soon as he and Mrs. Calverley were alone.

" Then sit down, that we may have a confidential chat," replied the lady.

III.

CHETWYND'S LETTER.

In such haste were the two girls to open the packet that they almost ran up the spiral staircase to Mildred's bedroom, in which was a deep bay window.

In this recess they sat down.

Mildred's hand trembled as she tore open the packet.

It contained a long, closely-written letter, inside which was a folded sheet of paper that looked like a document of some kind.

This document dropped on the table, and was not examined at the moment.

The letter was dated on the previous day, but bore no address.

Ere she had read many lines, a mist seemed to gather over Mildred's vision. Unable to proceed, she laid the letter down.

" You terrify me," cried Emmeline. " What has happened ? "

" He meditates self-destruction," replied Mildred. " But read the letter, dearest—I cannot."

Mustering up all her courage, Emmeline read aloud as follows :

" This is the last letter you will ever receive from me, dearest sister, and, in bidding you an eternal fare-well, I implore you to think kindly of me.

" With one exception, you are the only person in the world whom I love, and my latest thoughts will be of her and you.

" You know her, and will easily guess her name, but I shall not confide it to this sheet of paper. In all respects she is superior to the artful and treacher-ous woman by whom I allowed myself to be deceived —superior in beauty and accomplishments, and ami-able as beautiful. Had I been fortunate enough to wed her, I should have been a different man. Now it is too late, I see my folly, and comprehend my loss."

" You see that he dearly loved you, Emmeline, for it is to you that he refers," observed Mildred. " But pro-ceed, I entreat you ! "

" I have met with the basest ingratitude. Men

who have received from me favours innumerable—hangers-on who have sponged upon me, and professed the greatest regard for me, have shrunk from me, and avoided me in my misfortunes—men who have fleeced me, who have ruined me, and driven me to desperation ! My funds are almost exhausted, but they will last me out. I owe nothing, for I have paid that kind-hearted Sir Bridgnorth Charlton the exact sum he lent me. Had I not obtained it from him, I should have been called a defaulter. Fortune favoured me for the moment, for I won sufficient to discharge my debt to him. He would lend me more, I doubt not, but I will never borrow again. As to the woman who has robbed me of my inheritance, I have sworn I will accept nothing from her, and I will keep my oath. She will be responsible for her conduct before Heaven."

Again there was a pause, but neither made a remark and Emmeline went on :

" Fear nothing, dearest sister. I have changed my name, and have taken such precautions that my retreat cannot be discovered. Nothing will be found upon me that can establish my identity. A body will be found; that will be all ! "

" Gracious Heaven ! " ejaculated Mildred. " Grant that this dreadful catastrophe may be averted ! "

Emmeline's voice had been suffocated by emotion, but after a pause she proceeded :

" Mildred, I have been reckless and extravagant, and have led a most foolish and most useless life. I have been a gambler and have squandered large sums upon persons who profited by my follies; but I have done nothing dishonourable—nothing to tarnish my name as a gentleman. I think I could have retrieved my position, but it is not worth the trouble. I am weary of life; sick of the hollowness, the ingratitude, the perfidy of the world! Timon of Athens did not hate mankind more bitterly than I do. I would consent to live if I felt certain of revenge on some of those who have wronged me; but on no other condition. This is not likely to happen; so it is best I should go!"

"Alas, poor Chetwynd!" exclaimed Mildred. "His fancied wrongs have driven him to the verge of madness!"

"He seems extraordinarily sensitive, and to feel most acutely the slights shown him by his ungrateful associates," said Emmeline.

"Is the letter finished?" asked Mildred.

"No," replied Emmeline. "There is a farewell to you. But I cannot read it. My voice fails me!"

Mildred then took the letter, and went on with it:

"You know exactly how I am circumstanced, Mildred. I have nothing, that I am aware of, to leave; but I have made my will, and in your favour, and shall enclose it in this letter. I may have some rights of which I am ignorant; and if it should prove so, I desire that you may benefit by them."

"Here is the will," she remarked, taking up the little document and examining it. "I see he has observed all necessary formalities. Strange he should be able to do this at such a time!"

Though deeply affected, she resumed the perusal of the letter :

"And now farewell, dearest sister ! Again I implore you to think of me kindly ! My faults are inexcusable ; yet do not judge me harshly. The world has done that, and with sufficient severity. Do not suppose these lines are written to move your compassion. Long before they meet your eye, I shall be indifferent to scorn, neglect, and treachery !

" Should an opportunity ever occur of breathing my name to her I have loved, say that my chief regret was that I threw away the happiness that might have been mine ! "

Emmeline uttered an exclamation of despair, but it did not interrupt Mildred :

" Trouble yourself no more about me. Search will be in vain. Nothing can arrest my purpose. Ere to-morrow morn I shall have ceased to breathe, and have quitted a world I hate. Neglect not my last request ! Farewell, my sister ! May you be happier than your unfortunate brother ! "

" Heaven have mercy on his soul ! " exclaimed Mildred, dropping on her knees, and praying fervently.

Emmeline, likewise, knelt down and prayed.

After awhile, they arose.

" Sit down for a moment, dearest Emmeline," said Mildred ; "I have something to tell you. I believe the fatal act was committed at one o'clock this morning."

"Why at that precise hour?" inquired Emmeline.

"You shall hear. I was sleeping on yonder couch, and was awakened by the striking of the clock. The moon was shining brightly through the window, and I thought I saw a figure standing just where you are seated. I should have felt much more frightened than I did, if I had not been convinced it was Chetwynd; though how he came here at that time I could not imagine. I called out, but no answer was made, and I then became seriously alarmed. Suddenly, the figure, which had hitherto been looking down, raised its head, and fixed its mournful gaze upon me. I then saw that the features were those of Chetwynd, but pale as death! The phantom did not move from its position, but seemed to wave a farewell to me, and then melted away in the moonbeams."

"And this phantom you beheld?" said Emmeline, who had listened with intense interest in the narrative.

"I saw it as plainly as I now see you," replied the other. "Why it appeared to me, I now understand."

The silence that ensued was broken by Mildred.

After carefully replacing the letter and the will in the envelope, she said: "Let us go down-stairs and communicate the sad news to Sir Bridgnorth. It is right he should know it."

"True," replied Emmeline. "But oh! dearest Mildred, I can never like Mrs. Calverley again. I look upon her as the cause of this dreadful event."

"You do her an injustice, dear Emmeline," said

Mildred, who, however, began to regard her step-mother with altered feelings.

"We shall see how she bears the intelligence," said Emmeline; "and from that, some judgment may be formed."

IV.

HOW THE DIREFUL NEWS WAS RECEIVED BY MRS. CAL-VERLEY; AND HOW SIR BRIDGNORTH VOLUNTEERED TO MAKE INQUIRIES AS TO ITS TRUTH.

As the two girls entered the drawing-room, their changed appearance and mournful looks struck both Sir Bridgnorth and Mrs. Calverley, who were still seated on the sofa, conversing together earnestly.

Sir Bridgnorth immediately arose, and, advancing to meet them, said to Mildred:

"I am afraid you have not received very good news of Chetwynd?"

"Alas! no, Sir Bridgnorth," she replied, in a sorrowful voice. "You need give yourself no further concern about my unfortunate brother!"

"Why not?" he interrupted, anxiously.

"He is gone!" she replied, sadly.

"You shock me greatly!" he ejaculated. "Mrs. Calverley and myself have been considering what could be done for him, and have just devised a scheme that we hoped might be successful."

"All schemes for his benefit are now useless," said Emmeline. "He no longer needs our aid."

"Did I hear aright?" said Mrs. Calverley, starting

up, and coming towards them. "It cannot be that Chetwynd is dead?"

"It is so," said Emmeline.

"But how did he die?" asked Mrs. Calverley.

"By his own hand!" replied Emmeline, regarding her fixedly.

Mrs. Calverley looked aghast, and as if ready to drop.

"I did not understand he had destroyed himself," said Sir Bridgnorth. "When did this sad event occur? Can you give me any particulars?"

"I can only state that he contemplated suicide," replied Mildred. "This letter is a last farewell to me."

"Ah! then we need not despair of beholding him again," said Sir Bridgnorth, with a sensation of relief. "Many a man, now alive, has threatened to put an end to his existence. I hope it may turn out to be so in Chetwynd's case."

"I sincerely hope so!" said Mrs. Calverley.

"I have no such belief," observed Mildred, sadly.

"If you had read his most affecting letter, you would entertain no doubt as to his determination," added Emmeline, with difficulty refraining from tears.

"We shall soon be able to ascertain the truth," said Sir Bridgnorth.

"Not so," replied Mildred. "He has taken such precautions that his fate will remain a mystery."

Sir Bridgnorth shook his head.

"I can't believe that possible," he said. "It will be important, on several accounts, to have proof of his death. He may have made a will."

"He *has* made a will, and has sent it me in this letter," replied Mildred.

" Indeed ! " exclaimed Mrs. Calverley, surprised. " But he had nothing to leave."

" He seems to have thought otherwise," said Mildred. " He fancied he had certain rights and claims, and those he has left to me."

The slight shade that passed over Mrs. Calverley's countenance was not unnoticed by Emmeline.

" This shows it will be absolutely necessary to establish the fact of his death," observed Sir Bridgnorth. " What is the date of the letter you have received ? "

" It was written yesterday," replied Mildred. " But he is not alive now," she added, solemnly.

" You believe he destroyed himself last night ? " asked Mrs. Calverley.

" I firmly believe so," she rejoined.

Mrs. Calverley then turned to Sir Bridgnorth, and with a coldness that appeared revolting to Mildred and Emmeline, said :

" Is any case of suicide reported in the papers this morning ? "

" I have seen none," he replied. " But it might have escaped me. I seldom read such cases."

Emmeline rang the bell, and desired the butler to bring the newspapers.

The order was promptly obeyed, and search made, but no "mysterious death " or "supposed suicide" could be discovered.

" It is needless to ask if any address is given with your letter," remarked Sir Bridgnorth to Mildred.

" It is not likely there would be."

" And nothing mentioned that could serve as a guide ? "

" Nothing."

Sir Bridgnorth then bade them all a formal adieu, and made a final attempt to give them comfort.

" I hope Chetwynd may have changed his mind at the last moment," he said. " I believe it will turn out so. To-morrow I shall set out on my melancholy errand, and institute inquiries. You shall hear from me as soon as I have anything to communicate; and I promise you one thing—I will not remain idle. It shall not be my fault if the facts of this painful affair are not discovered."

End of the Second Book.

Book the Third.

WALTER LIDDEL.

I.

ON WESTMINSTER BRIDGE.

NEARLY at the same date as the incident related in the foregoing chapters, and about two hours past midnight, a strongly-built, middle-aged man, whose garb proclaimed him a mechanic, took his way across Westminster Bridge.

He was not walking very fast, but when the hour

was tolled forth from the lofty tower, he began to mend his pace, glancing occasionally at the sullen river that swept on beneath him.

The bridge was completely deserted. The last policeman he had seen was standing near New Palace Yard, and the belated mechanic was thinking how strange and solitary the usually crowded footway appeared, when he descried a figure leaning over the low parapet.

He had heard many tales of suicide, and something in the attitude of the figure caused him to hurry on.

As he advanced, he perceived, by the light of the lamp, that it was a young man, bare-headed, for a felt hat was lying on the pavement.

The person was muttering to himself, and his demeanour was altogether so wild, that the mechanic was convinced that his suspicions were correct, and he, therefore, called out.

He instantly turned at the cry, and exhibited a haggard visage; but instead of replying, made an attempt to spring upon the parapet.

But the workman was too quick for him, and seized him before he could execute his desperate purpose.

The intended suicide quite shook in the grasp of his powerful preserver.

He was a young man, and his brown hair and beard made the ghastly hue of his countenance yet more striking by the contrast. Moreover, he had the look of a gentleman, but it was difficult to judge of his condition from his grey tweed habiliments.

He offered very little resistance to his friendly captor, his strength apparently being gone.

"Let me go!" he said in a hoarse voice. "I don't wish to live!"

"Madman!" cried the mechanic. "What's the matter, that you would throw away life thus?"

"What's the matter?" echoed the other, with a laugh that had nothing human in it. "I am ruined—utterly ruined! Had you let me alone, my troubles would have been ended by this time!"

And he made another ineffectual attempt to free himself.

"Don't think to get away!" said the mechanic. "I'm sorry for you, but it's my duty to prevent you from committing this wicked act. I shall hold you till a policeman comes up!"

"No; don't do that!" cried the wretched man. "Though I don't know where to turn for a night's lodging, I don't want to be locked up! Leave go your hold; I promise not to make the attempt again!"

"Well, I'll trust you," replied the mechanic, releasing him.

They looked at each other for a few moments, and both seemed satisfied with the scrutiny.

The intended suicide was apparently about three or four and twenty; tall, handsome, well-proportioned. As already intimated, he had brown locks and a brown beard, and was dressed in such manner that no precise idea could be formed of his rank.

In regard to his preserver, there could be no mistake. His working attire and cap proclaimed his station. He had an honest, manly countenance. In age he might be about forty-five.

"Here's your hat, sir," he said picking it up. "I should like to have a word with you before we part.

Perhaps I may be warranted in asking you a question or two, especially as my motive is a good one. I'm not influenced by mere curiosity. I'll begin by telling you my name. It's Joe Hartley. I'm a stonemason by trade, and live in Lambeth Palace Road—at least, close beside it. The reason I'm out so late is that I've been doing a job at Paddington. But I don't regret it, since I've been the humble instrument of saving a fellow-creature. Now you know all you may care to learn about me, and, in return, I should like to hear something about you."

"I can't tell you who I am, Mr. Hartley," he replied, "nor can I acquaint you with my strange history. You may guess that I must have been brought to a desperate pass."

His voice changed as he went on.

"What's a poor fellow to do when he's utterly ruined? I've spent all my money, pawned my watch, my ring, and another little trinket. I've nothing left—not a sou."

"But have you no relatives—no friends?" inquired Hartley, kindly.

"Yes; I've relatives, but I've quarrelled with them, and would die rather than go near them!" he cried, in a bitter, desperate tone, that left no doubt of his fixed determination. "Friends I have none!"

"Well, well, I won't argue with you about that," said Hartley. "But there is no occasion for one so young as you are to starve. There are hundreds of ways in which you may earn a living. Amongst others, you might 'list for a soldier. I'm much mistaken if you don't stand six feet two. They'd take you at the Horse Guards in a minute.

"I did think of that; and, perhaps, might have done it, but I was goaded to this desperate act by a circumstance on which I won't dwell. I think I must have been mad. Very likely I shall enlist to-morrow.

"But you want rest, and have nowhere to go. Come home with me," said the stonemason.

"You are very good, Mr. Hartley," he replied, much affected. "This is real kindness, and I feel it—feel it deeply!"

"Come along, then," cried Hartley. "There's a policeman moving towards us, and he'll wonder what we are about. You won't tell me your name, I suppose?"

"Call me Liddel—Walter Liddel," replied the other. "It's not my real name, though I have a right to use it. At any rate, I mean to be known by it henceforward, and it will serve me with the recruiting sergeant."

"It will serve you with me as well," said Hartley. "So come along, Mr. Walter Liddel."

Presently they encountered the policeman, who eyed them rather suspiciously, but was satisfied with a few words from Hartley.

On quitting the bridge, the stonemason turned off on the right, into Lambeth Palace Road.

They walked on in silence, for Liddel did not seem inclined to talk.

Gradually the street became wider, and Hartley, noticing that his companion began to walk very feebly, told him he had not much further to go.

Their course seemed to be stopped by the high wall of the palace grounds; but Hartley turned into a narrow street on the left, called Spencer's Rents, and halting before the door of a neat little habitation, said :

" Here we are ! "

Walter Liddel replied, in a faint voice, that he was glad of it.

Hartley then knocked softly at the door, which was presently opened by his wife.

II.

THE HOUSE IN SPENCER'S RENTS.

PERCEIVING that some one was with her husband, Mrs. Hartley was about to beat an immediate retreat, but Hartley stopped her, and after a short colloquy between the pair, the stonemason entered with his companion.

Mrs. Hartley had disappeared, but there was a light in the kitchen, into which Walter Liddel was introduced.

The hospitable stonemason begged him to sit down, and, opening a cupboard, took from it some cold meat and bread, which he set before him, and bade him fall to.

Next proceeding to the scullery, Hartley drew a jug of beer. Walter Liddel ate as voraciously as a famished wolf.

Leaving him to enjoy the first good meal he had made for some days, Hartley went up-stairs, and his voice could be heard in consultation with his wife.

Evidently, some little preparation for their unexpected guest had to be made by the worthy couple, but it was completed before he had finished his meal. He was still engaged when Hartley reappeared.

"Glad to see you getting on so well, Mr. Liddel," observed the stonemason. "It ain't often we've a spare bed, but it so happens that our daughter Rose is away, so you can have her room."

"Anywhere will do for me," replied Walter, who by this time had devoured all the meat and bread, and emptied the jug of beer.

"Come on, then," said Hartley, taking up the candle, and signing to his guest to follow him.

A short, narrow staircase brought them to a landing, whence two or three doors opened, one of which admitted them to a small chamber, simply but very neatly furnished. It breathed an atmosphere of purity and innocence, with which Walter, exhausted as he was, could not help being struck.

"There's your bed," said Hartley, pointing to the neat little couch, the patchwork quilt of which being turned down, revealed the snowy sheets.

"Thank you, my good friend; I couldn't wish for a better," replied Walter, squeezing the mason's horny hand. "Heaven bless you for your kindness to me."

"Don't disturb yourself too soon," observed Hartley. "I'm not going out early myself to-morrow. I'll call you. Good night."

So saying, he retired, and closed the door after him.

As soon as he was alone, the penitent knelt down, and besought Heaven's forgiveness for the sinful act he had attempted, and which had been so fortunately frustrated. His contrition was sincere, and his resolution to lead a better life heartfelt.

His prayers ended, he took off his attire, and, lying down in the little couch in which innocence alone had hitherto reposed, almost instantly fell asleep.

His slumbers were sound, and he had not stirred when Hartley had entered the room on the morrow.

On opening his eyes, Walter could hardly make out where he was; but by degrees the recollection of all that occurred returned to him.

"Don't think any more of last night," said Hartley, noticing the pained expression of his countenance. "It's nearly noon, but if you feel tired I'll come again later on."

"Nearly noon!" cried Walter, preparing to spring out of bed. "I ought to have been up hours ago!"

Thereupon, Hartley retired, and his guest proceeded to make his toilette with a care that showed he had not forsaken early habits.

While thus employed he could not help casting his eyes round the chamber, and was more than ever struck by its extreme simplicity and neatness. Everything seemed in its place. It appeared like a profanation to invade such a temple of purity.

On going down-stairs, he found Mrs. Hartley, a middle-aged, matronly woman, decently attired as became her station, and still comely.

It was too late for breakfast, and the cloth was spread for dinner. On the table was a baked shoulder of mutton and potatoes.

Mrs. Hartley greeted him very kindly, and, with great good feeling and good taste, made no allusion to the circumstances that had brought him to the house, though she could not have been ignorant of them. But his appearance prepossessed her in his favour.

" Don't say a word about being so late, sir," she observed with a kindly smile. " I'm glad to see you looking so well. You must be content to make breakfast and dinner together to-day, sir."

While Walter was making a suitable reply, Hartley came in, and seemed quite surprised and delighted at his guest's improved appearance.

" A few hours' rest has done wonders with you, Mr. Liddel," he said. " This is my wife," he added; " and I will say it to her face, that no man could have a better."

" A good husband makes a good wife, Joe, as I always tell you," she replied, smiling. " Pray sit down, sir," she added, to Walter.

Both Hartley and his guest had good appetites, and a large hole was made in the shoulder of mutton before they had finished their meal. Far from begrudging Walter, Mrs. Hartley seemed pleased.

" Now, Mr. Liddel," said Hartley, as he laid down his knife and fork, " I must go to my work. The missis will take care of you till my return. We may have company in the evening."

" I must go and look after some employment," said Walter.

" Time enough for that to-morrow," rejoined the mason. " We'll have some talk together on the subject to-night. Meantime, keep quiet."

And the worthy fellow went about his business.

Mrs. Hartley showed her guest into the little parlour, and when she had cleared away the things,

joined him there, and they had a little chat together; but whatever curiosity she felt, she re-
strained it.

Limited as was her knowledge of the world, she
felt convinced that Walter was a gentleman. She
talked to him in a kindly, motherly tone, that soon
drew him out.

At last, after beating about the bush, she said, in
a straightforward way :

"You must excuse me, sir, if I take upon me to
give you advice, but don't you think you had better
go back to your friends?"

"Never!" he replied. "I will never go back to
them. If you knew all, you would agree that I have
been infamously treated! No, Mrs. Hartley, my
resolution is taken. I am down, but I will make my
way up in the world. To mount the ladder, one must
begin at the lowest step."

"I approve of your resolution, sir," she rejoined,
kindly; "and if you are determined, you cannot fail
of success. You have youth, strength, good looks.
I dare say, now," she added, unable to repress her
desire to know something more of him, "I dare say
you think you have been wronged?"

"I have had great injustice done me," he replied.
"But you must not ask me any questions, Mrs.
Hartley. I shall never speak of what I have been,
unless——"

"You reinstate yourself," she supplied.

"Exactly. And many years may elapse before I
can do that."

"Ah! you don't know," she replied with an encouraging smile. "But you must excuse me. I have

got the house to attend to. You may like to see the paper ? "

Having spent some little time over the daily paper which she gave him, Walter took up his hat, and went out.

Strolling leisurely along, he came to Lambeth Palace, and standing near the pier at the foot of the bridge, he watched the boats arriving and departing —landing passengers and carrying them away.

The lively scene served to amuse him. Among those who were embarking, he noticed a tall, thin man, dressed in black, whose sharp features were familiar to him.

The individual in question was only just in time, and as soon as he got on board, the boat was cast off, and took its course towards the other side of the river.

It had not gone far, when the tall, thin man, approaching the stern, descried Walter, and almost started at the sight of him.

They remained gazing at each other as long as the steam-boat continued in view, but no sign of recognition passed between them.

The sight of this person, whoever he might be, seemed to awaken a train of painful reflections in Walter's breast.

He sat down on a bench on the little esplanade, and remained there for some time contemplating the busy scene on the river.

By degrees he recovered his serenity, and it was in a more cheerful frame of mind that he returned to the house in Spencer's Rents.

III.

INTRODUCES MR. TANKARD, MR. LARKINS, AND MR. PLEDGER DAPP.

THE tea equipage was set out in the little parlour, and Walter enjoyed a cup of bohea with Mrs. Hartley very much, and passed the evening with her in tranquil converse. He began to feel a great regard for the good dame, and listened to her advice.

Hartley did not return till nearly supper time, and brought with him a friend—a neighbour—whom he introduced as Mr. Tankard.

Rather an important personage in his way was Mr. Tankard—stout, short, red-faced, possessing a rich mellow voice, consequential in manner, and respectably dressed in black. Some of his friends called him "Silver Tankard," but Hartley took no such liberty. Mr. Tankard had been a butler before setting up in business in the Lambeth Road, where he now kept a large china and glass shop.

Though generally distant and proud, Mr. Tankard unbent towards Walter, and was unusually civil to him.

"I like the looks of that young man," he observed, in a very loud whisper to Hartley.

Mrs. Hartley deemed it necessary to apologise to Mr. Tankard for the poorness of the supper, and told him if she had expected the honour and pleasure of his company she would have provided something better; but he begged her condescendingly not to mind—"he wasn't at all partickler."

Mrs. Hartley knew better. She knew he was ex-

I

ceedingly particular. However, she did the best that circumstances would allow, and as a finish to the rather scanty meal, gave him a dish of stewed cheese, and a jug, not a " tankard," of ale with a toast in it. With this he was tolerably well satisfied.

After supper, Hartley asked his guest if he would like to smoke, to which proposal Mr. Tankard made no sort of objection. A flask of Scotch whisky was likewise set on the table.

Scarcely were the pipes lighted, when the party was increased by the arrival of Mr. Pledger Dapp and Mr. Larkins, who it seems were expected by Hartley, though he had said nothing about them to his wife.

Pledger Dapp, a brisk little man, was a cook and confectioner in the York Road, and Larkins was a greengrocer in the same neighbourhood, and likewise went out to wait. They worked together with Mr. Tankard, and each recommended his friends whenever he had the opportunity.

More glasses were placed on the table, and more hot water, and everybody was puffing away.

The room was soon so full of smoke that Mrs. Hartley could stand it no longer, and retired to the kitchen.

A great deal of merriment prevailed among the company, and they laughed heartily at each other's stories. These related chiefly to their customers.

At last, Hartley contrived to bring Walter forward by making a direct allusion to him.

" I want to have your opinion about my young friend, gentlemen," he observed, taking the pipe from his mouth. " He thinks of joining the cavalry, but I think it is a pity such a fine young man should throw himself away. What do you say, gentlemen ? "

After a sip of whisky and water, the person chiefly appealed to replied :

" I think it would be a thousand pities. No doubt he would make a very fine Life Guardsman, but in my opinion, he would do much better as a figure footman."

" Much better," echoed Pledger Dapp and Larkins.

" I'm not ashamed to say I began life as a page," pursued Mr. Tankard; " and you see what I've arrived at."

" It's no secret that I was a cook in a gentleman's family before I set up for myself as a confectioner," said Pledger Dapp.

" And I was a gardener before I became a green-grocer," said Larkins. And he added, with a laugh, " I'm a gardener now, though no longer in service."

" Take the advice we all of us give you, sir, and become a footman," said Tankard. " I'll answer for it we'll soon find you a place."

" But I've no qualifications," replied Walter. " I don't know the duties—that is, I know what a footman ought to be—"

" Well, that's quite enough," interrupted Pledger Dapp. " You'll soon learn all the rest."

" It just occurs to me that Lady Thicknesse, of Belgrave Square, is in want of a footman," observed Tankard. " That would be a very good thing. It's a first-rate place."

" Lady Thicknesse ! I think I've heard of her," remarked Walter. " A widow, isn't she ?"

" Widow of Sir Thomas Thicknesse—middle-aged and rich. Besides her town residence, she has got a country house in Cheshire."

Walter reflected for a few minutes.

The proposition had taken him by surprise. The notion of becoming a flunky amused him vastly, and he could hardly entertain it seriously. However, there seemed to be no difficulty in assuming the part.

The result of his cogitations was that he felt inclined to adopt the expedient, and he told Mr. Tankard so.

"But I cannot offer myself under any false pretence," he said. "Lady Thicknesse must be made aware that I have never served in this capacity before."

All his auditors, except Hartley, laughed loudly at his scruples.

"Bless you, my dear fellow, you needn't be so diffident," cried Mr. Tankard. "If Lady Thicknesse is satisfied, that's all you need mind. I'll set about the business to-morrow. In a week I expect you'll thank me for my pains."

"You'll have a first-rate situation, if you get it, I promise you," remarked Pledger Dapp.

"Very handsome livery and powder," observed Larkins.

"Powder!" exclaimed Walter, in dismay. "Is it necessary to wear powder?"

"Indispensable," replied Tankard. "But you'll find it very becoming," he added, with a laugh. "Powder will suit your hair. You're above six feet in height, eh?"

"Six feet two," replied Walter.

"Capital!" cried Tankard. "Stay! One thing mustn't be neglected," he added, rubbing his chin expressively. "You must get rid of that handsome brown beard."

"S'death! must I shave?" cried Walter, amid the general merriment.

"Certainly, my dear fellow," replied Tankard. "Whoever heard of a footman in a beard? Follow my instructions, and you may make yourself quite easy about the place. I'll engage you shall obtain it."

"But I've not quite decided myself," said Walter.

"Pooh! nonsense! you can't do better," cried Tankard. "Can he, gentlemen?"

Everybody concurred with him in opinion.

Partly in jest, partly in earnest, Walter assented. So much, in fact, was said in favour of the plan, that he began to grow reconciled to it.

As the clock struck eleven, Mrs. Hartley came in, and her appearance was the signal for the breaking up of the party.

While shaking hands with Walter, Mr. Tankard renewed his promises, and said:

"I'm a man of my word. What I say I'll do. To-morrow I'll go to Belgrave Square, and see my friend, Mr. Higgins, Lady Thicknesse's butler. On my return I'll call and tell you all about it."

"Really, Mr. Tankard, you are taking a vast deal of trouble——"

"Not in the least, my dear fellow!" replied the other. "It is a pleasure to me—a very great pleasure."

"And if you knew him as well as I do, you'd feel that it must be, or he wouldn't do it," observed Hartley, laughing.

In another minute the company were gone, and shortly afterwards the whole of the little household had retired to rest.

Visions of his new life floated before Walter as he laid his head on the pillow. He slept soundly enough, but on awakening next morning he rather regretted the promise he had given.

"I don't like the idea of turning flunky," he thought; "but the livery will serve as a disguise."

IV.

SIGEBERT SMART.

Before going out to his work, Hartley had a little talk in private with Walter.

Fearing he might be inconvenienced from want of money—having heard him say, at their first meeting on Westminster Bridge, that he had none—the worthy stonemason, with great consideration, volunteered to lend him five pounds, on the simple understanding that this sum was to be repaid when Walter had earned so much wages.

Thus amply provided with funds, Walter sallied forth after breakfast to make a few necessary purchases preparatory to entering upon the situation, should he obtain it—and telling Mrs Hartley what to say to Mr. Tankard, in case that obliging person should call during his absence.

His first business was to seek out a hair-dresser's shop; and, hearing there were several in the Lambeth Road, he went thither.

He had not proceeded far, when he came to an establishment that bore the name SIGEBERT SMART, in large gilt letters, above the window, and promised all he desired.

Entering the shop, he perceived two persons—one a showy-looking female, stationed behind a counter laden with pots of pomade, flacons of oil, brushes, sponges, and perfumery; the other, a dapper, fair-complexioned young man, with his blonde hair brushed back from his forehead.

This was Sigebert Smart in person. Having been for a year in Paris, at a large shop in the Rue St. Honoré, he considered himself perfectly versed in all the arts and mysteries of a French coiffeur, and incomparably superior to any of his rivals in the Lambeth Road.

Walter thought the hairdresser stared at him rather inquisitively as he entered the shop; but the man's manner was perfectly polite, and, on learning his customer's requirements, he begged him to step into an inner room, communicating by a glass-door with the shop.

"Pray be seated, sir!" said Sigebert, pointing to a well-stuffed arm-chair. "Shaved, I think you said, sir?"

"Shaved!" repeated Walter.

"Before taking the irreparable step," said Sigebert, placing himself in front of his customer, and regarding him steadfastly, "let me ask if you have reflected?"

"What d'ye mean?" cried Walter, staring at him in surprise.

"Excuse me, sir," rejoined the hairdresser, "but have you positively determined to part with that magnificent beard?"

"I don't like to lose it, I confess," replied Walter. "But I have no choice."

"That's hard. Never in my experience have I

beheld a finer beard, nor better grown. I shall be loth to cut it."

" You are pleased to compliment me," said Walter.

" It is not my habit, sir, I assure you.   Generally I am frank to a fault.   *Apropos des barbes*, I will tell you a curious story.   A gentleman called here last evening, and inquired whether a very tall young man, dressed in a grey tweed suit, exactly like yours, sir, and having a particularly handsome brown beard, the very ditto of yours, sir, lodged in the Lambeth Road, or hereabouts.   I told him I had not remarked any such person ; but you, sir, answer precisely to the description.   Strange you should put in an appearance next day ! "

" That's why you stared at me so hard when I entered the shop ? " cried Walter.

" Couldn't help it, sir.   Quite startled."

" And now for a description of the individual who has taken the liberty to inquire about me ? " said Walter.

" Tall, thin, sharp features ; long, straight nose ; professional-looking," replied Sigebert.

" I know him," said Walter.   " I saw him yesterday."

" At Lambeth Pier ; he said he caught sight of you there.   He appears most anxious to find you, and has been making inquiries about you in the neighbourhood."

" Did he mention any name ? "

" No ; he was exceedingly reserved on that point. But I think he'll call again."

" I've no especial desire to see him.   But now to work."

"Must I really commit this outrage?" cried Sigebert, flourishing his scissors. "My soul revolts at the deed."

Walter, however, insisted, and, in a very few minutes, his luxuriant beard had vanished, and his cheeks and chin were perfectly smooth.

He had just got up from the arm-chair, when the glass-door opened, and a tall man came in.

"You have found your friend at last, sir," cried Sigebert, on beholding him. "I suppose my wife told you he was here?"

"She did," replied the other.

Walter, however, did not seem willing to acknowledge the intruder as a friend, but drew himself up, and regarded him sternly—almost angrily.

"Perhaps I had better retire, gentlemen," said Sigebert. "You may wish to have a little private converse."

With this, he went out, but we rather fancy the door was left slightly ajar.

"How is it that you have presumed to follow me about in this way?" asked Walter, in an offended tone.

"You must forgive me, sir. I saw you yesterday, and have searched for you here to-day. It is my earnest desire to induce you to return to your relatives and friends. They feared something terrible had happened to you."

"They need not trouble themselves about me," rejoined Walter. "I shall not trouble myself about them."

"But I have certain propositions to make to you."

"I reject all propositions. It is useless to talk to me."

"I have, also, a sum of money at your disposal. Will you not receive it?"

"If it comes from a particular quarter, and as an allowance, no!"

"Permit me to say, sir," remarked the tall gentleman in a grave tone, "that you are acting very injudiciously, and are throwing away a great piece of good fortune. All can be easily put to rights if you will only allow me to do it. And there are many other advantages that might accrue to you, to which I cannot now more particularly advert."

"I am the best judge of what concerns myself, sir."

"I don't think so," rejoined the other.. "You seem obstinately bent upon pursuing a wrong course. Have you any debts?"

"None!"

"Any liabilities?"

"None!"

"Then why not assume your proper position? You will have every aid. I understand your objections, and though I deem them ridiculous, I shall not attempt to combat them at this moment. But there are friends willing and anxious to assist you. Amongst others," he added, lowering his voice, "Sir Bridgnorth Charlton."

"Sir Bridgnorth is an excellent man—one in a thousand!"

"Then you cannot distrust him?"

"I do not distrust him! On the contrary, I have entire confidence in him! He is a gentleman and a man of honour!"

"Let him have the management of your affairs."

" Do you come from Sir Bridgnorth ? "

" Sir Bridgnorth is not certain you are alive. He fears you have committed suicide. It will be a great satisfaction to him and several others to learn that you have not executed your fell purpose."

" Suffer them to remain in ignorance. I would rather they supposed me dead. Keep this secret for me, I beg of you. It is the sole favour you can do me. I will reappear at the proper time."

" But, meanwhile, you will make several persons very unhappy—your sister, who has the greatest affection for you, as I can testify—and Miss Barfleur."

" Miss Barfleur ! " exclaimed Walter, starting. " She has no interest in me."

" You are mistaken," replied the other. " Sir Leycester Barfleur having recently died, she is now a great heiress."

" The very reason why she should not think of me."

" Don't despair ! Make your appearance ! "

" I have said I will appear at the proper time—not before."

" Won't you give me any idea of your projects ? "

" No."

" Do you want money ? I am ready to advance it to you."

" I want none."

" Then our interview is at an end."

" Once more, I must ask you not to mention that you have seen me."

" I cannot consent to keep those persons who are attached to you in doubt—nor ought you to ask it. If, for reasons of your own, you choose to live in concealment and under a feigned name, however I may

regret your determination, I shall not attempt to interfere with it. But I am persuaded you will speedily
change your mind."

"If I do, I'll write to you."

"No; write to Sir Bridgnorth. He is searching
for you. He ought to have a letter. Address him at
the 'Grosvenor Hotel.' He is now in town."

"I will do it. Before we separate, give me your
word that you won't follow me, nor attempt to find out
my abode. You will gain nothing by the discovery."

"I give you my word," replied the other.

"Enough," said Walter. "I thank you heartily for
the trouble you have taken about me. Adieu!"

On issuing forth into the shop, Walter found the
hairdresser standing rather suspiciously near the glass-
door. But he seemed to have some employment at the
counter. Walter, however, could not help remarking
that Sigebert's manner towards him seemed more respectful than it had been.

As he received payment for the task he had performed, the hairdresser exclaimed:

"Ah, sir, I fear you'll regret the loss of your beard.
Your best friend wouldn't recognise you—you're so
much changed. But don't lay the blame on me. I
did my best to dissuade you."

As he bowed the young man out, he looked after
him for a moment, and saw that he proceeded towards
the bridge, whereupon the wily Sigebert made a significant gesture to his wife as he returned.

At this juncture, the tall, professional-looking gentleman came forth, and having nothing to pay, merely
offered his thanks as he went out.

A hansom cab chancing to pass at the moment, he

immediately got into it, and ordered the driver to go to the " Grosvenor Hotel."

Meanwhile, Sigebert, having divested himself of his apron and put on a hat, nodded to his wife, and followed Walter, who was not yet out of sight—his tall figure rendering him easily distinguishable.

V.

ROMNEY.

On his way back, Walter stopped at a large linen-draper's shop to purchase some shirts and other articles, never dreaming he was followed by Sigebert. Having provided himself with all he required, and given orders where the parcel should be sent, he proceeded on his course.

Not till he had fairly housed him did the hairdresser discontinue the quest, and he then hovered near the spot for some time.

There was a mystery about Walter that greatly excited Sigebert's curiosity, and he determined to unravel it.

" Why, what have you done with your beard, sir ? " cried Mrs. Hartley, as Walter entered the house.

" Left it at the hairdresser's ! " he replied, with a laugh.

" Well, I can't say your appearance is much improved. I wish Rose had seen you as you were."

" What ! has your daughter come back ? " cried Walter.

" No; but I expect her very shortly. She has been at Harrow-on-the-Hill, on a visit, as I think I told you, and I've just got a letter from her, telling me she will return to-day. ' Father must meet me at Lambeth Pier at noon, and carry my carpet-bag '—that's what she says ; but I don't think he'll be back in time."

" Well, I'll meet her, and carry the carpet-bag, with the greatest pleasure ! " said Walter.

" But you won't know her."

" Describe her, and I shall. Not very tall, I suppose ? "

" Not very—rather short."

" Pretty figure ? "

" I think so."

" Blooming complexion ? "

" Odd you should guess that. Well, she has a pink complexion."

" That's why you call her Rose. What sort of eyes ? —black, blue, grey, or nondescript ? "

" I never heard of nondescript eyes. Rose's are light blue. But how stupid I am ! Here's her photograph. Very like her it is."

" And a very pretty girl it represents," replied Walter, examining it. " You might have said a great deal more in her praise without being charged with maternal vanity. Having seen this, I can make no mistake."

" Not easily; for she wears the same blue serge dress, and the same hat. I'm sorry you'll lose your room, but we'll find a bed for you."

" Oh, it can't be helped ! " he cried, affecting an indifference he did not feel. " Pray has Mr. Tankard been here to-day ? "

" I've seen nothing of him as yet," she replied.

" Well, then, I'll be off. I'll soon bring your daughter back to you."

" Dear me, how surprised she'll be ! " cried Mrs. Hartley. " She'll wonder who you are."

" Don't be afraid. I'll explain matters."

As Walter went forth, he noticed a stout ash-plant hanging up in the passage, and took it with him— very fortunately, as it turned out.

Pleased with the task he had undertaken, he marched along quickly, and did not remark that Sigebert, who had seen him come out, was on his track.

A boat had just landed its passengers as Walter reached the pier, but he saw no one among them bearing the slightest resemblance to the pretty damsel he was looking for. However, it was not yet twelve o'clock.

About a quarter of an hour later on, another steamboat could be seen crossing the river ; and on a near approach of the vessel, the deck not being crowded, he easily made out Rose.

Her photograph did not do her justice. She was even handsomer than he anticipated, and her good looks had evidently gained her the unwelcome attentions of a young but dissipated-looking individual, who was standing near her.

This person, whose looks, gait, dress, and manner showed that he belonged to the Turf, was well known to Walter, and with good reason, since he had won large sums of money from him. The young man's name was Romney ; and though he contrived to hold up his head in the betting-ring, he was not in very good repute, and was regarded as a blackleg. Walter held him in detestation, for he mainly attributed his ruin to him.

Though he must have perceived that his attentions were annoying to Rose, Romney did not discontinue them, but became more impertinently assiduous as the boat neared the pier, and seemed determined not to part with her.

Rose looked out anxiously for her father, but could not discover him, nor did she perceive any person she knew, or whose protection she could claim.

Stepping on shore before her, Romney offered her his hand, but she refused to take it, and his proposal to carry her bag was peremptorily declined.

At this juncture, Walter came up, and pushing the intruder forcibly aside, bade him begone, and no longer molest the young lady.

"What business have you to interfere?" cried Romney, furiously. "Who are you? Do you know him?" he added, to Rose.

"I never saw the gentleman before," she rejoined. "But I am greatly obliged by his assistance."

"*Gentleman!*" echoed Romney, scornfully. "He doesn't deserve the term!"

"Blackleg and scoundrel!" vociferated Walter. "Do you dare to speak thus of one you have cheated and plundered?"

And seizing him by the throat, he applied the ash-plant vigorously to his shoulders.

No one attempted to interfere; and when Romney was released, he made himself scarce as soon as he could; perceiving, from the observations that reached his ears, that the feeling of the bystanders was decidedly against him. He was followed by Sigebert, who had witnessed the encounter, and determined to have a word with him.

Meanwhile, Rose had found another protector. Mr. Tankard had come up, and was standing with her at a short distance. He had given her all needful explanation respecting Walter; and when the latter joined them, after the scuffle, she said to him:

"I never imagined you came from our house, Mr. Liddel. You have really done me a great service. But how on earth did you know me? I never remember seeing you before."

"I don't suppose you ever did," he replied. "I knew you from the photograph your mother showed me when I offered to go and meet you at the pier, in place of your father."

"Well, I declare, that *is* curious!" she cried.

"And I promised to carry your carpet-bag; but Mr. Tankard, I'm sure, is too gallant to surrender it."

"Quite right," replied the other. "I'm proud to be of use to Miss Rose. I was just coming to call upon you, Mr. Liddel. I've been to Belgrave Square, and have got you the situation. I saw Mr. Higgins, the butler, and he says you're to enter upon your duties the day after to-morrow."

"Quite soon enough," remarked Walter, laughing.

"There's something about the livery that I have to tell you; but that will do by-and-by," added Tankard.

"Dear me, Mr. Liddel!" exclaimed Rose, raising her finely-arched eyebrows in surprise; "you're not going to wear a livery, are you?"

"Livery and powder," supplied Tankard.

"Impossible!" exclaimed Rose.

K

"No; it's too true," said Walter.

By this time they had reached the house. Rose rushed in, and was welcomed by her mother with kisses and embraces.

VI.

ROSE HARTLEY.

ROSE HARTLEY was just nineteen, and had all the freshness and bloom of youth.

A remarkably neat, but rather plump, figure, comely features, brilliant complexion, sparkling eyes, nut-brown hair and particularly small feet, constituted the sum total of her charms; and she had considerably more than fall to the lot of nine girls out of ten.

Rose was puzzled upon one point. She could not exactly understand how Walter had found his way to her father's house; and her mother did not care to enlighten her. However, his appearance and manner pleased her, and she felt sure she should soon learn all about him.

"Mr. Tankard," said Mrs. Hartley, "I must get you to help us out of a difficulty."

"With the greatest pleasure, my dear madam, if it lies in my power."

"I needn't tell you our accommodation is very limited; and now Rose has returned, I fear——"

"I know what you are going to say," interrupted Tankard. "You wish Mr. Liddel to have a bed at my house. I expected the request, and am, luckily, able to comply with it. He *shall* have a room."

"Upon my word, Mr. Tankard, I'm very much obliged to you," said Walter.

"Not in the least," rejoined Tankard. "But we must have a merry meeting to-night, Mrs. Hartley. You must all come and sup with me. Mr. Higgins, Lady Thicknesse's butler, has promised to give the pleasure of his company; and, since Miss Rose has returned, I'll ask Harry Netterville, of Gray's Inn, as I'm well aware she likes the society of that amiable and agreeable young man."

"Pray don't ask Mr. Netterville on my account, Mr Tankard!" observed Rose, with affected indifference. "I'm not particularly anxious to meet him."

Mr. Tankard, however, knew better; and said that as soon as he got back, he would send off a note to the young gentleman in question. Mr. Netterville, he explained to Walter, belonged to the legal profession, being clerk to an eminent solicitor in Gray's Inn.

"And now, Mr. Liddel, I must take you with me," said Tankard. "I've got some arrangements to make with you. If we don't meet before," he added to Rose and her mother, "I shall see you all at nine this evening—that's understood."

Rose would have preferred Walter remaining a little longer, but as he promised to come round in the course of the afternoon, she felt quite reconciled to his departure.

Mr. Tankard first took his companion to the shop of Mr. Pledger Dapp, in the York Road. Mr. Dapp, as we have said, was a pastrycook and confectioner, and the numerous good things on the counter looked very tempting at that hour.

Mr. Dapp was delighted to see them, insisted on

serving each with a basin of mock-turtle soup, and stood beside them while they discussed it at a small table at the further end of the room.

"Well, is all satisfactorily settled, may I inquire, Mr. Liddel?" he said.

"Yes; all's settled, Dapp," said Tankard, answering for his friend. "The very livery is ready!"

"Indeed!" cried Walter, looking up in surprise. "Has it appeared by magic?"

"I've not yet had time to enter into details," rejoined Tankard; "but when I saw Higgins this morning, he told me Lady Thicknesse had left the arrangements entirely to him, so we had only to talk them over together; and it was then agreed that he should come to my house this evening, where he could have an opportunity of meeting you, and judge for himself, though he entertained no doubt, from description, that you would suit."

"So far good," remarked Walter. "But about the livery?"

"You shall hear," replied the other. "It seems that Charles Brownlow, the late footman, who was as near as possible your height and figure, was discharged at a moment's notice for impertinence. His livery, no doubt, will fit you."

"But has he worn it?" cried Walter.

"No; it has not been delivered. Higgins will order the suit to be sent to me, so that you can try it in the evening, and we can judge of the effect."

"A capital plan," laughed Dapp.

"A dress rehearsal, in fact," said Walter. "Well, it may be useful."

"No doubt you'll play your part to perfection," said Tankard.

" I shall see how I like it myself," rejoined Walter.
" This is why you've invited the party to supper, I
conclude ? "

" Exactly," replied Tankard, laughing. " You've
divined my purpose. By-the-by, Dapp, you must
send me a good supper to-night—a very good supper,
mind ! "

" For how many guests ? "

" A dozen ; and make one of them yourself. That'll
keep you up to the mark."

" I'll give you a supper worthy of the ' Silver Tankard,' " replied Dapp. " At what hour shall it be ? "

" Ten o'clock precisely. Direct Larkins to send me
some flowers—cut flowers ; and tell him to come, too.
We'll do the thing in style."

" Nothing shall be neglected. I know how particular you are," replied Dapp. " But won't you take one
of these ? " he added, placing a dish of patés before
them.

Just then he was obliged to leave his friends to
attend to some customers. When a couple of patés
had been devoured, Tankard and his companion arose,
and quitted the shop.

" Who is that tall young man ? " remarked one of
the customers at the counter.

" Mr. Walter Liddel," replied Dapp.

" I don't think that's the name," said the individual.
" I've heard it before, and feel almost certain it's not
Liddel."

Dapp made no remark at the time ; but he afterwards pondered a little upon the matter.

" He's a very singular fellow, that Walter Liddel,"
he thought. " I expect he'll turn out a Claimant of

some sort, or he may be a dook in disguise. Shouldn't wonder."

VII.

TOM TANKARD.

MR. TANKARD's establishment was larger and hand-somer than Walter expected to find it. In the windows there was a very good display of china and glass, and the shop was tolerably spacious.

Mrs. Tankard, to whom he at once was presented, and who received him very kindly, was still good-looking, though somewhat on the wane; but she was sharp and intelligent, and evidently very well able to attend to the business in her husband's absence.

The Tankards had an only son—an only child, we ought to say. Tom Tankard was a much smarter man than his father, and much more self-important. Like his father, he had a sobriquet, and was called "Cool Tankard." Tom ought to have attended strictly to the shop; but being allowed to do pretty much as he liked, as a natural consequence he did little or nothing.

Tom was not handsome. On the contrary, he was decidedly an ugly dog. Short, fat, snub-nosed, round-faced, he had deep-seated, grey eyes, and these had a cunning, though rather comic, expression. His pink cheeks were totally destitute of whisker, and his whity-brown hair was cut extremely short.

A brown Newmarket coat was buttoned over his broad chest; but his shoulders were out of proportion with his spindling legs, which were cased in very tight trousers.

Nevertheless, Tom was a smart fellow in his way, though rather loud in his style, and exceedingly particular about the flaming colour of his tie and the size of his gold pin.

Now and then he used to drive in the Park when he could afford to hire a drag, and took some smart young ladies with him. More than once he had ridden at the Croydon Steeple-chases, and he occasionally contrived to attend a meet of the Surrey hounds.

Tom chanced to be in the shop when Walter came in with his father, and, being struck by his appearance, condescended to pay him some attention.

Mr. Tankard lost no time in informing his wife that Mr. Liddel would occupy a bed in the house for a night or two; and then went on to explain that he had invited a few friends for the evening, and had directed Pledger Dapp to send in a little supper— thinking it would save trouble.

Mrs. Tankard received the intelligence with great good nature, and Tom was told to take Mr. Liddel up-stairs and show him the spare room, which proved to be a very neat little chamber.

They were still talking together, when Mr. Tankard came up with a large brown-paper parcel, and, deeming it advisable to mystify his son, winked at Walter, to let him into his plan, and then said to the hopeful youth:

"Do you know, Tom, Mr. Liddel is going to a fancy dress ball?"

"How jolly!" exclaimed Tom. "What costume?"

"As a footman," replied old Tankard. "Here's his dress."

"As a footman," exclaimed Tom, with a droll expression. "Jeames of Buckley Square—or Chawles. Well, he's just the figure for one of those gentry. Is he going to the ball to-night?"

"No; but I've persuaded him to appear in private at my little party this evening, that we may see how he looks."

"Oh! he can't fail to look well," said Tom, somewhat sarcastically. "But let's see the dress, guv'nor. Beg pardon, Mr. Liddel! I ought to have asked your permission."

"Oh, don't stand on any ceremony with me, I beg!" cried Walter.

The parcel was then opened, and a very handsome suit of livery produced. There was likewise another rather smaller parcel inside.

"Here's a gorgeous coat! here's a brilliant pair of plooshes!" exclaimed Tom, holding up the latter. "You'll look uncommon well in these, Mr. Liddel."

"No doubt he will," said Mr. Tankard. "But no more of your chaff, sir."

The smaller parcel was then opened, and was found to contain a pair of thin shoes, buckles, silk stockings, shirt, and white cravat.

"I was going to put you in mind, Mr. Liddel," observed Tankard, "that you'd want several articles to rig you out completely—but here they all are. I dare say the shoes will fit you."

"I'm certain of it," replied Walter, examining them.

"Another thing mustn't be forgotten, Mr. Liddel," said Tom. "Since you're going to appear as Jeames, or Chawles, you'll want your 'air powderin'. I'll get you a *coiffeur*. When will you have him ? "

" Not till evening," replied Walter.

" Very good," said Tom. " He shall be here at eight."

" Now, go down to the shop, Tom," cried Mr. Tankard. " Send off a note at once to Harry Netterville, and ask him to supper. Consult your mother, and if she approves, ask Mrs. Tripp and Clotilde, Mrs. Sicklemore and Flora, or anybody else agreeable to her, but don't exceed half a dozen, for we have got five or six already.

" Counting Harry Netterville ? "

" No ; not counting him."

" You've seen Rose Hartley, of course, Mr. Liddel ? " cried Tom. " Sweet girl, ain't she ? Harry Netterville is rather smitten in that quarter.'

" Then give him the chance of meeting her," said his father.

Thereupon Tom disappeared.

After an early dinner with the Tankards, Walter betook himself to Spencer's Rents, and saw Rose, who was alone in the little parlour. Evidently she regarded him with more interest than she had done.

" My mother has told me all about you, Mr. Liddel," she said, "at least, all she knows, and I feel exceedingly sorry for you. But I hope all will soon be right. I am neither old enough nor wise enough to give you advice, nor is it right or proper for me to do so, but I am sorry you are thinking of becoming a footman. I feel quite sure you are a gentleman—"

" I have been one," interrupted Walter. " But I have no money, and must do something. The offer

was made me, and I accepted it. Any honest employment is respectable."

"So it is, undoubtedly. What I fear is that you
may hereafter regret having taken the step."

"I can leave if I don't like the employment.
But I must say you talk very sensibly, Miss Rose. I
wish I had had such a counsellor a year or two ago,
before I committed my worst follies."

"You wouldn't have listened to me," she replied,
shaking her head.

"I don't know—I might have done. But your
remarks seem to produce some salutary effect upon
me, and that is more than I could say of myself
formerly."

"Then you are improved by misfortune."

"In some respects, I think I am. But there is
considerable room for further improvement."

"Mr. Liddel, I am convinced you have a great deal
of good in you. Only do yourself justice."

"I will try," he replied. "But how is it, I must
again ask, that you, who are so young, are able
to give such sensible advice?"

"I have a good mother," she replied.

At this very moment Mrs. Hartley came into the
room.

"I hope you heard what was said of you, ma'am?"
observed Walter. "Your daughter has just been
telling me how much she owes you."

"I owe quite as much to her," cried the good dame,
affectionately. "She is the joy of the house, and I
don't know what I shall do when I lose her. But I
suppose I must make up my mind to it one of these
days."

" Not yet, dearest mother," said Rose.

" I suppose we shall meet the fortunate individual this evening?" observed Walter. " Mr. Harry Netterville, eh?"

" Yes, that's the name; and a very nice young fellow he is," replied Mrs. Hartley. " I only wish he was a little richer."

" Well, we must wait contentedly till he becomes so," sighed Rose. " Poverty and happiness don't go together in married life."

" Again I must compliment you on your good sense, Miss Rose," remarked Walter.

" That's one of my mother's maxims," she rejoined. " But don't call me *Miss* Rose, please. After the service you rendered me this morning, I shall always regard you as a friend, and so will Harry!"

" I think I told you that Romney, the insolent fellow by whom you were affronted, was one of those who mainly contributed to my ruin?" remarked Walter. " He is a great libertine, and I hope you may experience no more annoyance from him. I may not always be at hand to protect you."

" Luckily, he doesn't know where I live, or I might feel some uneasiness," said Rose.

" Ah, those rakes are dreadful—no keeping them off!" cried Mrs. Hartley.

At this moment there was a knock at the outer door.

Rather startled, Mrs. Hartley went to see who it was; and presently returned with a letter in her hand.

" This is for you, Rose!" she cried. " It was left

by a stranger, who said no answer was required, and
went away immediately."

"For me!" exclaimed Rose, turning pale. "It is
certainly addressed to me, but I don't know the
handwriting."

She then opened the letter, and, after angrily
scanning it, read it aloud.

"The gentleman who had the great pleasure of meeting Miss Rose Hartley on the steam-boat this morning,
hopes soon to behold her again, as her charms have
made an ineffaceable impression upon him. He feels
certain that the incident that occurred on the pier
must have been as vexatious to her as to him; but
she may rest assured that the ruffian who committed
the assault shall not pass unpunished."

"So, then, he has discovered your address!"
cried Walter. "I wonder how he learnt it, since he
ran off."

"I could not have credited such audacity, without
proof positive!" exclaimed Rose, indignantly. "Does
Mr. Romney imagine I will ever exchange another word
with him, except to express my anger and scorn? Have
I given him any encouragement, that he should dare
to write me such a letter?" she added, tears of
vexation starting to her eyes.

"No, no! I am sure not," cried Walter. "But
it is part of Romney's system; he believes no woman
can resist him. I now begin to think he will persist
in the attempt, notwithstanding the chastisement he
has received, and the utter want of encouragement on
your part."

"Dear me! I declare I'm all of a tremble!" cried Mrs. Hartley. "I don't know what we shall do to get rid of him."

"Never mind him," cried Rose. "I'm not at all afraid."

"Leave me to deal with him," said Walter. "To-morrow I'll look after him."

"It is Harry Netterville's business to defend me," cried Rose.

"But I understand the man," rejoined Walter. "Besides, I have still an account to settle with him. Leave him to me."

"Yes; Mr. Liddel will manage him best," said Mrs. Hartley. "But I'll go and bring in tea; a cup will do us all good after this bother."

As the good dame had foreseen, the pleasant beverage soon produced a tranquillising effect, and enabled them to spend an hour or two in cheerful converse.

Walter then thought it time to go back to Mr. Tankard's, but offered to stay and take charge of them if they felt at all afraid. Mrs. Hartley said she expected her husband every minute, and he would bring them to the party.

"In that case, you can dispense with me," said Walter. "We shall meet again before long, and then you'll find me completely transmogrified."

"I am sorry to hear it," said Rose; "I like you very well as you are."

Walter laughed, and set out, taking with him his parcel of purchases.

VIII.

AS A FOOTMAN.

PREPARATIONS for the supper party had already commenced when Walter arrived at Mr. Tankard's. The shop had been closed at an earlier hour than usual, but was lighted up, and so arranged that the company could walk about it if they thought proper.

After casting a look around, and exchanging a word with Mr. and Mrs. Tankard, both of whom seemed very busy, Walter went up-stairs to his own room, which had now been converted into a nice little *cabinet de toilette.* No doubt he was indebted for this attention to Mrs. Tankard.

His first business was to try on the livery, and he was quite surprised to find how well it fitted him. We have already said it was a handsome, showy suit; and on Walter, who was very tall and extremely well proportioned, it produced its full effect.

What was his first thought as he contemplated himself in the glass, when thus metamorphosed, may be inferred from the loud laugh into which he burst.

Just at this juncture, Tom Tankard, who was now in evening dress, came into the room, and joined very heartily in the merriment.

"Excuse my laughing, Mr. Liddel," he said; "but yourself set me off. I never beheld such a swell footman before. You'll astonish 'em down stairs presently. But I've come to tell you the *coiffeur* is waiting outside. I suppose you're pretty nearly ready for him?"

The hairdresser proved to be Sigebert Smart; and great was the surprise of that inquisitive individual when he found that the customer who had so much excited his curiosity had assumed a new *rôle*, and found a new lodging.

"Can I believe my eyes?" he exclaimed, with a theatrical start. "Do I, indeed, behold the gentleman whom I was compelled to deprive of his beard? I now understand the meaning of that order. With a costume like this, a beard would be incongruous. But is the dress worth the sacrifice?"

"Cease this foolery, and begin!" said Tom. "The gent wants his 'air powderin'. He's goin' to a fancy ball, as I told you!"

Begging Walter to take off his coat, and flinging a loose gown over his shoulders, and giving him a napkin to protect his eyes, Sigebert set to work, and carefully powdered the young man's fine brown locks, pausing ever and anon in his task.

At length, he exclaimed, as he laid down the powder-puff:

"Now you'll do, sir—now you'll do! What do *you* think of the effect, Mr. Tom?" he added, appealing to our fat friend.

"Hum!" cried Tom, without delivering an opinion. "Wants a little more at the back, don't it?"

"Not a particle! Couldn't be better!" said Sigebert. "Now, let me help you on with your coat," he added to Walter.

And having thus aided in arraying him, he exclaimed, in affected admiration:

"Why, you're quite a picture, sir! You eclipse the

finest of the Court lacqueys! You'd get a first-rate
place, if you wanted!"

"That he would!" laughed Tom. "What's the
damage, Sigebert?"

"Would five shillings be too much?" said the
coiffeur, with a droll expression. "It's half a crown
for a real footman!"

"Well, here's a crown," replied Walter.

Sigebert received the money with a bow, and, while
putting his things together, said:

"May I inquire where the fancy ball takes
place?"

"Not far off," replied Tom.

"Here?" asked Sigebert.

Tom nodded.

"I guessed as much," said Sigebert. "Judging
from this specimen, it will be very good. But how
is it you're not in character, Mr. Tom?"

"Domino and mask easily put on!" replied Tom
not caring to enlighten him further.

Upon this, Sigebert bowed and departed, Tom attending him as far as the shop.

As he went out, the hairdresser saw Pledger Dapp,
whom he knew, with his assistants, bringing in the
supper; and he also saw Larkins, with some flowers,
but he did not say anything to either of them. In
fact, he was absorbed in thought.

When he got out into the street, he stood still for
a few moments, and reflected.

"What the deuce is he doing here?" he thought.
"He seems to have changed his quarters. And what's
the meaning of this disguise?—for disguise I believe
it is. Something may be made of the discovery."

Having arrived at this conclusion, he hailed a hansom cab, and bade the coachman drive to the Grosvenor Hotel.

***

IX.

IN WHICH MISS CLOTILDE TRIPP AND MISS FLORA SICKLEMORE MAKE THEIR APPEARANCE.

NOT long after Sigebert's departure, Mr. Higgins, Lady Thicknesse's butler, arrived, and was cordially welcomed by Mr. Tankard.

Stout, florid, bald-headed, well-mannered, quiet, wearing a white choker and a black dress coat, Mr. Higgins seemed the very model of a butler, and he certainly was most useful and important in the establishment over which he ruled. Lady Thicknesse confessed she could not do anything without Higgins.

" Odd things occurred this afternoon," remarked Higgins, after a little preliminary converse ; " and I'll mention it now, while there's an opportunity. Sir Bridgnorth Charlton called on my lady ; but, as she wasn't at home at the time, he conferred with me, and inquired whether I knew anything about Mr. Chetwynd Calverley. I told him 'no.' I had often heard the name in Cheshire, but had never, that I was aware of, seen the gentleman. This didn't satisfy Sir Bridgnorth. He next inquired whether we had recently discharged a footman, and I told him 'yes,' but we had just engaged another, though I myself had not yet seen the new man, but I expected he would enter on the place to-morrow. I had received a very good character of him from you. Sir

L

Bridgnorth then inquired your address, which I gave him, and likewise the young man's name—Walter Liddel—and he expressed his intention of calling upon you. I can't tell what he wants, or why he began by asking about Mr. Chetwynd Calverley."

"Sir Bridgnorth has not been here yet, and I've nothing to tell him when he does come," remarked Tankard. "I never heard of Mr. Chetwynd Calverley. Who is he?"

"The son of a rich gentleman who lived at Ouselcroft, in Cheshire. He was ruined on the turf, and disinherited by his father, and his stepmother has got the entire property. These circumstances happened about a year ago, and were the talk of the county at the time, so perhaps you may have heard of them."

"No; they're news to me," replied Tankard. "I never was in Cheshire—never heard of Ouselcroft, or the Calverleys. But the case is not very extraordinary. We *do* hear occasionally of youngsters getting ruined on the turf, and being disinherited in consequence. It's a piece of luck for the stepmother."

"Yes; and she's young and handsome!" said Higgins.

Their converse was here interrupted by the entrance of Mrs. Tankard and Tom, both of whom expressed themselves as very glad to see Mr. Higgins.

The lady wore a yellow satin dress, covered with black lace, and a rather showy cap; and Tom had the usual evening dress, with white tie and polished boots.

Tea and coffee had just been brought in by a female servant, when a knock was heard at the side-door, and directly afterwards a very tall, well-powdered footman advanced with stately step into the room, and announced, in agreeable tones, not too loud, but quite loud enough, Mr. Henry Netterville.

Nothing could be more effective than Walter's entrance.

Higgins gazed at him in astonishment. Prepared as he was to behold a fine, tall footman, he had not expected such a well-grown, handsome young fellow as this.

"By Jove! he'll do!" he exclaimed.

Harry Netterville, who was by no means a bad-looking fellow, and no smaller than the rest of his species, was completely dwarfed by the tall footman.

Tankard and his wife expressed their satisfaction in low tones; but the irrepressible Tom gave a little applause.

Walter, however, having done his devoir, immediately withdrew, being summoned by another knock at the door; but presently reappeared and ushered in Mrs. Tripp and her daughter, who were quite astonished at being thus introduced, and thought the Tankards must have taken leave of their senses.

Mrs. Tripp was a milliner, and Clotilde Tripp, who assisted her mother, was a very pretty girl, and looked upon Tom as an admirer.

But she had a formidable rival in Flora Sicklemore, whose mother kept a Berlin wool, fringe, and trimming warehouse in Kennington Road. Flora was quite as pretty as Clotilde—much prettier, in her own opinion—for had she not bright golden locks and a very fair skin—while Clotilde's tresses were coal-black, and her complexion olive-coloured!

Both charmers were smartly dressed, and both bent on captivating Tom.

L 2

Like the Tripps, the Sicklemores were filled with amazement at the sight of the grand footman, but they felt sure such an extraordinary addition to the establishment could only have been made by Tom.

Everybody had now arrived, except the Hartleys.

At last they appeared. Walter received them as he had done the others, at the side-door, and offered to announce them, but Rose wouldn't let him; so they entered the room quite quietly, but were very cordially welcomed by the host and hostess; and even Tom, for some reason or other, was particularly civil to them. He paid Rose a great many compliments; but they were appreciated by the young lady at what they were worth; and she gladly turned to Harry Netterville, who was dying to talk to her, and who devoted himself to her for the rest of the evening.

Meanwhile, Higgins, wishing to have a word with the new footman, went in quest of him with Mr. Tankard.

They found him in the shop, which communicated with the other rooms. Bows and presentations took place. Then the parties shook hands.

" 'Pon my word, Liddel," said Higgins, in a good-natured but extremely patronising manner, "you promise exceedingly well! Indeed, with a little instruction, which I shall be extremely happy to give you, I unhesitatingly assert you will ' *do !* ' "

" Such commendation from a gentleman of your judgment and experience is extremely encouraging, Mr. Higgins," said Walter, bowing. " I was really desirous you should see me before I was finally engaged, that you might form your own opinion as to my capabilities."

" I had perfect confidence in my friend Tankard,"
replied Higgins ; " nor did he mislead me. You have
great personal advantages, Liddel, and they count for
much in a footman. I will say this for you, and you
may take it as a high compliment, I have never before
seen our livery look so well."

" I am much gratified," replied Walter, again bowing.

" A single question, and I have done," said Higgins.
" Do you happen to know Sir Bridgnorth Charlton ? "

" I am aware there is such a person," replied Walter,
rather embarrassed.

" I've also a question to ask you, Liddel," remarked
Tankard. " Did you ever hear of Mr. Chetwynd Calverley ? "

" Not lately," replied Walter, without hesitation ;
" and I don't think I am likely to hear of him again
very soon. I fancy he has disappeared altogether.
But why do you inquire, sir ? "

" Sir Bridgnorth Charlton was asking about him
this morning," interposed Higgins : " and, somehow,
you got mixed up in the inquiry."

" That's strange," replied Walter. " Surely he
didn't suppose I was Mr. Calverley ? "

" No ; he didn't think that," rejoined Higgins,
laughing ; " but he wanted some information respecting the young gentleman."

" Well, I'm unable to give him any," said Walter.

X.

AFTER a brief conference with Pledger Dapp, Mr.
Tankard returned with Higgins to the company.

Presently, the gladsome announcement was made
by the fine footman that supper was ready.

Mr. Tankard showed his guests the way by taking
out Mrs. Tripp; Mrs. Sicklemore followed with Hartley, whose arm she took with some reluctance; then
came Larkins with Mrs. Hartley; then Harry Netterville with Rose, by far the best-looking couple in the
assemblage; then came the gallant Tom, with a young
lady on either arm, singing to himself, like Captain
Macheath, " How happy could I be with either; " and,
lastly, came the hostess and Mr. Higgins.

Walter stood at the supper-room door as the company entered, and Flora and Clotilde made some com-
plimentary remarks upon his appearance. Tom, however, would not allow them to stop for a moment, but
took them to their seats, and placed himself between them.

The table was not very large, but it was well covered
with dishes; for Pledger Dapp had been as good as
his word, and had given a capital supper.

The chickens, hams, and tongues being ready carved,
could be helped without delay; and the lobster salad
was pronounced faultless by Mr. Higgins, who professed to be a judge.

The creams, jellies, and *pâtisserie* were equally good,
and Tom took care the young ladies should have plenty.

Nor was Harry Netterville less attentive, though Rose was far more easily satisfied.

Claret-cup and sherry were the beverages, and the glasses were constantly replenished by Pledger Dapp.

Ever since the supper began, Walter had disappeared. At length, his absence was remarked by Flora and Clotilde.

" I don't see your fine footman, Mr. Tom," said the former. " I suppose he won't wait at supper ? "

" Can't say," replied Tom. " He does pretty much as he likes."

" Now, do tell me, Mr. Tom," said Clotilde, " is he *really* a footman ? "

" To be sure he is ! " cried Tom. What do you take him for ? "

" *I* take him for a gentleman," said Flora.

" And so do I," added Clotilde.

" Well, he *is* a gentleman, in his way," said Tom. " What wages do you suppose we give him ? A hundred a year—quarter in advance—separate meals. He's gettin' his supper by himself at this moment ; will have his pint of champagne, though the guv'nor only allows *us* claret-cup—ha ! ha ! "

" I don't believe all this stuff you're telling us about high wages and champagne, Mr. Tom," said Flora. " But I'm certain there's something extraordinary about your new footman. You may as well let us into the secret."

" Well, if you want to know his history, I must refer you to Miss Rose Hartley," said Tom. " She can tell you about him."

" Is this so, Rose ? " said Harry Netterville, who overheard the remark.

" Don't ask me for any explanation just now, please Harry," she replied; " I'd rather not give it."

" Why not ? " cried Netterville, who was rather of a jealous temper. " Have you known him long ? I never heard of him before."

" I have already said I shall not answer any questions concerning him just now."

" Ah ! yonder he is ! " exclaimed Flora. " I can see him in the shop, through the open door. I declare, he has changed his dress ! He doesn't look half so imposing now."

" But he is much more like a gentleman," said Clotilde, who also perceived Walter in the shop, now in his morning attire. " Do be good-natured, Mr. Tom, and tell us who he is ! "

" I would rather stop both your mouths with a little of this trifle," said Tom, helping them.

Harry Netterville's eyes had followed the same direction as those of the two girls.

He noticed the change that had taken place in Walter's exterior, and said, rather sharply :

" Clear up the mystery, Rose."

" Not to-night," she replied, quietly.

" I wish Mr. Liddel would come in and join us at supper," said Mr. Tankard to Pledger Dapp. " Do go and ask him."

" Yes ; pray do, Mr. Dapp ! " said Flora. " We can easily make room for him here."

But Walter was prevented.

Just before the message was sent, a knock was heard ; and, thinking it was a visitor, he went to open the street-door, and found himself face to face with Sir Bridgnorth Charlton and Mr. Carteret.

An instantaneous recognition took place on either side. Walter hastily retreated, but neglected to shut the door after him; and the two gentlemen followed him into the shop, where he checked their further progress.

"You must excuse this intrusion," said Sir Bridgnorth, "and attribute it to my anxiety to find you. I have been searching for you everywhere, and rejoice that I am, at last, successful."

"Not so loud, Sir Bridgnorth," said the young man, pointing to the party in the adjoining room. "I am only known here as Walter Liddel."

"What I have to say may be said very briefly; and it cannot matter who hears it," rejoined Sir Bridgnorth. "Your friends wish you to return to them."

"I have already given Mr. Carteret an answer," said Walter. "I refuse."

"But I would remonstrate with you on your folly."

"It is useless. I beg there may not be a scene. It will produce no good effect, and may do mischief, by interfering with my plans."

"But your plans cannot be carried out. Come to me at the Grosvenor Hotel to-morrow, and I will convince you of their utter absurdity."

"No," replied Walter; "I am inflexible in my purpose. The only favour I will ask of you and Mr. Carteret is not to reveal my name."

"But, my good fellow, listen to reason. Don't take a step you will most assuredly repent. Hereafter you will thank me most heartily for giving you this advice. You won't want money. Carteret has got five hundred pounds, which he will pay over to you. You won't want friends, for we will all rally round you. Come, don't hesitate ! "

It was clear that the worthy gentleman's earnestness had produced an impression. Walter seemed inclined to yield, but still hung back,

At this moment, Tankard, who had heard some conversation going on, came out of the supper-room, accompanied by Hartley and Higgins.

As they issued forth, they shut the door after them,

" I believe I have the honour of addressing Sir Bridgnorth Charlton," said Tankard, bowing.

" Yes, I am Sir Bridgnorth," replied the other; " and I feel persuaded you will assist me to restore this rather wrong-headed young gentleman to his friends."

" Then I am right in my notion that he is Mr. Chetwynd Calverley ? " remarked Tankard.

" It is useless to conceal his name, though he seems to desire it," rejoined Sir Bridgnorth.

" Yes, I *am* Chetwynd Calverley," said the young man. " I care not who knows it. I have been a great fool, and I suppose I shall continue one to the end."

" No, don't ! " cried Hartley, advancing towards him, and regarding him very earnestly. " Don't commit any more folly. Perhaps I have a right to advise you."

" You have, Hartley. I fully recognise it," replied Chetwynd, taking his hand " You saved my life. Whatever you advise me to do, I will do ! "

" Then, go back to your friends," said Hartley. " That's my advice."

" And mine," said Tankard.

"And mine, too," added Higgins. "I shall be sorry to lose you ; but that's of no consequence."

"Hartley," said Chetwynd, clapping him in a friendly manner on the shoulder, "you have decided me. I'll go back at once with Sir Bridgnorth."

"That's right, sir—that's right ! " replied the other.

"I owe you a large debt," continued Chetwynd. "But I'll not fail to pay it."

"You owe me nothing, sir," rejoined Hartley.

"Yes, I do," replied Chetwynd, earnestly ; " more than I can ever pay."

He then shook hands with the others, and, taking the hat and valise which Tankard brought for him, bade them all three farewell, and quitted the shop with Sir Bridgnorth and Mr. Carteret.

End of the Third Book.

Book the Fourth.

PROBATION.

I.

THE FIRST STEP.

WE will now return to Brackley Hall, where we shall find the two young ladies.

They were still in a great state of uncertainty in regard to Chetwynd, though Sir Bridgnorth had written them a letter calculated, in some degree, to relieve their anxiety.

Of the two, Emmeline seemed to suffer most—probably because her temperament was more vivacious than Mildred's ; but it is certain that the feelings she had formerly entertained for the inconstant Chetwynd had completely revived, if not become intensified.

Mildred, as we have shown, was strongly attached to her brother, and her affection for him remained undiminished, but constant and sad disappointment had taught her to control her emotions. She did not say so to Emmeline, but she scarcely hoped to behold him again.

Mrs. Calverley was at Ouselcroft, but she drove over almost every day in the pony phaeton, and remained for an hour or two.

As to Lady Barfleur, she had been almost entirely confined to her room since Sir Leycester's death.

Things were in this state at Brackley Hall, when one morning, about an hour after breakfast, the two girls went out into the gardon. They were in an uneasy and excited state, but the soft air and the fragrance of the flowers soothed them.

That morning's post had brought Mildred a brief letter from Sir Bridgnorth Charlton. It contained only a few words, but they stimulated curiosity and raised hopes.

"To-morrow, I shall send a messenger to you with some important intelligence. Expect him soon after the receipt of this letter.

"B. C."

They had been in the garden some little time, and were slowly returning towards the house, when they saw a tall figure, dressed in black, crossing the moat.

Evidently, it was the messenger from Sir Bridgnorth, as they had given orders that he should be sent out to them.

But who was he? Could it be Chetwynd in person? Not a doubt about it.

On making this discovery, Mildred uttered a slight cry, and flying to meet her brother, was clasped i his arms.

Emmeline stood still, and placed her hand upon her heart to check its palpitations.

In another minute, Mildred disengaged herself from her brother's embrace, and without stopping to make any inquiries, and scarcely to exchange a word of greeting, led him towards Emmeline.

As he approached, Emmeline became pale as death,

and felt as if she should sink to the ground; but she sustained herself by a great effort.

She thought him changed. He had a careworn look, and his features were sharper; but he was still very handsome—and, perhaps, he had more interest for her, looking thus, than if he had appeared full of health and spirits.

He raised his hat as he drew near, and took the hand she offered him, but did not venture to address her till she spoke.

"I am truly glad to see you again, Chetwynd," she said, in kind but tremulous accents. "We have been very, very anxious about you."

Having called him "Chetwynd" formerly, she did not hesitate to do so now. It is impossible to describe how much he felt her kindness. But he did not presume upon it, and scarcely dared to lift his eyes towards her.

"I should not have ventured to present myself to you, Miss Barfleur," he said, "after my unpardonable conduct, had I not been strongly urged to do so by Sir Bridgnorth Charlton, who told me you were good enough to still take an interest in me. I felt that I must have for ever forfeited your good opinion."

"Not for ever," she replied.

"I must go through a long period of probation ere I can hope to regain it," he rejoined. "I do not wish to make professions which you might naturally discredit, but I intend henceforward to become a very different man."

"It rejoices me to find you have formed such a praiseworthy resolution, dearest Chetwynd," said his sister.

"I have had a very serious conversation with Sir Bridgnorth," he replied, "and what he said to me carried conviction with it. I am determined to reform. As I have just stated, I do not expect you to believe in the sincerity of my repentance till I have proved it. It may be no easy task to change one's nature, to curb a hasty temper, and check a propensity to folly and extravagance; but I have promised to do it, and I will keep my word at any cost."

"I am sure you will," said Emmeline, "and the cost will be far less than you expect."

"But you must begin to reform at once," said Mildred.

"I have already begun," said Chetwynd. "Had I not done so, I should not be here. This is my first step, and it will lead to all the rest."

"But why should coming here be part of your probation?" asked Emmeline.

"You know not what I felt at the idea of appearing before you," he replied; "and had you treated me with scorn and contempt, it would only have been what I deserved. Blinded by the charms of an artful and deceitful woman, I threw away such a chance as rarely has fallen to the lot of man; but when I recovered my senses, I comprehended what I had lost. Bitterly did I reproach myself—but it was then too late to repair my error, or at least I thought so—and the sense of my folly drove me almost mad. I will not attempt to exculpate myself. My faults are inexcusable. But this is their explanation. Had it not been for Sir Bridgnorth's encouragement I should not be here."

"On all accounts, I am glad you have come," replied Emmeline. "I do not doubt what you tell me. Pass through the period of probation, and you may be fully restored to favour."

"How long a period do you enjoin?" he inquired, anxiously.

"A year," she replied.

"'Tis not too much," said Mildred.

"I am content," he answered. "Nay, more, I am deeply grateful."

"But you must likewise obey my commands—however hard they may seem," said Emmeline.

"I will cheerfully obey them all," he replied.

"Then the first injunction I lay upon you is to become immediately reconciled to your stepmother."

"Ah!" he exclaimed.

"Do you refuse?"

"No," he replied. "You could not have imposed a harder condition. Nevertheless, I will obey you."

"In all sincerity?"

"I promise to forgive her—if I can. At any rate, I will manifest no more resentment."

"But accept your allowance like a rational being," said Mildred.

"Yes; Sir Bridgnorth and Mr. Carteret have argued me out of my scruples."

"I am truly glad to hear it," said Mildred. "This is, indeed, a point gained."

"Mrs. Calverley generally drives over to luncheon," observed Emmeline. "I dare say she has arrived. Come and see her at once."

Chetwynd made no objection, and they proceeded to the house.

II.

THE SECOND ORDEAL.

MRS. CALVERLEY had arrived, and they found her in the drawing-room.

She appeared greatly surprised at the sight of Chetwynd, and perhaps not altogether pleased, but she quickly recovered herself, and greeted him in a friendly manner.

Certainly, she did not expect it, but he immediately stepped forward, and, for the first time for a lengthened period, shook hands with her.

" Let there be peace between us," he said.

" Willingly," she replied. " I never sought a quarrel with you, Chetwynd, and since you desire a reconciliation, I gladly agree to it. I am anxious to forget the past."

" You are very kind, madam," he replied. " I frankly own I have been much to blame, and have no right to expect your forgiveness."

" After this admission on your part, there is an end of all misunderstanding between us," said Mrs. Calverley. " Some painful, but clearly groundless, rumours having reached me," she added, " I must say that I am truly rejoiced to see you again."

" I have reason to thank Heaven, madam," he replied, gravely, " that I am still alive. But I ought still more to be thankful that my sentiments are changed. All my vindictive feelings are gone."

" Yes, I can answer for it, that my dear brother is now in a very proper frame of mind," observed Mildred, in a low tone.

M

Mrs. Calverley seemed much relieved by the assurance.

"Where are you staying, Chetwynd?" she inquired.

"With Sir Bridgnorth Charlton," he replied. "I rode over from Charlton Park this morning. I owe a large debt of gratitude to Sir Bridgnorth. He has behaved like a father to me, and has extricated me from all my difficulties. Without him, I know not what I might have become. Now the world is once more open to me."

"Dearest brother," exclaimed Mildred, "how thankful I am you have found such a friend!"

"I have found other friends, though in a very different sphere of life, who have rendered me great service, and shown me much kindness," he replied; "and I should be ungrateful indeed if I did not acknowledge my obligations to them. One day you shall know all, and then you will admit that poor men have as good hearts as their richer brethren. But for one of my humble friends I should not be here now."

Some bright eyes were dimmed at this remark, and a momentary silence ensued.

It was broken by Mrs. Calverley, who said, in a kindly tone:

"I hope you mean to make Ouselcroft your home, Chetwynd?"

"I shall be delighted to do so, since you are kind enough to ask me, madam," he replied. "I shall not give you much trouble, for I propose to live very quietly."

"Don't mistake me," she rejoined. "The house will be as much your own as during your father's lifetime. Come and go as you please. Your friends will always be welcome. In a word, do just as you like, and don't imagine I shall be any restraint upon you."

"You are too kind, madam," he rejoined, somewhat confused.

"I desire to meet you in the same spirit in which you have come to me," she said. "Now I hope you understand me."

"I do, madam, and I will avail myself of your offer, In a day or two I will again take possession of my old room."

"It has always been kept for you, as you will find; but you shall have any other room you may prefer."

"None can suit me so well as that. And since you permit me to ask my friends, I will mention a gentle-man I have just met at Charlton, as I feel sure he will be agreeable to you."

"Do I know him?"

"Perfectly—Captain Danvers. I will bring him with me, if you have no objection."

"Do so, by all means," she replied. "I shall be delighted to see him, and so, I am sure, will Mildred."

"Yes; he is very amusing," said that young lady.

"Captain Danvers is my cousin, and a great favour-ite of mine as well," observed Emmeline. "I am glad you have formed his acquaintance; and I am sure you will like him."

Luncheon being announced at this moment, they repaired to the dining-room, where they found Lady Barfleur, who had come down-stairs for the first time since the day of Sir Leycester's interment.

Being strongly prejudiced against Chetwynd, she received him very coldly, and as she could be very

M 2

rude when she pleased, she made several very unpleasant observations in his hearing, greatly to Emmeline's annoyance.

"I didn't expect to see your brother here," she remarked to Mildred. "I fancied he had got into some fresh scrape, worse than any of the others."

"Oh! no," cried Mildred, almost indignantly. "He has got out of all his difficulties."

"Since when?" asked Lady Barfleur, dryly.

Mildred made no reply.

"What is he going to do now, may I ask?" pursued her ladyship.

"Coming to reside with mamma, at Ouselcroft," replied Mildred.

"Oh! she is good enough to take him back again, eh?" observed Lady Barfleur. "Well, she is very forgiving, I must say."

"Mamma!" exclaimed Emmeline, reproachfully, and trying to check her.

"Nay, I meant nothing," muttered her ladyship. "It is her own concern, not mine. I have no right to interfere."

"I shall be greatly pleased to have him with me again—that is all I can say," observed Mrs. Calverley, rather offended, for she felt the matter was carried somewhat too far for Chetwynd's patience, and dreaded an outbreak.

Happily, none occurred. Chetwynd could not fail to hear all that was said, but appeared calm and indifferent.

Lady Barfleur, however, had not yet exhausted all her displeasure.

"What is he going to do?" she asked, after a pause. "I suppose he has nothing."

Mrs. Calverley smiled.

"Your ladyship is entirely mistaken," she said. "He has a very fair income, and," she added, with some significance, "extremely good expectations. You may trust *me* on this point."

"Of course," replied Lady Barfleur. "But allow me to say I was under a very different impression."

That Chetwynd felt highly indignant at this discussion in his presence, is certain, but he allowed no symptom of anger to appear. On the contrary, he seemed perfectly indifferent.

Emmeline was very anxious, fearing that his visits in future to the house might be interdicted. But she was needlessly alarmed, as it turned out.

Chetwynd's unwonted self-control served him well. Lady Barfleur began to relent, and to view him in a more favourable light. She made no more rude remarks; indeed, she seemed rather inclined to be friendly towards him; and he so gained upon her by his tact and good nature that, before luncheon was ended, she observed, in an audible whisper, to Mrs. Calverley:

"Upon my word, I must say Chetwynd is vastly improved!" And, to Emmeline's infinite delight, she added, "I shall be very happy to see him at Brackley whenever he likes to come over."

The two girls exchanged a look.

"I think he'll do now," whispered Mildred. "He has got through this ordeal remarkably well."

III.

THE RETURN TO OUSELCROFT.

THREE days afterwards, Chetwynd, accompanied by Captain Danvers, came to Ouselcroft.

Mrs. Calverley, who seemed to have buried her former quarrels in oblivion, gave him a very hearty welcome, and was particularly civil to Captain Danvers. Mildred had returned on the previous day, bringing Emmeline with her—so there was quite a little party in the house.

Everything look bright and cheerful, and Chetwynd was received like the prodigal son.

All the household appeared delighted to see him again, and old Norris declared it was the happiest day of his life. They all thought him changed, and that his manner was much more sedate than it used to be—the general impression being that he was greatly improved.

On entering the hall he stood still for a moment, and as he gazed around a singular and indefinable expression crossed his countenance. But it passed away quickly, and was succeeded by the grave composure that now habitually distinguished him.

The look, however, had not been unnoticed by Norris, who was close beside him, watching him anxiously, and made the old butler think he was acting a part.

But it was in his own chamber, where no one could observe him, that Chetwynd gave utterance to a few words that revealed the secret of his breast.

" Once more I am in my father's house," he murmured; "and I will never quit it till I penetrate the mysteries it hides. At length I have learned to dissemble, and my purpose shall not be thwarted by haste or imprudence. The part is hateful to me, but I will play it, and with care. My former want of caution will avert suspicion from my design. I will not even make old Norris my confidant."

He remained for some time in his room, occupied by a variety of reflections, until at last he was disturbed by a tap at the door, and on opening it, Norris came in.

Evidently, from his manner, he expected that Chetwynd would make him the depositary of some secret, but he was disappointed.

"Whatever may be your motive in coming back, I think you have acted most judiciously," he said; "and I am truly glad to find that a complete reconciliation has taken place between you and Mrs. Calverley, though I own I never expected it."

"Yes, Norris," replied Chetwynd. "We have become really friends. At one time I never supposed it would be so, as you are well aware. But strange things happen. I am very much changed since you saw me last."

"Well, I own you *are* changed, sir; but for the better—very much improved. I hope you mean to reside here altogether now?"

"I do, Norris. Mrs. Calverley has behaved with great kindness to me—with great generosity, I may say—and the animosity I felt towards her has been completely extinguished in consequence. She has asked me to make Ouselcroft again my home. I have accepted the offer, and here I shall remain!"

"It would have been very unwise to refuse the offer, sir," said Norris. "But are you convinced of her sincerity?"

"I cannot doubt it, after such proofs as she has given me. I only wonder she has shown so much forgiveness. But she shall have nothing to complain of in future."

"I approve of your determination, sir. Let bygones be bygones!"

Norris was completely puzzled.

He did not believe in the reality of the reconciliation, either on one side or the other. But he saw plainly enough there would be a suspension of hostilities.

Obviously, it was greatly to Chetwynd's interest to yield to his step-mother; but hitherto, the step-son had proved so obstinate, that any arrangement seemed impracticable. On the other hand, Norris had believed that Mrs. Calverley harboured great resentment against him; but now she seemed suddenly to have forgiven him.

Were they deceiving each other. He thought so.

IV.

WHICH OF THE TWO?

CAPTAIN DANVERS had never before been to Ouselcroft, and was charmed with the place.

The house was admirably kept up, and the garden in beautiful order. Mrs. Calverley had received him in the most flattering manner; and he had found

Mildred there, and his cousin Emmeline. Chetwynd had promised him a pleasant visit, and he felt sure it would turn out so. What can offer greater attractions than an agreeable country house, with two or three lovely inmates ?

Captain Danvers had not quite made up his mind whether he preferred the wealthy young widow or her pretty step-daughter.

There were reasons that inclined him to turn his thoughts exclusively to Mrs. Calverley, but Mildred's image would not be dismissed. He fancied he should be able to decide during his stay at Ouselcroft ; but it was not an easy matter, as he found out.

Possibly in accordance with some plan he had formed, Captain Danvers devoted himself on the day of his arrival to Mrs. Calverley.

Next day, he seemed inclined to go over to Mildred, but she did not give him so much encouragement as she had done at Brackley; and piqued by her indifference, he sought by every means to regain the ground he had apparently lost, and succeeded.

But Mrs. Calverley resented the neglect, and treated him coldly in her turn. He seemed, therefore, in danger of losing the grand prize. Though he found it next to impossible to go on with both, he was unwilling to give up either.

He then put the momentous question to himself—to which of the two should he propose ?

Clearly Mrs. Calverley would be by far the most advantageous match, in a pecuniary point of view; and being greatly governed by selfish considerations, he inclined towards her.

Still, he was really in love with Mildred, and the

thought of losing her was more than he could bear.

On reflection, he found he had put a question to himself that he could not answer.

That very morning an opportunity offered for saying a tender word to Mildred ; but his courage failed him. Loving her as he did, and feeling sure she loved him in return, he hesitated to commit himself.

They were walking in the garden, and the animated conversation with which they had commenced had gradually died away, and was succeeded by a silence that was almost embarrassing.

Clearly the moment had arrived. What could he do ?—what say ? He took her hand. She did not withdraw it, and he pressed it to his lips ; but, oh, disgrace to manhood ! no word was uttered. He heaved a deep sigh—that was all.

It was almost a relief to him when Mrs. Calverley and Emmeline were seen approaching.

" How provoking ! " exclaimed the captain, who, however, was secretly pleased by the interruption.

Had he thought proper, he might have moved on ; but instead of doing so, he turned round and met those who were coming towards them.

Mrs. Calverley, who had véry quick sight, had seen what took place, but did not of course make the slightest remark until she found herself shortly afterwards *tête-à-tête* with the captain, the others having walked on.

" I think I explained to you, Captain Danvers, what my intentions are in regard to Mildred ? " she said.

" Yes, I perfectly recollect," he replied. " You said you meant to give her a marriage portion of thirty thousand pounds; and I thought it exceedingly handsome."

"But you did not quite understand me, I fancy," said Mrs Calverley, regarding him steadfastly. "I ought to have added that she will have this sum on her marriage, provided I approve of her choice."

"Ah! that proviso makes all the difference!" exclaimed the captain. "The money may not be given, after all."

"I shall never withhold it unless I see some decided objection to the match," she rejoined. "Think over what I have told you."

No more was said; but the caution thus given him produced the effect intended on Captain Danvers. He saw that Mildred was completely in her step-mother's power, and that the latter would do nothing if offended.

He now rejoiced that he had not made a positive proposal, as he would then have been compelled to take the fair girl without a portion, and he was not disinterested enough to do that.

However, he put the best face he could on the matter, and said:

"I am obliged to you for the information you have given me. Had I meant to propose to Miss Calverley, it would not have deterred me; but I have no such intention."

"And you expect me to believe this after what I beheld just now?" said Mrs. Calverley, incredulously.

"I expect you to believe what I tell you," rejoined the captain rather haughtily. "And I again assert that I have *not* proposed to her."

"I am glad to hear it. It would have pained me to do a disagreeable thing."

"But you would have done it?"

"Undoubtedly. However, since you give me this assurance, I need say no more."

Later on in the day, Chetwynd and Captain Danvers were smoking a cigar in the dressing-room of the former, when the captain broached a subject on which he had been ruminating.

"Chetwynd, old boy," he said, "I want to ask you a question. Don't think me impertinent; but I should like to know whether it is true that Mrs. Calverley has the entire control of your sister's fortune?"

"I'll answer the question frankly," replied Chetwynd. "She has. My father, as you may be aware, made an extraordinary will, and it was the strange disposition of his property that caused the quarrel between myself and my step-mother. You talk of my sister's fortune. Properly speaking, she has none. She has a handsome allowance from Mrs. Calverley, who always declares she will give her a portion of thirty thousand pounds on her marriage."

"Provided she approves of her choice—is not that a condition?" said the captain.

"Yes; but it means nothing."

"Pardon me. I think it means a great deal. It might cause a match to be broken off."

"It might, certainly, if acted upon. But Mrs. Calverley is very much attached to my sister, and will never oppose her choice. At least I fancy not."

"I have reason to believe otherwise, my dear Chetwynd. She has already given me a pretty strong hint!"

"Have you said anything to her about Mildred?"

"No; but she has spoken to me, and has clearly

intimated that I am not the man of *her* choice. Were I to be accepted, depend upon it, Mildred would have no portion."

" You think so ? "

" I'm sure of it. Can you help me ? "

" I don't see how. I have no influence over Mrs. Calverley, and am determined not to meddle in any family matters. Besides, I should do no good. But I don't think there is any real ground for apprehension. As I have just said, she is extremely fond of Mildred, and if she felt my sister's happiness were at stake, she wouldn't interfere with any engagement she might form. I am certain of that. Though I cannot aid you, I will tell you who can, and most efficiently—your cousin, Emmeline Barfleur. I wonder she has not occurred to you."

" My dear fellow, I have had no time for consideration," rejoined the captain. " I have only just received this obliging hint from Mrs. Calverley. But I entirely agree with you. Emmeline is the person of all others who can aid me. Let us go and look for her at once. Most likely we shall find her in the garden, for they are not driving out this afternoon."

Chetwynd assented ; so they flung away their cigars, and went downstairs.

V.

HOW CAPTAIN DANVERS WAS THROWN OVER BY BOTH LADIES.

MRS. CALVERLEY was in the drawing-room occupied

with a novel; and feeling easy, as far as she was concerned, the two young gentlemen went out in quest of the girls, and soon found them.

At a sign from Captain Danvers, Emmeline came and sat down beside him on a lawn-chair, while Chetwynd and his sister walked on.

"Now, Charles, what have you got to say to me?" she inquired.

"I want to talk to you about Mildred."

"Well, I am prepared to listen. It would be quite superfluous to tell me you are in love with her, for I know that very well. Indeed, if I am not mistaken, you were interrupted in making a proposal this very morning!"

"I own the soft impeachment. But the interruption seems to have been fortunate, for I should have got into a serious scrape if the proposal had been actually made."

"How so?" she exclaimed in astonishment.

"Mrs. Calverley holds her step-daughter's destiny—that is, her fortune—in her own hands; and has since given me clearly to understand that, in my case, Mildred would be portionless."

"And pray what else could you expect? You have been flirting so outrageously with Mrs. Calverley herself, that you have caused her to regard her step-daughter as a rival. Were it not that Mildred may suffer from your conduct, I should say you were very properly punished. I declare I thought you had proposed to Mrs. Calverley!"

"Not quite!" he replied, laughing.

"Then you have misled her. No wonder she is angry when she finds you so inconstant."

"Will you do me a good turn, dearest Emmeline?"

"I can't promise. I feel greatly displeased with you myself."

" I'm sorry for that. But perhaps the mistake can be remedied."

" How can it be done? No! You have lost Mildred, and must put up with Mrs. Calverley!"

This suggestion threw the captain into a fit of despair.

"She is very handsome," pursued Emmeline, "very rich, and has got this fine house, with all the furniture, plate, pictures, horses and carriages. You won't be so badly off."

"I would rather have Mildred with her portion," sighed the captain.

" But you must take her without a portion you see. How will you like that?"

"It is not to be thought of! Give me some advice."

" My advice to you is to retire from the field altogether."

" You are laughing at me; that is cruel, under the circumstances."

" It is the best thing you can do."

"But I mean to stay, and hope to gain my point."

" Mildred's hand?"

" Yes, and the portion."

" You must cease to pay attentions to Mrs. Calverley."

" I have done so, and you see the result. I think I had better resume them."

"That would be most improper, and I cannot countenance such a proceeding. One or the other it must be—not both."

"But I must keep Mrs. Calverley in good humour, or there will be a quarrel; and that must be avoided."

"You are incorrigible," laughed Emmeline. "The sooner you go, the better!"

"I have just told you I don't mean to go! Ah! here comes Mrs. Calverley! Pray don't desert me!"

"Expect no assistance from me, deluder!"

As Mrs. Calverley came up, they rose to receive her.

"I am sorry to disturb you!" she said. "You seemed engaged in a very interesting discourse."

"We were talking about you," replied Emmeline.

"About me?" cried Mrs. Calverley, in affected surprise.

"Yes; but I can't tell you what we were saying. It mightn't be agreeable to you."

"I will take my chance of that."

"Well, then, I was just saying to Captain Danvers that if I had such a charming place as you possess, and such a good income, I would never marry again."

"I have no idea of marrying again," observed Mrs. Calverley, carelessly. "I may sometimes listen to the nonsense talked to me," she added, glancing at Captain Danvers, "but I rate it at what it is worth. I prefer being my own mistress. If I wanted companionship, I might think differently; but as things stand at present, I shall certainly adhere to my resolution."

" Such resolutions are never kept," said Captain Danvers. " Your sex are allowed to change their mind as often as they please."

" At all events, I shall wait till Mildred is married," she rejoined.

"Then I don't think you will have to wait long," remarked Captain Danvers.

" You are mistaken," rejoined Mrs. Calverley. " Mildred, I feel sure, will not marry immediately."

This was said with so much significance that both her hearers were struck by it ; and Emmeline gave her cousin a slight pinch, as much as to say :

" There, sir, you see what you have done."

At this instant Chetwynd and Mildred returned from the further end of the garden, and joined the party on the lawn.

Captain Danvers thought Mildred's manner colder to him than it had been before, but he soon received an explanation of the change from Chetwynd, who took him aside and said :

" I have had some conversation about you with my sister, and have ascertained her sentiments. It will be useless to propose to her. You will be refused."

" Is this quite certain, my dear Chetwynd ? "

" Quite certain. Whether she is acting by Mrs. Calverley's advice, I can't say ; but she has made up her mind to refuse you."

The captain was confounded.

Apparently he had lost his chance with both ladies.

VI.

MRS. CALVERLEY RENDERS CHETWYND AN IMPORTANT SERVICE.

NEXT morning while the party were assembled at breakfast, Captain Danvers announced his intention of terminating his visit, which he declared had been most agreeable; and, though pressed to stay by Mrs. Calverley, he declined.

"I have promised to spend a few days with Lady Barfleur before my return to town," he said, "and must not disappoint her. I have written to tell her she may expect me at dinner to-day."

"Then you really mean to leave us?" said Mrs. Calverley. "This is a very short visit. I hoped you would spend at least a week here. But you won't be far off, and can come back again if you are so inclined. I shall be very glad to see you."

Mildred did not say a word. If she had spoken, he would have assented.

"You are very good," he rejoined; "but it is possible I may be summoned to town."

"It is quite certain you will find Brackley very dull after this lively house, Charles," said Emmeline. "Take my advice and stay where you are."

"A little solitude will suit my present mood," he rejoined. "If I feel very, very lonely, I'll ride over here."

"Well, we offer you our society," said Mrs. Calverley.

"All of you?" asked the captain, glancing at Mildred, who was on the opposite side of the table.

But she did not look at him.

"If you are positively going, I'll ride over to Brackley with you this afternoon," observed Chetwynd.

"And stay to dinner," said the captain. "My aunt will be very glad of your company."

"That she will, I'm sure," observed Emmeline. "Suppose we all go? What say you?" she added to Mildred.

The young lady appealed to shook her head.

"The drive will do you good," said Emmeline. "Be persuaded."

"No, thank you; not to-day," replied Mildred.

Captain Danvers looked at her imploringly; but she remained steadfast.

"Well, since you are so perverse, you deserve to be left behind," said Emmeline. "You shall drive me in your pony-carriage, dear Mrs. Calverley."

"With greatest pleasure," replied the lady. "But I can't promise you an adventure—"

Then feeling that the remark might awaken painful recollections, she stopped short.

During the latter part of this discourse, Norris had entered the room, and, approaching Chetwynd, told him, in a whisper, that two persons wanted to see him on important business.

"Who are they?" inquired Chetwynd, thinking there was something strange in the butler's manner.

"They didn't give their names, sir," replied Norris; "and I've never seen them before. I've shown them into the library."

"Quite right. I'll come to them after breakfast."

" Better see them at once, I think, sir," observed Norris, significantly.

On this Chetwynd got up, without disturbing the party, and following the butler out of the room, repaired to the library, where he found the two personages.

Looks, dress, and deportment proclaimed their vocation. Coarse, stout, red-faced, vulgar-looking dogs, they seemed up to their business. Each was provided with a stout stick.

Having seen such fellows before, Chetwynd instantly understood what they were. But they would not have left him long in doubt.

As he entered the room, one of the twain stepped up to him, and said, with an attempt at a bow :

" Mr. Chetwynd Calverley, I presume ? "

Chetwynd replied in the affirmative.

" My name's Grimsditch," said the fellow, " and my mate's name is Hulse. We are officers. We have a writ against you for seven hundred pounds."

" But I owe no such sum," replied Chetwynd.

" Beg pardon, sir," said Grimsditch. " But we have the particulars. You gave a bill for six hundred pounds to Philip Marsh Romney, Esq. With costs and interest it now amounts to a hundred more."

" You'll find it quite correct, sir," added Hulse. " I dare say you'll recollect all about it."

" I recollect something about a gambling debt to Mr. Romney for six hundred pounds ; but I was told I ought not to pay it, and I won't."

" Sorry to hear you say so, sir," replied Grimsditch. " We hoped the matter would be quietly settled. But if it can't be, you must come along with us."

Chetwynd looked very angry for a moment, and seemed inclined to kick them both out of the room.

"We can't help it, sir," said Grimsditch. "We must do our duty."

"However unpleasant it may be to us," added Hulse.

"Make no excuses—I don't want them," said Chetwynd. "I'll be back directly."

"Can't part with you, sir!" said Grimsditch, planting himself before the door, so as to prevent egress. "Against rule. Hulse will ring the bell if you wish it."

"Do so, then," said Chetwynd.

The bell was rung, and the summons immediately answered by Norris, who must have been close at hand.

Chetwynd then sat down at a table on which writing materials were placed, and traced a few hurried lines on a sheet of paper, which he enclosed in an envelope.

"Take this note to Mrs. Calverley," he said to Norris.

"Instantly, sir," replied the butler, glancing indignantly at the officers.

While Norris went on his errand, Chetwynd remained seated at the table with his back towards the officers.

In a few minutes the door opened, and Captain Danvers came in with a note in his hand.

"Out of my way, men!" he said, as he marched past them.

"Mrs. Calverley has sent you a cheque on the Chester Bank for the amount you require—seven hundred pounds," he added to Chetwynd. "Pay these fellows, and get rid of them!"

"Here's the bill, with charges and all particulars," said Grimsditch, following him to the table.

"And there's the cheque," said Chetwynd, giving it to him after he had endorsed it.

"All right, sir," replied Grimsditch. "On Chester, I see; my own bank can't be better. Always glad to have one of them cheques in my pocket-book. And now, sir," he added, "if you'll allow me to sit down, I'll give you a receipt."

This business completed, Grimsditch got up, bowed, and was retiring with his companion, when Chetwynd called out to them.

"Stay a minute!" he said, in a stern tone. "I wish you to understand that I consider this as a most nefarious transaction. I have been robbed!"

"Sir!" exclaimed both officers.

"Not by you, but by your employer. Philip Marsh Romney is a consummate scoundrel! Tell him so!"

"We won't do you such a bad turn, sir," rejoined Grimsditch. "Mr. Romney might bring an action for libel."

"No, he won't," said Chetwynd. "He knows better. He may have done with me, but I have not done with him. Tell him that, at all events."

"We will," replied the officers, as they disappeared.

"I'm glad you've got rid of those rascals, Chetwynd," said Captain Danvers. "Upon my soul! I think Mrs. Calverley has behaved remarkably well. On receiving your note, she got up to write the cheque at once, and begged me to take it to you. She wouldn't bring it herself, you see, as her presence might have annoyed you."

"Yes, it was very well done, I admit; and I am greatly obliged to her."

"But you don't seem half grateful enough," said Danvers.

"Oh, yes, I *am* grateful—very grateful!" replied Chetwynd.

Shortly afterwards he went to Mrs. Calverley, and said :

"You have rendered me a great service; but I don't know when I shall be able to repay you."

"Repay me whenever it may be convenient," she replied; "or not at all. Just give me a memorandum that I have advanced you seven hundred pounds; that is all I require."

VII.

HOW CHETWYND AND EMMELINE PLIGHTED THEIR FAITH IN THE OLD CHAPEL.

No persuasion on Emmeline's part would induce Mildred to go to Brackley that day, nor would she bid Captain Danvers adieu.

The other arrangement was carried out; the captain's valise being sent on by his groom, who, at the same time, took a note from Emmeline to Lady Barfleur, to let her know whom she might expect.

About three o'clock the party set off; the two ladies in the pony-carriage, the gentlemen on horseback. The day was fine, but sultry; and as they crossed the heath, a peal of thunder was heard in the distance, but it came to nothing. Mrs. Calverley certainly did

not seem to regret Mildred's absence. She was unusually lively, and appeared quite to have forgiven the
captain's inconstancy, and to be willing to take him
into favour again. So he renewed his assiduities.

Chetwynd looked preoccupied. He rode by the
side of the pony-carriage, but did not converse much
with Emmeline, who was struck by his sombre expression of countenance. It was the same at Brackley.
They walked together in the garden, but he spoke
little, and did not breathe a word of love. Had he
something on his mind?

In the courtyard of the old Hall, as already stated,
there was an ancient chapel, in excellent preservation.
Originally, it was devoted to the rites of the Church
of Rome, as it must needs have been, since it was
built nearly a hundred years before the Reformation.

Chetwynd had often admired the exterior of the old
fabric, but had never been inside it, and Emmeline
offered to show it to him as they passed through the
court.

The door being unfastened, they went in. The
windows were filled with stained glass of the richest
hues, and there was a large sculptured monument,
that instantly caught the eye, to Sir Simon Barfleur
and Dame Beatrix, his wife, who flourished in the time
of Henry the Seventh.

Other monuments there were that somewhat en-
croached on the space of the little structure, but none
of the family had been interred in the vault beneath
for more than a century.

The chapel was provided with a large pew for the
family and guests, and seats for the household. A

venerable divine, the Reverend Mr. Massey, officiated as chaplain, and had done so for sixty years.

After advancing a few steps, Chetwynd paused, and looked round. Every object was coloured by the painted glass, now illuminated by the rays of the declining sun.

After admiring this glowing picture for a few moments, he joined Emmeline, who was standing near the precincts of the altar.

His countenance had still the melancholy look it had borne throughout the day; but he gazed earnestly at Emmeline, as he said, in a low, supplicating voice:

" I have not yet proved myself worthy of your love; but, if I dared, I would entreat you to plight your faith to me here."

For some minutes, she made no reply; but seemed occupied with serious reflection. She then said:

" I think I may trust you, Chetwynd."

" You may," he replied, in accents that bespoke his sincerity.

She hesitated no more, but freely gave him her hand.

" I hereby solemnly plight my faith to you, Chetwynd," she said. " If I wed you not, I will wed no other. That I swear."

His countenance underwent an instant change, and became lighted up with joy.

He repeated the words she had uttered; but added:

" I must not claim your hand. My task is not completed—scarcely begun."

" I am witness to the vow you have made," said a voice behind them.

Looking round, they perceived the old chaplain, Mr.

Massey, who had followed them unseen into the chapel.

A venerable man, in age more than fourscore, with silver locks, and a most benevolent expression of countenance.

" Heaven bless your union, whenever it takes place, and though I may not live to see it ! " he said.

" I trust you may unite us, reverend sir," said Chetwynd. " But you ought to know who I am."

" I *do* know, sir," replied Mr. Massey; "and I have perfect faith in you, or I would not have sanctioned this solemn engagement. Should it be carried out, as I doubt not it will, Mr. Chetwynd Calverley may esteem himself the most fortunate, and the happiest man in England. I have known the fair young lady who has just plighted her faith to him since she was a child, and have loved her as a father, and have met with none of her sex in any way comparable to her. Again, I say to you, Mr. Calverley, you are most fortunate; and, should the Almighty bless you with this treasure, guard it as you would your life ! "

"I will," replied Chetwynd, deeply moved.

They did not remain many minutes longer in the chapel, but repaired to the house, accompanied by Mr. Massey.

VIII.

THE HAUNTED ROOM.

THE day, as previously stated, had been fine, but exceedingly sultry, and the sunset portended thunder.

Just as those about to return to Ouselcroft were preparing for departure, a heavy thunder-storm came on, and as there seemed every likelihood of its continuance, they were easily induced to pass the night at Brackley.

A messenger was immediately sent off to Mildred to prevent alarm, and Captain Danvers undertook that Chetwynd should be put to no inconvenience in regard to his toilette.

There was no difficulty about beds, for there was a superfluity at Brackley. A large chamber was assigned to Chetwynd, containing an antique canopied bedstead with twisted oak pillars, and heavy brocade curtains, the splendour of which was somewhat dimmed by years. There were a couple of old black cabinets in the room, and the dark oak panels were hung with sombre tapestry, or adorned with portraits.

The only modern furniture was a card-table, set with two chairs in the centre of the room, opposite the end of the bed. Candles were placed upon the table, and a couple of packs of cards.

Very likely these preparations had been made by order of Captain Danvers.

Chetwynd had heard there was a haunted room at Brackley, but it never occurred to him that this was the identical apartment; and though Captain Danvers

was aware of its ghostly reputation, he thought it best
to say nothing about it.

He accompanied his friend to the room, having previously supplied him with such articles as he might
require for the night, and then pointing to the table,
said, " Shall we have a game at *écarté ?* "

" No, thank you," replied Chetwynd.   " I've vowed
never to touch cards again."

" Well, I won't tempt you to break your oath,"
replied Danvers, laughing.   " Good night.   I hope
you'll sleep well."

And he quitted the room.

Chetwynd sought his splendid couch, and though the
thunder rattled awfully overhead, and the lightning
blazed, he speedily fell asleep.

How long he slumbered he could not tell, nor could
he exactly say what awoke him, but when he opened
his eyes he perceived a light in the room.

At first he thought it must be the lightning, for he
was certain he had put out the bed-candle, but this
illumination was continuous.

Looking up, to his great surprise, he perceived two
elderly gentlemen seated opposite each other at the
card-table.   The wax candles were lighted, and the
two strange personages were playing at *écarté,* or some
other game.

An unaccountable dread seized Chetwynd as he
watched them, and he wondered how they came to be
there at that time of night.   Perhaps they might not
be aware of his presence, so he thought he ought to
apprise them of it.

Raising himself on the pillow to examine them
more narrowly, he perceived that one of them was Sir
Leycester Barfleur, and the other—his own father !

Astounded and dismayed at this discovery, he felt utterly unable to speak, and remained gazing at them, while they continued their game.

At last, they threw down their cards, and got up.

Then Mr. Calverley, as it seemed, exclaimed, in an unearthly voice, " I've won ! "

Upon which Sir Leycester, in accents equally unearthly, replied, " Not yet ! "

Then they both looked towards the occupant of the bed, and the expression of their countenance was so fearful that Chetwynd was unable to endure it, and fell back insensible.

When he recovered—or, rather, when he awoke— he did not feel quite sure that the supernatural appearance which he thought he had witnessed might not have been a dream.

On examination, the candles did not appear to have been lighted, and both packs of cards were untouched. This seemed to favour the idea that it must have been a dream, but Chetwynd could not believe so. He felt sure he had seen the two old men.

Captain Danvers was curious to learn how his friend had passed the night, and owned that the room was said to be haunted.

Chetwynd made an evasive reply.

" I'll tell you a strange thing," said Danvers. " My uncle, Sir Leycester, once lost a large sum to your father in this room."

" They have not yet finished the game," said Chetwynd. " I saw them playing during the night."

IX.

AFTER the stormy night came a magnificent day.

Brackley looked so charming, that the guests were in no hurry to depart. Captain Danvers took a stroll in the garden with Mrs. Calverley, resolved that the interview should decide his fate. It was idle to think any more of Mildred, who had behaved very heartlessly in refusing to bid him adieu. His selection was made. He would offer his hand to the beautiful and wealthy widow, who had given him every encouragement.

The bowling-green, though delightful, was rather too damp after the rain of the previous night, and the benches were not yet dried, so they moved on towards a shady walk, where the captain commenced :

" I hope you have quite forgiven me, my dear Mrs. Calverley ? " he said. " I can scarcely account for my folly, but I can assure you I am now quite sensible of it, and will never again offend in the like manner. Indeed, I will put it out of my power to do so, by binding myself indissolubly to you."

" Do you mean this as an offer ? " she said.

" Certainly," he replied. " What else can it mean ? "

" Then I must have a little time for consideration. I cannot make up my mind in a moment on such an important point."

The captain's ardour was very much damped. He had flattered himself he should be at once accepted.

" But you don't reject me ? " he said, anxiously.

"No, you must remain on trial for a month. If I am quite satisfied with your conduct during that interval, I may become yours."

"Then it is not to be an engagement?" he cried.

"Yes; I am quite willing it should be an engagement—but not binding on either party."

"Such an arrangement amounts to nothing," he said. "If you love me well enough to give me your hand, accept me now, and let the marriage be fixed for some early day."

"I cannot agree to that," she replied. "We shall have to come to an understanding on many points."

"We are sure to do that," he replied. "I agree to all beforehand. You shall have your own way entirely. I shall be a very good-natured husband."

"I am not so sure of that," she replied, with a slight laugh. "Men who make promises of compliance beforehand, often turn out most impracticable."

"That won't hold good in my case."

"Well, you sha'n't say that I take you in, for I announce that I mean to retain entire possession of my own property."

The captain could scarcely hide his confusion at this unexpected intimation. However, he did not make any objection.

"In a word, my house will be conducted precisely as it is now," pursued Mrs. Calverley.

"That is just what I should like," he rejoined. "Arrange it as you please. I shall never interfere. Have we come to a distinct understanding?"

"Yes; and if you retain these sentiments, we shall probably agree."

"Are we not now agreed?"

"On the main points," she replied. "But our engagement must be private for the present. I have my reasons for the request."

"I won't ask them, but comply. In all things you shall be obeyed."

She smiled very graciously, if not every affection-ately, and gave him her hand, which he raised to his lips.

Her beautiful features underwent a slight change at that moment, and the expression startled Captain Danvers so much that he almost repented the step he had taken; but it was now too late to retreat.

"Though our engagement will be secret, you can come to Ouselcroft whenever you please," she said. "Only remember there must be no renewal——"

"Fear nothing," he replied. "There shall be no more of that."

They then returned to the house, and on the way thither met Emmeline and Chetwynd. The former smiled on seeing her cousin and Mrs. Calverley to-gether, but made no remark.

Later on, however, when an opportunity offered, she said to Captain Danvers, "All is settled, I per-ceive, between you and the rich widow."

"What makes you think so ? " he asked.

"Both of you look as if you already repented," she replied. "But I hope you may be happy."

Captain Danvers rode back with them to Ouselcroft; but he did not stay, nor did he see Mildred.

However, he agreed to return in a few days.

Emmeline was distressed to find her friend looking less cheerful than usual. Indeed, she appeared de-cidedly low-spirited.

"I hope you are not troubling yourself about my unworthy cousin Charles," said Emmeline.

"I wish I could cease to think of him," replied Mildred, with a sigh. "I have tried, but in vain."

"You must think of him no more, dearest girl," said Emmeline.

Mildred looked at her anxiously.

"What is it? Don't keep me in suspense!" she cried.

"He is engaged to Mrs. Calverley," replied Emmeline.

Mildred became white as death.

"Engaged to *her!*" she ejaculated. "Oh, this is too much!"

She would have fallen if Emmeline had not caught her.

Fortunately, this occurrence took place in Mildred's own room, and, restoratives being at hand, it was not necessary to summon assistance.

X.

AN INVITATION TO TOWN.

NEXT day a letter was forwarded to Emmeline from Brackley.

It was from Lady Thicknesse, of Belgrave Square, of whom mention has been previously made. Lady Thicknesse, it may be stated, was a sister of Lady Barfleur, though several years her junior, and, consequently, aunt to Emmeline.

The letter, which had an enormous black border,

o

and was sealed with black wax, was to the following
effect :

"It will give me great pleasure, my dearest niece,
if you will come and spend a few weeks with me in
Belgrave Square—quite quietly, of course. I think
the change will do you good, and I shall be very glad
of your society, for I have been rather *triste* of late.
Poor Sir Leycester's death affected me a great deal.
I don't ask my sister to accompany you, for I know
she won't stir from Brackley, but I shall be very glad if
you will bring with you your friend, Mildred Calverley.
I remember her as a very charming girl, and know
you are much attached to her. She must not expect
any gaiety. You will be as quiet here as you are in
the country. Adieu, dearest Emmeline ! Come as
soon as you can, and don't fail to bring Mildred with
you. I write separately to your mamma."

Emmeline was in Mildred's room when Lady Thicknesse's letter was delivered to her. She read it aloud
to her friend, and, on finishing it, exclaimed :

"Now, Mildred, what do you say ? Will you go
to town with me ? I am sure my aunt, Lady Thicknesse, will be very glad to see you, and she is most
agreeable and kind-hearted—but I needn't describe
her, since you have seen her."

"Yes ; I know her slightly, and am persuaded I
shall like her much when I know her better."

"Then you will go ?"

"Certainly, since you wish me to accompany you.
I confess I don't feel happy here just now. It will be
an escape."

"Mrs. Calverley won't object, I suppose ?"

"On the contrary," replied Mildred, with a singular smile. "I think she will be glad to get rid of me for a time."

"I'm sure there will be no difficulty on mamma's part," observed Emmeline. "Why, here is a note from her that I have not read! As I expected!" she cried. "She urges me to accept the invitation, and hopes you will accompany me. Let us go downstairs, and settle the matter at once."

They found Mrs. Calverley seated with Captain Danvers in the drawing-room, engaged in a very interesting *tête-à-tête*, and the discovery increased Mildred's desire to be gone.

The captain rose, and bowed to her, and she made him a very freezing salute in return. It appeared that he had brought the letters from Brackley, and, having heard of the invitation from Lady Barfleur, had mentioned it to Mrs. Calverley, so that she was fully prepared.

"I know what you are come to tell me," she said. "Captain Danvers has already informed me of Lady Thicknesse's invitation, and I sincerely hope you intend to accept it."

"Since the plan is agreeable to you, we shall do so," replied Emmeline.

"And we propose to go soon," said Mildred.

"As soon as you please, my love," said Mrs. Calverley, smiling. "I won't delay you. You can set out to-morrow, if your preparations can be made in time."

"We have very few preparations to make," remarked Emmeline. "We are not going to any parties. I will write to Lady Thicknesse to prepare her for our arrival to-morrow evening."

"You will want some one to take charge of you," observed Mrs. Calverley. "You can't travel alone."

Captain Danvers was about to offer himself, but a look from Mrs. Calverley checked him.

"Chetwynd will take charge of them," she said.

This proposition was very agreeable to the two young ladies, and when Chetwynd made his appearance a few minutes afterwards, he readily agreed to it.

So the matter was settled.

Later on, Emmeline and Mildred went to Brackley, in order to spend the evening with Lady Barfleur. Captain Danvers remained to dine with Mrs. Calverley —so they saw nothing of him.

Next morning, Chetwynd came over, fully prepared for the journey; and Mrs. Calverley was with him, wishing to see them off.

With praiseworthy punctuality, all the boxes and portmanteaux were ready at the appointed time, having been packed by the young ladies themselves, as they did not mean to take a lady's-maid with them.

Lady Barfleur took leave of her daughter in private, and bedewed her cheek with tears when she embraced her at parting; but not many tears were shed on either side when Mildred bade her step-mother adieu.

Captain Danvers offered his hand to the offended damsel as she stepped into the carriage, but she declined the assistance.

Accompanied by Chetwynd, the two girls drove in the large, old-fashioned carriage to Chester, whence they proceeded by rail to London, arriving at Kensington about six o'clock.

Having conducted them to Lady Thicknesse's residence in Belgrave Square, Chetwynd took leave, promising to call on the morrow.

He then drove to the Grosvenor Hotel, where he engaged a room, and ordered dinner.

End of the Fourth Book.

Book the Fifth.

LADY THICKNESSE.

I.

IN WHICH CHETWYND LEARNS HOW A QUARREL HAS TAKEN PLACE BETWEEN ROSE AND HARRY NETTER-VILLE.

AFTER he had dined, Chetwynd took a hansom cab and drove to Lambeth.

Alighting at the foot of the bridge, he walked to Hartley's house in Spencer's Rents, wondering whether he should find any one at home.

He knocked, but not very loudly, and the summons was presently answered by Mrs. Hartley, who came from the kitchen with a light.

"Why, bless me! if it ain't Mr. Walter Liddel—or rather I ought to say Mr. Chetwynd Calverley!" she exclaimed, very nearly letting the candle drop in her surprise. "Who would have thought of seeing you here to-night, sir?"

"I've just come to town, Mrs. Hartley," he replied, "and I couldn't help calling to inquire how you all are. How is your worthy husband?—and how is Rose?"

"Both are well, sir," she replied, in a tone that did not sound very cheerful. "But pray come in, sir," she added, leading him to the little parlour, with which he was so familiar.

When another candle was lighted, and he had taken his seat, she remarked: "A good deal has happened since you went away, sir."

"Nothing unpleasant, I hope?" he inquired.

"You'll be sorry to hear that Rose's engagement with Harry Netterville is broken off."

"Broken off!" he exclaimed. "That is bad news indeed! On what account?"

"I was going to say on your account, sir; but that wouldn't be right," she replied. "However, this is what has taken place. An anonymous letter has been sent to Harry Netterville making reflections upon Rose's conduct with you; and as Harry is very jealous, he believed what was said, and reproached her; and Rose being very hasty, a quarrel ensued, and they both declare they won't make it up, but I hope they will, for I'm sure they're very much attached to each other."

"I'm surprised as well as grieved by what you tell me, Mrs. Hartley," replied Chetwynd. "I thought Harry Netterville had more sense than to be influenced by an anonymous slanderer. He ought to have treated the letter with scorn. He knows Rose too well to doubt her for a moment."

" Yes; and that's what makes her so angry with him. ' Harry has never had the slightest reason to complain of me,' she says; and now he gets this false, wicked letter, which is only written to make mischief, he thinks it all true ! "

" I fancy I can give a guess at the writer," said Chetwynd. "The villain had a double motive for sending the letter ! But I will see Harry Netterville myself to-morrow, and talk to him."

" I fear you'll only make matters worse, sir. He is very prejudiced and stupid."

" But the affair cannot be allowed to remain in this state. I owe it to myself to set it right."

" Well, you must talk to Rose, sir. I expect her back shortly. She's gone about a place."

" A place ? " exclaimed Chetwynd.

" Yes ; since her quarrel with Harry, she has determined to go into service, and our good friend Mr. Tankard has got her a situation as lady's maid. She is gone this evening to Belgrave Square to see Lady Thicknesse, who has engaged her."

" Now, indeed, you surprise me ! " cried Chetwynd. " This is a strange coincidence ! "

" Yes; I thought you'd be surprised when I mentioned the name, as you recollect that was the house ——But here she comes ! " she exclaimed, as a knock was heard at the door. " Rose, my dear," she added, " here's some one waiting to see you."

" I know who it is," replied her daughter. " I expected to find Mr. Chetwynd Calverley here."

In another moment she had taken off her hat and cloak, and came into the room, looking as pretty as ever, and, what could hardly have been expected under the circumstances, in very good spirits.

"I felt almost certain I should find you here, Mr. Calverley," she said, after salutations rather more distant than formerly had passed between them. "You will understand why I say so when I tell you I have just seen your sister and Miss Barfleur, and two more charming, amiable young ladies I never beheld. It will be quite a pleasure to me to attend upon them. And I must say they appeared equally well pleased with me. They seemed to know all about me."

"Yes; I had described you to them," remarked Chetwynd.

"So they told me," said Rose. "It's a curious thing altogether; but what makes it more singular is that I should go to the house at the very time of their arrival. I believe I was engaged by Lady Thicknesse expressly to attend to them."

Mrs. Hartley had uttered a great many exclamations as her daughter went on, and she now said:

"And how do you like Lady Thicknesse, Rose?"

"Very much indeed," was the reply. "She is a middle-aged lady, perhaps turned fifty, but still good-looking, and has a fine tall figure, and dresses very richly. I should have thought more of her if I hadn't been so much taken up with the young ladies. She received me very graciously, and said I should suit her perfectly, especially as her niece, Miss Barfleur, and Miss Calverley seemed pleased with me."

"Nothing was said to her ladyship in reference to any previous matter?" inquired Chetwynd.

"Nothing whatever, sir," replied Rose. "The young ladies spoke to me in private. I had likewise some conversation with Mr. Higgins, who cautioned me; but I told him I should never breathe a word on the subject. You needn't feel the slightest uneasiness, sir. To-morrow I enter upon my duties, and am sure I shall be very happy."

"I sincerely hope so, Rose," said Chetwynd. "I am very sorry for the misunderstanding that has occurred——"

"I've told Mr. Calverley all about the quarrel, my dear," remarked Mrs. Hartley.

"I'm very angry indeed with Harry," cried Rose, "and don't feel at all inclined to make it up with him."

"You'll think differently by-and-by, I dare say," observed Chetwynd. "My belief is that the writer of that mischievous letter to Harry is no other than the scoundrel who annoyed you in the steam-boat, and whom I chastised for his insolence."

"The same idea occurred to me," said Rose : "and I should have mentioned my suspicions to Harry, but he would listen to no explanations. Knowing his jealous temper, I never told him of that occurrence, as I fancied it would put him out. I also blame myself for not mentioning one or two circumstances that have occurred since your departure; but I really felt frightened."

"Has Romney made an attempt to see you again?" asked Chetwynd.

"More than once," she replied. "He annoys me dreadfully. When my father is with me, he keeps out of the way; but I cannot always have a protector at my side. This is one reason why I have resolved to go into service. I shall be secure from my tormentor."

"I hope he won't trouble you much longer," remarked Chetwynd.

Just then a knock was heard at the door. It was rather sharp, and surprised the hearers.

"Who can that be?" cried Rose, uneasily.

"I'll go and see," replied her mother.

The person at the door was no other than Tom Tankard. He inquired for Rose, and Mrs. Hartley begged him to come in, and ushered him at once into the little parlour.

Tom, who was dressed in evening attire, appeared very much surprised at the sight of Chetwynd, and would have retreated, if he could have done so with a good grace.

Declining to take a seat, he addressed himself to Rose, and said:

"I hope you will excuse this intrusion, Miss Hartley, but I am the bearer of a message to you from my friend, Mr. Harry Netterville. He wishes to know whether you will grant him an interview?"

"Shall I?" said Rose, in a low voice.

"Nay, don't appeal to me," replied Chetwynd. "Exercise your own discretion."

"I ought to say that Mr. Netterville is without," observed Tom; "so that he requires an immediate answer. When I inform him who his here, I don't feel quite sure that he will come in."

"He can please himself," said Rose. "Tell him, n reply to his message, that I will see him, but not alone."

"Have the goodness, also, to tell him from me, Mr.

Tom," abserved Chetwynd, " that I have a few words to say to him. I intended to call on him to-morrow."

" I will do your bidding, sir," replied Tom, " But I remark——"

" Pray, don't make any remarks at present, sir," interrupted Chetwynd. " Just convey my message."

Tom bowed, and left the room.

He was attended to the street-door by Mrs. Hartley, who waited to see whether he would return.

II.

HARRY NETTERVILLE'S JEALOUS RAGE.

SOME persuasion on Tom Tankard's part was evidently required to induce Harry Netterville to enter the house; but, at length, he reluctantly consented to do so, and followed Mrs. Hartley into the parlour.

As soon as he saw Chetwynd, he could no longer control himself, but flew into a transport of jealous rage, and would certainly have made a scene if Tom, who was close behind, had not checked him.

A sort of calm being restored, Chetwynd remarked, " Allow me, Mr. Netterville, before anything more is said, to offer a word of explanation. My presence here this evening is purely accidental. I have just arrived in town, and came to inquire after my good friends. It grieved me to learn that a misunderstanding has arisen between you and Rose; but I am sure it can be easily set right. The anonymous letter you have received was from a great reprobate, who, for purposes of his own, wished to destroy your confidence in this good and truthful girl, who is sincerely attached to you, and, unfortunately, he has succeeded in his object."

"Your explanation, though plausible, has very little weight with me, sir," replied Netterville. "I only consented to enter the house to convince myself by ocular demonstration that you are here. Having done that, I shall depart. Farewell, deceitful girl— farewell, for ever!"

"Stay, Harry!" cried Rose, rushing towards him, and seizing his arm. "I cannot allow you to depart thus! Listen to the explanation Mr. Calverley desires to give you. You have been made a dupe."

"I know it!" rejoined Netterville, bitterly; "but I will be duped no longer! It is idle to say how much I have loved you, faithless girl! I now tear you from my heart for ever!"

"Oh, don't say so, dearest Harry!" she cried. "It is all a mistake. You will be sorry when you find out your error. You have been very foolish."

"Foolish!" he exclaimed, in a tremendous voice. "Your conduct has been enough to drive me mad! If you really love me, as you pretend, come away with me now."

"No; I can't do that, dear Harry."

"You *shall*, whether you like it or not!" he said, seizing her arm.

Frightened by his violence, she uttered a cry, rushed back, and flung herself into Chetwynd's arms, who was coming forward to assist her.

As may be imagined, this occurrence inflamed the jealous lover to the highest pitch, and Tom Tankard had some difficulty in holding him back.

"Let me go!" cried Netterville, struggling with his friend. "My worst suspicions are now confirmed. Let me go, I say! I'll punish him!"

"No you sha'n't," cried Tom, who could scarcely refrain from laughing at the absurdity of the scene. "You've committed folly enough already. Come along."

And he dragged him out of the house.

"I didn't believe Harry could behave in such an extraordinary manner," said Rose, as soon as he was gone. "He terrified me so much that I scarcely knew what I was about. I hope you'll excuse me, sir."

"There's nothing to excuse," replied Chetwynd; "but you must judge your lover as leniently as you can. His violence only proves the strength of his affection for you."

"I would rather he didn't show his affection in this way," she rejoined.

"Certainly he allowed his passion to carry him a great deal too far," said Chetwynd. "But he will be very sorry to-morrow."

"When he comes here again, he will find me gone; and I sha'n't write to him," said Rose.

"Don't make resolutions you are sure to break," said Chetwynd. "And now, adieu. Possibly I may see you to-morrow in Belgrave Square."

Bidding good night to Mrs. Hartley, and leaving a kindly message for her husband, he then quitted the house.

III.

LORD COURLAND.

LADY THICKNESSE, widow of Sir Thomas Thicknesse, of Haslemere, Cheshire, was some four or five years younger than her sister, Lady Barfleur. In her day she had been considered a great beauty, and was still attractive, for her manners were extremely agreeable. She habitually resided in Belgrave Square, and not being fond of the country, seldom spent more than a couple of months in the autumn at Haslemere.

She still had a large establishment, much larger than she required, for the state of her health did not allow her to keep much company, and she no longer gave any of those grand parties that had once made her the fashion.

Lady Thicknesse had no children, but she was proud and ambitious, and her great desire was that Emmeline should marry a person of rank.

During Sir Leycester's lifetime she despaired of accomplishing her purpose, for he would allow no interference on her part. His demise, however, left the stage clear; and as Emmeline had now become a great heiress, the matter seemed quite simple and easy. The noble husband had only to be chosen.

After a little consideration, she fixed upon Lord Courland, the eldest son of the Earl of Lymington, who seemed to possess all the requisites, and in whom she herself felt an interest. Besides, he was a great friend of her nephew, Scrope Danvers, a circumstance that seemed very favourable to her design.

Lord Courland was about four-and-twenty, very

much liked generally on account of his agreeable manners, and sufficiently good-looking. She had never heard him express an opinion on the subject, but she fancied he was just the man who would desire to marry an heiress. The real question was whether Emmeline would accept him. On this point Lady Thicknesse had no misgiving, having perfect reliance on her own powers of persuasion.

Her plan settled, she wrote the letter we have seen to her niece. It quite answered its purpose, and excited no suspicion. All the rest followed as narrated.

On their arrival in Belgrave Square, Lady Thicknesse received the two girls with every demonstration of delight, and she appeared so amiable and affectionate, that they were charmed with her.

She was told that Chetwynd Calverley had brought them to town; but she attached no importance to the circumstance, not conceiving it possible that Emmeline could care for him.

Until now, she had never seen Mildred, and was quite surprised by her beauty. Had she known she was so good-looking, she didn't feel sure she should have asked her. She might outshine her niece.

Next morning the two girls, who were both in very good spirits, and looking very well after their journey, were seated in the large and splendidly furnished drawing-room, when Lady Thicknesse began to open her plan.

"By-the-by, Emmeline," she said, "I ought to mention that your cousin, Scrope Danvers, is in town, and will very likely call this morning, for he knows you will be here. I hope he may, and bring with him his friend, Lord Courland. I needn't tell you that Lord Courland is the eldest son of the Earl of Lymington ; but I may say he is very agreeable, and singularly unaffected for a person of his rank, and I am persuaded you will like him."

" I dare say I shall," replied Emmeline. " I have heard Charles Danvers speak of him as a very nice fellow."

" He is a great favourite of mine, I own," said Lady Thicknesse. " His father is in very bad health ; so it cannot be long before he becomes Earl of Lymington and master of Guilsborough Castle, one of the finest places in Hampshire. But I won't say any more about him. You'll see him presently, and judge for yourself."

The opportunity soon offered. Scarcely had Lady Thicknesse done singing the young lord's praises, than he and Scrope Danvers were announced.

Decidedly, he produced a favourable impression. Tall, and slight of figure, with features agreeable in expression, if not handsome, he was easy and refined in manner, and seemed to possess great tact. He had light-brown hair, a beard of the same hue, and very good teeth.

Both girls were pleased with him, and he was evidently struck by their beauty ; but he paid no exclusive attention to Emmeline, and talked quite as much to Mildred as to her. His sole aim seemed to be to amuse them, and his chat being very lively, and some of his stories very diverting, he perfectly succeeded. When he and Scrope rose to depart, after a visit of half an hour, during which there was no pause in the conversation, Lady Thicknesse asked them both to dinner, and the invitation was accepted—much to the delight of the girls.

" Well, what do you think of Lord Courland ? ' observed Lady Thicknesse, who thought the affair had commenced capitally. " Have I said too much in his praise ? "

" Not at all," replied Emmeline. " I never spent half an hour more agreeably."

" Nor I," added Mildred. " I feel quite ashamed of myself for laughing so much, but I really couldn't help it. He is an excellent talker ! "

" I hope you will see a great deal more of him during your stay in town," said Lady Thicknesse.

" I hope we shall," rejoined Emmeline. " He promises to be a very agreeable acquaintance."

" He may possibly be something more than a mere acquaintance, my love ! " remarked her ladyship, significantly. " I think you have made a conquest. He seemed quite captivated ! "

" Not by me, my dear aunt. If he was captivated by either of us, it was by Mildred. She has made the conquest ! "

" Quite unintentionally," replied Mildred. " But I agree with Lady Thicknesse ; you were the chief attraction."

Emmeline smiled, and shook her head.

" Well, whoever wins him will have good reason to congratulate herself," said Lady Thicknesse.

" We shan't quarrel about him, that's certain," said Emmeline. " I'm quite ready to retire from the field in your favour." she added to Mildred. " I should like nothing better than to see you Lady Courland ! "

" I fear we are getting on a little too fast, dear

girls," said Lady Thicknesse, who was not pleased by the turn things seemed taking. "I have raised expectations that may never be realised. I really don't think Lord Courland is a marrying man."

"I entertain quite a different opinion, aunt," said Emmeline. "Within a week I feel sure he will have proposed to Mildred."

"I hope Miss Calverley won't take what you say seriously," observed Lady Thicknesse. "She may be disappointed."

"No, indeed, I shan't," said Mildred. "I have no idea of catching this young lord. I am not dazzled by his rank, though not insensible to it. I am charmed with his affability and good nature, but that is all. You won't find a rival in me, dearest Emmeline."

"Never mind me, Mildred," said Emmeline. "You know very well I am out of the question. I ask you plainly, wouldn't you like to be Lady Courland?"

"I can't tell," replied the other. "I haven't thought about it."

"Then we'll talk it over, and I'll give you my reasons," said Emmeline.

"You'd better hear mine first," remarked Lady Thicknesse. "But tell me what you meant by bidding Miss Calverley 'not to mind you,' and adding 'she knew very well you are out of the question?' That is an ambiguous phrase."

"It is intelligible enough to Mildred, my dear aunt, and only means that I have no idea of marrying at present."

"But how came you to form such a silly resolution?"

"You mustn't ask me, my dear aunt."

"Not now; but at some more suitable time I shall think it my duty to require an explanation."

Rather fortunately, the discourse was interrupted just at that moment by Chetwynd, who was ushered into the room by Higgins.

Lady Thicknesse had never seen him before, and was very much struck by his appearance. She had no idea he was so handsome, and a suspicion of the truth then crossed her.

Could he be engaged to Emmeline? But she dismissed the notion as soon as formed.

She had been prejudiced against him by the accounts she had heard of his follies, extravagance, and impetuous temper; but his good looks and quiet deportment operated strongly in his favour, and he had not been in the room five minutes before she felt disposed to like him, and evinced her friendly feeling by asking him to dinner.

On his part, Chetwynd was very much pleased with her ladyship, and could not help smiling as he thought to himself what might have been the consequence if his original plan had been carried out.

IV.

A VIEW OF THE RING ROAD.

AFTER some little time spent in conversation, Emmeline remarked to Lady Thicknesse:

"As you don't mean to drive out till after luncheon, aunt, and as there is still plenty of time, Mildred and myself would like to take a walk in the Park, if you have no objection. Chetwynd will accompany us."

"With the greatest pleasure," he said. "You will see all the world, for people now go to the Park in the morning as well as later in the day."

"So I understand," she replied. "May we go, dearest aunt?"

Lady Thicknesse assented, upon which the two girls withdrew to make the necessary preparation for the promenade. In these they were assisted by their new lady's maid, Rose, who had commenced her duties that morning, to their great delight.

As soon as they were ready, they set out with Chetwynd, and took their way along Wilton Street and through Albert Gate to the Serpentine.

The morning being extremely fine, a great many people were about, and, even at that early hour, the banks of that lovely sheet of water were thronged with fashionable pedestrians, while the adjacent rides and drives were crowded with well-mounted equestrians of both sexes, and splendid equipages.

Unaccustomed to such a display, our two country girls were struck with admiration. How could they be otherwise? Passing in review before them, or grouped around, were some of the loveliest and best dressed women in the land; and certainly no better specimens of the youthful aristocracy could be found than might be seen mounted on those thoroughbred steeds, guiding those well-appointed drags and lighter vehicles, or lounging, cigar in mouth, against the iron railing. In its way the scene was very striking.

To the regular frequenters of the Ring, crowded as it was, it was not difficult to decide that the two

lovely girls, dressed in deep mourning, were stran-
gers.

Every one was struck by their remarkable beauty,
and wondered who they were. Information on this
point could not be had, since no one possessed it.
Some persons remembered Chetwynd Calverley, who
was standing beside the unknown fair ones, and fancied
they might be his sisters; and this notion being pro-
mulgated, soon obtained general credence.

Among the equestrians was one who instantly recognised them—this was Sir Bridgnorth Charlton.

Riding up to the railing, he made his presence
known to Chetwynd, who instantly went to speak to
him, and explained that the girls had just come to town,
and were staying with Lady Thicknesse in Belgrave
Square.

"Delighted to hear it," said Sir Bridgnorth, bowing
and waving his hand to the girls. "Tell them I'll
call to-morrow."

"Why not call to-day?" said Chetwynd. "They
will be charmed to see you, and so will Lady Thicknesse.
She was talking of you not an hour ago, but had no
idea you were in town. Come, if you can."

"I will," replied Sir Bridgnorth.

And with another friendly salute to the two girls,
he rode on.

Among the loungers collected near the rails when
Sir Bridgnorth pulled up, was Romney. His quick
ears caught all that was said. He learnt that the two
girls were staying with Lady Thicknesse, and that
Chetwynd was on intimate terms with her ladyship,
together with some other information that he thought
might be useful to him.

Though he was quite close at hand, Chetwynd did not observe him, but returned to the young ladies, who were very glad to learn that Sir Bridgnorth meant to call upon them.

It was now almost time to return, but the scene was so lively and amusing that they remained for a few minutes longer.

During this interval rather a smart mail-phaeton passed by slowly, containing a couple of showily-dressed but decidedly pretty girls, and driven by a young man who tried to look a swell, was rather loudly dressed, and seemed very vain of his coachmanship.

In the occupants of this vehicle, Chetwynd, to his great astonishment, recognised some acquaintances of his own—the loudly-dressed young swell, who appeared to think so much of himself, being no other than Tom Tankard, and the young ladies with him Miss Clotilde Tripp and Flora Sicklemore.

How Tom came to be possessed of such an equipage, and such a pair of horses, Chetwynd could not conceive.

Perhaps he had hired them? Perhaps some friendly coachman, whose master was out of town, had lent them to him? In any case, Tom paraded them as his own.

The supercilious air with which he gazed around, and which only excited ridicule and contempt, though he thought otherwise, was intended to convey that impression. He fancied people were staring at him in admiration, when they were merely laughing at him as a fool.

At last his eyes alighted on the tall figure of Chetwynd, conspicuous amid the throng, and he gave him a familiar nod; but Chetwynd pretended not to see it.

Enraged by the slight, Tom turned to the girls with him, and said :

"There's that tall fellow whom you saw dressed up as a footman at our house. He chooses to cut me, but I'll be even with him. He sha'n't ' cut and come again,' I can tell him ! "

"Perhaps he didn't see you," suggested Clotilde.

"Oh, yes, he did ! " rejoined Tom. "He couldn't help seeing me, since he was looking this way at the time. Never mind ; I'll serve him out ! "

"What two pretty girls those are with him ! " cried Flora.

"Not to compare with two others close at hand ! " rejoined Tom, gallantly.

"Ah, we can't accept that compliment, Mr. Tom," said Flora. "Those are two very stylish young ladies, indeed."

"I can't see it," remarked Tom. "I don't admire women in black. I like something bright—something in your style, Miss Flora."

"Or in mine ? " suggested Clotilde.

"Exactly," said Tom. "I hope that fellow won't tell the guv'nor that he saw me driving you in the Park."

"Good gracious ! I hope not ! " exclaimed both girls.

"But he's not likely to see Mr. Tankard, is he ? " observed Clotilde.

"Don't know—just possible ! If he should, there 'll be a jolly row. The guv'nor 'll never rest till he's found it all out."

"Well, don't let us spoil our pleasure by thinking about it," said Flora. "It's very charming ! never enjoyed anything so much in my life as this drive ! "

"Not even our drive to Hampton Races?" said Tom, with a knowing look.

"Not even that," she replied.

"I'm sure we shall always feel indebted to you for a most delightful day, Mr. Tom!" said Clotilde.

"Well, it is pleasant," cried Tom. "I like to see all these fine folks, and I like to be seen myself, but I don't like to be cut. Confound that fellow! I can't forget him!"

"That's not like you, Tom, to let such a small thing worry you," observed Clotilde.

"You're right," said Tom. "My maxim is—never bother yourself if you can help it. And now let us move on a little faster."

V.

LORD COURLAND CONTINUES UNDECIDED.

WHILE Tom and his fair friends were pursuing their course, Chetwynd and the two young ladies were quitting the gay scene.

As they made their way through the throng, they encountered Lord Courland and Scrope Danvers, who had been watching them from afar, and had both come to the conclusion that the two prettiest girls to be seen in the Park on that morning were Miss Barfleur and Miss Calverley.

Lord Courland did not know which he admired most; at one moment he thought Emmeline the prettiest, but the next he gave the preference to Mildred.

"Your cousin, Miss Barfleur, is certainly a most charming girl, Scrope!" he said; "but——"

" You prefer Miss Calverley," supplied the other.

"No; I don't say that," rejoined Lord Courland. " But Miss Calverley has lovely features, and an enthralling expression—at least, I find it so."

" I see you are half in love with her already, my lord," said Scrope, rather disappointed. " I quite admit that Miss Calverley is very beautiful; but don't forget that my cousin Emmeline is a great heiress."

" I am only indulging in a little sentiment, my dear boy," said Lord Courland. " Either of those girls must be admired for herself alone. Your fair cousin needs no large fortune to enhance her attractions—neither does Miss Calverley. Looking at them as equally well endowed in this respect, I should be puzzled to choose, even if choice were allowed me. But when to almost matchless beauty Miss Barfleur adds the possession of great wealth, there can be no hesitation."

" There I entirely concur with your lordship's opinion," said Scrope; " and had not my uncle, Sir Leycester, been a very crotchety fellow, she would have been married long ago. Even your lordship would have found some difficulty with him."

" I dare say," he replied. " But who is that with them ? "

" Miss Calverley's brother Chetwynd."

" I thought so. He is uncommonly handsome."

" He has been very wild and extravagant; but, I believe, has taken to better ways. I don't know him myself; but my brother Charles, who has seen a good deal of him, gives a very favourable account of him, and says he is an excellent fellow. By-the-by, Charles has been very much in love with Miss Calverley; but, I believe, all that is at an end."

" And Chetwynd Calverley is not a suitor to Miss Barfleur ? " asked Lord Courland.

" That would never be heard of for a moment," rejoined Scrope. " He has run through all his property; and, as far as I can understand, is entirely dependent upon his step-mother."

" He may desire to repair his fallen fortunes."

" He won't repair them by a marriage with Miss Barfleur," said Scrope, in a decided tone. " But see ! they are evidently going away. Shall we join them ? "

" By all means," replied Lord Courland.

So they went up to them, as previously mentioned; and the two gentlemen having been introduced to Chetwynd, with whom they were much pleased, the whole party walked on to Albert Gate, where Lord Courland and Scrope took leave, the others proceeding to Belgrave Square.

Lady Thicknesse had always been noted for her dinners, and she still maintained her reputation. She had a good French cook, and an excellent butler, as we know. Her *chef*, Monsieur Zephyrus, had been a pupil of the renowned Olivier Givors, of Orleans, and did credit to his master.

On this occasion, Zephyrus sent up a charming little repast, that pleased all who partook of it.

A small round table sufficed for the party, which only numbered seven. Among the guests was Sir Bridgnorth, who was asked at a very late hour; but he stood upon no ceremony, and was delighted to meet the two girls.

Again, it was quite impossible to say whether Lord Courland intended to devote himself to Emmeline or Mildred.

As a matter of course, he took down Lady Thicknesse to dinner, and sat between her ladyship and Emmeline; but he managed to talk a great deal to Mildred, who was placed opposite him; and had the girls been rivals, neither of them could have boasted of a triumph.

Next to Mildred was Sir Bridgnorth, and Emmeline was separated from Chetwynd by Scrope Danvers, who sat on her left, and prevented all conversation between them.

Chetwynd's deportment was very quiet during dinner, and he said little; but in the evening he talked a great deal to Lady Thicknesse, and pleased her so much that she gave him a general invitation to the house—a point he was very desirous to gain.

VI.

LADY THICKNESSE HAS A CONFERENCE WITH SCROPE.

NEARLY a week passed much in the same way.

The young ladies walked out in the morning with Chetwynd; drove out in the afternoon with Lady Thicknesse; and dined at eight, with nearly the same party, and on an equally good dinner.

Very little progress, however, seemed to be made with the important affair Lady Thicknesse had in hand. Her ladyship began to get tired, and had a private conference with her nephew, Scrope, but he could not help her.

"I cannot make out whether or not Lord Courland has spoken to Emmeline," she observed. "If he has, she has said nothing to me."

"Nor has his lordship said anything to me," rejoined Scrope, "though I have given him several pretty strong hints. The affair must take its course. We shall spoil all by precipitation."

"I sometimes think Emmeline has a secret attachment," observed Lady Thicknesse, after a short pause. "If my conjecture be right, it must be for Chetwynd Calverley."

"Impossible, my dear aunt!" exclaimed Scrope.

"No, it's not impossible," said Lady Thicknesse. "Chetwynd is an exceedingly fine young gentleman, and calculated to inspire an attachment. I have half resolved to question her."

"Better write to Lady Barfleur, I think."

"I *have* written to my sister, and very cautiously; but, as yet, I have received no answer to my letter."

"Well, then, wait till you do before taking any steps. Things are going on very smoothly."

"But very slowly—too slowly for me."

"That can't be helped. You must control your impatience, dear aunt."

"I didn't count on this delay. I expected the matter would be concluded in a week. I think I shall consult Sir Bridgnorth Charlton. If any one is in young Calverley's secrets, he is."

"But he won't betray them."

"He may give me some advice."

"His advice will be exactly the same as mine. He will recommend you to keep quiet. I really don't see any occasion for alarm. Things appear to me to be going on very well—if you could only think so. Courland won't be driven."

" Mildred Calverley is decidedly in the way. I'm very sorry I invited her."

" Perhaps it was a mistake. However, she can't be got rid of now."

" And I'm not sure Emmeline would have come without her."

A slight pause ensued, after which Lady Thicknesse said :—" By-the-by, your brother Charles is coming to town. I've just got a letter from him. I think I shall ask him to stay with me for a week. Is he really going to marry Mrs. Calverley ? He says nothing about her."

" I believe the match is broken off. She wants to keep all her property to herself. Had she behaved generously, as she ought to have done, and settled a handsome sum on Charley, it would have been a famous thing for him, no doubt. But it never does to be dependent upon an imperious woman like Mrs. Calverley. So he is quite right, in my opinion, to beat a retreat while there is yet time."

Lady Thicknesse seemed to take a different view of the matter.

" I'm sorry he has thrown away such a chance," she remarked. " Has she a large income ? "

" Four or five thousand a year, Charley tells me. Old Calverley was very rich, as you must be aware, and she has got all his money."

" Not *all*, surely ? Chetwynd and Mildred must have some of it."

" Both are dependent upon her. Chetwynd has had a very bitter quarrel with her, and has only just made it up. I think he acted very wisely, since he is completely in her power."

" What a singular position she is placed in ! "

" Old Calverley must have been in his dotage to give it her."

" She is still young and handsome ? "

" Not many years older than Mildred, and quite as good-looking. I saw her at Sir Leycester's funeral, and was charmed with her. No doubt, she is very fascinating."

" You excite my curiosity. I should like to see her."

" I dare say you will have the opportunity. But you won't see her as Mrs. Charles Danvers."

" Why not? They may still come to an understanding."

" Well, if you can bring them together again, and prevail upon her to make a handsome settlement on Charley, you will do a great thing," remarked Scrope, with a laugh.

" I will consider what can be done," replied Lady Thicknesse. " Meantime, I will write and ask Charles to come and stay with me."

Thus ended their conference.

VII.

THE VISIT TO MRS. HARTLEY'S.

Rose Hartley made a charming lady's maid.

She was so pretty, dressed so neatly, had such nice manners, and was so cheerful, good-natured, and obliging, that the two young ladies were enchanted with her.

They had a dressing-room in common, and nothing

pleased them better than a chat with the lively little damsel, while she dressed their hair, or assisted in making their toilettes. While thus employed, Rose appeared to the greatest advantage, and the pretty soubrette, whose figure rivalled those of her mistresses, in her neat morning dress, and the two lovely girls, in their very becoming dishabille, formed a picture of grace and beauty.

Brought together in this way, it was quite natural that she should relate her little story to them. They had listened to it with much interest, and expressed the greatest indignation at the annoyance she had experienced, but advised her not to trouble herself, as they felt sure her persecutor would not dare to annoy her now.

One morning, however, she showed them a letter she had just received, and evidently from the same source. In it the writer said he had just discovered her abode, and would pay her a visit ere long.

They were inclined to laugh at it, and treat it with contempt; but, as she seemed uneasy, they advised her to consult Mr. Higgins, the butler, who had been very kind to her, and treated her like a daughter.

Higgins recommended her not to go out unattended for a few days, as she might be annoyed; but added if the gentleman ventured to call at the house, he would have reason to repent his audacity.

When the young ladies heard what the butler said, they thought he was quite right; but Emmeline added, " You sha'n't be kept in-doors by this impudent varlet, who deserves to be horsewhipped. Lady Thicknesse says we can have the carriage whenever

we please. We'll take it out this morning, and you
shall go with us."

Delighted beyond measure, Rose essayed to express
her thanks.

"We'll pay your mother a visit," pursued Emmeline.
"We want to see her."

"But I should have liked to give her some notice
of your kind intentions," said Rose, rather embarrassed.

"No; that would defeat our object," said Mildred.
"We wish to take her by surprise."

Rose had nothing more to say, so the carriage was
ordered at once.

All three got into it, and were driven to the esplanade near Lambeth Bridge, where they alighted,
and walked towards Spencer's Rents. Emmeline
would not allow the footman to accompany
them.

Great was Mrs. Hartley's confusion at this unexpected visit.

She was busy in the kitchen at the time, and when
Rose rushed in to tell her Miss Barfleur and Miss
Calverley were at the house, she uttered a cry of
astonishment, and blamed her daughter for not letting
her know beforehand.

"Don't scold her, Mrs. Hartley," cried Emmeline,
who heard all that was passing. "We wouldn't allow
her to prepare you for our visit. We wanted to see you
just as you are."

"Dear me! it's very kind of you, miss!" cried the
good dame, not venturing to show herself. "Be
pleased to step into the parlour, and I'll come to you
as soon as I've put myself a little to rights. Rose
will show you the way."

Smiling as they went into the little room, which they thought very tidy and well furnished, the young ladies sat down, and sent Rose to her mother, who presently came in, and made many apologies for keeping them waiting.

Both were very much pleased by her appearance, and after she had been presented to each of them in turn, she said to Mildred :

"And so you're Mr. Chetwynd's sister, miss? Well, I don't see any great resemblance."

"I never was considered very much like my brother," observed Mildred, smiling.

"Ah, you might be proud of resembling him, miss; for he's a very fine young gentleman. Don't you agree with me, miss?" she added, turning to Emmeline.

"Yes; he is generally considered very good-looking," replied the young lady, slightly blushing—a circumstance that Mrs. Hartley did not fail to remark,

"Whoever gets Mr. Chetwynd for a husband will do well," she said. "Of that I'm certain."

And she would have launched still more strongly into his praises, had not Rose checked her.

"I'm very glad to have an opportunity of thanking you for your great kindness to my brother, dear Mrs. Hartley," observed Mildred. "He always speaks of you with gratitude, and says you were quite like a mother to him."

"I felt like one," she replied. "It touched my heart to see him. But, Heaven be thanked! all that's gone by, and I trust he's happy, as he deserves to be Nothing would please me better than to hear that he has found some charming young lady to——"

Q

" All in good time, Mrs. Hartley," interrupted
Mildred. " You shall be let into the secret, I promise
you, as soon as there is one to communicate."

Mrs. Hartley looked as if she thought that would be
very soon, but she didn't venture to give utterance to
her sentiments.

" And now let us speak about your daughter, Mrs.
Hartley," said Emmeline. " We came to talk of her.
She will tell you, I think, that she is happy in her new
place."

" I ought to be," said Rose ; " since every kindness
is shown me."

But she sighed as the words were uttered.

" Ah, you can't help thinking of Harry Netterville,
I suppose ? " observed her mother. " He doesn't
deserve your love. These dear young ladies shall
hear my opinion of him."

" Not unless it's favourable," said Emmeline.

" Well, I've nothing to say against him, except that
I don't want to have the engagement renewed,"
replied Mrs. Hartley.

" Why not ? " asked both young ladies, eagerly.

" Because I don't think it would be for my daughter's
advantage."

" I'm afraid she will never be satisfied without him,"
said Mildred.

" If I thought so, I wouldn't oppose it," rejoined the
good dame.

" Then take the assurance from us," said both
young ladies, earnestly.

" After that, I have nothing to say," observed Mrs.
Hartley. " Rose must decide for herself."

" Oh, thank you, dearest mother ! " exclaimed her

daughter, kissing her. " I should then say that
if——"

Her speech was here interrupted by a knock at the
door.

" Good gracious ! I hope nobody is calling," said
Mrs. Hartley.

" Don't mind us," cried the young ladies.

" You had better not let anybody in, mother,"
whispered Rose.

As Mrs. Hartley went out she closed the parlour
door after her.

But some conversation could be heard going on in
the passage. Familiar tones reached Rose's ears, and
she said to the young ladies :

" I do believe it is Harry Netterville himself ! "

" How strange if it should be ! " cried Mildred.

Next moment Mrs. Hartley returned, her countenance wearing a very singular expression.

" Who do you think has just come in ? " she said to
her daughter.

" I know very well—Harry Netterville," replied
Rose.

" Yes ; he knows you are here. What shall I say
to him for you ? "

Before answering, Rose looked at the young ladies,
as much as to ask, " What do you advise ? "

" See him, by all means," observed Emmeline.

" Alone ? "

" No ; here."

" Bring him in, my dear mother," said Rose.

No culprit ever presented a more abject appearance
than did Harry Netterville, as he entered the room
with Mrs. Hartley. He seemed thoroughly ashamed

of himself, and could hardly look at the young ladies.

"May I ask what has brought you here this morning, Mr. Netterville?" inquired Rose.

"I didn't expect to find you, dearest Rose," he replied, in a penitential tone, that touched all the listeners except the one it was meant to move. "I came to see your mother."

"Why do you address me as 'dearest Rose?'" said the young damsel, rather severely.

"You are still dear to me, and must ever remain so," he replied. "I confess I have behaved very badly."

"Well, the poor fellow can't say more," said Emmeline, moved by his looks and manner. "I hope you will forgive him."

"Do," added Mildred.

Netterville awaited his sentence with anxiety; but Rose did not seem inclined to pardon him at once.

"You have acted so unreasonably that I cannot forgive you till you have made some amends," she said.

"I am ready to do anything you may enjoin," he replied.

"You shall deliver me from the annoyance to which I have been subjected, and which has caused our disagreement," she replied. "You shall find out the writer of that anonymous letter to yourself, and who has likewise written other infamous letters to me, and punish him—punish him as he deserves. When you have done this, I will forgive you, but not till then."

"We quite approve of your decision, Rose," said Mildred; "and till Mr. Netterville has done this he doesn't deserve your regard. He ought not to hesitate."

" I don't hesitate," he replied, energetically.

" That's right," said Rose. " I begin to like you again. Here is the last letter I have received. Read it," she added, tossing it to him.

After scanning its contents, Netterville turned pale.

" And this has just reached you ? " he asked, with quivering lips.

" Yesterday," she replied.

" The writer must be discovered," he said.

VIII.

HOW HARRY NETTERVILLE FOUND ROMNEY.

WHEN the carriage came from Belgrave Square, those within it were not aware that it was followed by a hansom cab, from which a person having the appearance of a gentleman alighted near Vauxhall Pier, and addressing the footman, said, in a very civil tone, calculated to obtain a response:

" Pray is this Lady Thicknesse's carriage ? "

" It is, sir," replied the man, touching his hat.

" Is her ladyship with it ? " pursued the inquirer.

" No, sir. We only brought the two young ladies here."

" Are they gone to the Palace ? "

" I don't think so, sir. They have got the lady's-maid with them."

" Then I know where they are. Thank you very much."

And he walked off in the direction of Spencer's Rents.

As the individual we have mentioned, who was by no means bad-looking, walked on, he considered within himself what course he should take, and being utterly unscrupulous, he determined to go to the house and see Rose, whatever might be the consequences.

Just as he arrived at the corner of Spencer's Rents he encountered Harry Netterville, whom he knew by sight, and accosted him without hesitation.

" Can you tell me which is Mrs. Hartley's house ? " he asked.

Netterville had no idea who stood before him; but he was surprised at the inquiry, and rejoined rather sharply :

" Pray what business have you with Mrs. Hartley ? "

" I might decline to give an explanation to an inquiry put in such terms," said the other, " but I have no objection to tell you that I wish to speak to her about her daughter."

" Her daughter ! " exclaimed Netterville, starting back, and assuming an angry look. " Perhaps you are the very person of whom I am in quest ? Have you recently addressed a letter to Miss Hartley ? Have you written to me ? "

" I have written no letters at all," replied the stranger. " My object is to warn Mrs. Hartley against a certain individual."

" Who is he ? " demanded the attorney's clerk, eagerly.

" A very designing individual named Henry Netterville," replied the stranger.

So astounded was Netterville, that for a moment he could hardly reply. At length, he said :

" What have you to allege against the person whose name you have mentioned ? "

" Much ! But it is for Mrs. Hartley's ear. I am not likely to communicate to one unknown to me ! "

" Then learn, sir, to your confusion, that I am Henry Netterville ! "

" Indeed ! " exclaimed the other. " I shall not retract a word I have said. I shall convince Mrs. Hartley that she ought to get rid of you.

" For what reason ? " demanded Netterville. " Show cause why ! "

" I propose to do so. But since you force me to speak, I will say you are acting a most dishonourable part. You profess love for Rose, when you are making love to another. You offer her your hand, when you are already engaged."

" I engaged ! " exclaimed Netterville. " This is news to me. To whom am I engaged, pray ? "

" To Miss Clotilde Tripp, if I am rightly informed," replied the accuser. " If not to her, to Miss Flora Sicklemore."

" You must be confounding me with Tom Tankard," said Netterville. " I never paid the young ladies in question the slightest attention. And now allow me to ask a question ? Who are you, sir, who interest yourself so much in my concerns, and of whom I know nothing ? I am not aware that I ever saw you before ; but though you pretend ignorance, I strongly suspect that you know me very well. I believe you are the person who have been annoying Rose. I think you wrote the lying epistle to me, and the unmanly letters to

her. You imposed upon me for a time, but I have now
found you out.   Accident has delivered you into my
hands, and I don't mean to part with you.   Rose is at
home at this moment.   Come with me and apologise
to her, or I'll break every bone in your body ! "

" I will do nothing of the sort," replied Romney,
for it was he.

" We'll see that ! " cried Netterville.

And springing upon him suddenly, he caught him
by the collar and   dragged him towards the house,
which was not very far off.

Finding his struggles ineffectual, Romney submitted,
for he did not care to call out for assistance, as that
would have led to an exposure, which he desired to
avoid.

It chanced at this precise moment, that the door of
Mrs. Hartley's house opened, and the two young ladies
came forth, attended by Rose ; but the spectacle that
greeted their eyes sent them instantly back, for they
guessed what had occurred.

Another ineffectual struggle took place at the door ;
but Romney was dragged in by Netterville, and forced
into the parlour, whither the ladies had retreated with
Rose and her mother.

" Beg pardon, ladies ! " said Netterville, still keeping fast hold of his captive. " I hope you'll excuse
the intrusion ! "

" Oh, never mind us ! " they rejoined. " We are
glad you have caught the wretch ! "

" Is this the scoundrel who has annoyed you, Rose ! "
said Netterville.

" It is ! " she replied.

" Then down on your knees, and ask her forgiveness ! " said Netterville to his prisoner.

And he forced him to this humiliating posture.

"I have done nothing to call for this usage!" said Romney.

"You deserve a horsewhip!" cried Mrs. Hartley. "And if my husband were here, you'd have it!"

"Dare you say to my face that you have not several times annoyed me in the street?" asked Rose. "Do you deny writing those shameful letters to me?"

"I should not have written them if you had not given me encouragement!" he rejoined.

"It is false!" cried Rose. "I have never given you any encouragement. I detest you!"

"We do not believe a word he says, Rose!" cried Mildred, in accents of scorn and indignation. "Let him go, Mr. Netterville. The presence of such a creature is disagreeable to us!"

"Begone!" cried Netterville, releasing him, in obedience to the injunction. "Begone, I say, double-convicted liar and coward!"

And as Romney departed, he kicked him through the open door into the street.

The crestfallen blackleg stood for a moment before the house, as if about to return; but he had not the courage to face Netterville, and sneaked off.

"I think you have now got rid of him, Rose!" said Netterville, as he returned to the parlour.

"Yes; he won't trouble her again, I'm sure!" cried Emmeline. "You have served him quite right!"

"You are a brave fellow, Harry!" cried Rose, taking his hand, and gazing at him proudly and affectionately.

"And a lucky fellow as well!" he replied. "If this stupid scoundrel had not thrown himself in my way, I should not have caught him so quickly!"

IX.

CAPTAIN DANVERS ARRIVES IN BELGRAVE SQUARE.

Two days after the incident just related, the party at Lady Thicknesse's house in Belgrave Square was increased by the arrival of her nephew, Captain Danvers, whom she had invited to spend a week with her.

By this time, Mildred's resentment had, in some degree, abated, though she still treated him with coldness. But the captain looked so unhappy, that her heart was touched with compassion, and she soon showed a disposition to relent.

One morning on coming down to breakfast, he found her and Emmeline in the dining-room, and the latter perceiving she was rather in the way, good-naturedly left them together.

The captain immediately took advantage of the opportunity.

"Mildred," he said, in his softest tone, "will you allow me to offer an explanation?"

"I do not want any explanation, Captain Danvers," she replied. "I have ceased to take any interest in you."

"I hope not," he replied; "I trust I may be able to exculpate myself!"

"You will find that rather difficult!" she said.

"Yet hear me, I implore you!" he entreated in such moving accents, that she could not refuse.

"First, let me inquire whether Mrs Calverley has sent you any special information?" he said.

"I have not heard from her for nearly a week," she replied. "Indeed, I have not written to her."

" Then you are not aware that all is at an end between us ? "

" Your brother, Scrope, told me that the engagement was broken off."

" Did he tell you it was broken off by me ? "

" He did," she replied, colouring slightly.

" Mildred, I could not have married her. For a short space she seemed to cast a spell over me; but I soon recovered from it, and found that you alone are mistress of my heart, and that I could not live without you. But I had lost you—I had forfeited your regard, and could never hope to regain it."

" You judged correctly," said Mildred. But her looks rather belied her words.

" Though justly punished, I was resolved not to unite myself to a woman I cannot love, and who, I believe, is equally indifferent to me. A pretext for breaking off the engagement was easily found—nay, presented itself. Certain she would refuse, I required a handsome settlement to be made upon me. Her answer, as I anticipated, set me free ; and now, dearest Mildred," he added, venturing to take her hand which she did not withdraw, " you have heard my explanation, can you forgive me ? "

" You do not deserve forgiveness ! " she replied in a voice that showed she relented.

" I know it," he said, raising her hand to his lips. " But I feel that I am forgiven."

Further discourse was interrupted by the entrance of Lady Thicknesse and Emmeline, both of whom had witnessed the tender incident just described, and understood that a reconciliation had taken place, but neither made a remark.

"I've an agreeable surprise for you," said Lady Thicknesse. "Who do you think is coming to me to-morrow? You'll never guess; so I may as well tell you—Mrs. Calverley."

Exclamations of surprise rose from all; but no one seemed particularly pleased.

"I was not aware you knew her, aunt," remarked Captain Danvers, who did not care to conceal his vexation.

"I have never seen her," replied Lady Thicknesse. "But I wrote to say I should be delighted to make her acquaintance, and hoped she might be induced to spend a week with me while Mildred and Emmeline are in town. She has just answered that she accepts my invitation with the greatest pleasure, and I may expect her to-morrow. She will make a delightful addition to our little party."

"I am not so sure of that," muttered Captain Danvers.

"What put it into your head to ask her, dear aunt?" said Emmeline.

"A conversation I had with Scrope. He extolled her so much, that I longed to see her."

"I wish he had held his tongue," mentally ejaculated the captain.

Just then Higgins and a footman brought in breakfast, and an end was put to the conversation.

Later on, when she had an opportunity of saying a word to Lady Thicknesse privately, Emmeline observed:

"I think, aunt, you'll regret asking Mrs. Calverley. Though very handsome, very clever, and very agreeable, she's extremely mischievous. Everbody has been trying to get out of her way, and now we shall have her in our midst again. I shall be very much surprised if she doesn't cause some unpleasantness."

" Don't be afraid of that, my dear," said Lady Thicknesse, laughing. " I expect she'll be very useful."

" Useful in what way, aunt ? "

" I can't explain, but such is my opinion."

" I advise you to take care of her, aunt. Depend upon it, she's a very designing woman."

X.

MRS. CALVERLEY MAKES AN IMPORTANT CONQUEST.

NEXT day, Mrs. Calverley arrived in plenty of time for dinner.

She looked extremely well, and produced a most favourable impression upon Lady Thicknesse, who thought her one of the handsomest and best bred woman she had ever seen, and would not believe a word that had been said against her.

The meeting with Mildred was not very cordial; but Mrs. Calverley, who was a most accomplished actress, contrived to make it appear that there was no want of affection on her part, and completely imposed upon Lady Thicknesse.

With Emmeline it was the same thing. Whatever feelings she secretly entertained for that young lady, she professed the greatest regard for her.

Nor did she exhibit any coldness or resentment towards Captain Danvers, of whose conduct she had just reason to complain. No one could have guessed that they had recently quarrelled.

In short, Lady Thicknesse could see nothing in her but what was charming, and congratulated herself upon having invited her.

A splendid chamber was assigned her, with an adjoining room for her lady's-maid, Laura.

As usual, there was a small dinner-party on that day, consisting of Lord Courland, Sir Bridgnorth Charlton, Scrope, Captain Danvers, and Chetwynd.

Mrs. Calverley had a little talk with Chetwynd in the drawing-room, and they appeared on the most friendly terms; but their conversation was interrupted by the entrance of Lord Courland, who was presented to the beautiful widow, and claimed her attention.

Evidently the young lord was very much struck with her, and, seeing the effect she had produced, she exerted herself to the utmost, and before the end of the evening had completely enthralled her new admirer.

To Scrope, who knew his friend well, it seemed almost certain Mrs. Calverley would eclipse Emmeline. Hitherto, as we have shown, Lord Courland had divided his attentions between the two girls; but on this occasion he was engrossed by the fascinating widow, and had eyes for no one else.

Sir Bridgnorth came to the same conclusion as Scrope; and as he had taken Mrs. Calverley down to dinner, and found himself rather *de trop*, he was able to judge.

Even Lady Thicknesse began to see the error she had committed in introducing so dangerous a rival. Mrs. Calverley was far more to be feared than Mildred, and might carry off the prize.

However, the beautiful widow acted with great discretion. Apparently, she attached no importance to the conquest she had made. When rallied on the subject next morning by Lady Thicknesse, she owned that she had flirted a little with Lord Courland, but had not for a moment regarded his attentions seriously.

" I am glad to hear you say so," replied her ladyship. "Had it been otherwise, you would have run counter to a plan of mine. To tell you the truth, I rather wish to bring about a match between his lordship and Emmeline."

" Nothing could be better ! " said Mrs. Calverley. " I wouldn't interfere with it for the world. But I fear there is a little difficulty that you may not be aware of. I suspect Emmeline has an attachment."

" The same notion has occurred to me ; but I have never questioned her, and she has said nothing to me. To whom do you suppose she is attached ?—to Chetwynd ? "

" No ; it is only surmise on my part. But still I think I am right."

" If she won't accept Lord Courland, it will be monstrously provoking after all my trouble. He has met her every day for nearly a fortnight, and the affair has not advanced a single step. She seems to like his society, but nothing more, and he appears just as much pleased with Mildred as he is with her."

" Have you tried to bring him to the point ?   Have
you spoken to him ? "

"No; my nephew, Scrope Danvers, is strangely
averse to such a course."

" He is wrong.   Pardon me if I say you ought to
come to an immediate understanding."

" But Scrope advises me to proceed very cautiously."

" There may be excess of caution as well as too
little.   Something must be done.   I will speak to his
lordship if you like."

"I shall feel immensely obliged if you will.   I
should like to place the affair in your hands.   I
am confident you will manage it better than I can."

" I shall be able to put questions to him that your
ladyship could not.   Is he coming here to-day, may I
ask ? "

" I am not quite sure.   But he will dine here to-
morrow."

XI.

LADY THICKNESSE CONSULTS SIR BRIDGNORTH.

LORD COURLAND did not call on that morning; but
Scrope did, and had a private conference with Lady
Thicknesse in her boudoir.

He looked very grave as he addressed her.

" Your matrimonial scheme is at an end, my dear
aunt," he said.   " Courland has fallen desperately in
love with Mrs. Calverley."

Her ladyship uttered a cry of astonishment.

"He declares she is the most charming woman he ever met. I feel certain he will propose to her. Now what is to be done?"

"It seems embarrassing, certainly. But you need have no uneasiness. I have just been talking to her. He won't be accepted."

"Don't delude yourself, my dear aunt," he cried. "Mrs. Calverley would like very much to be Lady Courland, I feel quite sure. She may tell you otherwise. But it is so. She is an ambitious woman."

"What is to be done?" exclaimed Lady Thicknesse, in consternation.

"We must gain time. I have prevented him from calling here to-day."

"How did you manage that?"

"By telling him I wanted to ask Charles a few questions. Meantime, you must speak to Emmeline."

"But I very much fear she won't mind me," said Lady Thicknesse. "I'll get Sir Bridgnorth to do it."

"He's the very man for the purpose; and, fortunately, he's in the house. I left him just now with the ladies."

"Then beg him to come to me," said Lady Thicknesse.

Scrope needed no second bidding, but immediately quitted the boudoir, and reappeared a few minutes afterwards with the good-natured baronet.

"I won't interrupt the *tête-à-tête* which her ladyship wishes to have with you, Sir Bridgnorth," said Scrope as he left them together.

R

"Pray be seated, Sir Bridgnorth," said Lady Thicknesse. "I want your advice and assistance."

"Both are at your ladyship's service," he replied.

"I expected nothing less from you. You are a real friend. It is a very delicate matter on which I desire to consult you."

And she paused.

"Does it relate to a matrimonial alliance between Lord Courland and your niece, Miss Barfleur?"

"You have guessed right," replied Lady Thicknesse. You can assist me most materially in the affair, if you will. Emmeline, I know, has a very great regard, I may almost say affection, for you, and might possibly speak more freely to you than she would to me. Will you ascertain what her sentiments are respecting Lord Courland?"

"I can give your ladyship the information you desire at once," replied Sir Bridgnorth, "and shall really be glad to do so. Indeed, I have thought of speaking to you on the subject, but feared you might deem me impertinent. Any expectations your ladyship may have formed of such an alliance must be dismissed. It will never take place."

"You think so, Sir Bridgnorth?" said her ladyship, looking dreadfully chagrined.

"I am quite sure of it," he replied. "Miss Barfleur will never accept him."

"You would not make this assertion so positively without good reason, I am certain, Sir Bridgnorth," said Lady Thicknesse.

"I had the declaration from Miss Barfleur's own lips," he replied, "and was requested to repeat it to your ladyship. I am also permitted to mention a circumstance that will prevent any discussion on the subject."

" You are not about to tell me she is engaged, I hope, Sir Bridgnorth?" said her ladyship, manifesting fresh alarm.

" Such is the fact," he replied, quietly. " It is desirable you should know the truth."

" It is proper I should know the *whole* truth, Sir Bridgnorth," she rejoined. " To whom is my niece engaged? Speak frankly."

" To Chetwynd Calverley," he replied without hesitation.

Lady Thicknesse did not seem much surprised, for she expected the answer; but she said, in a haughty, decided tone:

" That union can never take place!"

A slight smile played on Sir Bridgnorth's kindly countenance.

" I do not see how it can be prevented," he said. " She is an heiress, and Lady Barfleur's consent has been obtained."

Lady Thicknesse looked thunderstruck, and remained silent for a few moments, and then said:

" Why have I been kept in ignorance of this engagement? I suppose Emmeline felt I should disapprove of it, as I do most decidedly!"

" I certainly think the matter ought to have been communicated to your ladyship," said Sir Bridgnorth. " But since the marriage, in all probability, will not take place for some time, I suppose it was not deemed necessary to mention it at present."

" That explanation does not satisfy me, Sir Bridgnorth! I feel highly offended. I suppose Mrs. Calverley has been in the dark as well as myself?"

"She has," replied Sir Bridgnorth. "And in her case, I think the caution was judicious. She is not to be trusted with any secrets but her own, and those she can keep. I shouldn't wonder if she wins the prize that has been offered to Miss Barfleur."

"It seems likely," said her ladyship. "There is one consolatory circumstance in this disagreeable affair; the marriage will not take place for some time. I trust it may be indefinitely postponed!"

Thinking the interview had lasted long, Sir Bridgnorth arose; but her ladyship would not let him depart thus, and said:

"Pray come and dine with me as usual. I shall expect you at eight. By that time, I hope I shall have got over my vexation. Don't imagine I shall make a scene! I never do make scenes. I shall say nothing to Emmeline till to-morrow. *Au revoir!*"

And she extended her hand to him.

As Sir Bridgnorth took the delicately white fingers, he felt inclined to raise them to his lips; but he didn't, and withdrew.

XII.

ANOTHER EXPLANATION.

MEANWHILE, another explanation took place in the drawing-room between Mrs. Calverley and Emmeline.

They were standing close beside a window, looking upon a square, and sufficiently removed from a central table, near which were seated Captain Danvers, with Chetwynd and his sister.

"I have brought you here, my love, to have a few words with you," commenced Mrs. Calverley. "I am commissioned by Lady Thicknesse to ask a question, which she doesn't like to ask herself. If you haven't already discovered it, I must tell you she has set her heart upon marrying you to Lord Courland."

"I am very much obliged to her!" said Emmeline. "But I suppose my consent will be first obtained?"

"That is the very point upon which I have undertaken to consult you," said Mrs. Calverley. "Should his lordship propose, are you inclined to accept him?"

"He is not likely to propose to me," replied Emmeline. "I may congratulate you on the conquest you have made."

"I am quite as indifferent to his lordship as you appear to be, my love," rejoined Mrs. Calverley.

"I shouldn't have supposed so!" laughed Emmeline. "But of course, I take your word for it. Pray tell my aunt I am sorry to disappoint her, but she has made a wrong choice for me!"

"May I add anything more? May I assign a motive for your conduct? May I tell her you are already engaged?"

"Tell her whatever you please, dear Mrs. Calverley; but make her clearly understand that no persuasion shall ever induce me to marry Lord Courland. I surrender him entirely to you!"

"Never mind me! But do tell me who is the highly-favoured individual you have chosen?"

"Can you not guess? There is but one person I could choose, and he is not very far off."

" Chetwynd ? " cried Mrs. Calverley.

" Yes."

" And you have accepted him ? "

Again the answer was in the affirmative. " He is indeed most fortunate ? " exclaimed Mrs. Calverley. " One question more and I have done."

" I know what you would ask," replied Emmeline. " Mamma has given her consent. But the marriage will not take place for some months."

" Oh, how delighted I am ! " cried Mrs. Calverley, with difficulty refraining from embracing her.

At this juncture Chetwynd arose. He had been watching them, and guessed what they were talking about.

As he approached, Mrs. Calverley sprang forward to meet him.

" Chetwynd," she said, " I have just received some information that has given me the greatest pleasure. I think I ought to have been let into the secret; but I am too much overjoyed to complain ! "

" I am glad the disclosure has been made," he said. " The maintenance of the secret has placed Emmeline in a false position."

" But no harm has ensued," observed the young lady. " I have only just discovered my aunt's scheme, or I should have acquainted her with the engagement. I now regret that I did not do so when I first came to town."

" And I am at liberty to explain all to Lady Thicknesse ? " inquired Mrs. Calverley.

" You will greatly oblige me," said Emmeline. " I shall be very glad to escape the task."

" I will go to her at once," said Mrs. Calverley.

And quitting the room, she repaired to the boudoir.

There she found that Sir Bridgnorth had been beforehand with her, and, explanations being unnecessary, she talked the matter over quietly with Lady Thicknesse, and endeavoured to reconcile her to the arrangement, apparently with some success.

Mrs. Calverley had quitted the boudoir rather more than half an hour, and Lady Thicknesse was alone, and lamenting the failure of her scheme, when Scrope again made his appearance.

His countenance had a singular expression, and he remained standing, while he said, in rather a stern voice :

" Don't give yourself any concern about Emmeline's imprudent engagement with Chetwynd Calverley, aunt. I have just learnt something that will enable me to put an end to it."

" You don't say so ! What is it ? " exclaimed Lady Thicknesse, in surprise.

" I cannot explain now," he rejoined. " Wait till to-morrow ! "

But finding her ladyship could not repress her curiosity, and determined not to gratify it, he abruptly quitted the boudoir, leaving her in a high state of excitement.

XIII.

A SOIRÉE DANSANTE.

A party was to be given that evening at the house in Belgrave Square ; but below stairs, not above.

Exceedingly indulgent to her servants, Lady

friends; and he had invited the Tankards, to whom he owed a return, and several others of our acquaintance—namely, Mrs. Tripp and the charming Clotilde; Mrs. Sicklemore and the fair Flora; Mr. and Mrs. Hartley, Harry Netterville, Pledger Dapp, and Larkins—to a *soirée dansante.*

Of course, the servants of the house were included, and they mustered very strong—footman, coachman, page, housekeeper, lady's-maid, housemaids, and kitchen maid. Nor must we omit to mention Rose, and Mrs. Calverley's lady's-maid, Laura, who had some pretension to good looks.

Most important, however, of all was the French cook, Monsieur Zephyrus, who next to Mr. Higgins himself, was the principal person in the establishment.

A very smart young man was Zephyrus, when not compelled by the duties of his vocation to disguise himself in a white apron, white *veste,* and white *bonnet-de-nuit.*

He now wore an evening dress, made by a fashionable tailor in the Boulevard Italien, the peculiar cut of which proclaimed its French origin; and, as he had a light figure, he looked very well in it.

Zephyrus was not bad-looking, and had a dark complexion, black eyes, and large black whiskers, of which he was not a little vain. When in full dress, as on the present occasion, he wore a *lorgnon* stuck in his right eye.

On the previous day he had paid a visit to his friend Sigebert Smart, whom he had known in Paris, and invited him and Madame Smart to the party. Both accepted the invitation with delight.

" In addition to a piano, brought from upstairs, and

on which Mrs. Tripp had kindly consented to perform, a violin, violoncello, and cornet had been provided by Mr. Higgins. Nothing, indeed, was neglected.

The large housekeeper's room, in which dancing was to take place, was brilliantly lighted up and decorated ; and supper, prepared by Monsieur Zephyrus himself, was to be served in the *salle à manger*. Nothing was seen of the kitchen.

Not till ten o'clock, when dinner and all other matters upstairs had been disposed of, did the company begin to assemble.

Of course they were obliged to descend the area steps; but, the passage once gained, and the doors thrown open, they were surprised by the splendour of the scene.

They were received by Mr. Higgins, who was supported by Monsieur Zephyrus.

First to arrive were the Tankards. Tom was very much struck by the appearance of Zephyrus, and wondered who he was, never supposing him to be a cook. His father told him he was a *cordon bleu*, but that did not enlighten him ; and the marked attentions paid by the gallant Frenchman to Madame Sigebert Smart, when she arrived with her husband, puzzled him still more. He could not understand how such a distinguished-looking personage could be on intimate terms with a *coiffeur* and his wife.

As soon as he got an opportunity, he said to Sigebert :

" Who's that very polite French gent talking to Madame ? "

" Monsieur Zephyrus," replied the *coiffeur*. " Don't you know him ? "

"I don't recollect seeing him before," remarked Tom. "The guv'nor says he's a *cordon bleu.* What does that mean?"

Scarcely able to refrain from laughing, Sigebert replied:

"It means that he's a knight of the Saint Esprit. The order was given him by Louis Napoleon. Chevalier Zephyrus is entitled to wear a broad blue ribbon, with a cross attached to it, but he doesn't put it on now."

"He seems a very condescending sort of fellow for a chevalier," said Tom. "No nonsensical pride about him."

"None whatever," replied Sigebert. "You'll find him very affable. But don't talk to him about cookery. He dislikes that subject."

"I'll take care to avoid it," said Tom.

By this time, the whole party having assembled—guests and inmates of the house—Mrs. Tripp was conducted to the piano by Higgins, and the musicians began to strike up.

Then it was that Zephyrus, who acted as master of the ceremonies, clapped his well-gloved hands, and exclaimed:

"*Messieurs, un quadrille—prenez vos dames!*"

"That means we're to take our partners for a quadrille. Ma'mzelle," said Tom, stepping up to Clotilde, "shall I have the honour?"

"Too late, Mr. Tom," she replied, coquettishly. "Already engaged to Monsieur Zephyrus."

"Ah, the Chevalier knows how to take care of himself, I perceive!" cried Tom.

"Yes. You'd better look quick, and secure Flora, or she'll be snapped up," said Clotilde.

Acting on the advice, Tom hurried off, but would have been too late if the thoughtful young lady had not reserved herself for him.

All the cavaliers seemed choosing partners, but the master of the ceremonies would only allow four couples in the first quadrille. These were himself and Clotilde, Tom Tankard and Flora, Harry Netterville and Rose, and Sigebert and Laura.

"Will you be our *vis-à-vis*, Monsieur Grandpot?" he said to Tom.

"With the greatest pleasure, Chevalier," replied our young friend. "But my name's not Grandpot; I'm Mr. Tom Tankard."

"*Mille pardons!*" exclaimed Zephyrus. "But we call a tankard a *grand pot d'argent*. Be pleased to take your place, Monsieur Tom."

The quadrille then commenced.

Monsieur Zephyrus danced with wonderful spirit and lightness, cutting cross capers, forward capers, side capers, back capers—now executing the *boree* step, the *courant* step, and the *gaillard* step—hopping, jumping, bounding, and ending with a pirouette that astonished all the beholders.

Tom Tankard tried to imitate him, but the performance was a mere caricature, and though it excited laughter, must be pronounced a failure.

Sigebert was more successful. He had figured at the Grand Chaumière at Paris, and treated the company to some of the fantastic steps he had seen performed there and at other *salles de danse* in the Bois de Boulogne.

Though very much amused by what he beheld, Harry Netterville did not indulge in any of these absurdities.

Both Flora and Clotilde danced very well, as they had had some practice at Cremorne, but Rose was very quiet.

A rigadoon followed, which again enabled Monsieur Zephyrus to display his grace and skill; then a valse, in which Flora fell to the share of the Frenchman, and Clotilde to Sigebert. Tom was obliged to content himself with Madame Sigebert, for Rose declined to dance with him.

When the valse was over, a country dance was called for by Mr. Higgins, who wished to dance with Mrs. Tankard, and led off with her. Almost everybody joined in this lively dance, which was carried on with the greatest spirit, and amid much laughter, for more than half an hour.

The elderly people seemed to enjoy it as much as the young folks, but Mr. Higgins and Mrs. Tankard could not go down a second time.

Monsieur Zephyrus, who was evidently quite captivated by Clotilde, induced her to dance with him, to the great disgust of Tom, who began to feel a little jealous of the gay Frenchman. However, Flora contrived to console him.

Harry Netterville and Rose thoroughly enjoyed the merry country dance, and did not feel in the least fatigued by their exertions.

The company then proceeded to supper; where, we have already explained.

The men-servants of the house, who were intended to wait, went in first. Mr. Higgins gave his arm to

Mrs. Tankard, and was followed by Mr. Tankard and Mrs. Tripp, Mr. Larkins and Mrs. Hartley, with the rest of the party.

A very elegant supper greeted them—quite a triumph of skill on the part of Monsieur Zephyrus, who had done his best. Iced champagne and moselle cup were to be had in plenty.

Tom Tankard was in raptures.

" By Jove ! " he cried ; " I never saw a nicer supper ! Lady Thicknesse must have a capital cook ! "

Monsieur Zeyhyrus, who chanced to be near him, smiled.

" Enchanted to find you are pleased with my performance, Monsieur Tom ! " he said.

" *Your* performance, Chevalier ! " cried Tom. " You don't mean to say you prepared the supper ? "

" *Mais oui, mon cher,*" said Zephyrus, proudly. " I, and no one else. Don't you know I am Lady Thicknesse's cook ? "

" Give you my word I wasn't aware of it till this moment," cried Tom. " I was told you are a *cordon bleu.*"

" And so I am," said Zephyrus. " But don't you understand that a *cordon bleu* means a first-rate cook ? —that's my description."

For a few moments Tom seemed lost in astonishment. He then exclaimed :

" The guv'nor's completely taken me in ! "

The company did not seem inclined to leave the supper table, and no wonder, considering the excellence of the repast and the abundant supply of champagne.

But Mr. Higgins, who was very careful, thought

they had sat long enough, and moved off to the ball-room, where the music again struck up, and dancing recommenced with even more spirit than before.

The only person who looked discontented was Tom Tankard. He had drunk a good deal of champagne, and it had got into his head and made him rather quarrelsome. He felt jealous and angry at the evident preference shown by Clotilde for Monsieur Zephyrus.

They were again engaged in a polka. Ordinarily, Tom was very fond of a polka; but on this occasion he refused to join in the dance, but stood on one side and noticed the passionate glances bestowed by the Frenchman on the inconstant charmer. His breast swelled; but he was obliged to devour his rage.

When the polka ceased several couples proceeded to the supper-room for a glass of champagne and amongst them were Zephyrus and Clotilde. In a minute or two the others came back; but the Frenchman and the fair syren did not appear.

Maddened by jealousy, Tom went in search of them.

As he approached the supper-room, the door of which was partly open, he perceived at a glance that they were alone together, and that Zephyrus, who was seated beside her, was still pouring forth tender speeches in her ear; but they were too much engrossed by each other to notice him.

His first impulse was to rush in upon them; but hearing his own name pronounced, he stood still.

" I hope you don't care for that *grand nigaud*, Tom Tankard," said Zephyrus. " Indeed, it is hardly possible you can—he is so frightfully ugly, besides being ridiculous and stupid. But I believe he flatters him-self you are in love with him."

"He certainly pays me a great deal of attention," replied Clotilde; "but if he fancies I am in love with him, he is very much mistaken. In fact, to confess the truth, I am becoming rather tired of him."

"That gives me hopes," said Zephyrus. "I shall try and please you better."

"You please me very much," said Clotilde. "You dance charmingly—much better than Tom."

"He cannot dance at all," said Zephyrus, contemptuously. "But dancing is the least of my accomplishments. I am a skilful musician; I ride well, drive well, shoot well——"

"And cook well," added Clotilde. "The supper you have given us was perfect."

"Ah, you shall taste a wedding breakfast; but not prepared for that odious Tom Tankard!"

"For whom, then?" inquired Clotilde.

Before an answer could be returned, Tom rushed into the room, and quite frightened Clotilde by his looks.

"So you are getting tired of me, are you?" he cried to the fickle girl. "How long have you been tired? Only this very morning you said you liked me better than any one else; but this French cook has made you change your mind. He may have you, and welcome. I've done with you for ever."

"You don't mean it, dear Tom?" she cried, penitentially.

"Yes, I do," he rejoined; "and I'm glad I've found you out in time. But I can't say much for your choice!" he added, casting a glance of scorn at his rival.

"What have you to say against me, saar?" cried

Zephyrus, with a fierce gesticulation, and shaking his clenched hand at Tom.

" You won't frighten me, monsieur," observed Tom, quietly. " Consider yourself thrashed."

" But I won't ! " cried Zephyrus. " I never was thrashed, and never will be ! "

" Yes you will ! " cried Tom.

And being somewhat of a bruiser, he dealt him a smart tap on the nose, or somewhere near it, that knocked him backwards against the table, upsetting a number of glasses with a tremendous crash.

Clotilde ran screaming out of the room.

" *Diable, vous avez poché mon œil au beurre noir, monsieur !* " cried Zephyrus, as he picked himself up. " But you shall pay for the affront with your life's blood ! "

" Don't be afraid, monsieur," said Tom, stoutly. " I'll give you satisfaction in any way you like ; sword, pistol, or this ! " he added, holding up his clenched fist.

" But the duel is no longer allowed in your country," said Zephyrus.

" Then we'll settle our quarrel in yours," rejoined Tom. " I'll go over with you to Boulogne, or Dieppe, whenever you please."

While these menaces were exchanged, Mr. Higgins, Mr. Tankard, and several others had entered the room, alarmed by the crash of glass and Clotilde's cries.

They instantly perceived that a conflict had taken place.

" What's the meaning of this disturbance, gentle-men ? " cried Mr. Higgins. " Can't you spend the evening quietly ? "

"I'm ashamed of you, Tom!" cried Mr. Tankard.

"The quarrel wasn't of my seeking, guv'nor," said the young man.

"But it won't end here," cried Zephyrus, holding a handkerchief to his face.

"I hope it will," rejoined Higgins.

"Tom," said his father, sternly, "I insist on your making an apology to Monsieur Zephyrus."

"*I* make an apology?" rejoined the youth. "Don't expect it, guv'nor."

"Nor will I accept an apology," said Zephyrus. "I will have his life! Sigebert," he added to the *coiffeur,* who had entered the room with the others, "you shall be my *parrain*—my second."

"With great pleasure," replied the other.

"If you talk of fighting a duel, I'll have you both bound over to keep the peace," said Higgins. "But come, we've had quite enough of this nonsense; shake hands like good fellows."

"I'm quite ready," said Tom. "I'll either fight or make friends, as suits Monsieur Zephyrus best."

This was said in such a good-natured way that it pleased the Frenchman, and he seemed disposed to make up the quarrel.

"I'm sorry I hurt you, for I don't believe you're half a bad fellow," said Tom. "There, will that suffice?"

"*Parfaitement,*" replied Zephyrus, taking the hand offered him.

"Bravo!" cried Higgins. "Now let us all have a glass of champagne, and then we'll go back to the ball-room. We must have a reel."

"No more dancing for me," said Tom.

s

"Nonsense!" cried his father. "I insist that you dance with Clotilde."

"Do you consent, Monsieur?" said Tom, with a droll look at Zephyrus. "She now belongs to you."

"You shall have her back altogether, if you like," replied the Frenchman.

"Nay, I won't tax your generosity so far," said Tom, with a laugh.

Champagne was here handed round, and, after the brimming glasses had been emptied, they all repaired to the ball-room.

Clotilde flew to Tom on his appearance, and he was foolish enough to forgive her.

A reel was called, in which all the company took part, except poor Monsieur Zephyrus, who was obliged to apply a piece of brown paper, steeped in brandy, to his injured orb.

<hr>

XIV.

AN UNPLEASANT INQUIRY.

Next morning, about eleven o'clock, Chetwynd found his way, as usual, from the "Grosvenor Hotel" to the house in Belgrave Square.

He had breakfasted very pleasantly with Sir Bridgnorth Charlton, who was staying at the same hotel as himself, and had not the slightest idea that anything disagreeable awaited him; but he was rather struck by Higgins's manner, as he let him in.

Evidently the butler had something to communicate.

It may be proper to mention that, since Chetwynd's resumption of his own name, and appearance in his true character at Lady Thicknesse's, no allusion to the past had ever been made by Higgins, who had always been particularly respectful.

"Mr. Calverley," he said, as they stood together in the vestibule, "I must prepare you for an interview with her ladyship and Mr. Scrope Danvers. They are in the dining-room, and I am directed to conduct you thither on your arrival. I know nothing, but should any questions be asked me, you may rely on my discretion."

"I am greatly obliged to you, Higgins," replied Chetwynd; "but you are at liberty to tell all you know respecting me. I desire no concealment. Of course, I should be glad to throw a veil over the past if I could; but that is impossible."

No more was said.

The butler ushered him into the dining-room, where he found Lady Thicknesse and her nephew.

Her ladyship received him with her customary good-nature, and begged him to be seated; but Scrope's manner was cold and haughty.

After a few preliminary remarks by Lady Thicknesse, Scrope interposed, and in a very grave tone said:

"Will you allow me to ask you a few questions, Mr. Calverley? I shall be sorry to give you pain, but circumstances compel me to adopt this disagreeable course."

"Since the questions you desire to put refer, no doubt, to a very painful period of my life, it might, perhaps, have been better if you had spoken to me in private," rejoined Chetwynd. "But proceed."

" Pray understand that it is at my particular request that Lady Thicknesse is present," said Scrope. " We have long been aware that some time ago you were in great difficulties, and on bad terms with your father and stepmother ; but, until very lately neither of us knew you had attempted to commit suicide."

" What you have heard is quite true, sir," replied Chetwynd. " I was driven to desperation by my own folly ; but I have never ceased to feel deep remorse for the attempt, and I daily thank Heaven that I was saved from the commission of the sinful act."

Hitherto Lady Thicknesse had looked down, but she now regarded him with an interest she had never felt before.

" These sentiments do you credit, sir," said Scrope. " But I must now ask what steps you took immediately after the attempt ? "

" I endeavoured to obtain employment."

" In what way ? "

" I decline to answer that question, sir," replied Chetwynd.

" As you please, sir," said Scrope. " I can easily obtain the requisite information."

And he rang the bell. The summons was promptly answered by the butler.

" Higgins," observed Scrope, " when Charles Brown-low, the former footman, was discharged, did Mr. Tankard apply for the place ? "

" He did, sir."

" For his son ? "

" No, sir ; for a young man named Walter Liddel."

" Are you certain that was his real name ? "

" I can't be quite sure, sir," replied Higgins. " At any rate it was the name given me by Mr. Tankard."

" Did you see the party spoken of? "

" Oh, yes, sir ! I saw him at Mr. Tankard's house, and was very much pleased with his appearance. The livery suited him extremely well."

" Oh ! then he had on the livery ? "

" Yes, sir. I wished to see how it fitted, and it *did* fit him to admiration. I never saw such a fine-looking footman in my life."

" And you engaged him ? "

" At once, sir. I thought him a great catch."

" Did he enter on the situation ? "

" Something prevented him. Either his father died quite suddenly, and left him a large fortune, or else he married ; I don't recollect which."

" Be serious, if you please, Higgins. Have you ever seen him since ? "

" Not that I am aware of, sir."

" Should you know him again if you saw him ? "

" I don't think I should, sir. I only saw him in livery, and a handsome livery like ours sets a man off to advantage. Are these all the questions you propose to ask me, sir? "

" One more, and I have done ; and I beg you will answer it distinctly. Do you see him now ? "

" Walter Liddel ? No, sir."

" You are a very cautious fellow, Higgins, but it won't do," said Scrope.

" Speak out, Higgins," said Chetwynd. " I have no wish for concealment."

" Now I look again," remarked the butler to Scrope, " I should say there is a very strong resemblance between Walter Liddel and Mr. Chetwynd Calverley."

"Enough!" cried Scrope. "You may retire."

Higgins bowed, and left the room.

"And now," said Chetwynd, "may I ask the meaning of this inquiry?"

"My object is merely to establish a fact," replied Scrope. "Lady Thicknesse and myself have just learnt, to our great surprise and annoyance, that our charming relative, Emmeline Barfleur, has had the imprudence to form an engagement with you."

"Imprudence, sir!" cried Chetwynd.

"I might use a stronger term, but that will suffice. It cannot be very agreeable to those connected with her, that the daughter of the proud Sir Leycester Barfleur, who might marry any one she pleases, should throw herself away upon a—footman!"

Chetwynd absolutely started, but controlled himself by a great effort.

"I now understand your anxiety to secure Lady Thicknesse's presence at our interview," he said. "You have aimed a cowardly blow at me, but it has failed in effect. I treat your observation with scorn!"

Then, turning to Lady Thicknesse, he added, "Since your nephew refuses to give me credit for acting like a gentleman, I must inform your ladyship that Emmeline is acquainted with the ridiculous circumstance of which so much has been made, and it merely excited her laughter. I have confessed all my follies and faults to her—*all!*—and she has forgiven me, because she believes in my promises of amendment."

As he spoke the door opened, and Emmeline herself entered the room, accompanied by Mildred and Sir Bridgnorth Charlton.

XV.

EVIDENCE IN CHETWYND'S FAVOUR.

"I THOUGHT I should be required as an important witness in the inquiry which I understood is going on here," said Emmeline, stepping quickly forward, "so I have come to give my evidence."

"You are too late, my love," said Lady Thicknesse. "The inquiry is over."

"Has it ended satisfactorily?" asked Emmeline.

"Not to me," replied Chetwynd. "Your cousin Scrope has endeavoured to show that if you had not intentionally been kept in the dark as to certain matters, you would not have entered into an engagement which he holds to be utterly unworthy of you. Nor has he acknowledged his error, though every assurance has been given him that he is mistaken."

"Will my amiable but incredulous cousin accept my assurance to the same effect?" observed Emmeline. "He shakes his head, and declines to answer. He is, therefore, out of court. Nevertheless, I will tell him, and all who choose to listen to me, that Mr. Chetwynd Calverley has behaved in the most honourable manner, and has concealed nothing from me. I will also tell my proud cousin, and he may make what use he pleases of the information, that I have engaged myself to as good a gentleman as himself, and that nothing that he or any one else can say will induce me to break my promise."

"Thank you, from my heart!" said Chetwynd.

"Now is your time to speak, if you have anything to say," observed Emmeline to her cousin.

But Scrope shrugged his shoulders, and declined the challenge.

"Then I will tell you one thing, which you don't know, and, perhaps, won't believe when you are told it," said Emmeline. "Chetwynd himself proposed to go through a period of probation before our engagement took place: and he readily agreed that the marriage should be deferred for a year. Will that content you?"

"I should be better pleased if it were postponed altogether!" muttered Scrope.

"Let me say a word for my friend Chetwynd," interposed Sir Bridgnorth. "As yet, it is somewhat early to declare that he has reformed, but I sincerely believe in his professions, and I feel persuaded he will carry them out."

"I won't disappoint you, Sir Bridgnorth!" said Chetwynd, earnestly.

"I have entire confidence in you," rejoined the baronet.

"And so have I," said Lady Thicknesse. "I am so well satisfied with the explanation that has taken place, that I give my full consent to Emmeline's engagement."

"I am delighted to hear you say so, dearest aunt!" cried the young lady. "You make me quite happy. It would have grieved me to incur your displeasure. I don't care a bit about Scrope!"

"Won't you even give me credit for the desire to serve you?" said Scrope.

"No. I am displeased by your uncalled-for interference. You do more harm than good!"

"Before deciding against my friend Chetwynd,

Scrope," said Sir Bridgnorth, "you ought to give him a fair trial."

" That is all I desire," remarked Chetwynd. " Six months hence, if I have not proved myself worthy of Emmeline, I will retire from the field."

" I take you at your word," said Scrope. " Am I to decide the point ? "

" No ; because you have shown yourself unfair and ungenerous," said Emmeline.

At this juncture, Captain Danvers entered the room, and uttered an exclamation of surprise on seeing so many persons present.

" I wondered where you all were," he said. " What important affair have you been discussing ? "

" A marriage ! " replied Lady Thicknesse.

" And everybody, except Scrope, is pleased with it ! " said Emmeline.

" Oh, never mind him ! " remarked the captain. " He'll come round to the general opinion."

" Don't be too sure of that ! " said Scrope.

" Ten to one you come round before a month ! " said his brother.

" Done ! " rejoined Scrope.

" I wish I could bet ! " said Emmeline. " I'd lay fifty to one that in less than a week Scrope will own his mistake, and ask my pardon ! "

" I'll back you ! " said Sir Bridgnorth, looking at Scrope.

" Taken ! " rejoined that person.

" And now let us go up-stairs," said Lady Thick-nesse.

" Not to the drawing-room, dear aunt," rejoined Captain Danvers.

"Why not there?" inquired her ladyship, surprised.

"Because we should interrupt a very tender interview," said the captain. "Lord Courland and Mrs. Calverley are in the drawing-room, dear aunt."

"I should think the affair must be settled by this time," observed Scrope.

"Give them another quarter of an hour," said the captain.

The proposition was unanimously agreed to.

That morning, Mrs. Calverley's lady's-maid, Laura, had delivered to her mistress a little *billet doux* from Lord Courland, entreating the favour of a private interview.

The request was granted, and, through the instrumentality of Mr. Higgins, who was consulted by Laura, it was arranged that the meeting should take place in the drawing-room, the obliging butler undertaking that the pair should not be interrupted.

Never had the charming widow looked more beautiful than on that morning.

As she sat in the drawing-room awaiting Lord Courland's appearance, her breast swelled with triumph, and her eyes shone with more than their customary splendour.

Great pains had been taken with her toilette by Laura, who assured her, with a smile, that she looked enchanting, and added that there was not another person in the house to be compared with her.

The fair widow believed what was said, and might be excused for doing so under the circumstances, since she had at once carried off the grand prize from those whom she regarded as competitors.

Lord Courland was enraptured when he beheld her.

He did not throw himself literally at her feet when the discreet Higgins, who had ushered him into the room, had retired, but he manifested all the ardour of an impassioned lover.

He gave utterance to a few expressions of delight as he sat down beside her on the sofa, and pressed her hand to his lips, but his looks were far more eloquent than his words.

XVI.

LORD COURLAND PROPOSES TO MRS. CALVERLEY.

To many a courageous man a proposal is a formidable business, but Lord Courland certainly did not appear to find it so; nor was it necessary for the beautiful widow to give him any encouragement.

"Need I say I adore you?" he exclaimed. "You must be conscious that from the first moment I beheld you I was fascinated by your charms."

She smiled softly, but made no audible response.

He continued in the same passionate strain.

"Let me have a word to say I am not an object of indifference to you—that you requite my love."

She regarded him more tenderly than before, but spoke not.

He could not misunderstand the look.

"You love me!" he cried. "Your eyes confess more than your lips are willing to avow! You force me to snatch an answer from them!" he added, suiting the action to the word.

"Now you are mine, Teresa," he continued, still holding her hand. "Soon to be Viscountess Courland, hereafter Countess of Richborough. But you are silent. Speak, I conjure you! Tell me you are content!"

"Can you doubt it?" she replied, with a look that seemed to penetrate the inmost recesses of his breast.

"And you really, truly love me?"

"Really, truly!" she rejoined. "I never loved till now!"

"May I credit this?" he remarked, somewhat incredulously. "I am willing to be deceived."

"I repeat, you are the only person I have ever really loved."

Another kiss followed the gratifying assurance, which might possibly have been correct.

"Are you ambitious, Teresa?" asked the enamoured young nobleman.

"I do not think so," she rejoined. "I am influenced by your agreeable qualities, not by your rank. Though a recommendation, your title would not have gained you my hand."

"But I ought to tell you I am not very rich, and I shall not have much during my father's lifetime."

"It matters not," she replied, with a smile. "I have a tolerably good income, and Ouselcroft is rather a pretty place, as I think you will own when you see it."

"No doubt. Scrope says you have one of the nicest seats in Cheshire."

"I cannot contradict him, since I entertain the same opinion myself. But you must come and see it.

I shall not prolong my stay in town. Possibly I may return to-morrow."

" So soon ? "

" I have nothing to detain me, and, under present circumstances, I shall be glad to get back."

" It will be far more agreeable to me to see you at your own house, than here," observed Lord Courland.

" Then be it so," she replied. " Come as soon as you please."

" Shall I bring Scrope Danvers with me ? "

" By all means ; I have plenty of room. Besides, Brackley, Lady Barfleur's residence, is only a few miles off."

" Miss Calverley resides with you, I believe ? "

" Yes ; and a great delight she is to me. I couldn't do without her."

" And Chetwynd—pardon my asking so many questions—is he also with you ? "

" For the present. I hope you like him ? "

" I like him immensely. I'm sure we shall get on together uncommonly well. And now, am I at liberty to inform Lady Thicknesse and Scrope that you have consented to become Lady Courland ? "

" Yes ; I think it will be quite proper to do so," she replied.

Not many minutes afterwards voices were heard without, the door was thrown open by Higgins, and Lady Thicknesse and most of the persons whom we left below entered the room.

As Lord Courland arose and advanced to meet her ladyship, she could not fail to be struck by his joyous air.

" I hope I may congratulate your lordship ? " she

"Do I look like a rejected suitor?" he remarked.

"Not exactly," she replied. "I should say all has gone well."

"Yes; my suit has prospered," he said. "But I am entirely indebted to your ladyship for the treasure I have gained."

"That you have gained a treasure, I am certain," rejoined Lady Thicknesse. "But I do not see how you owe it to me."

"Is it not here that I have found it?" he said. "But for you, I might never have met the only person who can make me happy."

By this time Mrs. Calverley herself had come forward to participate in the general felicitations.

"What think you of this proposed marriage?" observed Sir Bridgnorth, in a low tone, to Chetwynd.

"I think very little about it," replied the other. "It will never take place."

"Wherefore not?"

"I cannot explain myself," said Chetwynd; "but, depend upon it, I am right."

"Well, time will show," said Sir Bridgnorth. "I am going down to Charlton to-morrow. Come, and spend a few days with me. I feel certain there will be a general move."

And so it proved.

No sooner did Mrs. Calverley announce her intention of returning to Ouselcroft on the morrow, than Emmeline and Mildred said they should return at the same time, though Lady Thicknesse besought them to stay a few days longer.

At last, when she could not prevail upon them to remain, she declared she would go down to Haslemere for a short time, and while in Cheshire would come and spend a week with her sister, Lady Barfleur, at Brackley Hall.

Determined not to be left out, Captain Danvers likewise volunteered to go to Brackley. Indeed, from the various plans proposed and discussed, there seemed every prospect that the whole party would soon meet again in the country.

As it was quite impossible that Emmeline and Mildred could part with Rose, it was arranged that she should accompany them; and in the mean time the little damsel was allowed to take leave of her friends.

One of the best dinners Monsieur Zephyrus had ever served formed the farewell entertainment. The merit of the repast was fully appreciated; but the company was not so lively as heretofore.

Next day the party broke up.

Though the purpose for which she had assembled her guests had not been accomplished, good-natured Lady Thicknesse was content, and her congratulations to Mrs. Calverley were sincere.

As to the fair widow, who had now reached the summit of her ambition, she did not attempt to disguise her satisfaction.

Since she had formed the engagement with Lord Courland, a slight but perceptible change had taken place in her demeanour. Her manner to Mildred was more haughty.

Before her departure she had a private conference with her noble suitor, when a good many matters were talked over, but in the pleasantest way possible. In fact, all seemed *couleur de rose.*

Lord Courland attended her to the station, and, while bidding her adieu, she reminded him that in three days she should expect him at Ouselcroft.

"Doubt not you will see me," he rejoined. In the same railway carriage with Mrs. Calverley were two young ladies, a lady's maid, and two gentlemen. The gentlemen were Chetwynd and Sir Bridgnorth, who were about to accompany the ladies to Chester.

The lady's-maid was remarkably pretty; but there was a tear in her bright eye, the cause of which will be understood when we mention that on the platform stood a tall, black-whiskered young man, gazing wistfully at her.

Harry Netterville—for it was he—did not dare to approach the carriage, but waved his hand, as the snorting engine started on its journey and bore his love away.

End of the Fifth Book.

Book the Sixth.

THE CLAUSE IN MR. CALVERLEY'S WILL.

I.

OLD NORRIS QUESTIONS LAURA.

CARRIAGES, ordered by telegraph, were waiting for the ladies at Chester, and conveyed them to their respective destinations.

Mrs. Calverley, attended by Laura, drove direct to Ouselcroft. Emmeline and Mildred, accompanied by Rose, who had now got over her grief, and was full of curiosity to behold her new abode, proceeded to Brackley Hall.

Sir Bridgnorth and Chetwynd stopped to dine at the "Queen's Hotel," and then went back to the nearest point on the line to Charlton Hall, where they arrived about nine o'clock.

As a matter of course, the important news that their mistress was engaged to be married to Lord Courland was immediately communicated to the household by Laura, and caused a great sensation— some of the servants being pleased, while the others did not exactly know how their own particular interests might be affected.

The unexpected intelligence produced a singular effect upon Norris. For a time, he remained absorbed

T

in thought, neither expressing approval nor disapproval. He then called Laura into the butler's pantry, and, begging her to be seated, said :

"This is a very sudden affair, Laura. I can't understand it!"

"You must be very stupid, Mr. Norris! Can't you understand that a young nobleman like Lord Courland may easily fall over head and ears in love with such a captivating lady as Mrs. Calverley? I wasn't surprised at all. I felt sure she would carry him off, and so she did. The girls hadn't a chance with her. Mr. Higgins told me his lordship never said a tender word to either of them. I dare say it has been a great disappointment to Lady Thicknesse; but Mrs. Calverley can't help that."

"It's a great match to make," observed Norris— "a very great match! Is the wedding-day fixed?"

"Bless you, no!" exclaimed Laura. "Why, his lordship only proposed yesterday! A deal will have to be done before the marriage takes place."

"You're right," remarked Norris, drily. "What does Miss Mildred think of it?"

"I can't tell," replied Laura. "But it's perfectly immaterial what she thinks. Mrs. Calverley hasn't consulted her, and doesn't mean to consult her. But I don't fancy she likes it. Not that she cares for his lordship, for I believe she has made it up with Captain Danvers. However, I'm not in the secret, for the girls have got a lady's-maid of their own, and she doesn't talk much. But if that's the case we shall have a lot of marriages before long."

"How so, Laura?" inquired Norris.

"Why, it's certain Miss Barfleur has accepted Mr. Chetwynd!"

"Accepted Mr. Chetwynd!" exclaimed the old butler. "That's good news, indeed—too good to be true, I'm afraid!"

"Oh, no, it's quite correct," rejoined Laura. "Mr. Higgins told me there was a great consultation about it yesterday. Lady Thicknesse and Mr. Scrope Danvers, it seems, object to the match; but Miss Barfleur is determined to have him, and when a young lady makes up her mind opposition is useless, Mr. Norris!"

"Especially when the young lady is a great heiress!" rejoined the butler. "Now tell me something about our new master, Laura, for I suppose we shall have to call his lordship 'master' before long. Is he handsome?"

"Well, there is a difference of opinion on that point, Mr. Norris," she replied. "But he has a very stylish look, and is extremely affable in his manner. In short, he looks like a person of rank. But he's coming here in a few days, and then you'll be able to judge for yourself."

"Coming here, is he?" cried Norris, gruffly. "I'd rather he kept away. I suppose he wants to see whether the place will suit him?"

"Being engaged, he must take it whether it suits him or not," observed Laura.

"Ah, you are a wit, Miss Laura!" said the butler. "Well, the description you give of Lord Courland is satisfactory. But I shall be sorry to see my old master's property pass into other hands. Have you any idea what Mr. Chetwynd thinks of the match?"

"Not the slightest," replied Laura; "except that I feel certain it can't be satisfactory to him or his sister."

"Impossible—quite impossible!" cried Norris.

"Such is Mr. Higgins's opinion," observed Laura.

"Your Mr. Higgins seems a very sensible man," remarked Norris. "I should like to have some talk with him."

"You would find him most agreeable, as well as very shrewd," said Laura. "You will be pleased, I'm sure, to hear that he thinks very highly of Mr. Chetwynd."

"Another proof of his discernment," said Norris. "By-the-bye, where is our young master? Have you left him in town?"

"He came with us as far as Chester, but he has gone to Charlton Hall with Sir Bridgnorth for a few days."

"He would have done better to come on here. And Miss Mildred, you say, has gone to Brackley with Miss Barfleur? Well, a great change is at hand. It won't affect you, Laura; but it will affect me. Lord Courland will find me too old. He will require a younger and smarter butler, and I shall be dismissed."

"Oh, I hope not, dear Mr. Norris!" cried Laura. "That would grieve me excessively!"

"It will be so, my dear," he replied; "and I almost think Mrs. Calverley herself will be glad to get rid of me."

"If she does, she will provide for you."

"I am not sure of that. Old servants are not always rewarded—very rarely, indeed, I should say. Ah! if my good old master had lived, it would have been different! But I feel convinced I shall not retain my place unless something happens; and it *may* happen!" he added, significantly.

" What do you mean, Mr. Norris ? "

" I can't explain my meaning. But perhaps, on consideration, Mrs. Calverley may deem it expedient to keep me on."

" I'll give her a hint," said Laura, as she quitted the room.

II.

THE CABINET.

ON going up-stairs, after looking for her mistress in the bed-chamber, where she had left her, Laura proceeded to a small cabinet, in which the late Mr. Calverley was wont to transact his private business, write his letters, and hold consultations with his tenants and others. Here, in a large oak chest, all the old gentleman's deeds and bulky documents were deposited, while an escritoire contained his smaller papers, account-books, and memoranda.

On tapping at the door of the cabinet, Laura was bidden by her mistress to come in.

From the expression of Mrs. Calverley's countenance it was clear that something had gone wrong, and the sharp lady's-maid scarcely needed any information on the point when she observed that several of the escritoire drawers were pulled out.

" You can't find something, I perceive, ma'am ? " said Laura. " Can I help you ? "

" You'll do little good, Laura," replied the lady. " I've searched these drawers most carefully, and can't find what I want."

" Is it a letter, may I venture to ask ? " said Laura.

"No; it's much more important than a letter," replied Mrs. Calverley. "Nothing less than my late husband's will."

"Good gracious, ma'am!" exclaimed Laura. "I hope you haven't lost it?"

"Lost it?—no. Besides, it wouldn't much matter if I had, since the will has been proved, but I can't conceive what has become of it. I placed it in one of those drawers myself. I hope it has not been stolen."

"It couldn't be stolen, ma'am, if it was safely locked up in one of those drawers," said Laura. "I wish you'd let me search for it."

"It will be useless, but you may try."

On this, Laura turned over the contents of the drawers, which were chiefly old letters and memoranda, but without success.

"It's gone, no doubt, ma'am," she said.

"Yes; I felt sure you wouldn't find it," remarked her mistress. "The occurrence is most vexatious, but I won't worry myself any more about it now. I shall see Mr. Carteret in the morning. You know I've telegraphed to him to come to me?"

"Oh, yes, ma'am; and I guessed what you wanted to consult him about," rejoined Laura, with a knowing look.

"Tell me, Laura," said Mrs. Calverley, "what do your fellow-servants say about my engagement with Lord Courland? Speak freely; I should like to know the truth."

"In general, they are very much pleased, ma'am; but old Mr. Norris is rather afraid he shall lose his place. He fancies his lordship may prefer a younger butler."

" Well that is just possible," remarked Mrs. Calverley. " Norris is a faithful old servant, and I am greatly attached to him, but he is growing super-annuated."

" I think it might be prudent to keep him on for a time, ma'am," said Laura, with a certain significance, " since he has lived so long in the family."

Mrs. Calverley looked inquiringly at her.

" Has he said anything to you, Laura ? "

" Only that he hoped his services might not be forgotten, but he said it in a way that meant a great deal. I think it would be well not to get rid of him at present, ma'am."

" I have no intention of doing so," replied Mrs. Calverley. " I have a great regard for him, as you know."

" So I told him, ma'am."

" Does he doubt it ? "

" He seems uneasy and resentful; and, unless quieted, I think he may make mischief."

" In that case, his dismissal would be unavoidable. But I hope he will display better judgment. Assure him that I have not the slightest idea of parting with him, and that it will be entirely his own fault if he does not remain here for many years longer."

" I will tell him what you say, ma'am," replied Laura ; " and I am confident it will give him great satisfaction. You have no further commands for me, I suppose ? "

" I would rather you didn't mention down-stairs that the will is missing. It will be time enough to make inquiries about it to-morrow when I have

consulted Mr. Carteret. I shall see you again before
I retire to rest."

"Certainly, ma'am," replied Laura, as she withdrew.

Left alone, Mrs. Calverley locked up all the
drawers of the escritoire, and then sat down to
reflect.

That the will had been abstracted she now felt
certain; but by whom?—and with what design?

At one moment her suspicions alighted on old
Norris; but she instantly rejected the supposition, as
inconsistent with his character. Besides, she could
see no motive for the theft, since the instrument
would be valueless to him in every way. Again, how
could he know that it was placed in the escritoire?—
and had he a key of the drawer? No, no; Norris
could not be the thief.

But who else could have taken it?

Unable to answer the question, she turned her
thoughts to other matters.

Mrs. Calverley's feelings were of a mingled
character. Though pride and triumph predominated,
her anxieties had increased, and every step she took
seemed fraught with difficulty.

But she shook off all misgivings, and congratulat-
ing herself on her splendid achievement, determined
at whatever risk, and whatever might be the consequences, to carry out the important arrangement she
had made.

III.

HOW THE WILL WAS FOUND.

MRS. CALVERLEY, as already intimated, had sent a telegraphic message from London to Mr. Carteret, desiring him to come to her next morning at Ouselcroft; and she gave him a hint of the business on which she wished to consult him, by mentioning that she expected Lord Courland.

Accordingly, about ten o'clock next morning, in compliance with the summons he had received, Mr. Carteret made his appearance, and was conducted by Norris to the cabinet just described, where he found the beautiful widow seated at a desk, with writing materials before her.

"I am so much obliged to you for coming to me, Mr. Carteret," she said, giving him a very warm welcome. "I want to see you most particularly. Pray sit down!"

"If I am not mistaken, madam, you are about to form an important matrimonial alliance?" he remarked.

"You have guessed rightly, Mr. Carteret," she said, with a smile. "I went up to town a few days ago perfectly free, and have returned engaged."

"To Lord Courland?"

"To his lordship."

"Accept my congratulations," he said, rather gravely. "But I am obliged to treat the affair as a matter of business, and must dismiss all sentiment. Does his lordship propose to make a handsome settlement upon you?"

"No doubt he would, if it were in his power; but he is unable to do so."

"I feared not," replied Carteret. "But I hope he doesn't expect a settlement to be made on him?"

"I rather think he does," replied the lady.

"But surely you have not made any promise to this effect?" observed Carteret.

"Indeed, I have, sir," she rejoined. "You look surprised. But I really could not do otherwise. I have promised to settle half my property upon him."

"But how will you fulfil your promise?"

"I see no difficulty in the way," she rejoined. "I have only to give you the necessary instructions."

"If that were all, it would be easy enough. But I can scarcely conceive it possible you can be in ignorance of——"

"In ignorance of what?" she hastily interrupted.

"Of the clause in your late husband's will, which directs that in the event of your marrying again, the whole of the property shall go to Mildred. Thus you will have nothing more than the settlement made upon you before your marriage."

"Is this so?" asked Mrs. Calverley, with some astonishment. "I was not aware of it."

"It is exactly as I state," he replied. "I am amazed to find you have not read the will."

"I *have* read it," she cried. "But I did not notice the clause you mention."

"I will show it you in a moment if you will give me the will," he said.

"I fear the will has been stolen," she rejoined.

"Stolen?" he ejaculated.

"Yes; I wished to refer to it last evening, but could not find it."

"Had you put it in a safe place?"

"I put it in one of the drawers of this escritoire. The drawers were all locked, but the will was gone!"

"Have you examined the drawers to-day?" asked Carteret.

"I have not, because I consider further search completely useless."

"I should like to satisfy myself before making inquiries," said Carteret.

Mrs. Calverley unlocked the top drawer, and opened it, and had no sooner done so, than Mr. Carteret sprang forward, exclaiming:

"Why, there it is!"

Had it come there by magic?

Mrs. Calverley could scarcely believe her eyes.

"Are you certain you examined this drawer?" said Carteret.

"Quite. Laura searched it after me."

"But how came the will back?"

"That I cannot explain," replied Mrs. Calverley. "But it is clear one of the servants has a key that fits this lock. I scarcely like to say so—but I suspect Norris."

"I can't believe the old man capable of such an act," said Carteret. "However, we'll speak of that presently. First, let me convince you that my statement in regard to the will is correct. Here is the clause. It is at the very end of the instrument :—
'And I hereby declare that if my dear wife, Teresa, shall marry again, without the consent in writing first had and obtained of my dear daughter Mildred, then, and in such case, the whole of my property hereby devised to my said wife, shall go and revert to my said daughter Mildred, anything heretofore expressed

to the contrary notwithstanding.' Thus you see, madam," he pursued, " if you marry again, all your property, which may be roughly estimated at five thousand pounds per annum, will go from you, and you will have nothing but your settlement. I cannot imagine how this important clause escaped you."

" Neither can I," said Mrs. Calverley.

" But it will now be necessary to decide whether you will sacrifice your present large income, or break off the important match you have just formed. I don't think you can have much hesitation. In my opinion, when Lord Courland learns how you are circumstanced, he will be anxious to retire."

" I do not think so," exclaimed Mrs. Calverley.

" Well, you will have an excellent opportunity of testing the sincerity of his affection."

" I am taken quite by surprise, as you see, Mr. Carteret," said Mrs. Calverley, who was greatly agitated, " and must have time for consideration before I can decide. I anticipate no difficulty."

" It is certainly an awkward dilemma," said Carteret; " but I don't see how you can get out of it, unless you are content to remain single. I quite thought you understood your position, or I should have ventured to give you some advice before."

" I wish you had," said Mrs. Calverley. " I little imagined Mildred held my destiny in her hands. She cannot be aware of her power ? "

" I have no means of judging," replied Carteret. " But I fancy not."

" Then let her be kept in ignorance for a short time, till we are able to think the matter over. I cannot, will not give up Lord Courland—I love him ! "

" That alters the case, madam."

" But though I cannot give him up, I know not whether he is disinterested enough to take me with my small fortune."

" Fifteen hundred a year is not a small fortune," said Carteret; " and you have that, at any rate. If Lord Courland loves you as strongly as I am persuaded he does, I am sure he will be content with it."

" But he has been led to expect more," said Mrs. Calverley.

" Yes; that is unfortunate. His expectations having been raised so highly, a disappointment may ensue. But I do not anticipate a rupture is to be apprehended. Let me state that I did my best to prevent the introduction of this objectionable clause into the will. But my remonstrances were ineffectual ; Mr. Calverley was determined. ' If she marries again, the property shall return to my family,' he said. So I was obliged to carry out his instructions. I know not what are your plans, madam ; but my advice to you is to delay the marriage as long as you can, so that some arrangement may be made with Miss Calverley."

" I will follow your advice, Mr. Carteret. But, when Mildred discovers her power, I think she will prove impracticable."

" It may be so," he rejoined. " But you are still mistress of the situation. She may prevent your marriage, but she can do nothing more. Evidently, she is in the dark at present. Keep this matter secret till you have concocted your plans; you will then be able to make a better arrangement."

" But you forget that I have an enemy in the house. Whoever abstracted the will — and I still suspect

Norris—is in possession of the important secret, and will communicate it. That is certain."

Struck by what she said, Mr. Carteret reflected for a few minutes.

" Under the circumstances, it may be well to keep on good terms with old Norris," he said. " Chetwynd and Mildred, I find, are both absent, so that you need not apprehend immediate interference from either of them. Summon me, if you require my counsel, and I will come at once. I can render you no service just now. But mind! make no proposition to Mildred without consulting me."

And he left the cabinet.

As he went out, he found Norris in the hall, and took the opportunity of speaking to him.

" Well, Norris," he said, " you're going to have a great change in the house before long. How does it suit you ? "

" Not at all, sir," replied the old butler, who looked very gloomy. " I'd rather things remained as they are. But do you really think, sir, this marriage will take place ? "

" What's to hinder it ? " remarked Carteret, looking at him inquiringly.

" Nothing that I know of," replied Norris ; " but perhaps Mrs. Calverley may change her mind. She has got everything she wants now."

" Except a husband ! " replied Carteret, laughing.

" And he may cost too dear," said Norris.

" Too dear ! What do you mean ? "

" A young nobleman is not to be had for nothing," replied Norris.

" Well, Mrs. Calverley can afford to pay a high price

for such a luxury, if she chooses," said Carteret. "However, that's not the way to look at the matter, Norris. This is a very great match, and must be conducted in a befitting manner. A large settlement must necessarily be made."

"I don't dispute that, sir," said Norris. "But *can* a large settlement be made?"

"The rascal has read the will!" thought Carteret. "Of course it can!" he added, aloud. "Mrs. Calverley can do what she likes with her own."

"Well, you ought to know better than me, sir," said Norris; "but I fancy you're mistaken. I always understood my old master didn't wish his wife to marry again, and I concluded he would take precautions to prevent her doing so."

"I wouldn't advise you to make such observations as those to any one but me, Norris," said Carteret.

"Not even to Mr. Chetwynd, or Miss Mildred, sir?"

"I see what you are driving at, Norris; but you had better hold your tongue, and keep quiet; you'll do yourself no good by meddling in what does not concern you. Things are by no means settled. Most certainly, the marriage won't take place at present. Very likely it may not take place at all. But if it does, the testamentary directions will be strictly carried out."

"That's all I wished to know, sir," replied the butler. "I won't say a word more to any one."

And he attended Mr. Carteret to the door, where the solicitor's mail-phaeton was waiting for him.

IV.

A LETTER FROM LORD COURLAND.

On quitting the cabinet, the door of which was locked, and, taking the key with her, Mrs. Calverley went out into the garden, looking, apparently, quite cheerful, though she had an anxious breast, and had just sat down on a lawn chair, when a letter that had arrived by post was brought her by Laura.

As yet, Mrs. Calverley had said nothing to her lady's-maid about the restoration of the will, as she thought it best to leave that matter in doubt for the present, and she now allowed her to depart without any allusion to the subject. Indeed, she was dying to read her letter, which she saw was from Lord Courland.

It was just such a letter as might have been expected from him, but there were some passages in it that produced an effect contrary to that intended by her noble suitor, and heightened her uneasiness.

"I must write you a line, dearest Teresa," he began, "though I have nothing to say, except to tell you how supremely wretched I feel now you are gone. However, I try to console myself by the thought that I shall soon behold you again, and in your own house, which I long so much to see—as it will be my abode when I am made the happiest of mortals by the possession of your hand.

"I have to thank Mr. Calverley for two things—first, that he was considerate enough to die; and secondly, that he left his large property at your entire disposal. I shall always entertain the highest respect for his memory.

" This may seem rather heartless jesting, sweet Teresa, but it is the simple expression of my feelings. Really, very few men would have behaved so well as your late husband, but he fully appreciated you. I wish I could follow his example—not by quitting you, for I don't intend to do that, if I can help it, for many years to come—but by making a handsome settlement upon you.

" Fortunately, you have enough—enough for us both—and I cannot sufficiently thank you for your kind promises. My devotion shall prove my gratitude. Ouselcroft, you tell me, is a charming place, and I ought not to accept it, or any share in it ; but I can refuse nothing you offer me—not even that priceless treasure, yourself.

" I do not ask you to write to me, though one word would enchant me, and enable me to endure this separation.

" Adieu, sweet Teresa ! I shall count the minutes till we meet."

The perusal of this letter gave Mrs. Calverley infinitely more pain than pleasure, for she now feared she should never be able to carry out her noble suitor's wishes, and she saw plainly that he would not be content with the income derived from her settlement.

She read the letter again, and this conviction struck her even more forcibly on the second perusal.

She revolved the matter in her mind very deliberately.

What could she do ?

Dark thoughts possessed her. There seemed only one way of extricating herself from the difficulty. She shrank from it ; but it recurred again and again, till

U

she became familiarised with the idea, and it appeared less dreadful than at first.

The step seemed unavoidable.

She resolved to answer Lord Courland's letter, but very briefly, and to make no allusion to her promises to him, though he seemed to expect it.

She was still buried in thought when Laura came to her, and with the familiarity which this favourite attendant usually displayed, said:

"Dear me, ma'am, you look dreadfully pale! I hope nothing has gone wrong?"

"Nothing whatever," replied Mrs. Calverley, with a forced smile. "I have had a most charming letter from Lord Courland. But I feel rather faint. The air doesn't seem to revive me, so I shall go in-doors."

And she arose.

"I came to tell you, ma'am," said Laura, "that old Norris is greatly obliged by your kind promise to him. He says he now feels quite easy."

"There was no need to trouble himself before," observed Mrs. Calverley. "By-the-bye, I haven't told you that the will has been found."

"Indeed, ma'am! Where?" exclaimed Laura.

"In the top drawer of the escritoire!"

"I'm sure I searched that drawer, ma'am!"

"Mr. Carteret found it at once. But don't say anything more about it. I don't want the matter talked about. By-the-bye, I mean to drive over to Brackley in the pony-carriage this afternoon, and shall take you with me."

"I'm always pleased with a drive, ma'am, especially to Brackley," replied Laura.

As they entered the house, they met the aged butler, who bowed respectfully to his mistress.

" Much obliged to you for thinking of me, ma'am,"
he said. "You've always shown me great kindness."

"Not more than you deserve, Norris," she replied
graciously. " It was quite a misapprehension, I assure
you. I never intended to part with you, and should
never think of doing so without making you a comfortable provision."

" I'd rather stay where I am, ma'am," replied the
butler. "After living in it for half a century, a man
gets attached to a house."

"Then rest easy, Norris," she rejoined. " You shall
stay here to the last—that I promise you."

The old butler muttered his thanks, for he felt
rather husky, and Mrs. Calverley went up-stairs to her
own room.

V.

SHOWING WHAT MRS. CALVERLEY'S DRESSING-BOX CONTAINED.

AFTER closing the door, Mrs. Calverley approached the
large Psyche that stood opposite her, and ejaculated,
" No wonder Laura was struck by my appearance ! I
do look frightfully pale ! I must take care my looks
don't betray me."

But her countenance assumed a deathly hue, and
her limbs seemed scarcely able to support her as she
moved towards the door communicating with the
dressing-room.

There she stopped, her entrance, apparently, being barred by a shadowy figure resembling her dead husband.

But Teresa, as we have shown, was a woman of high courage, and not to be daunted by superstitious fears.

Convinced that the figure was a mere effect of her imagination, she passed into the inner room, and then, standing still for a moment till she had quite recovered her self-possession, proceeded to unlock a large dressing-box that stood upon the toilet-table, and took from it a small casket apparently containing scent bottles.

When the casket, in its turn, was unlocked by a diminutive and peculiarly-shaped key, four very small phials were disclosed.

Teresa selected one of them, filled, as it seemed, with a very bright spirit, held it up for a moment, and then, taking out the stopper, breathed at the contents of the phial.

Just then a slight noise disturbed her, and she became aware that she was watched by Laura, who was standing at the bed-room door.

Though appalled at the sight, she exhibited no sign of alarm, but with the utmost coolness said :

" I thought some *eau-de-luce* would do me good. I always take it for the *migraine* from which I am now suffering. But you need not stay. Order the pony-carriage in half an hour, and be ready yourself by that time, Laura."

Not for an instant doubting the truth of what she was told, Laura withdrew ; and she was no sooner gone than Mrs. Calverley wrapped the small phial in her embroidered pocket-handkerchief, and then re-placed the casket, and carefully locked the dressing-box.

VI.

POISON IN THE CUP.

HALF an hour later, Mrs. Calverley, who had completely recovered, and, indeed, looked remarkably well, drove over to Brackley in the pony-carriage, attended by Laura and a groom.

The two girls were in the garden when she arrived at the Hall, but Lady Barfleur, who was much impressed by the brilliant engagement Mrs. Calverly had formed, received her with great ceremony.

"Accept my congratulations, dear Mrs. Calverley!" she said. "I felt sure you would marry well, but I did not expect you would make such a great match as this. You are fortunate in every respect, it seems, for Emmeline tells me Lord Courland is exceedingly good-looking and agreeable. I hope he may like Ouselcroft. I should be very sorry if you left this part of the country."

"Don't be alarmed, dear Lady Barfleur," rejoined Mrs. Calverley. "I should never think of leaving Ouselcroft, and I am persuaded Lord Courland will be pleased with the place. I expect him on Thursday."

"You must all come and dine with me during his stay. I don't give dinners now, as you know, but I must see him."

"He will be delighted to dine with you, I am sure. But I must bring him over some morning to see the old Hall."

"By all means," replied Lady Barfleur. "You will always be welcome."

Here the two girls came in fresh from the garden. Emmeline looked blooming and full of spirits, but Mildred complained of slight indisposition, and, in fact, did not seem very well.

Mrs. Calverley noticed these symptoms with secret satisfaction. They favoured her dark design.

"You seem rather poorly this morning, my love," she said.

"I am a little out of sorts," replied Mildred. "I think I caught cold on the journey. But I shall soon be better."

"Better when a certain person arrives," whispered Emmeline. "Well, he will be here this evening, or to-morrow at latest. Don't fall ill before he comes!"

"Unfeeling creature!" exclaimed Mildred, with a sickly smile.

Just then, the luncheon-bell was rung, and the ladies proceeded to the dining-room.

It might have been noticed—if such a trifling circumstance could attract attention—that Mrs. Calverley carried her embroidered kerchief in her hand.

While they were crossing the hall, the Reverend Mr. Massey made his appearance, and after saluting Lady Barfleur and the others, went in with them to luncheon.

As they took their seats at table, Mrs. Calverley easily managed to get a place next her step-daughter.

Some little progress had been made with the repast,

which it is supposed ladies enjoy more than dinner, when Emmeline remarked :

"You must let us have some champagne to-day, mamma, please. Mildred is rather out of spirits."

The proposition was seconded by the chaplain, who was always exceedingly cheerful, and had been conversing very agreeably with Lady Barfleur. So the wine was brought and handed round by the butler.

"You must not refuse, Mildred," cried Emmeline. "The champagne was ordered expressly for you."

"And for me," added the chaplain, laughing.

"For you as well," said Emmeline. "You are entitled to a second glass."

Even as the words were spoken, with singular boldness and dexterity, and screened by the handkerchief, Mrs. Calverley contrived to let fall two or three poisonous drops from the phial into Mildred's glass.

The action passed completely unnoticed, Mildred's attention being diverted at the moment.

No peculiarity was perceptible in the flavour of the champagne. It seemed excellent, and really believing the exhilarating wine would do her good, Mildred emptied the glass.

In answer to a friendly sign from the chaplain, Mrs. Calverley raised the glass to her lips, but her handkerchief had disappeared.

The enlivening effect of the wine on the party was speedily apparent—except in the instance of Mildred, who began to feel ill, and was obliged to rise from table, and leave the room.

Mrs. Calverley, who seemed greatly concerned, and was very attentive to her, wished her to see Doctor Spencer, but she declined, insisting that it was a mere passing indisposition.

Emmeline was of the same opinion, but Rose Hartley, who had been summoned to attend her, thought otherwise, and prevailed on her to retire to her own room.

By this time, she had become so faint, that Rose had to assist her to mount the spiral staircase.

To disarm suspicion, Mrs. Calverley remained for an hour, conversing with Lady Barfleur and Mr. Massey, and played her part to perfection—charming them both.

Before setting out on her return, she went up-stairs to see Mildred, and found her lying on a couch with Emmeline and Rose by her side. The glow of the painted glass in the bay-window somewhat disguised the sufferer's paleness.

No touch of pity agitated Teresa's breast as she gazed at her victim. On the contrary, she secretly exulted in the success of her direful attempt. Nevertheless, she inquired with well-feigned solicitude :

"How do you feel now, my love ?"

"Somewhat better, I think, mamma," replied Mildred.

"I am so glad to hear you say so !" remarked Mrs. Calverley. "I hoped to take you and Emmeline back with me to Ouselcroft, but that is quite out of the question now."

"Quite, ma'am," observed Rose. "I think Miss Calverley ought to have medical advice."

"So do I," rejoined Teresa. "Shall I send for Doctor Spencer, my love ?"

"No, mamma," replied Mildred. "If he comes, I shall be laid up for a week, as I know from sad experience. You recollect how tiresome he was during

my last illness, and wouldn't let me stir. I won't
have him now, unless I'm obliged."

"Better let her have her own away," whispered
Emmeline, unconscious that she was playing into Mrs.
Calverley's hands. "She wants to see a certain per-
son on his arrival here."

"Well, you mustn't blame me if any harm ensues,"
rejoined Teresa. "I really think she ought to have
immediate advice."

Rose looked imploringly at her, but did not venture
to remonstrate.

"Well, I shall come over to-morrow morning," said
Mrs. Calverley; "and then——"

"What then?" asked Mildred, faintly.

"I shall go and fetch Doctor Spencer myself, unless you contrive to get well in the interim. However, I shall feel easy about you, knowing you're in
good hands."

"Yes; Rose and I will take every care of her,"
said Emmeline.

"Don't bring Doctor Spencer, or send him, till
you see me again, I beg, mamma," said Mildred.
"Promise me that."

Mrs. Calverley gave the required promise, though
with apparent reluctance.

As she bade her victim adieu, and kissed her fevered
brow, Mildred instinctively recoiled from the contact
of her lips.

———

VII.

PANGS OF REMORSE.

No trace of anxiety could be discerned on Mrs. Calverley's beautiful countenance as she drove back to Ouselcroft with Laura by her side. On the contrary, she seemed quite elated.

Struck by her want of feeling, the lady's-maid said :

"I am sorry to hear Miss Mildred has been taken ill."

"Oh, there is nothing much the matter," rejoined Mrs. Calverley. "She has been slightly indisposed all the morning, and something disagreed with her at luncheon."

"Glad to hear it, ma'am. I was afraid from what Rose Hartley said, it was a serious attack."

"Oh, no," replied Mrs. Calverley. "She thought so little of it herself, that she wouldn't let me send for Doctor Spencer. I shall drive over again to-morrow, and trust to find her quite recovered."

"I should think a little *eau-de-luce* would do her good, ma'am ?" remarked Laura.

"Why do you think so ?" asked Mrs. Calverley, startled.

"She seems to have had such a sudden seizure, like yourself, ma'am."

"Mine was merely a violent headache, Laura, accompanied by faintness. Ah !" she exclaimed, in real alarm, after vainly searching for it in her bag. "What did I do with my handkerchief? I hope I haven't left it behind ! "

" No ; it's here, ma'am," replied Laura, giving it her. " You had laid it on the seat."

" Oh ! thank you, Laura," cried Mrs. Calverley, looking inexpressibly relieved.

And squeezing the handkerchief to make sure the phial was safe inside it, she put it into her bag.

" I wonder why she was so agitated just now ? " thought Laura.

All signs of exultation had now vanished from Mrs. Calverley's countenance, and she looked thoughtful and uneasy during the rest of the drive, and scarcely made a remark to Laura, who could not account for the sudden and extraordinary change in her mood.

On arriving at Ouselcroft, she went upstairs almost immediately to her own room, but, contrary to custom, and greatly to the surprise of the lady's-maid, did not take her with her.

This time, on going into her dressing-room, she did not neglect to lock both doors.

Feeling now safe from intrusion, she sat down to reflect. But there was such a turmoil in her breast, such confusion in her brain, that she found it impossible to do so calmly.

The fancied loss of her handkerchief, with the phial inside it, which, if it had really occurred, must have inevitably led to the discovery of the terrible crime she had committed, had completely unnerved her.

All was now quiet, but when the dreadful catastrophe occurred, suspicion would be instantly aroused, and the slightest circumstance that bore upon the dark deed would be weighed and examined.

The will, which had been prepared by Carteret, and which, she could not doubt, had been read by Norris, supplied the motive of the crime; inasmuch as it showed that her step-daughter's death would be extraordinarily advantageous to herself—so advantageous, indeed, as almost to suggest Mildred's removal.

Evidence sufficient to condemn her could be furnished by Laura, whose strange curiosity had enabled her to become a fatal witness against her.

When she clearly understood the frightful position in which she was placed, her terror increased, and she would have given all she possessed, and all she hoped to gain, if the deed could be undone.

So agonising were her remorseful feelings, that life had become intolerable; she resolved to put an end to it, and by the same means she had employed to remove Mildred. She had not yet put by the phial, though she had come thither for the express purpose of doing so. With a terrible feeling of exultation at the thought of escaping the consequences of her last crime, and of another crime equally dreadful that still weighed upon her conscience, she raised the phial to her lips, with the intention of swallowing the whole of its deadly contents.

But her fatal purpose was arrested by a tap at the bedroom door.

For a few moments, she could scarcely collect her thoughts, and when she spoke, her voice was hoarse.

" Who is it ? " she demanded.

"Laura," replied the person in the bedroom. " May I come in ?"

" No," rejoined the wretched Teresa.

" I have only come to tell you that Mr. Chetwynd has just arrived with two young men," said Laura.

The mention of that name produced an instantaneous effect on Mrs. Calverley, and dispelled her fears.

Even if he had come to charge her with her crime, she would have met him and defied him.

" Tell Mr. Chetwynd I will come down directly," she said in a firm voice. " Who are the persons with him ? Do you know them ? "

" They are two young men whom I saw at Lady Thicknesse's, ma'am—Mr. Harry Netterville and Mr. Tom Tankard. I don't know what business they've come about, but I fancy it relates to Rose Hartley— Miss Barfleur's lady's-maid."

Completely reassured by this remark, Mrs. Calverley told Laura to go down at once, and desire Norris to offer the young men some refreshment ; and as soon as she found that the inquisitive lady's-maid had departed, she unlocked the dressing-box, replaced the phial in the casket, and then, having made all secure, went down-stairs.

VIII.

HARRY NETTERVILLE AND TOM TANKARD APPEAR AT OUSELCROFT.

MRS. CALVERLEY found Chetwynd in the library with the two young men, who bowed very respectfully as she made her appearance.

" What has happened ? " she said to Chetwynd. " I thought you were staying with Sir Bridgnorth ? "

"I have only just come from Charlton," he replied. "We have got a strange business on hand, as you will admit when you learn what it is. You have heard me speak of an infamous scoundrel named Romney. Well, it seems that this daring libertine, who for some time has persecuted Rose Hartley with his addresses, has resolved to carry her off from Brackley."

"Such audacity seems scarcely credible!" exclaimed Mrs. Calverley.

"It is, nevertheless, certain he is about to make the attempt this very night," said Netterville. "My friend Tom Tankard discovered his design in a very singular manner, as he will tell you."

"Yes, ma'am," said Tom, with one of his best bows; "I went to get my hair cut yesterday by a *coiffoor* named Sigebert Smart, and while I was undergoing the operation, Sigebert, who is rather too familiar, says to me, 'Do you remember Rose Hartley, Mr. Tom?' 'To be sure I do!' says I. 'And a very pretty girl she is. She has gone to Brackley Hall, in Cheshire, with Miss Barfleur and Miss Calverley.' 'But she won't remain there long,' remarked Sigebert. 'Why not?' says I. 'Don't she like the place?' 'Can't tell about that,' observed Sigebert. 'But there's a gentleman going to look after her.' 'Indeed!' says I, pricking up my ears—for I thought of my friend, Harry Netterville. 'It won't be any use if he does.' 'You're very much mistaken there, Mr. Tom,' says he, with a knowing look. 'I'm going with him!' 'You!' says I, in astonishment. 'Yes; and if we can't manage it, the deuce is in it!' 'Manage what?' says I. 'You don't mean to carry her off?' 'That will depend,' said he. 'There may be an *enlèvement.* But I dare say she'll come willingly enough.' "

" On hearing this, I said no more to alarm him, for I knew who he meant, and wished to catch the rascal. But I presently inquired, ' When do you set out on this expedition ? ' ' To-morrow,' he replied. ' We shall get down to Brackley Hall in the dusk of the evening. But don't go and talk about it—especially to Harry Netterville—or you'll spoil all.'

" I promised to keep silence, but had no sooner left the rascally hairdresser's shop than I took a cab, and drove to Gray's Inn to see Harry, and tell him what I had found out. At first, he didn't believe it."

" I couldn't," said Netterville. " The attempt seemed too wild; but Tom convinced me it would be made. We then arranged our plans, and having ascertained from Lady Thicknesse's butler, Higgins, that Mr. Chetwynd Calverley had gone to spend a few days with Sir Bridgnorth Charlton, we set off for Stafford early this morning, and saw Mr. Calverley, hoping he might feel disposed to accompany us, and he did not hesitate a moment."

" No," cried Chetwynd ; " and I confess the intelligence you brought gave me the utmost satisfaction, for I felt that at last Romney had delivered himself into my hands. I judged it best to come on here, instead of proceeding direct to Brackley," he added to Mrs. Calverley, " as I feared to alarm the rascals. But I shall send over a note to warn Rose, and give her some instructions. Romney must not escape me ! "

" I should be very sorry for that," said Mrs.

Calverley. "But it is rather unlucky that Mildre should have been taken ill this morning, and Rose i obliged to be in attendance upon her."

"She is not seriously ill, I trust?" inquire Chetwynd, anxiously.

"No; and Emmeline can stay with her, while Ros leaves her for a time," said Mrs. Calverley.

"Nothing more will be needful," said Chetwynd.

Then turning to Netterville, and pointing to th writing materials on the table, he added, "Sit dow and prepare a note to Rose, and I will send it off a once by a groom to Brackley, together with anothe letter from myself."

So saying, he quitted the library with Mrs. Cal verley, but presently returned for Netterville's lettei which he gave to the groom, enjoining him to se off at once.

Meanwhile, Norris came to the library, and invite the two young men to come to the butler's pantry where a substantial repast was set out for them together with a bottle of claret.

"I say, Harry," remarked Tom, as he discusse the pigeon-pie, and quaffed the claret, "I shouldn' mind an expedition like this every day, if I coul insure such prog. And what a beautiful creature tha Mrs. Calverley is! I declare I'm quite in love wit her myself. How do you feel?"

"Very comfortable," replied Harry. "I can thinl of nothing but Rose."

"Oh, Rose! lub'ly Rose!" chanted Tom. "Tak another glass of claret. That'll cure you!"

IX.

THE ATTEMPTED ABDUCTION.

On that same evening, about nine o'clock, two individuals, who had recently alighted from a hired
carriage at no great distance from Brackley Hall, and
had contrived to cross both bridges, traverse the court-
yard, and get into the garden—these two persons,
we say, were standing near a yew-tree alley, looking
towards the ancient mansion, which could be distinguished through the gloom, with its picturesque
outline of gables and windows.

There were lights in some of the windows, but the
general appearance of the house was exceedingly
sombre.

Fortunately for the two individuals we have mentioned, there were no dogs in the court-yard. These
protectors were all with the keeper, Ned Rushton.
Not even a watch-dog was kept at the Hall, so that
no alarm was given.

" Well, I think you may succeed in your design,"
said one of the pair, " if you can only contrive to get
the girl out of the house. There's the difficulty.
The carriage is not more than a quarter of a mile off."

" We must have it much closer at hand presently,"
replied the other. " I wonder we haven't seen Lomax.
He ought to be here by this time. I hope he has not
played us false. Let us go towards the house."

On this, they quitted the garden, crossed the moat,
and re-entered the court—proceeding with the utmost
caution. But there did not seem any one about.

However, they soon discovered that some slight preparations had been made for them.

Reared against the side of the house was a ladder which could easily be shifted to any other spot that was required; and not far from the ladder was an open bay-window without curtains, in the deep recess of which window a candle was set, that illuminated the chamber, and showed Rose was its sole occupant.

This arrangement of things appeared so promising, that it almost looked like a snare.

But Romney did not hesitate. Without giving himself a moment for reflection, he carried the ladder to the open window, mounted as quickly as he could, and sprang into the room, followed by Sigebert.

On seeing them, Rose flew towards the door, but was instantly followed by Romney, who fastened a scarf over her mouth, so as to stifle her cries.

All this was executed with wonderful success, but it is quite possible Rose might have made more noise if she had thought proper. She did not even struggle much when they proceeded to take her through the window.

"She goes very quietly," thought Sigebert. "I believe we shall have no trouble whatever with her. In my opinion, she's not at all disinclined to be carried off."

Having got first down the ladder, Sigebert received the precious burden from his principal; but, as soon as Romney landed, he once more took charge of the fair damsel, and endeavoured to get her out of the court.

Hitherto, she had been quiet enough; but she now made a grand disturbance.

She quickly succeeded in tearing the scarf from her face, and then the court rang with her cries; in answer to which came forth Harry Netterville and Tom Tankard, who had been hidden in the old chapel. Each being armed with a stout stick, they soundly belaboured both rascals.

After a while, both caitiffs were released, but only for a worse punishment. As they were running off, in the hope of gaining their carriage, they were stopped by Chetwynd, and taken in charge by a couple of police officers, by whom they were conveyed in their own carriage to Knutsford, where they were locked up in the gaol.

X.

HOW MILDRED RECOVERED.

ON going over to Brackley next morning, Mrs. Calverley found Mildred much better, and decidedly out of danger.

She had not expected such a favourable change, and could not very well account for it; but, for many reasons, she was glad the poison had not taken full effect.

Of course Mildred was still very weak, though rapidly recovering; but, as her symptoms differed in no respect from those of an ordinary illness now, it seemed quite unnecessary to consult Doctor Spencer. Thus the evil woman escaped that danger.

But, though she had been saved the perpetration of

this dreadful crime, and its consequences, she felt no regret. No pity touched her heart. Even as she looked at Mildred on that morning, while suffering from the poison she had administered, she resolved to complete her work—but more deliberately, so that there should be no possibility of detection. While thus planning Mildred's destruction, she feigned the greatest affection for her, and seemed beyond measure rejoiced at her recovery. Perhaps, she rather over-acted her part; for both Mildred and Emmeline doubted her sincerity.

However, since this favourable change had taken place, she now proposed that both girls should come over to Ouselcroft next day, and bring Rose Hartley with them. Mildred felt sure she should be quite well by that time, so the proposition was agreed to.

At this particular juncture, Mrs. Calverley's great desire was to render herself agreeable to everybody. She, therefore, pretended to take a great interest in Rose Hartley, and made her give her full particulars of the intended *enlèvement*. From Rose she learnt that all had been prepared for the intruders, and that Romney and his companion had completely fallen into the trap.

"Miss Barfleur was good enough to lend me her room for the occasion," said Rose, "as it was very conveniently situated for our plan, and we hoped they would venture into the house. And so they did. Taking the ladder, which had been placed close at hand, ready for them, they mounted to the window, got into the room, seized me, tied a scarf over my mouth, and carried me off. But I was soon free; while my assailants, after receiving a sound thrashing from Harry Netterville and Tom Tankard, were taken in their own chaise to Knutsford Gaol, where they are likely to remain some time ; so that, at last, I am rid of my persecutor ! "

" I am glad of it," cried Mrs. Calverley. " The business was capitally managed. But where are Harry Netterville and his friend ? "

" They are still here, ma'am," replied Rose. " And perhaps they may remain for a day or so."

" Ask them to come over to Ouselcroft to-morrow," said Mrs. Calverley. " I will direct Mr. Norris to take care of them. We shall have some festivities going on."

" I'm sure it is very kind of you, ma'am," said Rose. " They will be delighted with the invitation. The young ladies, I believe, are going to you to-morrow ? "

" Yes ; and you will come with them," said Mrs. Calverley. " Therefore I make this proposition in regard to your friends, thinking it may be agreeable to you."

" It is most agreeable to me, ma'am," said Rose. " And I am exceedingly obliged to you. A few days at two such charming country-houses as Brackley and Ouselcroft will be a great treat to Harry and his friend."

" Well, I hope they may enjoy themselves," said Teresa. " And now take care to get Miss Calverley quite well by to-morrow. We mustn't have any more illness."

" Oh, she'll get well to-day, ma'am, I'm sure," said Rose, with a significant look. " Captain Danvers is expected ! "

The tact and good-nature displayed by Mrs. Calverley quite charmed Rose, who had not previously a very great liking for her.

The two young men were enchanted by the invitation to Ouselcroft. Tom Tankard had fallen desperately in love with Mrs. Calverley. His egregious vanity made him imagine she was struck by his appearance, and he fancied it was on his account that he and Netterville were invited to Ouselcroft.

XI.

MORE LETTERS.

Next morning, several letters arrived at Ouselcroft, and were brought by Laura to Mrs. Calverley's dressing-room.

The first opened by the lady was one from Lord Courland, as full of ardour and passion as his last letter, but considerably shorter.

Its chief object was to mention that he and Scrope Danvers would make their appearance in plenty of time for dinner. But he added, as a postscript, that he was dying with curiosity to behold Ouselcroft.

" The place is not yet mine," thought Teresa. " But rest easy. You shall not be disappointed. My project is only deferred."

The next letter opened was from Lady Thicknesse. This was quite unexpected. Her ladyship had talked of coming to Ouselcroft, but at a later date. She now volunteered a visit. But we must give her own words :

" You have pressed me so strongly to come to you,

dear Mrs. Calverley, that I cannot resist. I propose to come to you to-morrow about mid-day. I have got a surprise for you. You will wonder what it is ; but as you will never guess, I must tell you I am bringing with me my *chef*, Zephyrus, and I place him at your disposal."

" Charming ! " exclaimed Teresa. " This will be a great delight to Lord Courland. I know how highly he appreciates Monsieur Zephyrus's performances. Nothing could please me better. But he is not the only one, it seems. I shall have an entirely new house-hold."

" I shall also venture to bring with me my butler, Higgins. He is a very clever man, and I think you will find him useful ; but if he is at all in the way, he can go on to Brackley."

" Oh, I am so glad Higgins is coming ! " cried Mrs. Calverley. " He will be of the greatest use, and will enable me to get rid of that suspicious old Norris, whose eye seems ever upon me. But stop ! I must not offend old Norris, or I shall arouse another enemy. He must be kept in the background as much as pos-sible. So far, my letters have been very satisfactory. Here is another, and I think it is from Sir Bridgnorth Charlton. Let us see what he says."

" Since Chetwynd does not seem disposed to return, I must come to Ouselcroft. Have you room for me for two or three days ? "

" Plenty of room, and shall be delighted to see him ! " remarked Mrs. Calverley. " Here's a note from Captain Danvers," she added, with indifference. "They all seem resolved to come here. Well, I dare say I shall be able to accommodate him."

But, besides these, there was one person on whom nobody counted.

This was Mr. Tankard. He had written a letter to Chetwynd, saying he was coming with his friend, Mr. Higgins, and hoping it might not be considered a liberty.

Chetwynd went at once to Norris; and the old butler, glad to find that Higgins was coming to see him, undertook that beds should be prepared for that important personage and Tankard—to say nothing of Harry Netterville, Tom Tankard, and Zephyrus.

With such a party below stairs, it seemed more than probable that some of the gaieties of Belgrave-square might be repeated at Ouselcroft.

Having ascertained the train by which Lady Thicknesse must of necessity arrive, Mrs. Calverley met her at the station in her pony-carriage.

The whole of the luggage, which was rather cumbrous, together with Zephyrus, Higgins, and Tankard, came by a special omnibus.

Lady Thicknesse was one of the very few persons whom Mrs. Calverley really liked, and she showed she was glad to see her. The day happened to be fine, so they had an extremely pleasant drive of five or six miles to Ouselcroft.

Lady Thicknesse was in high good humour, and disposed to be pleased with everything. The approach to the house charmed her. Properly speaking, there was no park, but there was a good deal of land that had a very park-like character, being tolerably well timbered, while all the hedges were taken down.

As the carriage was stopped for a moment at a good point of view, Lady Thicknesse exclaimed :

" You are most fortunate, dear Mrs. Calverley. This is just the house to live in ! I am sure Lord Courland will be of my opinion."

But her ladyship was quite as much pleased with the house on a nearer inspection, as she had been on a more distant survey. The gardens and grounds were perfection ; and, as she looked out on the smooth lawn from her chamber window, she thought she had never seen a lovelier place.

Mrs. Calverley had an interview with Zephyrus soon after his arrival, and expressed her great satisfaction at having the advantage of his services.

Flattered by her compliments, the distinguished *chef* promised her an excellent dinner, but, to achieve his object, he declared he must have absolute control of the kitchen. This was readily accorded him, and everything else he required ; so he proceeded to make his arrangements, and struck terror into the breast of the cook and her assistants by his arbitrary manner.

Pursuing her policy of conciliation, Mrs. Calverley was very kind and courteous in her manner to Mr. Higgins and Mr. Tankard, begged them to make themselves at home, and desired Norris to show them every attention.

Harry Netterville and Tom Tankard likewise came in for a share of her civilities. They had just been to Knutsford to attend the examination of Romney and his companion who were sentenced by a full bench of magistrates to six months' imprisonment. Mrs. Calverley expressed her great satisfaction at the result, and took the opportunity of complimenting the young men on their prowess. Her observations were very simple; but Tom was greatly elated by them.

"There! did you see how sweetly she smiled on me?" he said to Netterville: "I told you I was high in favour."

Tom was not particularly gratified by his father's unlooked-for appearance on the scene, thinking, perhaps, his own importance might be diminished.

"What the deuce has brought the guv'nor down here?" he remarked to Netterville. "We could have done very well without him."

"He's come to look after you, I've no doubt, Tom," observed Netterville, laughing.

"No; it's Higgins!" cried Tom. "He can't live without Higgins. Where Higgins goes, Tankard must go too. I believe if Higgins set off for Jerusalem by next train, if there is a railway to Jerusalem, Tankard would set off after him. But I must shut up! Here come the guv'nor and Higgins. I hope they didn't overhear my remarks."

But it seemed they did, for they both shook their hands at him.

XII.

LORD COURLAND ARRIVES AT OUSELCROFT.

When Lord Courland and Scrope Danvers arrived later in the day, a very pretty picture was presented to them.

On the lawn, which was charmingly kept, the

whole party now staying in the house were assembled, and, judging from the lively sounds that reached the ear, they were all amusing themselves very well.

The two girls were playing lawn tennis with Chetwynd and Captain Danvers; and Sir Bridgnorth, who had arrived about an hour previously, was conversing with Lady Thicknesse and Mrs. Calverley. It was rather unfortunate that all the ladies should be in mourning, but in spite of the sombre costumes the scene looked gay and pleasant.

Mrs. Calverley had sent her carriage to the station for Lord Courland and Scrope, and no sooner had his lordship alighted than, without waiting for any formal announcement by Norris, he flew to that part of the lawn where Teresa was seated.

She did not wait till he came up, but hastened towards him, and a very lover-like meeting took place. So much ardour as Teresa now displayed seemed scarcely consistent with her character, but either she was passionately in love with Lord Courland, or she feigned to be so.

After exchanging a few words, and we suppose we must add a few kisses, they walked off to another part of the garden, having, apparently, a great deal to say to each other that would not brook an instant's delay.

Lady Thicknesse and Sir Bridgnorth looked after them with a smile.

" Well, and how do you like Ouselcroft ? " inquired Teresa.

" I have hardly had time to look around me," he replied, gazing on her. " At present, I can behold only one object."

"But I really want to have your opinion. Does the place equal your expectations?"

"It surpasses them."

"You have seen nothing yet. You ran away from the lawn, which is the prettiest part."

"We will go back there presently, when we have had a few minutes to ourselves. Too many curious eyes were upon us. When one is desperately in love, as I am, one wants solitude. But you will soon be mine."

"Not quite so soon as we anticipated. Some little delay, I find, will be unavoidable."

"I hope not," said Lord Courland, with a look of disappointment. "I would rather the marriage were expedited than delayed."

"I am afraid that will be quite impossible," said Teresa. "I shall have to make some preparatory arrangements."

"I thought the property was entirely in your own hands?" he said.

"So it is," she replied. "And there is really nothing to prevent the marriage from taking place immediately."

"Then yield to my impatience, I beseech you!"

"I have consulted my lawyer, and he advises a little delay."

"Lawyers always are tedious. They have no consideration for one's feelings. Even when nothing has to be done but draw up a settlement, they will make a long job of it. I fancied all might have been arranged in a few days, signed, sealed, and delivered."

"Perhaps it may," said Teresa. "But we are

getting quite serious in our discourse. All matters of business must be deferred till to-morrow, when I doubt not they can be satisfactorily arranged."

" I think if I could say a word to your lawyer, I could make him use more despatch," said Lord Courland.

" I scarcely think so," replied Teresa, uneasily. " I have given him all needful instructions. But there is the first bell. We must go and dress for dinner."

By the time they reached the lawn, the whole party had gone into the house, so they had it to themselves, and remained there for a few minutes.

Lord Courland was positively enchanted with the place, and could scarcely find terms sufficiently strong to express his admiration.

" Then you *do* like the house ? " cried Teresa.

" It is everything I could desire," he replied.

" I hope to make it yours ere long," she said. " But you must not be too impatient."

" I am eager to possess you, sweetheart—not the house," he rejoined.

" Ah ! if I thought so ! " sighed Teresa. " But I know better."

They then passed through one of the drawing-room windows, and were met by Norris, who conducted Lord Courland to his room.

XIII.

A DANCE ON THE LAWN.

NEVER before had a dinner so perfect been served at Ouselcroft. But, in the opinion of the distinguished *chef*, sufficient justice was not done to it. He was very particular in his inquiries of Norris and Higgins, both of whom were in attendance, and discovered that some of his best dishes had been neglected by the guest for whom he had specially prepared them.

This was very vexatious, but Zephyrus endeavoured to console himself by reflecting that Lord Courland was in love, and about to be married, either of which misfortunes, as he termed them, was sufficient to account for his lordship's want of appetite.

However, the repast was not wasted, but appeared again in the servants' hall, where quite as large a party sat down to it as had done in the dining-room; and it would seem they were far better judges, since the very *recherché* dishes that were previously neglected were now completely devoured.

As it happened to be a lovely moonlight night, and very warm, Mrs. Calverley took out the whole of the guests upon the lawn, and they had not been there long when Captain Danvers suggested a dance.

With the drawing-room windows left wide open, it was found that the piano sounded quite loud enough; Lady Thicknesse, who was a very good musician, immediately sat down and played a waltz.

Lord Courland and Teresa, with two other couples, were soon footing it lightly on the smooth turf, and a very agreeable impromptu little dance was got up.

But this was not all. At the instance of Lord Courland, a servants' dance was got up at the farther end of the lawn, near the two cedars of Lebanon already described.

Notice of the proposed dance was given by Norris, at the very moment when the party in the servants' hall had finished supper.

Nothing could have been more agreeable to Tom Tankard and Zephyrus than the suggestion. They had heard that dancing was going on in the garden, and if they could not join it, they at least desired to look on; but this proposition completely satisfied them.

The main difficulty seemed in regard to the music; but on inquiry it was found that the footman could play the flute, the coachman the violin, and the groom the banjo, and, provided with those instruments, they proceeded to the lawn. When the band struck up, it was found very efficient, and elicited great applause.

It was decided to commence with a quadrille, and finish with Sir Roger de Coverley.

As may be supposed, Harry Netterville had already secured a partner in Rose, but a contest occurred between Tom Tankard and Zephyrus for the hand of Laura; and the Frenchman proving successful, Tom was obliged to content himself with Clarissa, the rather smart upper housemaid.

Both the portly Mr. Higgins and the still more portly Mr. Tankard took part in the quadrille—the one dancing with the cook, and the other with the second housemaid, Lucy, who was quite as pretty as Clarissa.

Owing to the bright moonlight, the quadrille could be distinctly seen by the party near the house, and afforded them great amusement. Indeed, when Zephyrus danced his *cavalier seul,* Lord Courland and Teresa came forward to witness the performance. Tom Tankard was likewise stimulated into an extraordinary display by the presence of Mrs. Calverley and the other ladies.

But Sir Roger de Coverley was the real success of the evening. In this cheerful dance, form was set aside. Mrs. Calverley led off with Lord Courland, and danced down the long lines, making Tom Tankard supremely happy by giving him her hand for a moment. She was followed by Emmeline and Chetwynd, after whom came Mildred and Captain Danvers. Sir Bridgnorth induced Lady Thicknesse to walk through a part of the dance with him, but her ladyship retired long before she got to the bottom. The dance seemed interminable, and was not brought to a close till long after the great folks had withdrawn.

Old Norris declared this was the merriest evening he had ever spent at Ouselcroft since Mr. Chetwynd was christened, and he thought the good times were coming again.

Before retiring to her own room, Teresa accompanied Lady Thicknesse to her chamber, and sat with her for five minutes, during which they talked over the events of the evening—her ladyship being of opinion that everything had gone off remarkably well; and that, so far as she could perceive, Lord Courland's affability and good nature had produced a very good effect upon the establishment.

" I think his idea of a servants' dance on the lawn was excellent," she said, " and I am very glad you allowed it. Higgins told me they were all greatly pleased."

" It was particularly kind in your ladyship to take part in it," observed Mrs. Calverley.

" Well, I haven't danced for many a year, but Sir Bridgnorth seemed so anxious, I could not refuse him."

" I was delighted to see that he had prevailed," remarked Mrs. Calverley, with a smile. " I think your ladyship will very soon have to consider whether you are inclined to give him your hand altogether. He is certainly very devoted."

" I have a very great regard for Sir Bridgnorth," said Lady Thicknesse, " and think him very kind-hearted——"

" And as it seems to me, exactly suited——"

" In some respects, perhaps he is," said Lady Thicknesse. " At all events, I don't dislike him."

" And Charlton is really a very fine place," remarked Teresa.

" So I'm told," said Lady Thicknesse. " By-the-bye, I didn't expect to find Sir Bridgnorth here."

" I owe the pleasure of his company entirely to your ladyship," said Mrs. Calverley. " Had he not expected to meet you, I am certain he would not have come."

" You flatter me ! " said her ladyship, evidently pleased.

" When I beheld you together on the lawn this evening," pursued Mrs. Calverley, " and especially when I saw you together in the dance, I was rejoiced

Y

that the meeting had taken place, as I knew how it must end. And now, good night, and pleasant dreams!"

Teresa entered her own room in a very lively mood, and continued so as long as Laura stayed with her, and diverted her with her chat.

The lady's-maid had nothing but what was satisfactory to say of Lord Courland. He had produced a most agreeable impression upon the household, and his good-natured deportment in the dance had carried all the suffrages in his favour.

"Even old Norris is pleased with him," said Laura; "and if to-morrow goes off as well as to-day, everybody will be enthusiastic. Do you think we shall have another dance, ma'am? Monsieur Zephyrus is so anxious to try the polka with me! I said I'd ask you."

"We shall see," replied Mrs. Calverley. "I can't make any promises. I hope you're not falling in love with Zephyrus, Laura? I thought he seemed very attentive to you!"

"There was nothing particular about him, I assure you, ma'am," replied Laura. "It's his way!"

"But you seemed to encourage him."

"Well, there's no choice between him and Tom Tankard, and I can't bear that forward young man. Would you believe it, ma'am, the vain little fool flatters himself you are struck by his appearance?"

"I think him a most ridiculous object," said Mrs. Calverley. "But now, before you go, I have an order to give you, and I wish particular attention paid to it. Should Mr. Carteret come to-morrow morning, I wish him to be shown at once to my cabinet."

" It shall be done, ma'am, depend upon it ! " replied Laura, who thereupon withdrew.

XIV.

HOW MRS. CALVERLEY PASSED THE NIGHT.

UNTIL lately, it had not been Teresa's custom to fasten her chamber door. But as soon as Laura was gone, she locked it, and the dressing-room door as well.

She then sought for the phial of poison, and placed it on a small table near her bed. Why she did this, she could scarcely tell. Probably she felt that if an impulse of self-destruction assailed her during the night, she would yield to it, and get rid of the ceaseless mental torture she endured.

Though all had gone well since Lord Courland's arrival, she had been greatly alarmed by some remarks he had made, and had vainly endeavoured to tranquillise herself by thinking that the difficulties and dangers that beset her could be easily overcome.

Now she was left alone, she saw the folly of such reasoning. She felt that her marriage project could only be accomplished by the commission of another crime. Lord Courland had given her several hints that convinced her he would claim the fulfilment of her promise, and how could she fulfil it, if Mildred were not removed ?

But the contemplation of this crime awakened such horror in her breast, that sleep fled, and her thoughts drove her almost distracted.

Unable to rest, she arose, wrapped herself in a

dressing-gown, and sat down, trying to calm her thoughts. But in vain.

A lamp burning on the table on which the phial was placed, kept that terrible object constantly before her, and seemed to prompt her to have recourse to it.

Being long past midnight, it was to be supposed that all the inmates of the mansion, except herself, were buried in slumber, but the restless woman felt sure she heard footsteps in the gallery outside.

Who could be there at that hour? She was not left long in doubt. A tap was heard at the door, and to her inquiry who was there, a voice answered, " Rose."

Everything alarmed her now, and even this visit terrified her.

But after a moment's delay, she opened the door, and saw Rose in a *robe de chambre* belonging to one of the young ladies, and holding a taper in her hand.

" Pardon me for disturbing you, madam," she said. " But Miss Calverley has been taken suddenly ill, and is very faint, and Miss Barfleur has sent me to you for some *sal-volatile,* or some other stimulant, to revive her."

On hearing this, an infernal idea crossed Teresa.

" Give her three or four drops of *eau de luce* from this phial," said Teresa, giving her the poison. " I have just taken that quantity myself, for I have not felt well to-night. Not more than four drops, mind. Be very particular. And when you have given her the dose, bring back the phial to me."

" Won't you give it to her yourself, ma'am ? " said Rose.

" No ; I would rather not leave my room," replied Teresa. " Lose no time."

" The spirit of darkness has aided me," cried Teresa, as Rose departed on her terrible errand. " The deed will now be done."

Though not many minutes elapsed before Rose returned, it seemed a century to Teresa. She could scarcely restrain herself from going to the room occupied by the victim.

At length, Rose reappeared, bringing the phial with her. Teresa received it with trembling fingers.

" Has she taken the drops ? " inquired Teresa, in a scarcely articulate voice.

" She has," replied Rose. " She was very un-willing to take them, but Miss Barfleur and myself persuaded her."

" You did right," observed Teresa. " She will be well before morning."

" I hope so," said Rose. " But you look very ill yourself, ma'am."

" I *am* ill," replied Teresa. " But don't mind me. Go back to Miss Calverley. I hope I shall now get some sleep."

As soon as Rose was gone, Teresa again locked the door.

Amid the turmoil of thoughts that agitated her, she preserved a sort of calm that enabled her to go through the business she had to do.

Without a moment's loss of time she unfastened the dressing-box, replaced the bottle of poison, took out another phial resembling it, and really containing *eau de luce,* and then made all secure again.

This done, she drank a very small portion from the phial, and placed it where the poison had stood. Before seeking her couch she unlocked both her doors, judging it best to manifest no uneasiness.

Did she sleep?

How are we to account for it? She had scarcely laid her head on the pillow, than she fell into a deep, sound slumber, that was not disturbed by a dream, and that lasted till daybreak.

XV.

HOW DOCTOR SPENCER WAS SENT FOR.

LITTLE did the many guests staying at Ouselcroft imagine what had occurred during the night. They slept on, undisturbed by any idea that a direful deed was being enacted in an adjoining chamber.

Rose's nocturnal visit to Mrs. Calverley was heard by no one; and, since then, all had been tranquil. Was Mildred better? Was she sleeping? At all events, those with her were quiet.

Thus, when the large establishment arose, at an early hour, for they had an unusually busy day before them, no alarm whatever had been given.

No report was brought down-stairs that Miss Calverley had been taken ill during the night; but the housemaids were bustling about, and getting the rooms ready for the guests, who might be expected to make their appearance some two or three hours later.

Rose had promised Harry Netterville overnight that she would meet him in the garden at six o'clock, and they would have a stroll together; but, though the morning was charming, the young damsel did not make her appearance, greatly to Harry's disappointment.

Monsieur Zephyrus was more fortunate. Laura had engaged to meet him at the same early hour, and she was true to her appointment.

She must have been up soon after it was light, for she had evidently spent some time over her toilette. Zephyrus was enraptured by her costume and looks, and paid her many high-flown compliments in French, the import of which she understood. Undoubtedly she looked very captivating.

The amorous pair did not remain long on the lawn, though they met there, but sought a retired walk. They had not, however, proceeded far, when they saw another couple advancing towards them, whom they instantly recognised as Tom Tankard and Clarissa.

Salutations were exchanged in the most approved style, praises bestowed on the beauty of the morning, and on the delightful singing of the birds; and they were about to separate, when Laura thought proper to give Tom a friendly caution.

"If you don't want to meet your father," she said, "I advise you to keep clear of the lawn. He's there with Mr. Higgins and our old butler, Mr. Norris."

"Since that's the case, we'll turn back, if you please, Miss Clarissa. My guv'nor's an odd sort of man, and he don't like my paying attention to young ladies."

Clarissa, who was very good-natured, did not mind which way she went, so Laura suggested they should walk together to the fish-ponds, which were about half a mile distant, and they set off in that direction.

Amongst those who were early astir on that fine morning, and who had come forth into the garden, was Chetwynd.

Of course, he knew nothing that had happened during the night; but a strange foreboding of ill oppressed him. He found old Tankard and Higgins on the lawn; and, after a brief converse with them, he was proceeding to the stables, when Norris came up and begged to have a word with him, and they went into the library together.

"I am going to ask you a singular question, sir," said the old butler; "and I will explain my motive for doing so presently. Do you think this marriage with Mrs. Calverley and Lord Courland will really take place?"

"I believe it will, Norris," replied Chetwynd. "I see nothing to prevent it. I don't know whether all the preliminary arrangements are settled; but his lordship appears perfectly satisfied. And so he ought to be, if what I hear is true."

"It will be more advantageous to you than to him," said Norris.

"I don't understand you," rejoined Chetwynd, regarding him fixedly.

"When I say advantageous to you, sir, I mean to your sister," observed the butler. "But it cannot fail to be beneficial to you. You ought to pray that the marriage may take place, instead of opposing it."

"What the deuce are you driving at, Norris?"

"It appears to me, sir, that you have never read your father's will."

"You are right; I have not. But I know that the property is left entirely to his wife."

"Very true, sir—very true. But there is a most important proviso, of which you are evidently ignorant. In the event of the widow marrying again, she forfeits the property, which then goes to the testator's daughter, Mildred."

" Are you sure of this, Norris ? " cried Chetwynd, astounded.

" Quite sure, sir," replied the old butler. " I have read the will myself, most carefully. As I have already said, the best thing that can happen to you is that your step-mother should marry again. But will she make this sacrifice ? I fear not."

" Can she be aware of the proviso you have mentioned, Norris ? "

" Impossible to say," rejoined the old butler. " I should think so. She has the will in her possession. I do not see how it can fail to act as a bar to a second marriage, unless she comes to some arrangement with Miss Mildred."

" That she will never do," said Chetwynd. " My sister, I am certain, will never surrender her rights to her."

" Has the matter been broached to Miss Mildred ? " inquired Norris.

" Impossible, or I should have heard of it."

" Then nothing is left Mrs. Calverley but to break off the match, and that is the point from which I started," said Norris.

" It is incomprehensible she should have allowed the affair to proceed so far," said Chetwynd. " I am altogether perplexed. But I will have an early interview with my sister this morning, and hear what she has to say. Something must be done forthwith. She cannot give a tacit assent to the arrangement."

At this moment Rose Hartley appeared at the open window, and Chetwynd called her in.

"I was looking for you, sir," said Rose, who appeared very anxious. "I came to tell you Miss Calverley is very ill."

"Indeed!" exclaimed Chetwynd, surprised and alarmed.

"She was taken ill in the night with a renewal of the attack she experienced the other day at Brackley, but recovered for a time, and obtained some hours' sleep; but she is worse again this morning."

"What ails her?" asked Chetwynd.

"I can scarcely describe her illness; but she suffers a great deal of pain. I think she ought to have immediate advice."

"She shall," replied Chetwynd. "I should wish to see her myself."

"Not now, sir; later on."

"Has Mrs. Calverley seen her?" he asked eagerly.

"No, sir; but she sent her some *eau de luce* by me."

"Some *eau de luce?*"

"Yes, sir. I knocked at her chamber door in the middle of the night, and she gave me a small bottle that was standing by her bedside. Miss Calverley only took a few drops of it."

"Quite enough, I should think," muttered Norris.

"Well, don't give her any more at present," said Chetwynd.

"I haven't got any more to give her," replied Rose. "I took back the phial."

"Mark that, sir," observed Norris.

"Why mark it?" inquired Rose.

"Never mind him," said Chetwynd. "Go back to my sister at once, and remain with her till Doctor Spencer arrives. Don't give her anything more, and don't let Mrs. Calverley come near her if you can help it."

"Mind that!" said Norris, emphatically.

Rose looked at him, but made no remark.

"Tell her I have something to say to her, and must see her this morning; but don't make her uneasy," said Chetwynd. "I suppose Miss Barfleur is with her?"

"Yes, you may be sure she won't leave her, sir," replied Rose. "Your message shall be delivered to your sister, and your instructions attended to."

As soon as Rose was gone, Norris could no longer contain himself.

"Here we have it as plain as possible, sir," he cried. "The sole bar to the marriage is to be removed. Don't you see it, sir? I do, plainly enough. How else should she fall suddenly ill just at this time?"

"Whatever you may think, Norris; and however difficult you may find it to do so, I insist upon it that you hold your tongue," said Chetwynd, authoritatively. "If you disobey me, you'll ever afterwards lose my favour. Now go and send for Doctor Spencer at once, and leave the rest to me."

"Don't fear me, sir," said Norris. "I'll keep silence as long as you enjoin me."

And he proceeded to the stables, and sent off a mounted groom for Doctor Spencer.

XVI.

CHETWYND MAKES COMMUNICATION TO SIR BRIDGNORTH.

CHETWYND was pacing to and fro on the lawn, occupied

with painful and distracting thoughts, and scarcely knowing what course to pursue, when he was joined by Sir Bridgnorth Charlton, who saw he was greatly disturbed, and kindly inquired what was the matter.

Chetwynd found it somewhat difficult to explain, as he did not desire for the present to enter into details; but he mentioned that his sister had been taken ill during the night, and was still rather seriously indisposed. This was quite sufficient to account for his anxious looks.

However, Chetwynd desired to consult his friend; and, therefore, said to him:

"I have a communication to make to you, dear Sir Bridgnorth, which I am convinced will give you great surprise, and very likely induce you to take a totally different view of certain matters now before you. My sister and myself have hitherto been completely in the dark in regard to a very important provision of my father's will."

"Indeed!" exclaimed the baronet. "I should not have conceived that possible. What is it, pray?"

"From examination of the will, it appears that if Mrs. Calverley marries again, the whole of the property bequeathed her by my father goes to Mildred."

"Now, indeed, you surprise me!" exclaimed the baronet. "And is it possible this very important proviso has only just been discovered? Such negligence is inconceivable!"

"The proviso cannot, I think, have been known to Mrs. Calverley, or she would not have proceeded so far with her present matrimonial arrangements. But, whether known to her or not, it is the fact. Now comes the important question—does she mean to marry Lord Courland?"

" I have no doubt of it," replied Sir Bridgnorth. " Unless prevented, she will marry him."

" Most assuredly, then, she will forfeit her property. Besides, she can make no settlement upon him."

" Yes ; she has property of her own. She can settle that."

" True ; but will that be sufficient ? "

" I cannot say," replied Sir Bridgnorth. " I am not in Lord Courland's confidence."

" As yet, I don't think his lordship has been let into the secret."

" Nor is it desirable he should be. He must look after his own affairs. It is not your business to prevent the marriage, but to forward it. If Mrs. Calverley does not choose to tell her noble suitor how she is circumstanced, that is her own concern. She is a very clever woman, and can take care of herself. I should not have thought her capable of making such a sacrifice as this for any man. But she seems to be really in love with Lord Courland ; or, perhaps, she is resolved at whatever cost to make an important match. At any rate, her scheme must not be thwarted."

" Not unless it should turn out to be mischievous," observed Chetwynd.

" It cannot be mischievous to Mildred," said Sir Bridgnorth. " Lord Courland, probably, will be disappointed when he finds the property pass away from him ; but that will be the worst that can happen. And if his lordship is a loser, Charles Danvers will be an immense gainer. How oddly things turn out ! After all, Charles may become master of Ouselcroft, in right of his wife. Ah ! here he comes ! " he added, as the captain made his appearance. " I wish I could tell

him what a brilliant prospect he has before him ; but
I musn't."

" Well, are you laying out your plans for the day ? "
said Captain Danvers, as he came up.

"No; we were talking about you," replied Sir
Bridgnorth. "I was wishing you might be able to
reside here."

" Ah, that's out of the question now ! " rejoined the
captain. "It's a charming place, but I fancy both
Chetwynd and myself shall soon be shut out of it.
Lord Courland is certain to make a great change, and
bring in a new set. If I had been master here, my
aim would have been to keep my old friends about me.
Chetwynd should always have had his room, and old
Norris should have remained in his place."

" I'm glad to hear you say so," remarked Sir Bridgnorth. "I'm certain Mr. Calverley never meant his
property to be disposed of in this fashion. It's a
great pity half didn't go to Mildred."

"Ay; it ought to have been divided between Chetwynd and his sister. That would have been the right
thing to do. Now, Mildred is not even to marry except
with her step-mother's consent."

"You need have no uneasiness on that score,"
remarked Chetwynd. " Mildred will have her marriage
portion, and something besides."

" You think so ? " said Captain Danvers.

" I'll answer for it," rejoined Chetwynd.

"And if you require an additional guarantee, I'm
ready to give it," said Sir Bridgnorth. " But mind !
should you ever come to be master here, I shall hold
you to your promise to make us all at home."

" You shan't need to remind me of it, should that
fortunate day ever arrive," said the captain.

At that moment, the person who seemed to stand most in the captain's way came forth, and wished them " Good morning."

They all fancied he assumed a little of the air of the master of the house.

" I must consult you on a little matter after breakfast, Sir Bridgnorth," he said. " I know you are a man of great taste. It strikes me some alterations might be made in the garden."

" I hope your lordship won't touch the lawn," remarked Sir Bridgnorth. " It is very much admired."

" The lawn itself is charming," said Lord Courland ; " but I don't like those two sombre cedars."

" They were my father's especial favourites," observed Chetwynd. " I hope your lordship will spare them."

" I should consider it a sacrilege to remove them," said Sir Bridgnorth.

" I don't carry my veneration for trees quite so far," rejoined Lord Courland ; " and, as I have no particular associations connected with the two cedars, I shall merely consider whether my lawn cannot be improved."

" *My* lawn ! " whispered Chetwynd to Captain Danvers. " He is master here already."

" I will get you to walk round with me presently, Sir Bridgnorth," said Lord Courland, " and favour me with your opinion on the general arrangements."

" If I may venture to give your lordship my opinion, without walking round," replied Sir Bridgnorth, " I would strongly advise you to let the gardens and grounds alone. It is allowed to be one of the prettiest places in the country, and I should be sorry if it was destroyed."

" But I don't mean to destroy the place ; I desire to improve it."

" Such improvements as your lordship contemplates, I fear would destroy its character," said Sir Bridgnorth; "and that is what I should regret."

Just then the breakfast bell put an end to the discourse, and attracted the party to the house.

XVII.

DOCTOR SPENCER.

LADY THICKNESSE and Scrope Danvers were in the breakfast-room when the others came in, and her ladyship said to them, " I am very sorry Mrs. Calverley will not be able to make her appearance at breakfast, this morning."

" I hope she is not unwell," remarked Lord Courland.

" She is not very well," replied her ladyship. " But she wishes to confer with Doctor Spencer. He has been sent for to attend Miss Calverley, who has been taken ill during the night."

" Indeed ! " exclaimed Captain Danvers, anxiously. " She seemed quite well, and in excellent spirits last evening."

" Perhaps she took cold," observed Lady Thicknesse. " I fear we remained out rather too late. Only think of my dancing Sir Roger de Coverley in the open air ! If I had been laid up, like Mildred, you would have been to blame," she added, to Sir Bridgnorth.

" But your ladyship is looking better than ever,"

he rejoined gallantly. "You ought therefore to thank me."

"Well, I don't think I'm the worse for it, and I certainly enjoyed the dance very much."

Breakfast was then served and Lady Thicknesse presided at the table.

She took care to have Sir Bridgnorth beside her, and they seemed the most cheerful persons present, for the absence of the three other ladies cast a gloom over the rest of the party.

Meanwhile Doctor Spencer was with Mrs. Calverley in her dressing-room, she having given orders that he should be brought there immediately on his arrival.

An elderly man, with white hair, jetty eyebrows and black eyes. The expression of his countenance was kindly and composed, his accents agreeable, and his manner singularly pleasing. All his patients liked him.

Mrs. Calverley had been a great favourite with the doctor, and he had hitherto had a very high opinion of her, founded not only upon his own notion of her character, but on the praises bestowed upon her by her late husband.

She thought his manner less cordial than it used to be, but she was so troubled she could scarcely judge.

"I am very sorry Miss Calverley is ill," he said, taking a seat. "What is the matter with her?"

"I can't exactly tell," she rejoined. "I have not yet seen her this morning. We were all dancing on the lawn rather late last evening, and she may have taken cold."

"Dancing on the lawn!" exclaimed Doctor Spencer

z

shaking his head. "That was imprudent. Mildred is delicate. She has got a chill, I suppose?"

"I can't tell. Her maid came to me in the middle of the night, and said Miss Calverley felt very sick and ill, so I sent her a restorative. She took a few drops of *eau de luce*, as I understood, and I thought she was better, for I heard nothing more till the morning, when I learnt that the sickness was not gone, so I sent for you."

During this explanation, Doctor Spencer kept his eye fixed on Mrs. Calverley in a manner she did not like.

"This is not a feverish cold, as I thought," he observed. "But I shall be better able to judge when I see her."

"Emmeline Barfleur and their maid occupy the same room with her, so she has had plenty of attendance. I should have gone to her if she had been alone."

At this moment a tap was heard at the door, and Emmeline came in.

She looked very much frightened, and said, hastily:

"Pray come and see Miss Calverley at once, Doctor Spencer! She has just fainted!"

Doctor Spencer instantly prepared to obey.

"Take these restoratives with you," said Mrs. Calverley, giving him several small bottles; "and come back to me when you have seen her."

"I will," replied the doctor, as he followed Emmeline.

Some little time elapsed before Doctor Spencer appeared again.

To the guilty woman, who awaited her sentence, it

was an interval of intense anxiety; but she endeavoured to maintain her calmness, fearing to betray herself.

Thinking she ought to be employed, she sat down to write a letter, but had not got very far with it when Doctor Spencer came into the room.

Closing the door after him, he fixed a strange and searching glance upon her, and so terrified her by his looks that she could not speak, nor did he break the silence.

At length, she gave utterance to these words:

"I am afraid you bring bad news, doctor. Is she seriously ill?"

"She is," he replied, sternly. "But I think I shall be able to save her."

"What ails her?" inquired Mrs. Calverley.

"Have you no idea?"

"None whatever," she replied, looking perplexed.

"Poison has been administered to her!"

"Impossible!" she exclaimed.

"I cannot be deceived!" said Doctor Spencer. "The attempt has been twice made. In each instance the dose was, fortunately, too small to be fatal."

The slight nervous tremour that agitated Mrs. Calverley was not unnoticed by the doctor.

"This is a terrible accusation to make!" she said.

"But it can be easily substantiated," he rejoined. "Indeed, it would be difficult to conceal the evidence of the crime!"

"On whom do your suspicions alight, doctor?" asked Mrs. Calverley, as firmly as she could. "On any one in attendance upon her?"

"One of them has been an unconscious instrument,"

he replied. "But the hand that really provided the poison was elsewhere."

After a short pause, he added, in a stern tone:

"Madam, yours is the hand by which the deed has been done!"

"Mine!" she exclaimed, fiercely and defiantly.

"Nay, it is useless to deny it!" he rejoined. "I have but to search this chamber to find proof of your guilt."

"Search it then!" she cried, in the same defiant tone.

Doctor Spencer glanced around, and his eye quickly alighted upon the dressing-box.

"Open this box!" he cried, seizing her hand, and drawing her towards it. "Open it, I say!" he reiterated, in a terrible voice. "There the poison is concealed!"

So overpowered was she by his determined manner, that she did not dare to disobey.

Without offering the slightest resistance, she unlocked the box, and disclosed the casket.

He uttered a cry of satisfaction on beholding it.

"Now unlock this!" he said, giving her the casket.

Again she obeyed; but instantly took forth a phial containing the poison, and would have swallowed its contents, had not Doctor Spencer snatched it from her.

"Why do you treat me thus cruelly?" she cried. "Why not let me die?"

"Because I desire to give you a chance of life," he rejoined. "If your intended victim escapes the fate you designed her, I will not denounce you. If she dies, you know your doom!"

"Do you think she will live?" asked Teresa.

"Her life hangs on a thread. But a few days—perhaps a few hours—will decide. For the present, I will keep your terrible secret, and screen you from suspicion. But only on the condition that you remain here, and abide the result of your dreadful crime. Attempt to fly, and I will instantly check you. Now you know my fixed determination."

"And you will remain in constant attendance on Mildred?" she asked.

"I shall," he replied. "And rest assured I shall do my best to save her."

With this he left the room, taking the phial with him.

XVIII.

DOCTOR SPENCER HAS AN INTERVIEW WITH CHETWYND.

WHILE the terrible scene just described was taking place up-stairs, Chetwynd had quitted the breakfast-table and repaired to the library, where he proposed to have an interview with Doctor Spencer, after the latter had seen Mildred.

He subsequently learnt from Norris that the butler had had a private conference with the doctor on his arrival, and had given him some information that would serve to guide him in his proceedings.

Chetwynd thought the doctor a long time in coming down, and when at last he entered the library, the young man did not augur very well from his looks.

"I am afraid you find my sister worse than you expected, doctor?" he said.

"She is in a very precarious state," replied Doctor Spencer. "Still, I hope to save her life."

Then assuming a different manner, he added, "I had better mention at once that Norris has made certain disclosures to me, the truth of which I have just ascertained."

"You are satisfied, then, that an attempt has been made to poison my sister?"

"I am," replied the doctor.

"By her step-mother?"

"By Mrs. Calverley. I have discovered the poison in her room, and have it now in my possession."

"Then what should prevent us from instantly delivering her up to justice? No pity ought to be shown her."

"I think differently," said the doctor. "I have promised that if I can save your sister's life—as I hope I can—her own shall be spared."

"She does not deserve such consideration," cried Chetwynd.

"Perhaps you will think differently," said the doctor, calmly, "when I tell you that it is your sister's wish that she should be spared for a life of penitence. The dear girl entreated me so earnestly to screen her intended murderess, that I consented."

Chetwynd was deeply moved.

"Mildred is an angel of goodness!" he exclaimed, in a voice half suffocated by emotion.

"You would say so, if you had seen her, as I have done," said the doctor. "No one could be more gentle and patient, though she suffers much, and she is perfectly resigned to her fate, whatever it may be. But she desires spiritual counsel, and Miss Barfleur has written to Mr. Massey, the chaplain of Brackley, requesting him to come to her forthwith, and it is certain he will promptly obey the summons. Under such painful and peculiar circumstances, and where it is necessary that secrecy should be observed, no better man could be found than Mr. Massey."

"I am certain of it," said Chetwynd. "I have had experience of his goodness. He is as judicious and discreet as he is strict in his religious duties."

"I must now go," said the doctor; "but I shall return again ere long. I need not say more to you about the necessity of attending to your sister's wishes. Should she be disturbed or excited, I will not answer for her life. I have already cautioned Norris, and I think he will attend to my injunctions."

"I will also speak to him," said Chetwynd. "But you need not fear any indiscretion on his part. Since you have made him aware of my sister's wishes, he will attend to them—for he is strongly attached to her, though he detests Mrs. Calverley. Unluckily, the house is full of company; and you are also, I conclude, aware under what circumstances Lord Courland is invited ?"

"Yes; I understand that a matrimonial arrangement has been all but concluded between his lordship and Mrs. Calverley. It is idle to speculate as to what will now be the result. But I counsel you in no way to interfere. Impossible you can do so without some explanation, which cannot now be given. Your sister's wishes ought to be your paramount consideration."

With this injunction, the doctor took his departure.

XIX.

WHAT PASSED BETWEEN LORD COURLAND AND MR. CARTERET.

LORD COURLAND was in the drawing-room after breakfast, amusing himself as well as he could, and hoping Mrs. Calverley would soon make her appearance and dispel his *ennui*, when Norris brought him a message from Mr. Carteret, who said that, if perfectly convenient to his lordship, he should be glad to see him for a few minutes.

Lord Courland was delighted. He was aware that Mr. Carteret was Mrs. Calverley's lawyer, and was particularly anxious to have a little conversation with him.

" I'll come to him at once," he said. " Where is he ?"

" I'll take your lordship to him," replied the butler.

And he conducted him to the cabinet, in which, as we have explained, Mrs. Calverley was wont to transact her private business.

Mr. Carteret was alone, and bowed very respectfully as his lordship entered.

After a little preliminary discourse, Lord Courland remarked, in a very easy tone, as if everything was satisfactorily settled :

" I hope we shall be able to complete our arrangements, Mr. Carteret."

" I hope so, my lord," replied the solicitor. " But I am desired by Mrs. Calverley to offer you some explanation, as she fears there has been a slight misunderstanding on your lordship's part. It is always better these affairs should be arranged by professional men, who don't hesitate to ask each other questions."

"I thought there were no questions to ask," said Lord Courland, rather surprised. "Everything appeared clear."

"So it seemed. But I find, on conferring with Mrs. Calverley, that she was under a misapprehension as to her power——"

"What do you mean, sir?" cried his lordship, quickly. "If I am rightly informed, she has absolute control over her late husband's property?"

"She has so now, my lord," replied the solicitor.

"You don't mean to insinuate that she forfeits the property, in case she marries again?" cried his lordship, in dismay.

"That is precisely her position, my lord," replied Mr. Carteret, calmly. "The property will go to her step-daughter, Miss Mildred Calverley!"

"Why was I not informed of this before?" cried Lord Courland, looking very angry.

"It is on this point that I desire to offer your lordship an explanation," said the solicitor. "Until Mrs. Calverley conferred with me about the settlement, she was quite unaware of her ability to make one."

"This is incredible, sir," cried Lord Courland. "I shall make no remarks, but it is useless to proceed with the business."

"Your lordship seems to form a very unjust and improper opinion of my client," said Mr. Carteret. "She was greatly distressed when she made the discovery I have mentioned—but more on your lordship's account than on her own. Though she will lose this large property, she can still settle fifteen hundred a year on your lordship, and has instructed me to say that she will do so."

"I do not feel inclined to accept it, sir!" replied Lord Courland, haughtily.

"Then I am to understand that the match is broken off?"

"It is," replied Lord Courland, in the same haughty tone.

"Permit me, then, to remark, on my own part," said Mr. Carteret, "that I think Mrs. Calverley is much better off with her large property than with a title. I will communicate your decision to her. I have the honour to wish your lordship a good morning."

And he quitted the cabinet.

XX.

THE PARTING BETWEEN TERESA AND LORD COURLAND.

LEFT alone, Lord Courland did not feel by any means satisfied with what he had done.

He was really in love with Mrs. Calverley, and now that he seemed likely to lose her, his passion revived in all its force. He had made certain of a large fortune, and vexation at his disappointment had carried him farther than he intended. It was disagreeable to lose so charming a place as Ouselcroft, and such a splendid income as he had been promised, but it was far more disagreeable to loose the object of his affections. Moreover, fifteen hundred a year, though it would not bear comparison with five thousand, was not to be despised. Altogether, he blamed himself for his precipitancy, and resolved, if possible, to set matters right.

With this determination, he was about to quit the cabinet, when Teresa made her appearance.

She looked exceedingly pale and ill, and, thinking he was the cause of her suffering, he felt inclined to throw himself at her feet, and entreat forgiveness.

But she checked him by her manner, which was totally changed, and almost freezingly cold.

"I have learnt your decision, my lord," she said, in accents devoid of emotion, "and entirely approve of it. I would not have it otherwise."

"But I was wrong, dearest Teresa!" he cried. "I retract all I have said, and pray you to forgive me! I will take you without fortune! I cannot live without you!"

A melancholy smile played upon her pallid features.

"Would I had known this before!" she said. "But it is now too late!"

"Why too late?" he exclaimed, despairingly. "I have told you I will take you as you are. Do as you please with your own. I will ask nothing!"

"Alas!" she exclaimed, sadly. "I repeat it is now too late. I cannot wed you!"

Lord Courland uttered a cry of anguish.

"Not wed me!" he ejaculated. "What hindrance is there to our union that did not exist before? Pardon me, sweet Teresa; I feel I have deeply offended you by my apparent selfishness, but I will try to make amends! I am sure you love me!"

"I do!" she replied, earnestly, and with a look of

inexpressible tenderness. "You are the only person I have ever loved—not for your rank, but for yourself. Had I been fortunate enough to wed you, I should have been happy—happier than I deserve to be!"

"Not than you deserve to be, dearest Teresa!"

"Yes," she replied, in accents of bitterest self-reproach. "I have no right to expect happiness!"

"What is the meaning of this?" he exclaimed, regarding her in astonishment.

"Do not question me," she replied. "Some time or other you will understand me. I merely came to tell you it is best that we should part, and therefore I approve of your decision as conveyed to me by Mr. Carteret."

"But I recall it," he cried. "Think no more of it, sweetest Teresa."

"Again I say it is too late," she rejoined, in a sombre tone. "It is idle to prolong this discourse, which can lead to nothing. Farewell!"

"Do you, then, bid me depart?"

"I do not bid you; but we cannot meet again."

"If so, it would be useless to stay. But you will think differently when you become calmer."

"You mistake," she said. "I was never calmer than now. Had I not felt so, I would not have seen you. But the parting moment is come. Again, farewell!"

And with a look that remained for ever graven on his memory, she disappeared.

Bewildered as if he had been in a troubled dream, Lord Courland remained for some time in the cabinet, seriously reproaching himself with having caused the mental malady with which he thought Teresa had become suddenly afflicted.

He then went down-stairs, intending to consult Lady Thicknesse, but found she had gone to Brackley Hall with Sir Bridgnorth Charlton, who had driven her thither in his phaeton.

However, as his lordship could not rest in his present anxious and excited state, he determined to follow her; and, explaining his difficulty to Scrope, though without entering into particulars, the latter offered to accompany him, and they went at once to the stables to procure horses.

XXI.

HOW MRS. CALVERLEY MADE HER WILL.

ON returning to her dressing-room, after the painful interview with Lord Courland, Mrs. Calverley sat down for a few minutes to collect herself; and then, taking a large sheet of paper from a drawer, began to write out a formal document.

She pursued her task, without intermission, for more than half an hour; and then, having completed it, rang the bell for Laura.

" Shall I bring your breakfast, ma'am ? " asked the lady's-maid.

" No; I do not require any breakfast," replied Mrs. Calverley.

" Let me persuade you to take some, ma'am. You look very ill."

" I am too busy just now," rejoined Mrs. Calverley.

"Beg Mr. Carteret to come to me. You will find him in the library. I also wish to see Mr. Higgins. Request him to come up to me in about five minutes—not before."

"I understand, ma'am."

"Stay!" cried Mrs. Calverley. "I have several letters to write, and shall not want you. If you like you can drive to Brackley in the pony-carriage."

"Oh! thank you, ma'am! May I take Monsieur Zephyrus with me?"

"Monsieur Zephyrus, and anybody else you like. You needn't take the groom."

Laura departed, full of glee.

Shortly afterwards, the attorney made his appearance.

"Pray sit down, sir," she said. "I wish you to read this document."

"Why, you have been making your will, I perceive!" he cried, as he took the paper.

"Will it suffice?" she asked, briefly.

"It seems to me, from a hasty glance, that it will answer perfectly," he replied. "But we will go through it. You divide your property equally, I find, between Chetwynd and Mildred. Quite right. But I do not approve of the bequest of five thousand pounds to Lord Courland. However, I suppose it must stand."

"It must," she observed in a peremptory tone.

Mr. Carteret then went on.

"I am much pleased that you have remembered your late husband's old servant, John Norris. The faithful fellow well deserves the thousand pounds you are good enough to leave him. I also observe that you have made several minor bequests, and have not forgotten your attendant, Laura Martin."

" I believe Laura is attached to me," remarked Mrs. Calverley.

" I have no doubt of it," said Mr. Carteret. " As executors, I see you have appointed Sir Bridgnorth Charlton and Chetwynd, with a legacy to the former of a thousand pounds. No appointment could be more judicious. The will requires no alteration."

" I wish to execute it at once," said Mrs. Calverley.

" In that case, we shall require another witness. We cannot have Norris, since he is a legatee."

" I have provided for that," said Mrs. Calverley ; and have told Laura to send up Lady Thicknesse's butler, Higgins. He may be without."

" I will see," replied Carteret.

Finding Higgins at the door, he explained the business to him, and brought him in.

The butler bowed respectfully, and seemed greatly struck by Mrs. Calverley's changed appearance, but he made no remark.

" I want you to witness my will, Mr. Higgins," she said.

" I am ready to do so, ma'am," he replied. " But I would rather witness any other document."

The attorney then placed the will before Mrs. Calverley, and she executed it with a firm hand—the two witnesses duly attesting her signature.

This done, Higgins was about to depart, when Mrs. Calverley gave him a purse that was lying on the table.

" This is far more than I desire or deserve, ma'am," he said, with a grateful bow. " But I trust you may live many and many a year, and make half a dozen more wills."

" I do not think I shall," she murmured, faintly.

With another profound bow, Higgins retired.

" All is now finished, madam," said Carteret. " Shall I take charge of the will ?"

" No; leave it with me," she rejoined.

Seeing she did not desire to say more, the attorney hastened to depart.

She remained sitting firmly upright till he was gone, and then sank backwards.

XXII.

CHETWYND IS SUMMONED TO HIS SISTER'S ROOM, AND IS SENT BY HER TO TERESA.—THEIR INTERVIEW.

MEANWHILE, Chetwynd had been summoned by Rose, and a very touching spectacle met his gaze as he entered his sister's chamber.

Near the couch on which Mildred was lying, looking the very image of death, sat Mr. Massey. Before him, on a small table, was the sacred volume from which he had been reading, and he was offering up a prayer for the preservation of the sick girl. Kneeling by the bedside, and joining fervently in the prayer, was Emmeline.

With the appearance of the venerable divine—his silver locks and benignant aspect—the reader is already familiar ; but his features now wore a saddened and anxious expression. He was really alarmed by Mildred's state, and scarcely thought it possible she could survive.

Chetwynd and Rose had entered so noiselessly that they did not disturb the others, and good Mr. Massey continued his prayer, quiet unconscious he had other hearers except those close at hand.

At length he ceased, and Chetwynd advanced, and bending reverently to the good chaplain, took his sister's hand.

Hitherto, she had not perceived him, but a smile now lighted up her pallid features, and she murmured his name.

On hearing his approach, Emmeline rose from her kneeling posture.

"I am glad you are come, dear Chetwynd," said Mildred. "I was afraid I might not behold you again."

"I would have come before, had I thought you desired to see me, dearest sister," he replied. "But how do you feel?"

"Somewhat better," she replied. "Mr. Massey's consolatory words have done me as much good as the medicines I have taken—more, perhaps! Doctor Spencer tells me I shall recover, and I have great faith in him."

"Trust only in Heaven, dear daughter," observed Mr. Massey, who did not wish her to delude herself.

"I hope I am now prepared," she said, in a tone of perfect resignation. "I shall quit this world without regret."

"A frame of mind attained by few—but the best," said the chaplain.

Here Emmeline could not restrain her tears, and Rose sobbed audibly.

"I will retire for awhile, dear daughter," said the good chaplain, rising. "You may have something to say to your brother."

And he moved to a little distance with Rose.

"What would you with me, dearest sister?" asked Chetwynd, "Any injunctions you may give me shall be strictly fulfilled."

"I wish to see Mrs. Calverley," she said.

"Better not," he replied.

"I think so, too," added Emmeline. "Her presence will only disturb you."

"I must see her before I die," said Mildred. "Bring her to me, if you can. She is in her own room."

Chetwynd made no further remonstrance, but proceeding to Mrs. Calverley's chamber, which was on the same floor, and at no great distance, tapped at the dressing-room door.

A faint voice bade him come in.

He found Teresa lying back in the chair, as last described, and was quite shocked by her appearance.

"What brings you here, Chetwynd?" she asked. "Has Mr. Carteret sent you?"

"No," he replied. "I have come to tell you that Mildred desires greatly to see you."

"I am unable to move, as you perceive, or I would go to her. What does she desire to say to me? Any question you may ask me in her name I will answer."

"In her name, then, I ask you—as you will have to answer at the bar of the divine tribunal—have you endeavoured to take away her life by poison?"

The wretched woman made an effort to speak; but her power of utterance completely failed her.

"Since you do not deny the charge, I hold you guilty," he said.

"I am guilty," she replied. "The attempt has been twice made."

" Twice ! " ejaculated Chetwynd. " Had you no pity on her ? "

" None," replied Teresa. " My heart was hardened. She stood in my way, and I did not hesitate to remove her."

" Horrible ! " exclaimed Chetwynd. " But your murderous design has failed. She will recover."

" You may not believe me when I tell you I am glad to hear it," replied Teresa. " Nevertheless, it is so. The infernal fire that burnt for a time so fiercely in my breast is extinguished. I had listened to the promptings of the Evil One, and bartered my soul to him for worldly gain that will profit me nothing. If I could, I would pray for Mildred's recovery; but Heaven would not listen to me."

" You cannot judge of the extent of Heaven's mercy. If your repentance is sincere, you may be forgiven."

" Alas ! I have sinned too deeply ! I have no hope for the future ; but I have striven to make atonement for my crimes."

" Atonement !—in what way ? " demanded Chetwynd.

" By restoring the whole of the property I have wrongfully taken from you and your sister. There is my will," she added, pointing to it. " When you examine it you will see what I have done, and I trust you will be satisfied."

Chetwynd stared at her in astonishment, almost doubting whether he heard aright.

" Convince yourself that I have spoken the truth," she said.

Chetwynd opened the will, and glanced at its contents. 2 A 2

She kept her eye fixed upon him as he did so.

"I see it is in your own handwriting," he remarked.

"But do you perceive that I have left my entire property, excepting certain bequests, to yourself and Mildred?"

"I do," he replied.

"Do you likewise notice that I have appointed you and your friend, Sir Bridgnorth Charlton, joint executors of my will?"

"I do."

"Are you satisfied?"

He made no reply.

"You do not answer."

"You have deceived me often, and may be deceiving me now," he rejoined.

She uttered something like a groan, and then said:

"I cannot blame your incredulity. But keep the will—keep it securely. It will soon come into operation."

"I cannot misunderstand the dark hint you have just thrown out," cried Chetwynd. "You have swallowed poison."

"Seek to know no more," she rejoined. "You had best remain in ignorance."

"Instant assistance must be obtained!" he cried. "You must not die thus!"

"Nothing will save me," she replied.

"Do you refuse spiritual aid?" he cried. "Good Mr. Massey is with Mildred; will you see him?"

"I will," she rejoined. "Send him to me—send him quickly, or it may be too late."

Chetwynd hastily departed, but in a very short space of time returned with the chaplain.

Mr. Massey had been told why he was summoned, and regarded the dying woman with profound compassion, being greatly touched by her appearance.

"We must be alone and undisturbed," he said to Chetwynd.

"I will keep watch outside," replied the other. "No one shall enter."

And, with a pitying look at Teresa, he quitted the room.

XXIII.

SIR BRIDGNORTH PROPOSES TO LADY THICKNESSE, AND IS ACCEPTED.

On that morning, as previously intimated, Sir Bridgnorth Charlton had offered to drive Lady Thicknesse to Brackley Hall; and as Mrs. Calverley did not make her appearance, and no other arrangements were made, in consequence of Mildred's illness, she accepted the proposal with delight, secretly hoping that a proposal of another kind might follow. Her ostensible purpose was to spend the day with her sister, Lady Barfleur, and return to dinner.

Everything promised well. The weather was propitious, and as Sir Bridgnorth assisted her to her place in front of his well-appointed and well-horsed mail-phaeton, he squeezed her hand in a manner that seemed to proclaim his intentions.

But his deportment and discourse when they had started on the drive left her in no doubt. He lowered his voice, and bent down his head when he addressed her, so that what he said could not be overheard by the two grooms behind.

For an elderly gentleman, he acted the part of a suitor very creditably. If his looks were not impassioned, his manner was devoted. Lady Thicknesse was pleased, and with good reason, for the match, if it took place, would be satisfactory in all respects.

A better *parti* than Sir Bridgnorth could not be found. He had the recommendation of an excellent social position, rank, and wealth. Moreover, he was extremely good tempered.

Though somewhat of an invalid, Lady Thicknesse was a most charming companion, and a great deal more amiable than so-called charming people usually are. Besides being very rich, very well bred, and very agreeable, she had a special recommendation to Sir Bridgnorth—she had no family. He had resolved never to marry a widow with incumbrances.

Lady Thicknesse looked remarkably well that morning. Her pale and delicate complexion was a little warmer than usual, and her eyes rather brighter; but she was not in high spirits. Indeed, she never was in high spirits; her manner being always subdued. She questioned Sir Bridgnorth about Charlton, and seemed delighted with his description of the place.

"I hope you will see it ere long," he said, with a peculiar smile, that made her heart flutter, and caused her to cast down her eyes.

Now seemed Sir Bridgnorth's opportunity.

After clearing his throat he remarked:

"It appears to me that such a residence as Charlton, with a large park attached to it, and a house in Belgrave-square, would form a remarkably nice combination of town and country. What does your ladyship think ? "

" As a rule I am not very fond of the country," she replied. " But I fancy I could be happy anywhere, under certain circumstances."

" Under what circumstances ? " he asked, bending down his head.

" Don't ask," she replied, avoiding his ardent gaze.

" But I am particularly anxious to know," he said, " my own happiness being dependent upon the answer. Could you contrive to spend six months at such a dull place as Charlton ? "

" Yes, very well," she replied, raising her eyes, and looking him full in the face, " provided you will agree to pass the other six months in Belgrave Square."

Sir Bridgnorth could scarcely believe what he heard.

" Is that a bargain ? " he exclaimed joyously. " If so, let us conclude it at once."

" With all my heart," she replied. " I am quite satisfied with the arrangement."

" And I ought to be, and am," said Sir Bridgnorth. " I am sure I have got the best of it."

" You say so now," she rejoined with a smile. " But you may alter your opinion after six months' experience of Belgrave Square."

" Never ! " he exclaimed. " My only fear is that your ladyship may get tired of Charlton ! "

" Then dismiss that apprehension," she rejoined. " I cannot feel *ennui* if you are there."

Just then the clatter of hoofs was heard behind them, and the baronet's spirited horses, startled by the sound, set off at a pace that gave her ladyship a momentary fright.

But the runaways were quickly checked, and Sir Bridgnorth looking round, saw that Lord Courland and Scrope Danvers were galloping after them.

" What the deuce is the matter? " he shouted.

" Nothing," replied Scrope.

" Then take it quietly," said the baronet. " My horses won't stand that noise."

Thereupon, the pace was slackened on both sides, and Lady Thicknesse asked Lord Courland if he was going to Brackley.

" I hope you are," she added. " My sister, Lady Barfleur, will be charmed to see your lordship ! "

" I want to consult your ladyship," he replied, bringing his horse as close to her as he could, and speaking in a low voice.

" I hope nothing has gone wrong? " she inquired, rendered rather uneasy by his looks.

" I'm very much afraid the match won't come off," he replied ; " unless your ladyship will kindly act for me."

" I will do anything you desire," she rejoined earnestly. " It would grieve me beyond measure if any *contretemps* occurred."

" I cannot explain matters fully at this moment," he said. " But it is certain I am entirely to blame."

" Since your lordship so frankly makes that admission," she rejoined, " there can be no difficulty in arranging the quarrel—for quarrel I suppose it is."

" I will tell you all when we get to Brackley," he said. " But meantime, I may mention a circumstance of which I am quite sure neither your ladyship nor Sir Bridgnorth are aware."

"Your lordship must speak in a lower tone, if you would not have me hear all you say," remarked the baronet.

"But I do wish you to hear this," rejoined Lord Courland. "Mrs. Calverley has only just discovered that if she marries again, the whole of her property goes to Chetwynd and Mildred."

"You amaze me!" cried Sir Bridgnorth.

"When this piece of information was first communicated to me by Carteret," continued his lordship, "I yielded to an impulse of anger for which I now reproach myself, and declared I would break off the match."

"I don't wonder at it," said the baronet.

"But when I subsequently had an interview with Mrs. Calverley herself, my purpose changed. I found my affections were so strongly fixed, I could not execute my threat."

"I am delighted to hear it," said Lady Thicknesse. "Such disinterested conduct does your lordship the greatest credit. Then I presume all will go on as before?"

"I hope so," he replied. "But I am in doubt. Mrs. Calverley seems quite firm in her determination to break off the engagement."

"But she has nothing to complain of," remarked Sir Bridgnorth. "On the contrary, she is the sole cause of the misunderstanding. I take a totally different view of the matter from your lordship, and I suspect I am much nearer the truth. If she is now resolved to break off the match, it is because she is unwilling to lose her property."

"Oh, pray don't put that unfair construction on her conduct!" exclaimed Lady Thicknesse.

"It seems to me quite natural," said Sir Bridg-north; "quite consistent with her character," he added, in a whisper, to Lady Thicknesse.

"She seems very greatly troubled," observed Lord Courland; "and if anything occurs in consequence, I shall never forgive myself."

"Your lordship alarms yourself without reason, I think," said Lady Thicknesse.

"You have not seen her this morning, I suppose?"

"I have not," she replied.

"Then you don't know how ill she looks."

"I am very sorry to hear it," replied Lady Thicknesse. "But she will soon get well again if the matter is settled, as I am persuaded it will be."

"I ought to tell you she has bidden me farewell," said his lordship.

"Don't despair," rejoined Lady Thicknesse. "I'll undertake to bring you together again. I'm sorry you didn't call me in at the time; but it's not too late now."

"Your ladyship gives me hopes," said Lord Courland retiring.

"If she marries, as I trust she may," observed Sir Bridgnorth, as soon as his lordship was out of hearing, "it will be an immense thing for Chetwynd and Mildred. But I doubt whether she will make such a sacrifice for Lord Courland."

"I believe she is very much in love with him," remarked Lady Thicknesse.

"Possibly," said Sir Bridgnorth. "But this is too much to pay. As to her being in ignorance of the contents of her late husband's will, I never can credit that. Yet it puzzles me to conceive what she meant to do. Somehow or other, her plan has failed. Your ladyship thinks the matter will be easily settled. I am not of that opinion."

"To tell you the truth, dear Sir Bridgnorth," said Lady Thicknesse, "I do feel rather uneasy about Mrs. Calverley."

"If your ladyship knew her as well as I do," he replied, in an indifferent tone, "you wouldn't feel uneasy at all. My firm conviction is that she won't marry Lord Courland."

"If she doesn't, I shall alter my opinion of her," said her ladyship.

Sir Bridgnorth smiled, and giving his horses a slight touch with the whip, he quickened their pace, and the newly engaged pair soon arrived at Brackley.

XXIV.

THE RACE BETWEEN ZEPHYRUS AND TOM TANKARD.

ABOUT a mile in the rear of Sir Bridgnorth was Mrs. Calverley's pony-carriage, driven by Laura, by whose side was Zephyrus, very smartly dressed indeed, and wearing a Paris hat, while in the groom's place at the back, and looking very like a groom himself, sat Tom Tankard. Tom thought himself rather slighted by being placed in an inferior situation to the *chef*, but he was obliged to submit, or stay behind.

The first part of the drive was pleasant enough. Zephyrus was charmed with the carriage and the ponies, and declared the equipage was as pretty as any to be seen in the Bois de Boulogne. He was likewise enchanted with Mademoiselle Laura's skill as a whip;

and it was a gratification to him that Tom Tankard, of whom he entertained a secret jealousy, should be kept in the background.

But this latter circumstance, together with Laura's evident preference for Zephyrus, vexed Tom, and made him ready to pick a quarrel with the Frenchman. He soon grew very sullen, and took no part in the conversation. But this they did not mind. They did not care for his company, and Laura only brought him because she didn't like to drive out alone with the Frenchman.

Precisely the reverse of Tom, and full of life and spirit, Zephyrus had something amusing to say about everything. Laura was quite enchanted. Never before had she enjoyed so pleasant a drive. But then she had never before driven anybody except her mistress and the groom, and she didn't condescend to talk to grooms.

When they reached the heath, Tom shook off his sulkiness, and surveying the scene, called out :

" Look here, monsieur; here's a famous place for a steeple-chase ! "

" A fine place, indeed ! " observed Zephyrus. " I should say you could here have all the dangers you desire."

" I wouldn't advise you to try the heath, Mr. Tom," observed Laura. " Sir Leycester Barfleur lost his life in that dreadful quagmire."

" But a capital foot-race might be run on the hard turf," said Tom. " How say you, monsieur ? Shall we have a trial of speed ? Half a mile for half a sov'rin' ? "

" Shall I run, mademoiselle ? " said Zephyrus.

Laura gave him a look, as much as to say, "By all means; you'll beat him!"

"Agreed!" cried Zephyrus. "Mademoiselle Laura shall hold the stakes, and decide."

So saying, he placed a small piece of gold in her hand, his example being followed by Tom.

"Our mark shall be yonder tree," said Zephyrus, pointing to the shattered oak near which the ladies had been robbed by the gipsies.

"There and back?" asked Tom.

"There and back, of course," replied Zephyrus.

"Before we start," said Tom, "let it be clearly understood whoever wins is to sit beside Miss Laura."

"Bon!" cried Zephyrus. "I shall be certain to occupy that envied place!"

"Not so certain," rejoined Tom, with a knowing wink.

Ready in a minute, and in another minute off, at a signal from Laura, who had great difficulty in holding in the ponies when the start was made.

There seemed very little doubt that the Frenchman would win, for he was extremely agile, and ran far more lightly and fleetly than our fat friend Tom.

But it soon appeared that young Tankard intended some ruse, for he was still more than a hundred yards from the oak, and sixty or seventy behind Zephyrus, when he suddenly turned round, and ran back as fast as he could.

Zephyrus did not at first see what his opponent was about, but the moment he did, he likewise turned, and set off after young Tankard at such a pace that even then it seemed probable he would overtake him.

But by dint of extraordinary exertion, Tom managed

to reach the pony-carriage in time to spring into the coveted seat beside Laura, just as the Frenchman came up.

"Come out, sir!" vociferated Zephyrus; "you've lost!"

"Lost the race—but won the seat!" rejoined Tom, with a triumphant laugh.

"Come out, I insist!" cried the Frenchman.

To prevent the conflict that seemed imminent, Laura interfered; but she could not induce Tom to surrender the seat, so she tried to pacify Zephyrus by giving him the stakes, adding that they should soon be at Brackley, where a change could be made quietly.

Matters being thus arranged, though by no means to Laura's satisfaction, she drove on, and had just entered the park when Captain Danvers dashed through the lodge gate, and soon came up to them.

Apparently surprised at the sight of Laura, he stopped for a moment to speak to her.

"What are you doing here, Laura?" he inquired.

"My mistress allowed me to drive the pony-carriage to Brackley, captain," she replied, rather quickly, for she didn't like to be thus questioned; "and I brought these gentlemen with me."

"But don't you know your mistress is dangerously ill?" cried the captain.

"Not the least idea of it, I assure you, captain, or I shouldn't be here!" cried Laura, looking dreadfully frightened. "But I'll go back immediately."

"I don't think you'll find her alive," was the captain's consolatory remark; "but you may be of some service."

"What is it, sir?" cried Laura; "what is it?"

Captain Danvers, however, paid no attention to the inquiry, but dashed off as hard as he could to the Hall.

"It's something terrible—I'm sure of it!" said Laura. "I feel ready to faint."

"Change places, and I'll drive you back," said Tom. "It's lucky I'm here."

"I don't know what I should have done without Mr. Tom," said Laura, as she took his seat, and gave him the reins and whip. "Don't lose any time."

"I won't, depend upon it," rejoined Tom. "The ribbons are in good hands now they're in mine. Take my advice, dear girl, and don't make yourself uneasy till you get there. Time enough, then. All's for the best, you see, monsieur. If you hadn't given up that place, you'd 'a been forced to give it up, since you can't drive."

"You're mistaken, sir, I *can* drive—and very well, too," rejoined Zephyrus.

"But not so well as me," said Tom. "I'll bring you to Ouselcroft in no time," he added to Laura.

And he soon got the ponies into such a pace as they had never travelled before.

XXV.

CAPTAIN DANVERS BRINGS DISTRESSING NEWS.

LEAPING from his steed in the court-yard of the old Hall, Captain Danvers inquired for Lady Thicknesse; and learning that she was with Lady Barfleur, in the drawing-room, he hastened thither, and found the two ladies in question, with Lord Courland, Sir Bridgnorth, and his brother Scrope.

His looks caused general consternation, since all could perceive from them that some direful calamity had happened.

Lord Courland rushed up to him, and, taking his hand, said:

"You bring us bad news, I'm afraid, Captain Danvers?"

"I do, indeed, my lord," he replied in a sorrowful tone; "very painful news."

At these words, the whole party gathered round him.

"To whom does your bad news relate?" inquired Lady Thicknesse.

"Chiefly to Mrs. Calverley," he replied.

"Great Heaven, my worst fears are realised!" exclaimed Lord Courland, in a voice of anguish and despair. "Does she still live?"

"Death would be a release in her present state!" replied Captain Danvers. "She has swallowed poison."

"Poison!" echoed several voices.

"And I am the cause of this dreadful act!" cried Lord Courland.

"Calm yourself, my lord, I entreat you!" said Captain Danvers. "It is not exactly as you suppose. That love for you has led this unhappy lady into the commission of a dreadful act is certain; but the attempt at self-destruction, which no doubt will end fatally, has been made solely to escape the consequences of her crime."

The whole assemblage listened in horror to what was said.

"I will not ask you for any further explanation," cried Lord Courland, "unless you feel justified in giving it to me. But you have made certain dark allusions that ought to be cleared up. You charge Mrs. Calverley, whom I love dearly in spite of all, with the commission of a dreadful crime, to which she was instigated by love for me. What has she done? Is it a secret?"

"No, my lord," replied Captain Danvers, with great feeling. "It is perfectly well known at Ouselcroft. She has attempted to poison her step-daughter, Mildred."

"But what was the motive?" demanded Lord Courland.

"To prevent Mildred from profiting by her father's will. Had she died before the projected marriage, the property would have remained with Teresa."

Lord Courland looked aghast.

"There is every reason to hope Mildred will recover," pursued the captain. "Doctor Spencer is confident he can save her. He cannot save Mrs. Calverley, because remedial measures were too long delayed."

A groan burst from Lord Courland.

"Pardon me, Lady Barfleur," he said, turning to her, "if I quit you thus abruptly. I know you will excuse it under the circumstances. I shall return at once to Ouselcroft."

"I will go with you," said Scrope.

And they quitted the room together.

"I am quite as agitated and distressed as his lordship," observed Lady Thicknesse. "You must take me back, Sir Bridgnorth."

2 B

"I will order the horses at once," he replied. "In a few minutes the phaeton shall be ready."

And he departed on the errand.

"I grieve to leave thus, dearest sister," said Lady Thicknesse. "But it cannot be helped."

"I know it cannot," Lady Barfleur replied. "Let me see you to-morrow. But nobody has told me how Emmeline is?"

"You needn't be uneasy about her, dear aunt," replied Captain Danvers. "Through all this anxiety and trouble, Emmeline has kept up most wonderfully. I saw Rose, her attendant, not much more than an hour ago, and she said her young mistress had scarcely suffered from a headache. And now, dear aunt, I must take a hasty leave. Like the rest, I shall return to Ouselcroft, to see the end of this sad business. Adieu!"

Shortly afterwards Sir Bridgnorth appeared at the door to give Lady Thicknesse notice that the phaeton was ready.

"It is fortunate you have got Sir Bridgnorth with you, sister," observed Lady Barfleur. "He is one of the most sensible and most agreeable men I know."

"I am glad to hear you say so, sister," replied Lady Thicknesse. "He proposed as he drove me here this morning, and I accepted him."

"Bless me! That *is* news!" cried Lady Barfleur. "Come here, dear Sir Bridgnorth," she added, signing to him. "I must have a word with you. I have just heard something that has enchanted me. You are made for each other. Now don't stop here a moment longer, but take her to the carriage. Good-bye!"

XXVI.

TERESA'S CONFESSION.

ALONE with the dying Teresa.

"Take comfort," said the good chaplain, regarding her with tenderness and compassion. "Ease your breast by a full confession, and then, if your repentance is sincere, doubt not Heaven's goodness and mercy. Our blessed Saviour will not desert you."

On this, Teresa knelt down before him, and, though he strove to raise her, she would not quit the humble posture.

"Prepare yourself for a dreadful relation, reverend sir," she said, clasping her hands. "I had the best and kindest of husbands, who studied my every wish, and strove in every way to make me happy. I persuaded him I was happy; but I deceived him. The yoke I had put on was unsupportable.

"An evil spirit seemed to have taken possession of my breast. I strove to dismiss the wicked thoughts that assailed me; but they came back again and again, and with greater force than before.

"I had not a fault to find with my husband—he was kindness itself. Yet I sought to get rid of him by poison. It was long before I could make up my mind to the dreadful act; but I was ever brooding upon it.

"At last I obtained the poison, minute doses of which would kill without exciting suspicion. But not till my husband was attacked by some slight illness did I administer the first dose.

"He grew worse. But it seemed only a natural

2 B 2

increase of the malady, and the symptoms excited no suspicion whatever in his medical attendant, the progress of the poison being so slow and insidious. Moreover, I was constantly with my victim, and acted as his nurse."

The good chaplain covered his face with his hands, and a short pause ensued, which was broken by Teresa.

"And now comes the astounding part of my narration," she said. "I can scarcely credit my own hardness of heart. As I saw this kind and excellent man, who loved me so dearly, gradually wasting away— literally dying by inches—I felt no compunction— none! I counted the days he could live."

Here there was another pause, and the guilty woman had to summon up resolution before she could proceed.

"To free myself from my marriage fetters was only part of my scheme," she said. "My greedy spirit would not be content without my husband's property, and this I felt certain I could secure. He doted upon me. I had obtained his entire confidence. I knew his inmost thoughts. He had quarrelled with his son. I aggravated the dispute, and took care to prevent a reconciliation, which could have been easily effected had I so desired it.

"My ascendancy over my infirm husband was now so great that he acted upon all my suggestions; and by hints cunningly thrown out, I easily induced him to make a will in my favour, persuading him I would carry out his wishes in regard to his son and daughter."

"Did no suspicion cross him?" inquired the chaplain.

"Not till the last night of his life," she replied. "But I think it did then. If he suspected me, he never taxed me with my guilt."

At this moment a sudden change came over her, and she gazed strangely into the vacancy.

"What troubles you?" inquired the chaplain.

"I thought I saw my husband standing there!" she replied, with a shudder.

"'Tis fancy. Proceed with your confession. You have more to tell?"

"I have," she replied, with a fearful look. "The dark tragedy was over. Intoxicated by the power and wealth I had acquired, I contrived to stifle remorse. I kept Mildred constantly with me. Her presence seemed to shield me, and I sought to make some amends by befriending Chetwynd.

"But vengeance was pursuing me, though with slow feet. My punishment was accomplished in an unforeseen manner. Hitherto my heart had never known love, and I thought myself proof against the tender passion. But it was not so. I met Lord Courland at the house of Lady Thicknesse in London, and he at once won my affections and offered me his hand.

"Loving him, and thinking to bind him to me, I promised him half the large property I fancied at my disposal. All was arranged, and my destined husband had come down here to see his future abode, when almost at the last moment I discovered that if I married again the whole of the property would go to Mildred.

"This discovery roused all the evil passions in my heart, and I determined to remove her in the same manner I had removed her father.

"Provided with the means of executing my fell purpose, I did not delay it. You were present, reverend sir, when I dropped poison, unperceived, into her wine, and you may remember how soon it took effect ? "

"I remember she was suddenly seized with illness after drinking a glass of champagne," he replied, with a look of horror; "but I little thought the wine had been drugged—nor did any one."

"She recovered," pursued the guilty woman; "and all might have been well if I could have resisted the dreadful temptation to which I was subjected. But I yielded.

"Again I contrived to give her poison, and another seizure followed. Doctor Spencer was sent for. The symptoms could not be mistaken; the terrible crime was discovered, and quickly traced to me. The poison being found in my possession, my guilt was established."

"It may comfort you to learn that Mildred will recover," observed Mr. Massey. "The medicines given her by Doctor Spencer have produced a wonderful effect. At first I had little hope. But now I have every confidence that her life will be spared."

"'Tis well," she replied. "But my doom is sealed. Doctor Spencer took away the phial containing the poison; but I had enough left for myself."

"And you have done this desperate deed ? " he asked.

"I could not live," she replied. "I should go mad. But that Mildred will live is the greatest possible consolation to me. If I could see her, and obtain her forgiveness, I think I could die in peace. But I have not strength to go to her."

" She is here," said the chaplain.

The dying woman raised her eyes, and beheld Mildred standing before her, wrapped in a loose robe, and supported by Emmeline and Rose Hartley.

Behind them was Chetwynd, who closed the door after him as he came in.

Mildred's countenance was exceedingly pale; but her eyes were bright, and her looks seemed almost angelic to the despairing Teresa, who crept humbly towards her.

"I do not deserve pardon," said the penitent woman. "Yet for the sake of Him who died for us, and washed out our sins with His blood, I implore you to forgive me!"

"I do forgive you," rejoined Mildred. "I have come hither for that purpose. May Heaven have mercy upon you!"

"Since your repentance is sincere, daughter," said the chaplain, "may your sins be blotted out, and the guilt of your many offences be remitted."

"Amen!" exclaimed Chetwynd.

"Then farewell!" said Teresa, in a faint voice. "Farewell, Emmeline! farewell, Chetwynd! Think not of me with abhorrence; but, if you can, with pity!"

Without a word more, she sank backwards, and expired.

Chetwynd caught her before she fell, and placed her on a couch.

All those who had witnessed her death had departed, except Mr. Massey, who was still in the room when Lord Courland entered.

On beholding the body, he uttered a frenzied cry, and rushed towards it.

"I would have given five years of my own life to exchange a few words with her ere she breathed her last!" he exclaimed, in a voice of bitterest anguish and self-reproach.

"You loved her, then, deeply, my lord?" said Chetwynd.

"She was the only woman I ever loved," replied Lord Courland. "Farewell, Teresa!"

Bending down and kissing her brow, he quitted the room with Chetwynd.

XXVII.

A MONTH LATER.

A MONTH must now be allowed to elapse.

During the interval, the dark clouds that hung over Ouselcroft have dispersed, and the place has once more assumed a pleasant aspect.

Unhappy Teresa will never again trouble those connected with her.

Mildred, we rejoice to say, under the care of Doctor Spencer, has entirely recovered, and looks more beautiful than ever. She is at Brackley with Emmeline, who has quite regained her spirits and good looks, both of which had suffered from her recent anxiety. Rose Hartley is still with them.

Master of Ouselcroft, Chetwynd has already won the hearts of his dependents. He looks somewhat older and much graver, and Norris says he discerns a likeness to his father that he never perceived before.

As to Norris himself, we need scarcely say he still

holds the most important post in the household, and will continue to hold it as long as he is able to do so.

Chetwynd has two guests staying with him—Sir Bridgnorth Charlton and Captain Danvers—and they will remain at Ouselcroft till certain contemplated events come off.

Lady Thicknesse is at Brackley with Lady Barfleur, and means to stay there for a short time longer. She has engaged Laura, and is very well satisfied with her. The talkative lady's-maid suits her exactly. Sir Bridgnorth drives out her ladyship daily in his phaeton, and they then discuss their future plans, but she has not yet seen Charlton, nor will she visit her future residence till she goes there as its mistress. She has every prospect of happiness with Sir Bridgnorth, who really devotes himself to her, and strives to anticipate all her wishes.

Charles Danvers and Mildred pass all their time together. At first, they contented themselves with the gardens of Brackley; but since Mildred has grown stronger, and is able to take equestrian exercise, they have begun to take long rides, and are seldom seen between luncheon and dinner. Captain Danvers considers himself a most fortunate man, and with good reason, for he will have a most lovely bride, and a very large fortune.

But what of Chetwynd? Ought he not to be esteemed fortunate? As far as wealth is concerned, he has far more than he ever dreamed of, and if he weds the heiress of Brackley, he will become one of the richest men in the county. But his chief wealth, in his own esteem, is in the prize he has won, and he looks forward eagerly to the day—now not very far distant, he hopes—when he shall make her his own.

Such is the present state of things at the two houses the inmates of which are constantly together, dining with each other daily, either at Ouselcroft or Brackley; but we shall, perhaps, learn more, by assisting at a confidential talk that took place one afternoon in the butler's pantry at Ouselcroft, between old Norris and Laura.

"Well, Mr. Norris," she said, "I am come to see how you are getting on. We are quiet enough just now, but we shall soon have plenty to do."

"In what way?" asked the butler.

"In the matrimonial line," replied Laura. "Three weddings will come off very shortly."

"Are any of them fixed?" inquired Norris.

"Not that I am aware of," replied the lady's-maid; "but they cannot be long delayed. All depends upon Lady Thicknesse. When she names the day, the other two are sure to follow suit."

"Her ladyship, I suppose, has positively accepted Sir Bridgnorth?" asked Norris.

"Positively," replied Laura; "and a very good choice she has made, according to my notion. For my own part, I should prefer the old baronet to either of the young men."

"Pooh, pooh! He won't bear comparison with my young master. Of course, he's very suitable to a middle-aged dame like Lady Thicknesse."

"He's very agreeable, I repeat, and I think my lady uncommonly lucky in securing him. I believe they've agreed to spend half the year in town, and the other half in the country. That'll just suit me."

" At any rate, they'll have no lack of money," said
Norris. "But, after all, Lady Thicknesse is nothing
like so rich as her niece—to say nothing of Brackley,
which must come to the young lady by-and-by."

"Yes; they'll have too much," observed Laura.
" I wonder where Mr. Chetwynd and his lady will
reside ? "

" Why, here—at Ouselcroft—of course," replied
Norris.

" I don't feel sure of that," said Laura. " I sometimes fancy they'll live at Brackley."

"Nonsense ! " exclaimed Norris. " Mr. Chetwynd
will never leave his father's house, now he has got
possession of it. I'm certain of that."

" Then Captain and Mrs. Danvers may as well take
up their quarters at Brackley," said Laura.

" You're settling all very nicely ! " said Norris, with
a laugh. " But I don't know that Lady Barfleur will
consent to take them. I should think not. All very
well as visitors, but not for a permanence."

" Well, then, Mrs. Danvers must buy a place," said
Laura. " She'll have money enough."

Norris laughed ; but, directly afterwards, his countenance changed, and he said, gravely :

" Ah, Laura ! we live in a strange world. A month
ago, who would have thought things would be in this
state ? Then we were talking over Mrs. Calverley's
contemplated marriage with Lord Courland. Now she
is gone, and other weddings are about to take place."

" Don't mention the poor dear lady, Mr. Norris, if
you wouldn't make me cry," said Laura, taking out
her pocket-handkerchief. " She had dreadful faults,
no doubt ; but she was always very kind to me, and I

will say this of her, she was the loveliest creature ever beheld."

"She contrived to do a great deal of mischief in her time," observed Norris.

"Granted," rejoined Laura. "But you ought to feel some sorrow for her, seeing how very handsomely she behaved to you, Mr. Norris. I'm sure I feel very much obliged to her for my fifty pounds, though I wish it had been five thousand, like Lord Courland's legacy."

"Yes, that's a good lumping sum," observed Norris, "and will console his lordship for her loss."

"I suppose he has got the money?" remarked Laura.

"Yes; the legacy has already been paid," replied Norris.

"I thought it had," said Laura. "But do tell me, Mr. Norris—is it true the poor lady has been seen since her death?"

"Clarissa declares she certainly beheld her the other evening in the dressing-room," replied the butler.

"Dear me, how dreadful!" exclaimed Laura, "I should be frightened to death. Clarissa saw her in the dressing-room, you say. How was it? Do tell me!"

"Clarissa's tale is this. She was in the poor lady's bedchamber the other evening, just as it was growing dusk, when fancying she heard a sound in the dressing-room, she opened the door, which was standing ajar, and then beheld an apparition exactly resembling Mrs. Calverley, and holding a small phial, at which the figure was looking. So scared was

Clarissa at the sight, that she could neither cry out nor stir till the apparition turned its head and fixed its eyes upon her. Their expression was so terrible that she rushed back, and fell senseless on the bedchamber floor. This is the account she gives, and most of the women-servants believe it, but I regard it as mere fancy."

"*I* believe it, Mr. Norris," replied Laura, shuddering. "I once saw Mrs. Calverley myself in the dressing-room, in the exact posture you describe her, with a little phial in her hand, containing *eau de luce,* she said, but I am now sure it was poison. I shall never forget the look she gave me. Depend upon it, Clarissa has seen her spirit."

"May be so," observed Norris.

"The poor thing can't rest, and I don't wonder at it," observed Laura. "I suppose these rooms will be shut up, Mr. Norris?"

"Nobody has slept there since the poor lady's death," he replied; "but I can't say about shutting up the rooms."

"I wouldn't sleep there for the world," remarked Laura. "Indeed, after this occurrence, I don't think I shall ever venture into the dressing-room again. I should always expect to find her there."

Just then a bell was rung, and Norris instantly prepared to answer the summons.

"My young master wants to see me before he sets out for Brackley," he said. "Stay where you are for a few minutes. I may have something to tell you."

When Norris reappeared, he had a very joyful expression of countenance.

"I can tell you something you don't know, Laura," he said—"something about Lady Thicknesse."

"I know what it is. The wedding-day is fixed."

"Right!"

"When is it to be?" she exclaimed, eagerly.

"This day week," replied the butler.

"Then her ladyship will get the start of the others," said Laura.

"I'm not sure of that," replied Norris, significantly. "I can't tell you any more now. All I know is, my young master and Captain Danvers have just ridden off to Brackley."

XXVIII

ALL IS SETTLED.

When Chetwynd and Captain Danvers were about half a mile from Brackley Park, they saw Sir Bridgnorth and Lady Thicknesse coming slowly along in the phaeton.

The pair looked so happy, and so completely engrossed by each other, that the two young men scarcely liked to interrupt them. However, Sir Bridgnorth pulled up, and then the others stopped likewise.

After a few words had passed, her ladyship signed to Chetwynd to come close to her, and said, in a low voice:

"I have had some talk with Lady Barfleur this morning, and I think she has consented that your marriage with Emmeline shall take place immediately. Sir Bridgnorth, who was present at the time, lent his aid, and spoke so urgently, that I think he decided the point."

"I am infinitely indebted to you both," said Chetwynd, glancing at Sir Bridgnorth.

"You will find Emmeline in the garden," said Lady Thicknesse; "and by the time we come back from our drive, I hope all will be satisfactorily settled."

"This day week, mind!—not later!" added Sir Bridgnorth, leaning towards him. "All is ready for us at Charlton."

The baronet then moved on, while the others rode off in the opposite direction.

Arrived at Brackley, our friends ascertained that both young ladies were in the garden, and immediately went in quest of them, and found them seated near the bowling-green.

This being the first time we have seen them since their deliverance from Teresa, we are bound to say they were both looking charmingly, and in capital spirits. Mildred's illness hadn't left a trace on her fair countenance. On the contrary, she seemed prettier than ever.

No sooner did their lovers appear than they arose, and flew to meet them; and a very lover-like meeting took place.

But the couples then separated, and Chetwynd and Emmeline, whom we shall accompany, moved off to a short distance.

"Emmeline," said Chetwynd, "I had resolved not to ask you to fulfil your promise to me till I had gone through a year's probation; nor should I have done so had I not been placed by circumstances in a totally different position from what I was at that time. If you have confidence in my reformation—if you think I have proved myself worthy of you—if you can trust me—I will beg you to abridge my term, and give yourself to me now. But if you have any doubt remaining—if you deem it better to wait till the appointed time—I pray you to do so! Your happiness is my chief concern; and, however irksome the delay may be, I shall not complain!"

"I have entire faith in you, dear Chetwynd," she replied, in a voice of much emotion. "In every respect you have proved yourself worthy of my love, and I am prepared to give you my hand whenever you claim it."

"I claim it at once," he said, eagerly. "And as there is now no obstacle—for Lady Thicknesse tells me your mother has given her consent—I pray that our union may take place on the same day as the marriage of her ladyship with Sir Bridgnorth."

"Be it so," said Emmeline; "and I hope another marriage will take place at the same time."

Just then, the voice of Captain Danvers was heard at a little distance, and he called out:

"Don't let me interrupt you; but Mildred won't fix the day till she is satisfied you are agreed."

"Then tell her we *are* agreed," replied Emmeline. "Will this day week suit?"

"It will suit her perfectly," replied the captain.

"You answer for me!" said Mildred, laughing; "but, though you speak without authority, it is really the day I should choose."

" I felt certain of it, or I should not have ventured to say so," observed the captain. "But, since all private arrangements are made, and we are to be wedded at the same time, won't it be more convenient to talk matters over together ? "

" I am quite of that opinion," said Chetwynd.

No dissentient voice was raised. So they all came together, and began to discuss the general arrangements.

Ere long they were joined by Lady Barfleur, who gave her formal consent to her daughter's union with Chetwynd, and then took part in the discussion.

It was agreed they should be married in the private chapel belonging to the Hall, and that the Reverend Mr. Massey should perform the ceremony.

This was the chief matter, but they had a good deal to talk over besides, and they were still engaged in the discussion when Lady Thicknesse and Sir Bridgnorth returned from their drive.

Having already decided upon the private chapel of Mr. Massey, the last-mentioned pair had only to express their satisfaction that their own plans had been adopted, but they had many congratulations to offer to Chetwynd and Emmeline.

XXIX.

CONCLUSION.

THE auspicious day had arrived on which the three marriages were to take place, or rather we ought to

2 c

say four, since it had been arranged that Rose Hartley was to be married to Harry Netterville at the same time.

Harry had come down two days before to Ousel-croft, and had brought with him, on Chetwynd's special invitation, Mr. and Mrs. Hartley, together with Tom Tankard, who was to act as Harry's best man. Higgins was now staying at Brackley, and Mr. Tankard had been invited there. Captain Ponsonby, an old friend, had agreed to act as Chetwynd's best man, and Scrope Danvers would perform the same office for his brother. Sir Bridgnorth dispensed with a friend, and Lady Thicknesse had no brides-maid. Emmeline's bridesmaids were to be the two Miss Bretons, the beautiful Emma Ashton, and Hortensia Biddulph; Mildred's attendants were the Miss Leighs, Eugenia Radcliffe, and Blanche Dukin-field. It was not deemed advisable to increase the number, considering the small size of the chapel. Sir Gerard Danvers and Scrope were staying at Brackley, but Sir Bridgnorth, Captain Ponsonby, and Captain Danvers were at Ouselcroft.

A wedding portion of five hundred pounds had been jointly bestowed on Rose by Emmeline and Mildred, and Harry Netterville was to be appointed to the post of steward at Brackley.

The general arrangements was these. Chetwynd and his bride were to spend their honeymoon in perfect retirement at Ouselcroft; Captain and Mrs. Danvers meant to proceed to Windermere and the Lake country; and Sir Bridgnorth and his lady, like sensible folks, intended to drive at once to Charlton.

Such were the arrangements, and it was a matter

of congratulation to all when the morning proved fine.

An early and very cheery breakfast took place at Ouselcroft, for all three bridegrooms were in excellent spirits. Another early breakfast also took place in another room at the same house, at which Mr. and Mrs. Hartley, Harry Netterville, and Tom Tankard assisted.

After they had finished breakfast, Chetwynd came into the room and shook hands with them all.

"I'm right glad to see you here, Hartley," he said, clapping him kindly on shoulder. "Without you, my good friend, I should neither have been master of this house, nor wedded to her I love. I told you then I would some day prove my gratitude; and I mean to do so now. I have got a nice comfortable farm-house, which I shall bestow upon you and your wife, and where Harry Netterville can live with you. He will have a post as steward. I shall be glad to have you all near me."

"Heaven bless you, sir!" exclaimed Hartley, much affected. "You could not have conferred a greater kindness upon me, nor one I shall more appreciate!"

Mrs. Hartley was so overcome that she could hardly get out her thanks, but she did so at last.

We must now repair to Brackley.

As the day advanced, the old Hall presented a gayer appearance that it had done for many and many a year. The large court-yard was entirely filled with the tenants and retainers of the lord of the mansion —who henceforward would be represented by Chetwynd—their wives and daughters, some of the latter being very good-looking, and very well-dressed.

Among our acquaintances was Marple, the farmer, who had been present when Sir Leycester Barfleur was lost in the morass, and honest Ned Rushton, the keeper.

Already a brilliant assemblage was collected in the large room up-stairs, which was beautifully decorated with flowers, as were the drawing-room and the Hall. In fact, there were flowers everywhere.

At length the bell began to ring, the several bridal parties assembled in the Hall, and marshalled by Higgins and Norris, issued forth.

Preceded by a dozen young damsels dressed in white, who scattered flowers in their path, they then moved through the crowded court to the chapel, amid the audibly-expressed good wishes of the beholders.

Sir Bridgnorth and Lady Thicknesse took the lead, and her ladyship looked magnificent in her bridal array.

Then came Emmeline, escorted by her uncle, Sir Gerard Danvers, and followed by Chetwynd and Captain Ponsonby. She excited general admiration, as did Mildred, who followed on the arm of Mr. Talbot Hesketh, her mother's first cousin. Close behind them came Captain Danvers and his brother Scrope. Lastly came Rose, charmingly and simply attired in white, and looking quite as pretty as the others. Attended by her mother, and leaning on her father's arm, she was followed by Netterville and Tom Tankard. Laura and Clarissa were to act as her bridesmaids, but they had already gone into the chapel.

The little chapel presented an exceedingly pretty sight; but it was so full that very few of the tenantry could be admitted.

The chaplain was already at the altar, and his venerable figure completed the charming picture.

A few minutes elapsed while the several couples were being placed; but at length this preliminary proceeding was accomplished, and the ceremony commenced.

At this juncture the scene was exceedingly interesting, and long lived in the memory of those fortunate enough to behold it.

Rarely have two more beautiful brides than Emmeline and Mildred appeared at the altar—nay, we may say three, for Rose was little their inferior in beauty; and Lady Thicknesse, if she had not youth, had remarkable grace and elegance.

Grouped around were the bridesmaids, all of whom were young, exceedingly pretty, and charmingly attired.

Placed somewhat apart was Lady Barfleur, but being in deep mourning, she would not mingle with the group.

The ceremony proceeded, and the different couples were united.

Lady Thicknesse became Lady Bridgnorth, greatly to the delight of the excellent baronet. Chetwynd was made supremely happy by the hand of Emmeline. Nor had Charles Danvers less reason to be content, for in Mildred he obtained a treasure; while we doubt whether any one was happier than Harry Netterville, when he could really call Rose his own.

The ceremony is over.

We will accompany the happy couples—and they really deserve to be so described—as they cross the still crowded court, and pass through lines of bowing tenantry into the hall; but we will not join the throng in the drawing-room, nor sit down with the large party in the dining-room to the admirable breakfast prepared by Monsieur Zephyrus.

We will make passing bows to the beautiful brides; we will say farewell to our kindly Sir Bridgnorth, whom we rejoice to say still flourishes; we will bid adieu to Chetwynd and Charles Danvers, and wish them all happiness.

We will visit for a moment another table in another room, at which we shall find our blooming little Rose and her happy husband—now the happiest couple possible—her worthy father and doting mother; Tom Tankard and *his* father, who keeps him in order; Marple, the farmer; Ned Rushton, the keeper; and a great many more, all of whom are enjoying a most plentiful and excellent repast, at which, besides wine, there is no lack of good strong ale, a couple of casks having been broached that morning for the tenantry and general guests.

Our task is done.

THE END.

PRINTED BY TAYLOR AND CO.,
LITTLE QUEEN STREET, LINCOLN'S INN FIELDS.

THE SELECT LIBRARY 2/- VOLUMES.

Squire Arden.

By Mrs. Oliphant.

" Mrs. Oliphant's new book will not diminish her already established reputation. The plot is interesting and well managed, the scene well laid, and the characters various and forcibly described."—*Athenæum.*

—o—

Wild Georgie.

By Jean Middlemass.

" ' Wild Georgie' will add considerably to the author's reputation. The charm of the novel is the deep interest of the plot, which never flags for a moment. The characters are drawn with life-like vigour."—*Court Journal.*

—o—

In the Days of My Youth.

By Amelia B. Edwards,

Author of " Debenham's Vow."

" A novel which cannot fail to charm ; being written in a bright, sparkling, happy manner."—*Morning Post.*

—o—

The Lost Bride.

By Lady Chatterton.

" An ingenious and picturesque story, in which there is a good deal of character-drawing and some pleasant and lively sketches of society occur."—*Spectator.*
" ' The Lost Bride' will add considerably to Lady Chatterton's literary reputation. It is replete with interest, and the characters are perfectly true to nature."—*Court Journal.*

—o—

Mr. Arle.

By the Author of " Caste," etc.

" ' Mr. Arle' is a work of a very high order, and we are offering it no light tribute when we say that, in style and conception, it reminds us of the writings of Mrs. Gaskell."—*John Bull.*

(E)

Harry Muir:

A STORY OF SCOTTISH LIFE.

By Mrs. Oliphant.

" We prefer ' Harry Muir ' to most of the Scottish novels that have appeared since Galt's domestic stories. This new tale, by the author of ' Margaret Maitland,' is a real picture of the weakness of man's nature and the depths of woman's kindness. The narrative, to repeat our praise, is not one to be entered on or parted from without our regard for its writer being increased."—*Athenæum.*

—o—

For Love and Life.

By Mrs. Oliphant,

Author of "Squire Arden."

" ' For Love and Life ' is equal in all respects to the reputation of its writer. It will be read with delight."—*John Bull.*
" This novel is well worth reading. The story is interesting, the plot is original, and every character is a study."—*Daily News.*

—o—

Debenham's Vow.

By Amelia B. Edwards,

Author of " Miss Carew," etc.

" Debenham's Vow ' is decidedly a clever book. The story is pure and interesting, and most of the characters are natural, while some are charming."—*Saturday Review.*

—o—

Beautiful Edith.

By the Author of " Ursula's Love Story."

" We have no hesitation in placing ' Beautiful Edith ' among the very best novels that have been issued for a long period. It will become widely popular. The author possesses a charming style, and a talent for quiet humour."—*Messenger.*

THE SELECT LIBRARY 2/- VOLUMES.

Madonna Mary.

By Mrs. Oliphant.

"From first to last 'Madonna Mary' is written with evenness and vigour, and overflows with the best qualities of its writer's fancy and humour. The story is thoroughly original, as far as its plot and leading incidents are concerned; and the strength of the narrative is such that we question if any reader will lay it aside, notwithstanding the fullness in his throat, and the constriction of his heart, until he has shared in the happiness which is liberally assigned to the actors of the drama before the falling of the green curtain. But the principal charms of the work are subtle humour, fineness of touch, and seeming ease with which Mrs. Oliphant delineates and contrasts her numerous characters."—*Athenæum.*

—o—

Lost for Gold.

By Katherine King,

Author of "The Queen of the Regiment."

"Our readers will find much to interest them in this novel. It is the work of a writer of lively imagination and real ability."—*Messenger.*

—o—

Colonel Dacre.

By the Author of "Caste," "Pearl," "Bruna's Revenge," etc.

"There is much that is attractive both in Colonel Dacre and the simple-hearted girl whom he honours with his love."—*Athenæum.*
"Colonel Dacre is a gentleman throughout, which character is somewhat rare in modern novels."—*Pall Mall Gazette.*

—o—

The Days of My Life.

By Mrs. Oliphant.

"The author writes with her usual fine capacity for the picturesque, and her invariable good sense, good feeling, and good taste. No part of the narrative is uninteresting."—*Athenæum.*

May.

By Mrs. Oliphant,

Author of "Magdalen Hepburn."

"'May' is one of the best novels of the year. The Fifeshire scenes are admirable bits of that quiet landscape painting in which Mrs. Oliphant excels."—*Athenæum.*
"'May' is one of the freshest and most charming of Mrs. Oliphant's creations."—*Blackwood's Magazine.*

—o—

The Queen of the Regiment.

By Katherine King,

Author of "Lost for Gold."

"A charming, fresh, cheery novel. Its merits are rare and welcome. The glee-fulness, the ease, the heartiness, of the author's style cannot fail to please. Her heroine is a captivating girl."—*Spectator.*

—o—

Ombra.

By Mrs. Oliphant.

"This story is very carefully constructed. It has been written with sedulous pains, and there is no lack of individuality about any of the characters. The customary grace of the author's style, the high tone of mind, the ready and frank sympathies which have always characterised her, are found in this book, as in its predecessors; but here is something that they, not even the best among them, have not. She has never produced a rival to Kate Courtenay."—*Spectator.*

—o—

Miss Carew.

By Amelia B. Edwards,

Author of "Debenham's Vow," etc.

"Never has the author's brilliant and vivacious style been more conspicuously displayed than in this very original and charming story."—*Sun.*

THE SELECT LIBRARY 2/- VOLUMES.

Bella Donna.

By Percy Fitzgerald.

"There are certain characteristics in this novel which give it a peculiar place apart from most of the other novels of the season. It is not often, now-a-days, that we see the attempt made—or, if made, carried out with success—to construct a tale out of the development of sheer force of character. The interest of 'Bella Donna' lies in the skilful manner in which the plot is worked out by the subtle brain, and artful carriage of the heroine. There is a degree of originality and vigour about the writer, etc. .
The end is hurried on with an abruptness . . . . unless, indeed, he has intentionally acted upon the hint of Mr. Weller, and designed to make ns wish there was more of it."—*Saturday Review.*

—o—

Woodleigh.

By F. W Robinson,

Author of "Wildflower," etc., etc.

"This book has sterling merit: it is likely to sustain and extend an already high reputation."—*Press.*

—o—

The Constable of the Tower.

By W Harrison Ainsworth.

"Is an exceedingly entertaining novel. It assures Mr. Ainsworth more than ever in his position as one of the ablest fiction writers of the day."

—o—

Woman's Ransom.

By F. W Robinson,

Author of "Milly's Hero."

"'A Woman's Ransom' will fascinate the attention of the reader to the very end."—*John Bull.*
"The interest of this story is unflagging."—*Observer.*

The Young Heiress.

By Mrs. Trollope.

"The best of Mrs. Trollope's novels."—*Standard.*
"The knowledge of the world which Mrs. Trollope possesses in so emicent a degree is strongly exhibited in the pages of this novel."—*Observer.*

—o—

Ned Locksley,

THE ETONIAN.
FOURTH EDITION.

"A splendid production. The story, conceived with great skill, is worked out in a succession of powerful portraitures, and of soul-stirring scenes."

—o—

Wildflower.

By F. W Robinson,

Author of "Woodleigh."

"One of the best novels it has lately been our fortune to meet with. The plot is ingenious and novel, and the characters are sketched with a masterly hand."—*Press.*

—o—

Under the Spell.

By F. W Robinson,

Author of "Wildflower," "Milly's Hero," etc.

"This is the best story hitherto written by a very pleasant novelist. It is throughout a good story, that nobody will leave unfinished."—*Examiner.*

—o—

Tilbury Nogo.

By Whyte Melville.

"A capital novel, of the 'Charles O'Malley' school, full of dashing adventure, with scenes of real history cleverly introduced in the narrative."

(K)

THE SELECT LIBRARY 2/- VOLUMES.

The Second Mrs. Tillotson.

By Percy Fitzgerald.

"The jovial and unconscious hypocrisy of Mr. Tilney is delicious; and the way in which he mixes up ideas, and jumbles together quotations is charming. . . . We laugh at the old schemer; but we pity and admire him all the same. He is a man in whom Thackeray would have delighted. . . . He is an excellently drawn character."—*Saturday Review.*

—o—

Charles Auchester.

DEDICATED TO THE RIGHT HON. B. DISRAELI.

"The life of an enthusiast in music, by himself. The work is full of talent. The sketches of the masters and artists are life-like. In Seraphael all will recognise Mendelssohn, and in Miss Benette, Miss Lawrence, and Anastase, Berlioz, Jenny Lind, and another well-known to artist life, will be easily detected. To every one who cares for music, the volumes will prove a delightful study."—*Britannia.*

—o—

Two Marriages.

By the Author of "John Halifax, Gentleman," etc.

"We have no hesitation in affirming the "Two Marriages" to be in many respects the very best book that the author has yet produced. Rarely have we read a work written with so exquisite a delicacy, full of so tender an interest, and conveying so salutary a lesson."—*British Quarterly Review.*

—o—

Married Beneath Him.

By James Payn.

"A very clever, interesting, and well-written novel. The story is not less remarkable for excellence in point of plot and skill in construction than for the bright, pure, tender strain of feeling by which it is pervaded."

(M)

Christie's Faith.

By the Author of "Owen : a Waif," "Mattie : a Stray."

"This book deserves to be singled out from the ordinary run of novels on more than one account. The design and execution are both good. The characters are original, clearly conceived, and finely as well as strongly delineated. Christie herself is a delightful sketch."—*Pall Mall Gazette.*

—o—

The Country Gentleman

By "Scrutator,"

Author of "Checkmate."

"There is plenty of stirring interest in this novel, particularly for those readers who enjoy manly sport."—*Messenger.*

"An exceedingly well written and admirably told story. The characters are cleverly drawn. The incidents are very interesting."—*Sporting Review.*

—o—

Tales of all Countries.

By Anthony Trollope.

"These well-written and descriptive tales have already appeared. In their collected form they will be received with pleasure by the reading public, more especially at this season of the year. The tales which will give most satisfaction are 'The O'Connors of Castle Connor,' 'John Bull on the Guadalquiver,' 'Miss Sarah Jack, of Spanish Town, Jamaica,' and 'The Chateau of Prince Polignac,' but all of them testify to the talent of Mr. Trollope as a clever writer."—*Morning Advertiser.*

—o—

The Jealous Wife.

By Miss Pardoe,

Author of the "Rival Beauties."

"A tale of great power. As an author of fiction, Miss Pardoe has never done anything better than this work."—*Globe.*

THE SELECT LIBRARY 2/- VOLUMES.

Theo Leigh.

By *Annie Thomas,*

Author of "He Cometh Not," "Two Widows," etc.

"The author has surpassed herself in 'Theo Leigh.' The characters are distinctly drawn. The story is simple and spiritedly told. The dialogue is smart, natural, full of character. In short, 'Theo Leigh' takes its place among the cleverest novels of the season, and deserves to be popular. It is the cream of light literature; graceful, brilliant, and continuously interesting.

"In every respect an excellent novel. The interest is unflagging."

—o—

Giulio Malatesta.

By *Thomas A. Trollope,*

Author of "La Beata," etc.

"Will assuredly be read with pleasure. The book abounds in merit and beauty."

"This work will be read to the very last page with unbroken interest. It is one of the very best stories we have had from the author. It is full of the same power of observation, refinement, and grace which marks all his books."

—o—

Agatha's Husband.

By the Author of "John Halifax," "Olive," etc.

"One of Miss Muloch's admired fictions, marked by pleasant contrasts of light and shade — scenes of stirring interest and pathetic incidents. The theme is one of touching interest, and is most delicately managed."—*Literary Circular.*

—o—

Denis Donne.

By *Annie Thomas.*

"We can conscientiously recommend 'Denis Donne' to everyone who is sensible to the attractions of a well-written and more than commonly interesting novel."

"A good novel."—*Athenæum.*

(N)

Lindisfarn Chase.

By *Thomas A. Trollope,*

Author of "Beppo, the Conscript."

"The lovers of fictional literature will be glad to find that Messrs. Chapman and Hall have issued 'cheap editions' of the works of Thomas A. Trollope, a writer who has the tact of always sustaining the interest of his readers, and the experiences of a 'Lindisfarn Chase' and 'Beppo, the Conscript' are among the most popular works of this author. They are full of incident, and written with the pen of a man who is a keen observer of character and an excellent story-teller."

—o—

One and Twenty.

By *F. W. Robinson,*

Author of "Milly's Hero," etc.

"This remarkable novel is every way worthy of notice, whether as regards the veri-similitude of the story, or the simple and unaffected, yet exceedingly graphic style with which it is written. It reads more like a spirited memoir, than a mere creation of the author's brain."

—o—

Maurice Tiernay:

THE SOLDIER OF FORTUNE.

By *Charles Lever.*

"These are days in which the public should furnish their libraries, if they ever intend to do so. Who would be satisfied with the loan of the much thumbed library-book, when, for two shillings he can procure, in one handsome volume, a celebrated work of fiction, which often is seen swelling three books? This sprightly and original novel is now offered at a low price."

—o—

The Queen of the Seas.

By *Captain Armstrong.*

"With the exception of Marryat, Captain Armstrong is the best writer of nautical novels England has ever had."—*Sun.*

THE SELECT LIBRARY 2/6 VOLUMES.

Charles O'Malley, the Irish Dragoon.

By Charles Lever.

" The whole character of Mickey Free is indeed inimitable. We have no hesitation in affirming it to be the most perfect type of Irish humour that has ever been given to the world. It is perfectly sustained from first to last, and nothing in the conception of it is exaggerated or incongruous. Mickey Free is the Irish Sam Weller. He has, in fact, this advantage over Sam Weller, that he is the more thoroughly national and comprehensive type of the two. It is impossible but what this creation, which is in many respects the most felicitous of all Mr. Lever's creations, should live for ever as a distinct embodiment of national character."

—o—

Maurice Tiernay,

THE SOLDIER OF FORTUNE.

By Charles Lever.

" These are days in which the public should furnish their libraries, if they ever intend to do so. Who would be satisfied with the loan of the much-thumbed library-book, when, for two shillings he can procure, in one handsome volume, a celebrated work of fiction, which often is seen swelling three books ? This sprightly and original novel is now offered at the low price of half-a-crown."

—o—

The Daltons.

By Charles Lever.

"This work contains scenes from the late Italian campaign, and from Mr. Lever's well-known talent for depicting stirring scenes and faithful portraiture of character, it is needless for us to say much. The author of ' Charles O'Malley,' 'Harry Lorrequer,' &c., is too well known to require recommendation. We have no doubt the work will be well received." *Derby Reporter.*

18

The Knight of Gwynne.

A TALE OF THE TIME OF TH UNION.

By Charles Lever.

" The ' Knight of Gwynne' is certainly one of the most lovable characters that Mr. Lever has ever drawn; and he monopolises so much of our sympathy, that we hope to be forgiven for extending less of it than he probably deserves to Bagenal Daly, notwithstanding the vigour with which that character is drawn, the remarkable originality of it, and the fidelity with which it represents and sustains a most peculiar combination of qualities, intellectual as well as moral."—*Blackwood's Magazine.*

—o—

The Bramleighs of Bishop's Folly.

By Charles Lever.

" Mr. Lever has excelled himself in this capital novel, which possesses the merit of a carefully planned plot, the mystery of which is so artfully contrived that the reader does not suspect the very simple and natural solution until it is unfolded to him, combined with a group of thoroughly original personages who play their several parts with life-like dignity and grace; with charming naïveté and sweetness; or with refined craft and cunning."—*The Examiner.*

—o—

The Martins of Cro' Martin.

By Charles Lever.

" Mr. Lever has two capital qualities for a novelist, inexhaustible invention, and untiring spirits. His sketches are in a broad panoramic style, rudely drawn, and highly coloured, but full of striking effects. His fictions are of the full-blooded kind. All his characters have an excess of vitality, and when they are in full play it makes sober people almost go giddy to watch them."—*The Press.*

THE SELECT LIBRARY 2/6 VOLUMES.

Ralph the Heir.

By Anthony Trollope.

"A very interesting novel. The episodes of Sir Thomas Underwood's electioneering experiences and the whole of the Neefit courtship are, in our opinion, the strong points of the book. Probably no man alive, now that Charles Dickens has departed, can write on such subjects so humorously and so truthfully as Mr. Trollope. Sir Thomas Underwood and his clerk Stemm, Mr. Neefit and his daughter Polly, together with her lover, Ontario Moggs, are creations of which any writer of fiction might be proud."—*The Times.*

Orley Farm.

By Anthony Trollope.

"When a voluminous author writes a work of sustained power, the reader, fresh from the perusal of it, is apt to say, 'This is his best.' As a whole, some of his other novels may be better; but in parts he has attempted and he has achieved something higher in 'Orley Farm' than in any of his works. The character of Lady Mason is an exceedingly difficult one to grasp, and the position into which she is forced by her own acts is difficult to manage. She commits a great crime; she is in effect a swindler; there is to be no doubt as to the enormity of her guilt; and yet we are to love and admire her, and like all her friends to part from her with kisses and benedictions. During twenty years the lady bears in secret the load of her guilt, and tries to avoid the society of her neighbours; but at the end of twenty years, in the prospect of her guilt being discovered, she is to break down, she is to court the society of her friends, and she is to get elderly gentlemen to fall in love with her, one of them even proposing to marry her. These contrasts are presented to the reader with power and plausibility, and the lady, who has committed a very daring piece of villany in order to gratify her maternal feelings, is depicted in all her weakness, the victim of remorse, of terror, of shame unspeakable."—*The Times.*

16

Can You Forgive Her?

By Anthony Trollope.

"Mr. Trollope's last work may perhaps be a favourite with its author, for he tells us that he has had the story of it before his mind for many years, and that he has decided that the question asked in the title, 'Can You Forgive Her?' ought to be answered in the affirmative. The lady about whose forgiveness the public is thus questioned is a Miss Vavasor, and the offence for which pardon is needed is the heinous one of having been foolish enough to jilt a very estimable, though somewhat too perfect, gentleman. In fact, for Mr. Trollope's purposes she is made rather an adept in the art, as she breaks an engagement with one man twice, and another once, before she is finally married to the latter of the two. We shall not unravel the plot of the story further than to remark, that in no case is the 'jilting' process brought about, as is probably most usual in real life, by another attachment; and that though there are, no doubt, excellent reasons given for her breaking with her cousin George—the rascal of the piece—once and again, there is really no satisfactory cause assigned by Mr. Trollope for her giving up the admirable Mr. Grey, or for her second acceptance of George in his place."

The Knight of Gwynne.

A TALE OF THE TIME OF THE UNION.

By Charles Lever.

"The 'Knight of Gwynne' is certainly one of the most lovable characters that Mr. Lever has ever drawn; and he monopolises so much of our sympathy, that we hope to be forgiven for extending less of it than he probably deserves to Bagenal Daly, notwithstanding the vigour with which that character is drawn, the remarkable originality of it, and the fidelity with which it represents and sustains a most peculiar combination of qualities, intellectual as well as moral."—*Blackwood's Magazine.*